THE BONUS

T L SWAN

Arndell

Arndell

Keeperton Australia acknowledges that Aboriginal and Torres Strait Islander people are the Traditional Custodians and the first storytellers on the lands of which we live and work. We pay our respects to Elders past, present and emerging. We recognise their continuous connection to Country, water, skies and communities and honour more than 60,000 years of storytelling, culture and art.

First Published by Arndell, an imprint of Keeperton
1527 New Hampshire Ave. NW
Washington, D.C. 20036

First edition 2024

Paperback ISBN: 978-0-9756638-0-6
eBook ISBN: 978-1-9229055-2-9

Library of Congress Control Number: 2024935446

Printed in the United States of America

Sydney | Washington D.C. | London
www.keeperton.com

ALSO BY TL SWAN

Standalone Books

The Bonus

Our Way

Play Along

Kingston Lane Series

My Temptation

The Miles High Club Series

The Stopover

The Takeover

The Casanova

The Do-over

Miles Ever After

The Mr. Series

Mr. Masters

Mr. Spencer

Mr. Garcia

Mr. Prescott (Coming 2025)

The Italian Series

The Italian

Ferrara

Valentino (To be released)

ACKNOWLEDGMENTS

There are not enough words to express my gratitude
for this life that I get to live.
To be able to write books for a living is a dream come true. But not
just any books, I get to write exactly what I want to,
the stories that I love.

To my wonderful team,
Kellie, Christine, Alina, Keeley and Abbey. Thank you for
everything that you do for me,
you are so talented and so appreciated.
You keep me sane.

To my fabulous beta readers, you make me so much better.

My beautiful mum who reads everything I write and gives me
never-ending support. I love you mum, thank you xo

My beloved husband and three beautiful kids, thanks for putting
up with my workaholic ways.

And to you, the best most supportive reader family in the entire
world.
Thank you for everything, you have changed my life.

All my love,
Tee xoxo

GRATITUDE

The quality of being thankful;
readiness to show appreciation for, and to return kindness.

DEDICATION

I would like to dedicate this book to the alphabet.
For those twenty-six letters have changed my life.
Within those twenty-six letters, I found myself
and live my dream.
Next time you say the alphabet remember its power.
I do every day.

1

Grace

MY NAME IS GRACE PORTER, and I am the personal assistant to Gabriel Ferrara, CEO of Ferrara Media in New York.

And it's the perfect job, great pay, beautiful office, everything I ever dreamed of, if not for one small detail.

I am utterly and hopelessly in love with my boss.

Every day it starts the same, at precisely 8:20 a.m. I make my way into his office. By this time, he's already run on his treadmill, had an infrared sauna and showered. We run through his day while he dresses.

Watching Gabriel put on his suit each morning is the highlight of my day—who am I kidding, it's the highlight of my fucking life.

I pick up my notes and knock softly.

"Come in," his strong voice calls.

I tentatively open the door to see him standing at his coffee machine, white towel around his waist. Tanned muscles, broad back and dominance for miles, the lethal trifecta.

"Morning, Gracie."

"Good morning, Gabriel," I reply, my eyes drink him in while he has his back to me. I know most PAs make their boss's coffee, but each morning he likes to make mine, and besides, it's the only time I can stare uninterrupted.

He turns and passes me my cup and saucer. "Your coffee, madam."

"Thank you." I take a sip, warm and delicious, even his coffee is smooth. He goes back to making his coffee while I take a seat at his desk. I open his computer and log into his diary.

My eyes flick over the screen to his sculptured back. Damn it.

Why is he so delicious? How could any female work in these conditions and not be completely besotted with him?

And then he opens his mouth...and I remember why.

"Did you sleep at all last night? You look like shit."

"Thanks," I mutter as I refocus on his day.

"I didn't sleep much either, actually, can you remind me later to send flowers."

I bite the side of my cheek.

Fucker.

Not only do I have to watch him date every beautiful woman in the world, I send them fucking flowers too.

"Of course," I reply as I act unaffected.

I'm positive that I could win an Academy Award for the acting of casual that I do.

"What have we got today?" he asks as he disappears into his large closet. From my peripheral vision, I see the white towel drop as he puts his briefs on.

Focus.

I exhale as the screen jumbles, he's busy.

Even reading his schedule is exhausting. "Board meeting at nine."

"Let's run through that agenda." He walks out of the closet in black briefs, his suit and shirt on hangers.

"You are talking about the flow-on effect from the defamation case against Noble Industries," I reply.

"Yes, that's right. Did we get that information?"

"Bryce has sent it to your email, and it's saved in your Noble Industries file."

"Thank you." He pulls on his white shirt and slowly does up the buttons. "And do I have the graph?"

"Uh-huh." I bite my bottom lip as I try to focus on the screen. Something about him standing there in his briefs doing up a white shirt...it scrambles my brain.

Every.

Single.

Morning.

"Okay, so what then?" he asks.

"You have a meeting with Roger at ten fifteen." My eyes flick up to him. "Why do you have a meeting with Roger?"

"I'm letting him go." He pulls up his navy suit pants and zips up.

"What?"

He shrugs. "He's not performing."

"You can't fire Roger; he's going through a lot right now. His wife left him."

"Probably wasn't performing in bed either," he mutters dryly as he puts his gold cuff links on. "Wouldn't surprise me."

"Now is not the time, can you just give him a warning, please?"

"It's amusing that you think you have a say in this matter." He pulls his suit coat on. "Next appointment?"

"You have a phone conference with Holly, you are closing on the land for the shopping mall at one p.m. today and she needs to run through a few details."

"Uh-huh."

"At eleven you have a walk through the finance department to see the new refurbishment of their office."

He screws up his face in disgust. "Why?"

"Because you do," I snap in frustration. "You paid for it, the least you can do is be excited."

"You're getting a bit lippy this morning, Grace," he mutters dryly. "Don't piss me off before nine."

He walks back into his wardrobe and the scent of his aftershave wafts through the office.

Fuck it...why does he spray that when I'm in his office?

It's morally wrong.

I keep reading through his calendar. "You have lunch at twelve thirty with..." I frown and my eyes rise to meet his, "...Veronica."

"Uh-huh," he says casually. "Drink your coffee so I can collect your cup."

I sip my coffee as I plot his death.

Is it Veronica Rothchild?

It's a new name. I don't know a Veronica other than Veronica Rothchild the supermodel, and I know that they met two weeks ago at a charity event.

I'm happy with his regular women because I know that he sees them just as that...regulars. But every time he meets someone new, I panic a little, knowing this could be the woman he finally falls in love with.

As well as acting, another job I excel at is as undercover detective. I know who he is sleeping with before he does.

"Well, you don't have long for lunch, you have to be back at the office at one thirty for a very important meeting." I focus on the screen.

"Cancel it."

"Impossible." I keep typing and try to change the subject. "Who am I sending flowers to today?"

"Hmm." He purses his lips as he thinks. "Melissa."

"The card should read?" I act uninterested.

"You were incredible last night."

I clench my teeth so hard I nearly break my jaw. "Is that it?"

"Umm." He walks over to the window and looks down over New York. "Come away with me this weekend."

My eyes linger on his back as sadness sets in.

I can't do this anymore.

4

Every time I send one of his girls flowers or gifts, I die a little inside.

I'm twenty-nine years old, and for seven years I have hung on Gabriel Ferrara's every word, waiting for him to notice me.

Waiting for even just a shred of his attention, for him to admit his undying love and sweep me off my feet.

But it's never going to happen, is it?

He doesn't see me like that, he is *never* going to see me like that.

I run through the rest of his day on autopilot, my mind off in another place, and I know that while he is away with Melissa this weekend, I will be at home, wishing the time away until Monday so that I can see him again. So that I can be a personal assistant to his full and exciting life.

Pathetic.

"What are you waiting for?" he snaps.

I glance up. Huh? Was he talking?

"I beg your pardon?" I ask.

He gestures toward his door. "Leave, I have work to do."

"Oh...right." I stand, embarrassed. I walk toward the door.

"Gracie," he calls and I turn back to him.

"Yes."

"Don't wear that perfume again."

I frown in confusion.

"I don't like it."

I bite my lip to hold my tongue and make my way out of his office. I take a seat at my desk, deflated.

He doesn't like my perfume.

Well, fuck him!

I do, asshole, and I'm going to slather it all over myself tomorrow until he throws up.

I might even spray it in his eyes for added effect.

One by one, the office fills up, and then, like clockwork, right on nine, his office door opens, and he marches out like the king of the people.

Gabriel Ferrara in all his bossy glory.

5

"Gretel," he barks.

"Yes, sir," she stammers.

"Why isn't the advertising report in my email?"

"I...I..."

"You what?"

"I haven't finished it yet, I thought you didn't need it until tomorrow."

"You thought wrong." He strides through the office and stops in front of Allen's desk and his eyes roam over it. "Why does your desk look like a fucking dumpster fire, Allen?"

"Ahhh." Allen begins to nervously collect the coffee cups and stacked papers. "Sorry, Mr. Ferrara. I'll clean it now."

Gabriel glances up and his eyes meet mine. He strides back to my desk. "Miss Porter." He calls me Miss Porter in front of everyone, I'm only ever Gracie in private.

"Cancel my one thirty appointment," he demands.

He wants to extend his lunch date with fucking Veronica.

"Impossible, Mr. Ferrara, I told you that already. Please listen," I fire back.

You have *one* hour with her, motherfucker.

That's it.

"Then you can go in my place, because I won't be at the meeting." He marches back into his office and slams the door.

The staff all let out a collective sigh of release that the tyrant is gone. I tap my pen on the desk while my blood boils.

Asshole.

The sun shines down on me as I sit in the park. My lunch break is the best part of my day. I love the fresh air, watching the dogs play off leash and the birds fly around. I never realized how much I loved nature until I hardly saw any. As beautiful as New York is, it's the city of concrete.

When I moved here seven years ago, I was going to work for

twelve months, get some experience with a big firm and then move back to the suburbs somewhere.

Being infatuated with my jerk of a boss was never in the plan.

A dog runs up to me and I bend and pat him, he's big and brown. "Hey there, cutie." I smile as I pat him.

His owner walks up. He has a beard and longish hair with a big warm smile, he has a real chilled-out hippie vibe about him. "He likes you."

"I like him." I smile.

"Do you have a dog?" the guy asks.

"No, I wish." I keep ruffling up the dog's ears. "What's his name?"

"Dusty."

I giggle. "Hello, Dusty."

"You should get a dog," the guy tells me.

"I will one day, when I buy a house in the suburbs." I smile.

"One day?" He frowns.

"When I get my act together."

Code for when I get over *him*.

"You should do it now," the guy says.

I shrug.

"What are you waiting for, life is now. Decide what you want and take it."

I smile sadly. "I wish."

"Don't wish for it. Do it. If you want a house in the suburbs, save and buy one. You never regret the things that you do, only the things that you didn't." He throws the ball and Dusty takes off after it. "Catch you later."

"Bye." I frown after him as he runs off.

You never regret the things that you do, only the things that you didn't.

Hmm...

8:20 a.m., and I inhale deeply to calm the beast within.

I'm furious.

Like a cornered animal waiting to strike.

Mr. Ferrara didn't come back from lunch yesterday. He messaged me to say he was taking the rest of the day off and to cancel all appointments.

Must have been some lunch date, he's never done that before.

This is it, she's the one. It's finally happening, and I have no one to blame but myself.

Stupid fucking fuckface.

I hate him, I hate everything about him.

I collect my diary and pen and knock on his door. "Come in," his deep voice purrs.

I open the door and with one look at him, I melt into a puddle of patheticness. He's just gotten out of the shower; the towel is around his waist. Water is beading all over his skin, and his black hair is hanging in curls. "Good morning, my Gracie." He smiles.

My eyes drop to his big red lips, and I want to stab my eyes out with my pencil.

Anything to stop me seeing this perfection.

"Good morning, Gabriel," I reply. "Last time I looked, I was not your Gracie."

He lets out a deep chuckle. "You will always be my Gracie." He walks to the coffee machine and begins making us coffee. "What's on the agenda today, boss?" He smiles.

I stare at him as a clusterfuck of emotion runs through me.

Did you fuck her?

Of course you did. I slump into my chair at his desk.

I open his computer and see him bend and pick something up from the floor. "What's this?" he asks.

"What?"

He opens a booklet. "It's a pamphlet on Sardinia."

"Oh, it must have fallen out of my diary."

His eyes rise to meet mine. "Why do you have this?"

"Because I never want to go there, what do you think?" I roll my eyes as I click through to his diary.

"You want to go to Italy?" he asks, as if surprised.

"Of course I want to go to Italy," I scoff. "Everyone wants to go to Italy."

He sits down on the corner of his desk. "I'll take you one day."

I twist my lips, annoyed. *I hate you...remember?*

Get with the program.

"What, you don't believe me?" he asks.

I exhale heavily. "Will you just get dressed."

He holds his hands out as if surrendering. "You don't like me in a towel?"

"No. I don't, actually," I lie.

I love you in a towel.

"It's off-putting having to watch you get dressed every day, and frankly, very annoying. I don't make you watch me get dressed."

"Ahh..." He laughs. "Wouldn't that be something, Gracie Porter getting dressed in my office."

I glare at him as I point to the coffee machine. "Make my coffee, Gabriel. You have a very busy day, seeing as you didn't come back from lunch yesterday." I widen my eyes to try to stop myself from throwing a tantrum on the floor.

He smiles, amused, and begins to make our coffee.

Calm, calm...keep fucking calm.

"At nine thirty you have a teleconference with London." I begin to read through his day. From my peripheral vision I see his towel drop in his wardrobe, I glance up to see his bare bottom and I die a little inside.

I really can't do this anymore.

I love him, completely and utterly love him, and I'm just...I don't count to him at all.

The calendar on the screen blurs as my eyes fill with tears.

Focus.

I continue to read out his day as he dresses in his power suit and puts his aftershave on...and shock of the century, I didn't wear the perfume he hates.

"And that's your day." I smile as I close my diary. I stand and make my way to the door.

"Gracie," he calls.

"Yes." I turn back.

"Can you book me a hotel for the weekend, somewhere hot and heavy."

I stare at him, my heart breaking in my chest.

Ouch...

"Of course, sir," I reply through the lump in my throat.

He gives me a sexy wink. "What would I ever do without you?"

Fall in love.

I fake a smile and walk out to my desk and slump in my chair.

That's it.

This is the sign.

I've got to get out of here.

As much as I love Gabriel Ferrara, I can't do this to myself anymore. I'm getting older, my biological clock is ticking, and I won't even date anyone because I'm so blinded by my fatal attraction to my boss. Nobody stands a chance while I work with him.

I need to start thinking with my head and do what I know is right for me.

Make a future without him.

My heart constricts at the thought of not seeing him every day.

How could I bear it?

But then, it could be worse. Staying here, watching him fall in love and marry, start a family with someone else is a torture I cannot deal with.

It's time to rip off the Band-Aid, I need a fresh start.

I open Google and type into the search bar.

Properties for sale in Greenville, Maine

I went to Greenville for my cousin Debbie's wedding a few

years ago and I just fell in love with it, and for some reason, it's always been in the back of my mind that one day I'm going to move there.

Maybe one day is now.

I scroll through the pages, wow, it's cheap, you can buy a three-bedroom home on a quarter of an acre for a fraction of the price of New York.

I scroll through the towns and options with my mind going into overdrive.

I could get a dog of my own.

I smile, and for the first time in a long time, hope blooms in my chest.

I'm going to do it.

Gabriel's office door opens, and we all jump to attention. I quickly close my real estate screen. He marches through the office. "Geoffrey," he snaps. "This isn't a fucking marathon. Hurry up."

"Yes, Mr. Ferrara," Geoffrey stammers.

Without another word, Gabriel walks to the elevator and gets in, I stare at the doors as they close.

You're right, Gabriel, it isn't a fucking marathon.

I'm going for a sprint.

2

___

Grace

Six months later.

I PRINT the letter out and carefully fold it, with my heart in my throat, I slide it into the envelope.

Today's the day.

I've bought a house on the lake in Greenville and am moving out of state.

It's my last week working at Ferrara Media.

My last week with him.

I'm about to resign; I'll only have to work the four days until Christmas. I have the Christmas party, which I've decided that I'm going to look shit hot at. Then I've already booked my owed four weeks' vacation leave for January and that will count toward my one month's notice that I must give.

I'm trying to make this as seamless as possible, and in a perfect world, everything will run smoothly, but I know Gabriel is going to make my life a living hell once I tell him. I've already trained Greg to cover my position while I'm away, and I'm hoping that he will get to keep my job in the new year. And yes, it's true, I know what you're thinking, and to answer your question, yes.

Yes, I did. I trained up Greg, do you really think I'm going to hand over Gabriel to another female PA to watch him get dressed every morning?

I'm moving on...not stupid.

Right, this is it.

I let out a deep breath and knock on the door.

"Come in," his deep voice calls.

I push the door open and there he stands, wearing white briefs, his suit and shirt in his hand. I could just cry. I would give anything to see him get dressed at the end of my bed, even just once.

Focus.

"Good morning, Gracie," he says as he takes his suit pants from the hanger. "You look lovely today."

So do you.

"Morning." I smile, my heart is racing, and I just know this isn't going to go down well.

"Before I forget, can you drop down to Tiffany's and pick up a gift for me today?"

Huh?

Actually...good...a reminder of why I'm doing this, thank you, universe, I needed this.

Hit me straight in the face with it.

"Sure thing, what am I getting?" I ask.

He pulls his shirt around his shoulders. "I don't know. Earrings, necklace...some bullshit."

I roll my eyes and take out my notepad. "Umm...what are we talking? Gold, silver...platinum?"

He twists his lips. "Gold."

"What's the budget?"

"I don't know, you pick."

I exhale as I write it down. "Diamonds?"

"Fuck no." He fakes a shiver as if disgusted.

13

I glance up. "Why fuck no?"

"I'll only ever buy a diamond for someone I love."

"You should probably buy yourself a few, then," I mutter, deadpan.

He smirks as he buttons up his shirt. "I *am* the diamond."

No shit, Sherlock. A diamond python. Looks pretty...but if left unattended, will suffocate you to death.

"Okay...if you say so." I roll my eyes.

Thump, thump, thump goes my heart. I can't wait until the end of our meeting; I need to tell him now. I pull out the envelope and hold it out to him. "I've got something for you."

He turns and his eyes fall to the envelope and then rise to meet mine.

"What's this?"

I swallow the lump in my throat. "It's my resignation."

His face falls. "What?"

"I...."

"No."

"Gabriel...I'm not asking for your permission. I *am* leaving."

He snatches the envelope from my hand and tears it in half and then throws it in the wastepaper basket. "You will do no such thing."

Here we go.

He marches to the door and opens it in a rush. "Go back to your desk and get to work."

"No."

"Do. As. I. Say," he growls.

"No."

"Do not tell me no!" He's about to go into cardiac arrest. "You work for me, not the other way around."

"You're in your underpants, you know?" I gesture down at his body. "The whole office could walk in and see you."

"I fucking know that," he screams, but he must realize that I'm right, and he slams the door shut again. He marches over to his suit as it lies on the chair.

"And where do you think you're going to work, hey?" He picks up his pants, and being so angry, he struggles to put them on. "Do you think you are going to work with a competitor? Because I call fucking bullshit."

"I'm taking some time off for me." I cross my arms as I watch his tantrum unfold.

He flicks his pants angrily in front of him. "You can't afford to take time off."

"Yes, I can."

"Well, you can get this harebrained idea out of your head right fucking now, Grace," he yells. He pulls his pants up so fast that his leg gets caught and he nearly falls over. "Fuck off," he cries in frustration.

I roll my lips to hide my smile.

"Get out," he screams, the veins in his forehead are bulging and he's going red.

I let out a deep exhale. "There is no need to be this dramatic, Gabriel."

"I tore up your letter, it doesn't count. Take the day off and come to your senses."

"That's not happening, I've already emailed my resignation to HR and will be finishing up on the twenty-second of December."

"What?" he explodes. "That's four days away."

"I know."

"Get out," he screams as he loses all control.

"Fine." I walk out and he slams the door behind me, it echoes through the whole of New York.

Jeez.

I sit for a moment.

Bang.

I jump when I hear something hit the back of his door; I think it was his pen holder.

Ugh...he's always so over the top.

Bzzzzz.

I push the button to answer my intercom. "Yes, Mr. Ferrara."

"Get to work!"

I smirk. Man...I need caffeine, it's way too early for all this drama.

I make my way to the kitchen, and I hear the elevator ding.

Gabriel comes flying out of the office like a hornet.

"There is a gas leak on this floor, go away," he yells to Geoffrey.

"What?" poor Geoffrey stammers, wide eyed. "Should I call someone?"

"I already have. Work from level two today," he barks. "Tell everyone else from this floor to work from there too, put a note in the elevator."

I pinch the bridge of my nose...seriously?

This is going to be the day from hell.

I walk back out into the office with my cup of coffee.

"We need to work from level two today," Geoffrey tells me. "There's a gas leak."

"Oh, okay." I act oblivious. "I'll grab my things."

Gabriel narrows his eyes and points to his office. "A word, Miss Porter." He sneers.

Geoffrey looks between us in confusion.

"It's okay, Geoffrey, you go on without me. Mr. Ferrara has been sniffing too much gas, he's having a meltdown."

Geoffrey's eyes widen as he looks between us. "Oh no. Should I call an ambulance?"

"Go to level two, Geoffrey!" Gabriel screams.

Geoffrey scrambles to get his things and half runs to the elevator.

I sit down and open my computer. Gabriel paces back and forth in front of my desk, his hands are on his hips, and his eyes are crazy.

"Fine, twenty percent pay raise, that's it," he snaps.

I stay silent.

He continues to pace. "Hardball, hey...twenty five percent and that's it."

I begin to type as I act uninterested. "No thanks."

"What do you mean, no thanks?" he barks.

"It's not about the money."

"Everything is about money," he fires back.

I roll my eyes and go back to my computer.

"Fifty percent pay raise and that's totally fucking it."

I keep typing. "No."

"Double your wage and do not talk to me again. This is daylight robbery," he screams. "You are trying to fuck me up the ass, and I won't have it."

I was expecting a tantrum, but this is over the top. I shake my head in disgust. "Can you even hear yourself right now? The last thing I want to do is fuck you up the ass."

He puts his hands on his hips and begins to pace again, his mind is racing.

I continue to pretend to type, and I do have to admit, him groveling is doing wonders for my confidence.

"Fine, don't go to Tiffany's today, it doesn't matter. I won't get her the gift."

Huh?

I look up from my computer. *Does he know?*

"Why would you say that?"

"That's it, isn't it?" he says.

"We are not having this conversation, Gabriel," I snap.

"Yes. We. Fucking. Are."

"I'm leaving because I've bought myself a house."

He takes a step back, completely shocked. "You bought a house?"

I nod. "In Greenville."

"Where's that?"

"Maine."

"Why the *fuck* would you buy a house in Maine?" He screws up his face in horror.

"Because...it's time."

"For what?" he bellows. "To turn fucking Amish?"

"I want a family home with a garden and a dog, maybe even a

family. Renting a tiny apartment in New York is never going to get me there."

He blinks as he processes my words.

"I need to get out of New York, Gabriel."

"New York is your home."

"New York is *your* home. I've been here for seven years and I..." I shrug, not wanting to elaborate on my loneliness. "I haven't met anyone and it's time for me to pull up my big-girl panties and move on."

He pauses for a moment as if processing my words.

"You're leaving me?" he whispers.

"I have to."

His eyes search mine.

"I'm sorry."

His jaw clenches, and then without another word he marches back into his office and slams the door, it echoes as the walls shake.

Hot tears burn my eyes.

You were supposed to beg me to stay.

It's 6 p.m. and everyone has cleared out for the day. Gabriel hasn't left his office all day, not even for lunch.

I've been hoping to have a quick word on his way out, but there's still no sign of him.

The office is deathly silent, and I quietly knock on his door.

"Yes," he calls.

I open it and peep in. "I'm going to head off soon."

He doesn't look up from his computer. "Okay."

I wait for him to look up at me...he doesn't.

"Close the door on your way out," he replies flatly as he picks up a pen and starts signing some documents.

Great, now the tantrum is over, he's going to give me the silent treatment. "Are you not talking to me?" I ask.

"I have nothing to say." He keeps writing.

"Gabriel..."

He lets out an over exaggerated sigh as he glances up. "What is it?"

"I don't want this to end badly."

"It's already ended. You can finish now. No need to come back and work this week, I've signed the last of your leave documents. You are free to go."

I get a lump in my throat as I stare at him...that's it?

He really doesn't care.

He keeps his head down as he writes, seemingly totally unaffected.

I will not cry in front of this selfish bastard, it's all about him... it's always been about him.

I quietly close his office door and walk to my desk. I take my bag from the drawer and, with one long last look around the office, I feel my heart break.

Maybe he's right, maybe I *am* doing the wrong thing. Who's to say I'm going to like Greenville, anyway?

No.

This is what he wants. If I give up on my dream now, I'm only cheating myself.

No pain, no gain.

The thing about being a glutton for punishment is this...

Nothing.

Turns out that I'm a total ho for gluttony punishment and there is no excuse for my needy behavior. After tossing and turning all night, there's only one thing I know.

I am *not* a quitter.

Just as I said I would, I will work until the end of the week and then I'm going to the Christmas party looking shit hot and then I'm walking out on my terms. He cannot finish me up on a whim.

Who the fuck does he think he is, anyway?

Right on 8:20 a.m., I knock on his door.

"Yes," he barks.

I smirk, he's annoyed that I came back. Well...prepare to be angered, fucker. I open the door in a rush and step back as my eyes widen in horror.

He's making coffee in his briefs. Black, sexy Calvin Klein ones.

Lingerie for men.

He turns toward me, giving me a full frontal. "What are you doing here?"

I open my mouth to say something, but no words come out.

"Ahhh." My eyes bulge from their sockets. "What are you doing...?" I put my hands up toward his body. I'm flabbergasted as my eyes drop to the bulge in his briefs. "Doing that," I gasp.

"I'm making fucking coffee, what does it look like?"

Something snaps in my brain. "It looks like you're being a poser, that's what it looks like. This isn't a Calvin Klein runway show, you know."

"Nobody has a gun to your head to look." He angrily tips the coffee into his cup. "I think you like what you see, that's what I think."

"Oh...you think that!" I yell, horrified that he's onto me. "I think you're...hideous."

"Hideous?" he screams back, infuriated. "*You're* hideous."

Something about my boss standing there in his underpants, yelling that I'm hideous, tickles my fancy and I burst out laughing.

"Nothing is funny about this," he fumes. "Look away while I dress."

"Oh please, I've seen it all now," I scoff. "Stop acting frigid, we both know you're not." I sit down and open his computer.

"Apparently I'm too hideous to look at," he mutters as he disappears into his closet.

I smirk as I open his diary.

Not really.

I take one long last look in the mirror.

This is it.

My last time at Ferrara Media, the Christmas party at the office.

Most people stayed back straight from work, but I wanted to duck home and shower, try to pull a miracle together and make myself irresistible.

I'm wearing a red wrap dress, and I feel as self-conscious as all hell.

I never wear red; I have red hair and that's enough. Well, it's not really red, it's a deep auburn, but you get the gist. It's out and full, my makeup a little sexier than usual.

The dress has a vee neck that shows a peek of cleavage and a tie around the waist, it feels happy and Christmassy. I wanted to wear something different, he's never seen me in something like this before, so I wanted it to be wow...not sure if it actually is, but that's the plan.

I am waxed, fake tanned and moisturized to within an inch of my life, who knew it takes so much work to look hot. I really need to step up my self-care routine when I get on the dating scene in Greenville.

I smile to myself, *the dating scene in Greenville.*

That's the first time I've let myself consider the possibilities of dating in my new life.

Apart from the leaving Gabriel part, I'm really beginning to get excited. I've been saving for years, and with the cost of the house being cheaper than I thought, I have enough money to buy myself new furniture and do up the house exactly how I want it.

I even booked myself a trip to Hawaii, all by myself.

Who even am I?

Right, I collect my coat and bag, let's do this.

"Jingle Bell Rock" by Bobby Helms rings out as the band on stage does their thing.

The ground floor of Ferrara Media has been transformed into a magical wonderland. The Christmas decorations are over the top and waiters are walking around with silver trays of eggnog and champagne.

People are wearing bright dresses and Christmas outfits; laughter rings out as people chatter and the mood is jovial and jolly. I'm glad I wore my red dress now; I feel better knowing that everyone else is dressed up too.

It was the last day of work today, and everyone is pumped for the holidays and celebrating together.

I walk in, and feeling self-conscious, I flag down the first waiter I see. "I'll have one of those, please."

He smiles as I take a glass of champagne. "Thank you." I smile.

I wonder could I take two?

No, don't be an animal.

"Grace," I hear someone call. I turn to see Geoffrey and some of the others from our floor.

"Hi." I make my way over.

"Wow, you look gorgeous." Geoffrey smiles as he looks me up and down. "Like, really, really good."

"She does, doesn't she," says Paul.

"Who knew you were so hot, Porter."

I smile as I take a sip of my champagne.

Awkward...

Fuck it.

Don't tell me this dress is going to bait the wrong one. I try to act casual as I look around. "Where is everyone?"

And by everyone, I mean your boss.

"The girls are at the cocktail bar and accounting is dancing. Marlene from level three flashed her tits on stage."

I giggle as I scan the room, and then I stop still as my eyes meet Gabriel's.

He's wearing a dark gray suit, white shirt, Santa hat and my heart on the bottom of his shoe. He gives me a slow, sexy smile and raises his glass.

I smile and raise my glass right back.

He goes back to talking to the people he's standing with, and I watch him, waiting for him to glance back over at me.

He doesn't.

My heart free-falls from my chest at his totally unaffected demeanor, it's not going to happen...is it?

I don't know who I was kidding.

"Tell us about your new house." Geoffrey smiles excitedly. "I can't believe you're actually doing this."

"Me neither," chimes in Paul.

I smile, grateful to the people who actually do give a crap about what I'm doing.

I drain my glass. I need to forget about my asshole boss and just enjoy the night.

It's 11:30 p.m. and Gabriel left hours ago, he didn't even say goodbye.

Wow.

More than wow, *fucking* wow.

What a prick!

I'm going to get going, my eyes linger on the elevator and I just...I want to see my office one last time. I don't know why, but I do. I take the elevator to the top floor and make my way to my desk.

I look out over the view, it's so different at night up here, the lights of New York light up the entire skyline.

Unlike the busy and bustling daytime.

It's peaceful.

Serene.

I sit at my desk and look around.

So, this is what closure feels like. The end of one era and the beginning of another. I swivel on my chair, feeling proud of myself.

I did it, I made a plan and stuck to it. Did exactly what I needed to do.

I'm moving on.

I sit for a long time as I process everything that has happened over the last seven years, the dressing diary sessions, the fights and tantrums. The sarcastic snark. The laughter, the crush.

Oh...the crush. I crushed hard, but in my defense, I am only human.

I walk to his office and open the door; it's darkened, lit only by a lamp and his bathroom light. I look over his desk and smile sadly. It's hard to believe I'll never see him sitting here again. I run my hand over his desk, the back of his chair, over the keyboard that houses his fingers all day.

His presence is so strong in here, I can almost feel him.

"Couldn't even say goodbye," I mutter to myself as I cross my arms and look out over the view.

"Goodbye," a deep voice says.

I spin to see Gabriel sitting in the darkened corner of the room.

He has an amber drink in his hand, his elbows resting on his thighs as he watches me.

"Gabriel," I gasp, "I...didn't see you."

He stands and puts his drink down; his eyes are dark and dangerous and he walks over to me and stands so that his face is an inch away from mine.

The air leaves my lungs as I feel the heat from his body.

"I didn't give you your Christmas bonus yet," he murmurs.

I swallow the lump in my throat.

He raises his hand and rubs the back of his fingers over my breast as his eyes follow.

What the hell is happening right now?

"I..."

He puts his finger over my lips. "Don't. Say. Anything."

He puts his two hands around my waist and walks me back to his desk and then pushes me down onto it.

Thump. Thump. Thump...goes my poor weak heart.

He puts his hand on my chest and pushes me back so that I am lying down.

I stare at him, unsure what the hell is going on right now.

His large hands glide up my thighs and he slides my panties down my legs and takes them off.

Lifting them to his nose, he inhales deeply.

Goose bumps scatter all over.

Dear god.

He pushes my legs apart and his eyes linger on my sex. "Hmm." He lets out an aroused purr as he parts the lips on my sex with his fingers. I can hardly breathe.

What the actual...

With his dark eyes locked on mine, he bends and licks me.

Deep and intimate.

"You taste fucking good."

3

Grace

I NEARLY CONVULSE on the desk, and he licks me again. Deeper...better.

I see stars.

His grip on my thighs tightens as he begins to lose focus, his stubble burning the most tender part of my body.

He reaches under his desk, and I hear the door click as he locks it.

Oh hell... Here we go.

He lets loose and really lets me have it, licking and sucking.

He lifts my legs up over his shoulders as he drops to his knees.

"I have needed to do this...for years," he murmurs into me.

What?

The puzzle finally clicks together, of course. That's it.

Oh my god, how didn't I work this out before? He obviously never made a move because he was my boss. Now that I've resigned we can finally be together.

My back arches off the desk as he slides three thick fingers deep into my sex, his tongue flickers at just the right place. I let out a deep moan.

"Oh... God."

My body convulses around him and he lets out an evil chuckle.

"You're going to fucking get it, Gracie," he warns. "Parading this perfect ass around my office all this time. Driving my cock fucking crazy."

Ahhh!

"Do you know how many times I've jerked off in my office bathroom, imagining it was you on your knees, sucking me off?" He works me hard with his fingers and I grip the desk.

Say something sexy...anything.

Quick.

I'm so shocked by what's happening that my mind is completely blank.

"I fucked myself with your computer mouse."

He stills, and his eyes rise to meet mine.

Oh hell...that did not just come out of my mouth.

His eyes flicker with arousal. "You fucked yourself with my computer mouse?"

I think he liked it.

"Uh-huh..." I cringe, this could go either way.

He stands. "And what else of mine have you fucked yourself with?" He unzips his suit pants and pulls out his super-sized cock.

My eyes bulge from their sockets, nothing as fun sized as that.

He's engorged and hard, thick veins course down the length of it, and it's a wonder there's any blood left in his body.

"Ruler."

"My ruler?" he gasps.

Oh, for the love of god. Stop. Talking.

"How dare you use my stationery in this manner." He widens his eyes; he likes this game.

I do too.

"That's right." I grab a handful of his hair and drag him back down to me. "Less talking, more licking."

He chuckles into me and kisses my thigh. "In a minute."

Standing, he undoes my dress at the waist and tears it open, I lie on his desk in only my bra.

His eyes linger on my skin, he trails his finger from my jaw down between my breasts and then down to the lips of my sex.

"Pink," he murmurs almost to himself as he spreads me wide. "I've watched a lot of redheaded porn to try and imagine what you'd be like." His eyes rise to meet mine. "But nothing could prepare me for your beauty."

"You've thought about my body."

"Every fucking day."

The air crackles between us.

"Have you thought about mine?" he asks.

"Every fucking night."

"When you fuck yourself?"

I nod. "Yes." I take his hand in mine. "When you stretch me open and give me what I need."

He inhales sharply, his eyes flutter. "Gracie," he whispers darkly.

I sit up and pull him close, our lips touch as we kiss.

Softly at first, barely a whisper.

But it's so good, he takes my face in his two hands and I kiss him again. He frowns against me as our kiss deepens.

An intimate kiss in a sea of arousal, it's unexpected.

Confusing.

"Gabriel."

"Don't." He cuts me off with another kiss and I can feel his arousal grow, hitting fever pitch.

Something changed with our kiss.

The fire is out of control, a blazing inferno.

He pushes me back down onto the desk and with his eyes locked on mine, he unbuttons his shirt and drops his pants.

His huge dick springs free.

My eyes widen... Is this really happening?

He bends and licks me between my legs and spits a little to lubricate me.

Oh my god.

He did not just do that.

Don't wake me up because if this is a fantasy dream...I am all in. This is porn sex, big-dick, spitting, fucking-your-boss-on-his-desk porn sex.

His skin has a sheen of perspiration all over and with his dark eyes fixed on me, he licks his lips in anticipation.

My arousal hits fever pitch.

He's just so... Never have I seen someone so ridiculously hot.

He stands and swipes the tip of his cock through my swollen lips as we stare at each other.

Then, without hesitation, he pushes forward and slides in to the hilt. "Ohhh..." My body ripples around his.

The air leaves my lungs at his size. "Good lord," I moan.

Thankfully, all the stationery fucking has prepared me for this wide load.

Ouch... That smarts.

I'm grateful for my trusty vibrator right now. *Well done, Bob.*

All our intimate nights alone have paid off, if I hadn't been fucking you all this time, I would have just been split in half.

He slowly pulls out and slams in hard.

Actually, I still might...ahhhh.

I'm completely at his mercy like this.

He slams into me again and the air is knocked from my lungs. It's a wonder the desk doesn't break.

"Gabriel..." I whimper. "Easy..."

Fucking hell.

"Sorry," he mutters, distracted. He slows, and in a more measured and controlled way he slowly loosens me up.

With his hands gripping my hip bones, we fall into a rhythm. Strong, thick pumps and I can't speak, I can't breathe, and hell...I can't even see.

"Oh fuck," he moans, his breathing labored as he struggles for control, perspiration beads on his brow. "So fucking good, Gracie."

He pumps me hard. "So." He pumps me again. "Fucking." Another deep pump. "Good."

The sound of our skin slapping echoes throughout the office.

Looking up at him, doing that...is too much, and I explode headfirst into an orgasm as I cry out loud.

His eyes roll back in his head and he really lets me have it, deep punishing hits, and then he holds himself deep and lets out a guttural moan.

We pant, trying to get precious air into our lungs. Both red and puffing, covered in perspiration.

He moves slowly to completely empty himself into me and then he pulls out. His chest rises and falls, and his eyebrows shoot up as if surprised. "Well..."

I giggle. "Well..."

He takes my hand and pulls me up to a seated position and then cups my face and kisses me, soft and tender. His lips lingering over mine.

Oh...

"I've been wanting to do that for seven years." He smiles against my lips.

"And now that you have?" I whisper.

"I'm glad I didn't, we would never have gotten any work done." He grabs my sex and tugs it. "Having this perfect pussy in my office would have been a major distraction." He turns and picks up my dress.

I giggle, feeling relieved.

Perfect pussy.

"Get dressed." He kisses me quickly before collecting my clothes and passing them over.

"I'm a hot mess, I need to use the bathroom."

He gives me a slow, sexy smile as he opens his bathroom door. "Okay."

Okay? I walk past him into the bathroom and he closes the door behind me.

Oh...

He's not coming in, then?

I was dreaming of having round two in his shower. I've only fantasized about it every day for seven years.

I clean myself up and quickly dress, and then I stare at my flushed reflection in the mirror and smile goofily.

"Oh my fucking god," I mouth to myself.

"I know," I mouth back.

I walk back out into his office to see him completely dressed in his suit, looking completely calm and unaffected. "We should get back to the party."

Oh...

"Okay."

He pushes the hair back from my face as he stares down at me. "You were incredible."

Were is all I hear.

He walks to his desk and takes a small, long black box with a black silk ribbon and passes it over to me. "Your Christmas present."

I smile. "Thank you." I go to undo the ribbon.

"Open it later, it's a pen. Nothing exciting."

"Oh." I smile, feeling embarrassed. "I got you something too." I walk out to my desk and take out the oversized parcel.

He frowns as he looks down at it.

"Open it later, it's a robe." I shrug.

He smiles. "Thank you."

It's a robe with the letter *G* embroidered on it. The *G* is code for Grace so I can always be with him... But I know he will think it's for Gabriel because it's all about him.

The gift that is sneaky but relevant.

He gestures to the elevator. "Let's go." He walks to the elevator, seemingly unaffected. "I have to get back to the party."

"Oh."

He's just going back to the party? What the hell?

That's it?

I get into the elevator beside him and we turn to face the doors.

He straightens his tie and twists his neck as he stares straight ahead. My mind is racing a million miles per minute, what the hell is going on here? I glance over at him, and rather than make eye contact with me, he looks down and fiddles with his cuff links.

He's hard and cold.

There's no banter, no conversation.

Nothing.

The elevator dings as we hit the ground floor and the doors open. The party is in full swing now.

"Let's get a drink," he says casually as he looks around.

I stare at him, what the actual fuck is happening right now?

Did I just imagine that whole entire thing?

"No, I'm going to head off," I reply coolly.

"Okay." He puts his two hands into his pockets. "Do you want me to walk you out?"

I'm taken aback that he would even have to ask that.

Wow.

"No. I'm fine." I fake a smile. "Goodbye, Mr. Ferrara."

"Goodbye, Miss Porter. My car will take you home."

I glare at him. "Have a nice life."

He tilts his chin to the sky as if angered. "You too."

Ha, and there it is.

Proof.

That he's an asshole and I'm pathetic.

Well, screw you.

I turn and walk out the front doors as my angry heartbeat sounds in my ears.

Fucking fuckface, big dick, fucking twathead, asswipe.

His blacked-out Range Rover is parked in his bay, and I storm over to it. His driver, Mark, is behind the wheel, and he jumps out when he sees me. "Good evening, Grace." He smiles.

"Hi, Mark, could you give me a lift home?"

"Sure thing." He opens the door and I climb in.

"Did you have a good night?" He smiles as he pulls out into the traffic.

32

I fake a smile as I look out the window. "It was just okay, a bit boring if I'm honest."

He chuckles. "Aren't all work Christmas parties?"

I stare out the window as New York flies by.

The sky is red as my apocalyptic anger begins to burn.

Fuck. You.

4

_____

Grace

I CANNOT BELIEVE that just happened.

All those years of longing and pining...and damn it. I hate that the sex was as good as I imagined it would be. But...to act like that after it? Just, what the fuck?

The car comes to a halt as a crossing guard holds up a stop sign for a delivery truck that is reversing onto a building site.

My mind is running at a million miles per minute, I'm shocked. Shockder than shocked, and shockder isn't even a word.

We wait for the delivery truck as I go over the last hour's events. You know what...this is good.

This is the closure that I needed. The proof that the man I stupidly pined over for all these years doesn't even exist. He's not sweet and loyal underneath. He doesn't care about anyone but his selfish self.

Gabriel Ferrara is a bona fide bastard to the bone.

Just like the world thinks he is.

"Just going to take a call," Mark tells me. He's wearing a head-piece, so I didn't hear it ring.

"That's fine."

He taps his ear to answer. "Hello," he says, he listens for a moment. "Yes, okay." He listens again. "Tomorrow is fine." He listens again. "Okay, I'll chase it up. Goodbye." He hangs up.

Must be Mark's girlfriend or something, I wonder what it's like to date someone like him where he's working all hours.

I go back to my daydream, also known as the murder plot.

You know what...fuck him.

Who the hell does he think he is, seduces me in his office, fucks me on his desk, comes inside of me? He didn't even offer a condom; I probably have an STI now.

I run my hand down my face in disgust.

Ugh.

What the hell, that was a complete fucking disaster.

Thank god I'm moving and I never have to see him again.

I picture how cold he was: *Do you want me to walk you out?*

No.

I want your dick to fall off, that's what I want, asshole.

How dare he have a good dick!

I'm infuriated.

Rich, handsome, endowed...selfish, motherfucking fuckface.

I glance up, why is it taking so long to get home? Where even are we?

"What's this way?" I ask.

"I had to take a detour for the accident back there," Mark replies.

"Oh." I didn't even notice an accident, that's how preoccupied I am. "Okay." I slump back into the seat and continue my pity party for one.

The car finally pulls up. "Here you go, Grace."

I frown as I peer out the window. "This isn't my house, Mark."

"Mr. Ferrara called and asked that you be dropped back at his place."

"He did what?"

The door opens from the outside, and Gabriel looks down at me. "Get out."

35

"Go to hell," I spit.

He grabs my hand and pulls me out of the car and I snatch my hand out of his. "Do *not* fucking touch me."

The doormen on his fancy building all turn to see the commotion.

"Up. Stairs," he growls in a whisper. "People are watching."

"I am *not* going anywhere with *you*," I whisper angrily. "You think you can treat me like that."

"What did you want? The whole office to know that we just fucked on my desk?" he whispers angrily. "Upstairs now."

I stare at him, my mind a cluster of confusion.

What?

He grabs my hand and leads me into the building, but I'm too mad to focus on a thing, next minute we are in the elevator, the doors slowly close and we turn to face them.

My angry heartbeat is hammering in my chest, and I rip my hand from his. "Do *not* touch me, Gabriel. I swear to god, I'm about to lose my living shit with you."

He smirks, clearly amused. "Anger is an aphrodisiac to me, Grace. I wouldn't push your luck; my control is hanging by a thread as it is."

I cross my arms and glare at the back of the doors. I have never been so infuriated.

"You're an asshole," I spit.

"I have been told that once or twice."

"Per hour, no doubt," I fume. "And just what the hell makes you think you can ejaculate inside of me without asking? How selfish can you be? I probably have an STI now."

"I always wear condoms; trust me, you do *not* have an STI," he snaps. "And I know you're on the pill. I just...I couldn't help myself."

"How the hell do you know I'm on the pill?" I fume.

"I see them in your purse all the time, and on occasion, I even look at where you are in your month."

"What?" I explode.

36

"Well, some days you hate me more than others and I want to know why."

"Because you're an asshole, Gabriel. That's why I hate you more on some days. Today being a prime example." I can hear my angry heartbeat in my ears. "I don't even know why I'm here with you."

"But you *are* here."

"I was ambushed."

He does smile this time, and it's like waving a red flag in front of a bull.

"I'm not one of your bimbos, Gabriel."

"I am well aware of that."

"So why bring me here?" I huff.

I want answers, all of them. *Start talking, motherfucker.*

He stands silently as if contemplating my question and the elevator doors give a soft ding as we arrive at the floor. They open and my heart drops.

Fuck.

The elevator has opened up straight into his apartment, or should I call it an...Italian Colosseum.

He steps out of the elevator but I stay still as I look around.

I'm too shocked to move.

"Out." He grabs my hand and pulls me out of the elevator, and I stumble forward.

I swallow the lump in my throat as I look around.

Jeez.

I always knew that Gabriel Ferrara had expensive taste, but this is next level. The walls are a soft hue of gold. The ceilings are sky high, and huge dark wooden archways interconnect the rooms. The arches remind me of something you would see in an historic church or something. Grand and oversized.

The furnishings are all beautiful dark wooden antiques. Huge navy and maroon Aubusson rugs are on the dark timber floors. Beautiful artworks in huge gold gilded frames are hanging on the walls.

It's like a step back in time to a king's palace or something.

"Welcome to my home." His eyes twinkle with pride.

Suddenly, I remember the mission. *That's right, I hate you.*

"It's nice," I lie through gritted teeth. It's not nice, it's fucking fabulous, but I'm not giving him the satisfaction of gushing over it.

His dark eyes hold mine.

"Don't look at me like that." I drop my shoulders to try to look tough and in control.

"Like what?" Before I can answer the question, he cuts me off. "Like I want to taste every inch of your skin?"

I feel myself melt into a puddle. Don't start talking dirty, I won't stand a chance.

"Yes."

"But I do, Gracie. I cannot hide it. I won't even try to. I haven't even touched the surface with the things I want to do to you."

Arousal begins to steal my brain. "You shouldn't be such an asshole, then," I whisper. That didn't sound convincing, even to me.

"Do you know me at all?" He smiles as he lifts my hand to his lips and kisses my fingertips. The hairs on the back of my neck stand to attention.

Oh...

I watch him softly kiss my hand. "That's the problem, I do," I whisper, distracted.

He's just so...

"I'm not your plaything, Gabriel," I say as I pull my hand from his grip.

"But I *am* your toy to play with." He smirks. "Only too happy to donate my body to science."

"You think I'm a science experiment?" I squeak.

He tips his head back and laughs out loud, and I bite my bottom lip to stop myself from smiling too.

"Would you like a drink?" he asks.

"That depends."

"On what?"

"On whether I'm getting an apology for your assholeness or not."

His eyes dance with delight, and I get the feeling that it is me who is the toy. "Gracie." He takes me into his arms and drops his lips to my neck. "I am sorry for acting like myself at the office." He bites me, and goose bumps scatter up my arms. "I should have acted like someone else." He teases me as he bites me again. "Because the very least you deserve is for me to act like I want the entire office to know my business."

He bites me again, and my body melts against his as I grab his hair.

Okay, what the hell is this?

He's taunting me while not apologizing and my body is lapping it up.

Asshole.

I take a step back from him. "I'd like that drink now, please."

"Of course." He licks his lips as his eyes hold mine and the darkness behind them sends a shiver down my spine.

I get the feeling that I'm going to get it.

Hard.

He walks into another room off the living room and down a corridor and I tentatively follow.

Holy...what the?

It's a bar. A fully fledged huge bar, the walls are dark green and the bar is a rosewood timber.

He begins to pour the drinks as my eyes look around the space.

There's a pool table, a card table, even a roulette table. It's like a damn casino in here. To the right, there's a sunken room with a black circular leather couch around a pole.

Huh?

"What's the pole for?" I ask.

"Strippers," he says casually as he takes a sip of the drink he's just poured.

I stare at him as my brain misfires, what do you even say to that?

"You have strippers to your house?" I gasp.

"Of course I do. I certainly don't want to go to their houses," he replies casually as he passes me a heavy crystal glass.

What the...

I'm shocked, shocked to my core. He has a fucking stripper pole in his bar room.

I take a sip and wince, so strong. Ugh, it's horrible. "Is this stripper juice?"

He raises his glass in the air with a cheeky wink. "Something like that."

"Figures," I reply dryly. I imagine all the hot women he must have here, and insecurity creeps in. What could he ever see in me?

Damn it, maybe I do need this liquid bravery. I take a huge gulp and it burns all the way down.

Ugh... Oh, hell.

Perhaps tonight's stripper may be throwing up after drinking this, but whatever. He asked for it.

"Sit." He points to a stool at the bar, and without thinking I do as he says and drop to the seat. He sits down beside me; his eyes linger on my lips as he takes a slow sip of his drink.

He's imagining something, god knows what, but it's perverted, I know.

I glance over to the sunken lounge and the pole; I imagine him sitting there watching a naked girl writhe and dance for him, it's too much to bear and I snap my eyes away.

Seriously...what am I doing here? He isn't in my league. We aren't even in the same stratosphere.

This is going to break me.

"What is it?" he asks.

"Nothing," I say softly.

He puts his finger under my chin and lifts my face to his. "Gracie?"

My stupid eyes well with tears, betraying my bravado act.

His face falls. "What is it?"

I put my drink down on the bar. "I should...I'm going to get

40

going." I stand. "Have a merry Christmas." I force a smile. "It was really..." I pause as I try to get a hold of my emotions, "...nice working for you.

He stands abruptly. "Gracie, the night is young. Don't go."

"I'm not a stripper, Gabriel. I'm not even a player. The last time I had sex was over a year ago, and this is...." I gesture to the room. "Isn't..." I shrug, embarrassed that I'm not the bad girl I want to be, that my heart is already broken after one cheap fuck on his desk. "It's not who I am. I'm sorry if I gave you the wrong impression." I rush back out to the living room with him hot on my heels.

"Gracie."

I keep walking.

"Grace."

"Don't."

"Grace." He grabs my hand and spins me toward him. "Forgive me." He pauses as he searches for the right words. "I shouldn't have taken you in there...it's been a long time since." He pauses.

"Since what?"

"Since I've been with someone like you."

Someone who stupidly loves you?

I stare at him, hating myself that I can't forget tomorrow and be lost in the moment tonight.

He cups my face in his hands and kisses me softly, his lips linger across mine. "Don't go." He kisses me again. "Please?"

His demeanor has changed, somehow, he's gone from hunter to something softer, more in tune.

"Sweetheart, I'm sorry. I shouldn't have..."

His lips linger over mine and my feet start to float from the floor.

"Tomorrow, you're leaving me forever."

My hands rise to his face, don't even say that. I can't bear the thought of never seeing him again.

"Can't we just spend the night together to say goodbye properly?" he murmurs against my lips.

Oh...

His kiss deepens. "I've wanted you for so many years, Gracie. Give me one night. It's all I ask."

"I can't deal with this alpha bullshit, Gabriel," I whisper, our foreheads touching.

There's a tenderness between us, the one we have when we are alone in the mornings at work, before the world gets in the way.

He kisses me softly. "It's who I am, Gracie."

"It's not," I whisper. "You're in there somewhere, I know you are." We kiss softly. "Show me the man I care about, it's him that I want."

He frowns as he kisses me as if internally torn, then he bends and in one sharp movement picks me up, and with his lips locked on mine, he carries me up the hallway to a large bedroom. He walks into the bathroom and carefully puts me down and turns the shower on.

When he turns back toward me, the air is electric.

Finally, he's here.

This is him, the man that I want.

His gaze is fixed on his hands as he slowly undoes my dress, it falls open and he takes it over my shoulders and throws it to the side, his eyes linger over my body.

"Your skin," he breathes. "It's perfect, so peaches and cream."

He bends and kisses me softly on the chest. "I've wanted you for so long, Gracie. I can hardly believe you are here with me, my love."

My love.

My heart somersaults in my chest at his tenderness.

He slides my panties down my legs, his lips follow his hands as he drops to his knees in front of me.

I have an out-of-body experience and it feels like I'm watching us from way up above. Him kneeling before me, my heart beating out of my chest.

And the alarm bells scream all around me. Like a car crash waiting to happen.

This is bad.

Gabriel being tender and loving is a new level of dangerous.

Because unlike the alphahole that I love to hate, this version of him is...

He takes my bra off while we kiss and then undoes the buttons on his shirt. I take it off over his shoulders and am blessed with the sight of his broad muscular chest with a scattering of dark hair. I unzip his pants and he steps out of them and I slowly slide down his briefs. His large, engorged dick springs free and I bend and softly kiss him there.

Oh... Physically, he's a beautiful man, in every way.

This is weird, I know we've already done it.

But it feels like the first time.

He pulls me into the shower, soaps up his hands and carefully washes my body, up over my back, down my stomach and between my legs.

The feeling of his big hands, along with the hot water, is so good, and for the first time tonight, I feel the adrenaline slowly begin to leave my body.

We kiss, long and slow. Like we have all the time in the world and damn it, why isn't he like this all the time? A little voice from deep in my psyche says something stupid.

He's been saving it for you.

We stay in the shower for a long time, our hands roaming over each other's bodies. Exploring all the things we wondered about.

I look up at him and can hardly believe what I'm seeing, his dark hair hangs over his face, beautiful big brown eyes look down at me and the water is beading on his skin. "Bed," he mouths.

"I want you," I whisper. "God, how I want you."

He smiles, his first genuine smile of the night, and it sends my heart free-falling from my chest.

"Not half as much as I want you." He dries us both and leads me into his bedroom and lays me down on the bed, he spreads my legs and lies beside me. We kiss as his fingers slide through my wet flesh. "You're so fucking creamy," he whispers. "Waiting for my cock."

43

I smile into his mouth as we kiss. My hand finds his dick, it's rock hard and pre-ejaculate is dripping from the end.

I can't wait any longer.

"Now," I whimper as he rolls over me. He nudges my opening as he stares at me, a beautiful warm glow growing between us, and it's too much.

He's too intense, my heart can't take it.

Fucking hard on his desk was a lot safer than this, whatever *this* is.

He slides home in one deep movement, and I cry out as my body ripples around him.

"Fuck...Gracie." He moans as if pained. "So. Fucking. Good."

We hardly move, kissing and taking our time, and fuck.

This is next level.

His body is huge, stretching me to the hilt. His lips are on mine and he stays close, holding me as he loves me.

He moans into my mouth and I feel the telling jerk of his cock as he comes.

"I'm sorry," he murmurs. "It's too good."

But I can't focus on a word he's saying because my own orgasm is hitting me like a freight train. My back arches from the bed as I moan into his mouth. He pumps me harder to let me work it out, and we pant against each other as we kiss.

Holy hell.

Perfection.

It's late, later than late.

I'm lying with my leg over Gabriel's body and he's facing me on his side.

We've been at it for hours; I've lost count of how many times we've come. What started out as gentle lovemaking has turned into a rough and ready fuckfest.

I loved every single minute of it.

We are freshly showered now, and I can hardly keep my eyes open.

Gabriel's fingers are slowly sliding through my swollen sex as he stares at me. It's not a sexual kind of fingering, it's a worship kind of touch. He's feeling where his body is inside of mine.

My eyes are so heavy and they slowly close, he slides his finger inside me and I flutter my eyes back open.

"Sleep, sweetheart," he whispers. "You're exhausted."

My heavy eyelids close, and I feel his fingers deep inside me, his lips on my neck.

"Hmm."

"Can I touch you while you sleep?" he whispers, his fingers slowly sliding in and out of my body. I'm so wet, my body is filled with him.

I smile sleepily. "Please," I whisper.

I battle to keep my eyes open, to keep up with his needs, but I can't.

Exhaustion takes over.

Dreams of Technicolor.

I'm dozing through the ecstasy. Not awake and yet not deeply asleep.

In between worlds.

Kisses and nibbles, fingers and tongue.

Gabriel's quivering breath in my ear, whispering beautiful things in Italian.

My body being rolled one way and then the other as it fills his every craving.

Pillows underneath me.

His tongue on my behind, his soft moans as he comes deep inside my body.

Again, and again...he takes me.

He worships my body and uses it for his pleasure.

Unable to stop himself, he keeps going and going.

Taking it all.

Sleep robs me of my time with him, and I'm not sure if I'm dreaming or if this is truly happening.

But whatever it is, don't wake me up. This is the best night of my life.

I'm in heaven.

5

___

Grace

I wake with a start.

The room is dark, but I can tell that it's morning. I sit up and look around. Gabriel is nowhere to be seen.

I drag my hands down my face as I go over the night we had. *Wow.*

Incredible doesn't come close for words to describe it.

I go to the bathroom and stare at my reflection. I look a right wreck, raccoon eyes and all. I tame down my hair and wash my face and throw on his robe that was hanging on the back of the door.

He must be making breakfast. A thrill of excitement runs through me, and I go in search of my man.

I walk up the hallway and out into the kitchen, no sign of him. I can smell freshly brewed coffee, he's been up.

I walk through the living room and the television is on CNN news. "Gabriel," I call.

"In here," he calls back.

I smile and make my way up another corridor; this apartment

is so huge. I find him sitting behind a desk in his office, he's fully dressed in a suit and on his computer, typing away.

Oh...

I linger at the door and finally he looks up. "Good morning."

"You're working?" I frown.

"I am."

I know for a fact that he finished for the year yesterday. "I thought you finished?"

"You thought wrong." He smiles, but it doesn't touch his eyes, and I instantly know that the sweet man who made love to me all night is gone.

Gabriel Ferrara is here in his place.

Maybe I'm imagining it. I walk over, sit in his lap and he kisses me quickly. "Give me a minute to finish up here, Grace, and I'll take you home." He taps my behind to get me off his lap. "Go get dressed."

What?

I walk to the door, feeling awkward, not quite the greeting I expected. I make my way up to the kitchen and pour myself a cup of freshly brewed coffee.

What the hell was that?

With my heart in my throat, I drink my coffee. I'm not getting dressed. We need to talk.

I wait and wait and wait...

Twenty minutes later he walks out, his back ramrod straight and he looks me up and down. "I thought you were getting dressed."

My eyes search his and he snaps them away. He goes to the coffee machine and pours himself a cup of coffee, he can't even look me in the eye.

"Is this about me leaving?" I ask softly.

He stays silent and sips his coffee, his eyes are wild as if he's about to lose control.

It is.

"I guess..." I smile hopefully, "...I could rent my house out and..." I shrug. "We can't work together anymore, but..."

He walks over and stares out the window with his back to me.

Yes, why not? I could stay. After the magical night that we had, *I have to see where this goes.*

"I'll get another job, and I mean..." I begin to pace as I think out loud, "...I'll have to rent another apartment, but as long as the rent covers my mortgage...then."

He remains silent, his back still to me.

"I mean, of course, I'll have to go for a week to collect the keys and stuff, but I'll come right back."

"You need to go to Connecticut."

I frown. "Connecticut?"

"Wherever the fuck it is you're moving to," he spits angrily.

I step back, shocked by his venom. "But... I thought—"

"You thought wrong." He cuts me off.

"What?"

He stays staring out the window, back straight, shoulders squared.

"Look at me?"

He turns. "You need to go," he whispers.

"Why? I don't understand. We had the most incredible night?"

"I know." His haunted eyes hold mine.

"Then why?"

"Because I can't give you what you want, much less what you deserve."

"It's okay." I take his hand in mine and lift it to kiss his fingertips. "We can work out this dating thing together." I smile softly.

"I can't marry you."

I frown. "Well, we just got together." I chuckle. "Who knows what will happen?"

"I know." His jaw ticks as it clenches, his eyes hold mine. "I am to marry an Italian girl."

"What?" I drop his hand.

49

"My heritage is very important to me. It is expected that I deliver a strong bloodline; my children's first language to be Italian." He thinks for a moment before adding, "I need an Italian wife."

I step back from him, the sting from his words cuts like a knife.

"I'm sorry," he murmurs. "I..." He pauses. "There is no excuse for my selfishness last night."

"It's the twenty-first century, Gabriel. Why would you think that you need to marry an Italian?" I snap as my anger rears her ugly head.

"Because I want to, Grace," he snaps. "Because I want to."

His silhouette blurs.

"So...last night..." I screw up my face in tears. "Meant nothing?"

"It meant everything," he whispers, his nostrils flare. "It was a gift that we gave to ourselves. One that I will hold dear forever." He pushes the hair back from my forehead. "You will never be forgotten."

And I feel it coming, the pain, like a tidal wave, as my heart shatters into a million pieces. I turn and march up the hall to the bedroom. I rush into the bathroom and see my clothes folded neatly on the chair, and I put my hands over my mouth and sob. When he folded these...he knew.

He knew that we never stood a chance, all along. He knew.

I thought resigning had given us a solution to our problem, but I had no idea what was really going on in his head.

He doesn't care at all, he never did.

My god.

I'm such a lovesick fool.

I just need to get the hell away from him.

I throw on my dress and shoes and rattle through my handbag for a pair of sunglasses. I put them on and walk back out.

His eyes hold mine. "Gracie..." he whispers as he reaches for me.

"Don't fucking touch me," I whisper. I march to the elevator and push the button.

He stands quietly behind me, unsure if I'm about to take a swing at him.

The elevator doors open and we ride to the basement in silence.

With my dark glasses on he can't see my tears, but the lump in my throat hurts so bad as I try to hold them in.

Once in the basement parking lot, he strides in front, and I follow him as pieces of my heart drop onto the concrete like confetti.

He gets to a black fancy car and the lights flash twice as he pushes the button. I don't even know what kind of car it is, only that it's cold.

Like him.

We drive to my place in silence, and I pray to god that he's going to change his mind once we get there.

How could he not, we are meant to be together.

He pulls the car to the curb outside my building, and we sit in silence. "Gracie..." he whispers. "Don't hate me."

I close my eyes, verging on a full meltdown. "Goodbye, Gabriel."

"Goodbye," he whispers.

I can't even see him through the tears, but I know I need to get the hell out of this car before I start to beg for his love.

I would give anything...

I get out and slam the door and as I walk up the steps, I hear his sports car roar up the road, he didn't even wait until I got inside.

I sob my way through the foyer and into the elevator. After the best night of my life came the worst day in history.

He's gone.

The mover loads the last box onto the truck and pulls the door down. "That's the last of it."

"Thanks." I smile.

"I'll see you in Greenville tomorrow?" he says.

"Uh-huh." I step back from the truck. "Drive safe."

"I will."

I watch on as the truck pulls out into the traffic and I look up the road.

He's not coming.

It's been seven days since Gabriel dropped me home, and for some reason, I thought he'd come back. In the back of my mind I hoped that it was going to be a fairy-tale romance, where the hero comes back at the last second to declare his love.

But he's not.

He's in Italy, he flew out the night after we were together.

I know this because I checked his email that confirmed the flight. The next day he changed the passwords to everything, pushing the finality of our situation home.

I get a vision of him in Italy with all of those beautiful Italian women and my heart twists, he's probably looking for his future wife right now...that's if he doesn't already know who it is.

Of course he knows, *she's not me.*

I drag myself back up to my apartment to start the final cleanup. I'm staying in a hotel tonight and fly out first thing in the morning.

I can't cry anymore, there are no tears left.

My heart is an empty vessel, broken beyond repair. And the worst part is that I miss him.

I miss him so bad that I can hardly breathe.

And I want to hate him, but I can't even do that right.

I look around my apartment and there are a few odds and ends on the floor, my red clutch purse is sitting on the counter, the mover found it under the cushion on my lounge when they were moving it.

I walk over and throw it into my suitcase. I've packed a bag of clothes to get me through the next few days. It clunks as it hits the side, what's in there that's hard? I pick it up and look inside to see the black box with silk ribbon. "Gabriel's pen." With all the heart-breaking, I completely forgot all about this. I quickly undo the ribbon. "Maybe he had it engraved." I open the box and frown, there's another felt box. I open that and gasp, I take it out and my eyes widen, it's a diamond tennis bracelet. He bought me a diamond.

Not one diamond, but an entire bracelet.

His words come back to me: *I'll only ever buy a diamond for someone I love.*

"What?" I whisper. "The hell?"

There's a small card underneath and I take it out of the envelope.

To my Gracie,
Forever yours,
Gabriel

xo

I screw up my face in tears as I hold the bracelet to my chest, he loved me.

In his own messed-up way, he loved me.

Six weeks later.

Greenville is new, different to New York. I've met a few people and have taken my time unpacking, trying to find a new normal.

I still suffer from my affliction; I miss him every day.

I haven't spoken a word to Gabriel Ferrara, he never called, and I couldn't bring myself to talk to him now, even if I wanted to.

He broke something between us that can't be repaired.

I wear my diamond bracelet all the time, I will never take it off.

It is my most prized possession, and as messed up as it is, knowing that he did care makes me feel a little better.

I hope he suffers too.

I sit on the side of my bathtub and stare at the stick in my hand.

"Please be negative, *please be negative.*"

I'm late, and I shouldn't be because I was on the pill.

With my heart in my throat, I watch as two lines light up, and I put my hand over my mouth in shock.

No...it can't be.

I do another test and get the same result.

Oh my god...no, this can't be happening.

How? I was on the pill. My mind rolls over the last few months.

Oh...the antibiotics for my sore throat, was that it?

It has to be.

Gabriel's words from that morning come back to me, loud and clear.

It was a gift that we gave to ourselves.

Did he know?

I put my hand over my stomach and look down at myself...a baby.

What the....

I'm having his baby.

A little piece of him that I can love forever.

Oh...

I smile softly.

I imagine the future with just the two of us, and a weird sense of calm falls over me.

I can do this, me and bub, we will work it out...together.

We can build a new life for the two of us.

Gabriel gave me the ultimate gift.

His child.

6

Grace

MIDNIGHT.

Where darkness lives and anxiety thrives.

It's been four days since I found out I was pregnant. Four days of swinging between elated and shocked to horrified and sad.

I haven't told a single soul.

I don't know what to do and I'm scared.

The enormity of carrying Gabriel Ferrara's baby has just hit me.

He doesn't want me or a child, and having a baby on my own is not something I ever envisaged for myself.

To be honest, I don't know if I can do it.

This house is big and quiet...and now lonely.

I imagine myself coming home from the hospital with my little bundle of joy...all alone, how will that feel?

I see my future of sitting up in the middle of the night and feeding a tiny little baby, nobody to help me, nobody to love me... or him. This poor little baby deserves to have a dad who loves it, this isn't his fault...or hers.

And what do I tell the baby as it grows up?

Daddy wants nothing to do with you... He wants an Italian baby and you just don't cut it.

The hot tears run down my face and drip into my ears.

I've never felt so alone, so confused.

My heartache was bad enough when I thought I just lost him, but now this...everything seems magnified and I'm no longer grieving my loss of him, that seems irrelevant if I'm honest. I'm grieving for my baby and the happy family that I can't deliver him.

I picture the moment when I tell my parents and my brothers that I'm pregnant with my former boss's baby and that he doesn't want anything to do with me.

My mom will cry, my dad will be outraged with Gabriel... Everyone will feel sorry for me.

Poor Grace, her boss got drunk at the Christmas party and had her on his desk for kicks, got her knocked up and now wants nothing to do with her... *I hate that it's true.*

And then there's the Ferraras, Gabriel's mother is going to go ballistic. His father, his brothers and sister...oh god.

I feel sick to my stomach.

The tears flow onto my pillow like a river, my mind is jumping from one nightmare thought to the next and I know exactly how this looks.

A grab for cash from one of America's wealthiest men, the ultimate trap.

I imagine the tabloids and the media coverage.

Gabriel Ferrara's former PA falls pregnant after having sex on his desk at the Christmas party.

I screw up my face in tears...oh my god, this is a disaster of epic proportions.

Gabriel's going to hate me, and who could blame him.

All the plans he had for an Italian family...his hopes and dreams altered forever too.

I close my eyes at the horror, how the hell did I let this happen?

Why didn't my pill work? What's the damn point of taking it if the fucker doesn't work?

Everything is changed now, and I can't take it back no matter how much I want to.

This isn't how I imagined my life would go, I'm supposed to be happy and fulfilled, feeling safe and secure, building a family and a home with a man that I love.

My husband.

I roll onto my side and curl up in a ball as I try to protect myself from my own thoughts.

I have to talk to someone; I have to get out of my own head, I can't keep going round and round like this.

Tomorrow I'll talk to Deb, she'll know what to do.

10 a.m., I sit in the café; the morning sun is beaming onto the bench seat through the window as I wait. There's a window planter box with pansies in every color, and the village feels alive.

"The two coffees," the waitress says as she puts them down on the table.

"Thank you." I smile.

Things look better today. Along with the sunlight, I feel stronger. But that's how I seem to roll at the moment, brave by day, terrified all night.

My favorite thing about Greenville is my best friend, Deb. She also happens to be my cousin and the reason I found this place. It was her wedding that I came here for five years ago, and from the moment I stepped out of the car, I instantly fell in love with the place.

Deb married a local boy she met at college, his name is Scott and this is his hometown, they moved back here permanently after their wedding.

Deb bounces through the door and her broad smile lights up the entire café. "Hey you." She trips on a chair leg as she sees me and stumbles. "Sorry," she apologizes to the person who was nearly thrown out of their chair.

I giggle at her dramatic entrance. "Hi." Deb is...how can I explain her?

Chicken soup for my soul...for everyone's soul. Blond and pretty with a can-do attitude to everything.

She kisses my cheek and sits down. "Tell me you have good news."

"What?"

"Well..." Her eyes dance with excitement. "You said you had something to tell me. He called, didn't he?"

I stare at her as my brain misfires.

Oh...

"I knew he would." She smiles. "I knew he would come back begging on his knees."

I exhale heavily, one thing about Deb is she's the ultimate optimist. "He didn't call."

"He didn't call?" She scrunches up her nose. "What's wrong with this dickhead, why didn't he call?" She sips her coffee. "You know, you keep saying this Gabriel Ferrara is super intelligent, I'm finding it very hard to believe."

I exhale heavily.

"Well..." She sips her coffee again. "What do you have to tell me?"

"I'm pregnant," I blurt out.

She puts her coffee cup down onto the table with a thud and coffee sloshes over the side. "What do you mean?"

"What else could I mean? I'm pregnant."

"Are you sure?"

"Positive, I've done six tests."

Her eyes widen. "It's his?"

"Well...I haven't had sex with anyone else, have I?"

"Fuck." She puts her hands up to her temples as her eyes hold mine. "When did you find this out?"

"Monday."

"It's Saturday." She frowns.

"Yes...so?"

"So you haven't told me for five fucking days?"

"I was trying to get my head around it."

"Fuck," she whispers as her head begins to catch up. "Oh fuck...Grace."

"You said that already," I snap.

"What did he say?"

"Gabriel?"

"Yeah."

"He doesn't know."

"He doesn't know." She gasps loudly.

"Sshh." I look around at the people in the tiny café. "And neither does anyone else. Keep your voice down."

"Oh my god," she whispers. "He doesn't know." She puts her head into her hands. "He didn't wear a condom?"

"No."

She holds up her hands in question.

"I'm on the pill."

"You forgot to take it, didn't you?"

"No. I did not forget to take it," I snap.

"Well, how...?"

"I don't fucking know, okay." I cut her off. "All I know is it happened and now I'm pregnant and I have no idea what to do, and if your reaction is anything to go by, I am totally fucking screwed."

"Sorry." She winces as she sits back in her chair. "I'm just shocked." She puffs air into her cheeks. "It's a shock."

"For me too."

We sit for a moment and both sip our coffee. "What are you going to do?" she asks.

"I don't know."

"Are you..."

"I'm having the baby." I finish her sentence.

Her eyes hold mine.

"Deb, I'm twenty-nine, I'm very single, and who knows, this

59

might be my last chance and..." I shrug, lost for words, "...I'm having it."

"Okay." She nods. "Well... Congrats...I guess." She gives me a lopsided smile.

"Thanks...I guess."

"When are you going to tell him?" she asks.

I exhale heavily. "I don't know." I think for a moment. "I don't know if it's the hormones or what's going on, but I feel so vulnerable and fragile. I'm not sure I could even see him at the moment without having a full mental breakdown, and that's without the baby."

Deb gives me a sad smile and takes my hand in hers. "Have you been to the doctor's, like is it *confirmed* confirmed?"

"Well, I've done six pregnancy tests and they were all positive, and it's been seven weeks since we had sex."

"So if I were a betting man, I would bet that you're seven weeks pregnant?" Deb thinks out loud.

"Last time I looked you're not a better or a man."

"I hope your baby has your wit," she mutters dryly. "Or not."

I exhale heavily as I think about the next steps I have to go through. "I'll go to the doctor on Monday."

"I'll come with you." She squeezes my hand in hers. "A baby," she whispers as she hunches her shoulders up. "This is a little bit exciting."

For the first time, a glimmer of hope runs through me, and I smile. "Maybe."

"It's positive." Dr. Moran smiles. "Congratulations, Grace, you are eight weeks pregnant."

My stomach flutters as if this is the first time I have heard it.

"Thank you."

"I'll write you a referral for an obstetrician." He begins to type into his computer. "Ring in the next few days and make an appointment for when you are twelve weeks along. I've also written a pathology request for some blood tests, get those done before your appointment."

"Okay."

He gets out a little wheel thing and spins it. "I have your due date estimate as the twenty-seventh of September."

"Oh." I smile goofily. "Okay."

Deb bounces in her chair beside me, unable to hide her excitement.

Is this really happening?

"Any questions?" the doctor asks.

"No." I stand. "Thank you."

"Congratulations again." He smiles.

"Thanks." I walk back to the car in a daze, Deb is chatting on and on but I hardly hear a word she's saying.

I'm having a baby.

His baby.

I put my hand over my stomach, a little piece of Gabriel is growing inside of me right now.

"Are you going to open the door?"

"Huh?" I glance up.

Deb widens her eyes. "Unlock the car."

"Oh. Right." I unlock the car and stare down at it.

"Do you want me to drive?" she asks.

"Maybe. I'm so distracted."

"No shit."

The drive home is made in silence, well, not really, because Deb is chatting away and having a conversation, but I don't hear a word.

I'm lost.

My mind is swinging between fear to the dream that he really loved me and maybe this baby was meant to be.

I get a vision of him being excited and lifting me up in the air and swinging me around as we laugh...

"Earth to Grace." She waves her hand in front of my face. "Are you even listening?"

"Oh, sorry." I glance over at her, almost embarrassed by my fantasy. "What?"

"You need to go to New York and tell him."

"I know. I just need to get my head around it first."

"No. You need to get your head around it together."

My stomach sinks because I know he's going to be devastated and I'm not sure I can handle one more rejection from him and survive it.

"Do you want me to come?" Deb asks.

"Where?"

"To New York," she says. "Then if things turn to shit we can at least have a few days in New York shopping and drinking cocktails."

I look at her deadpan.

"Oh right." She winces. "You can't drink cocktails. Eish, this is boring already. Shopping then."

"You don't mind?"

"I'd love to come and besides, I don't want you going alone." She takes my hand in hers. "We've got this and if Gabriel Ferrara doesn't want his baby then screw him. We do...and we will love this little baby so fucking hard."

I smile through tears and give a weak nod. "Yep."

She continues driving. "When are you going to tell your parents?"

"Can we just concentrate on telling the father first?" I hold my temples. "This is all too much."

"Right." Deb nods, she glances over at me casually. "Because your mom is going to freak out, you know that, don't you?"

"Not. Helping."

One week later.

The traffic whizzes by as we sit on the park bench, our eyes firmly fixed on the front doors of Ferrara Media.

"Okay, so let's run through this again," Deb says.

I glance at my watch. "He's going to be walking out to have lunch with his brothers at any moment, and I'm waiting until he comes into view and I'm calling him."

"Why don't you just call him now?"

"Because I want to see his face when he sees it's me calling, I want to know what to expect when I go to see him."

"Okay."

We wait, and we wait...and we wait.

"What if he isn't having lunch today?" she asks.

I shrug.

"What if he isn't even in town...the country."

"He's in the country."

"How do you know?"

"His jet is at JFK."

"How do you know that?"

"Because I do," I snap in frustration. "You are forgetting that I spied on this man for most of my adult life, I know where his fucking jet is."

"Right."

We sit some more and then I see Mark get out of his car and loiter around the front door. "Gabriel's coming out now."

"How do you know?"

"That guy in the black suit by the door is Mark, his driver."

"Why would his driver be going to lunch with him?"

"He's his bodyguard."

She screws up her face. "He has a bodyguard?"

"Of course he has a bodyguard, he's a rich bastard who pisses off a lot of people."

We watch Mark as he stands by the door.

"Hmm." Debbie smiles as she looks him up and down. "That Mark is a bit of alright, isn't he?"

"He used to be in the army or something." I shrug. "I don't know, something manly and tough."

"Mmmm."

"He and Gabriel fight like cats and dogs but I know that Gabriel must like him."

"Why do you say that?"

"Because he bought him a Corvette for his birthday last year."

"What?" she gasps. "How do you know?"

"Because I organized the registration on it."

Deb screws up her face in disgust. "Are you fucking kidding me, you sucked his dick and all you got was a stupid bracelet, where's your fucking Corvette?"

"It's diamonds." I widen my eyes; she doesn't get it at all. "It was about the sentiment."

"Big shit." Deb drinks the last of her thick shake through the straw and it makes a loud sucking sound. "Fuck him and his stingy sentiment. Give us a Corvette next time, asshole. Actually, make it a Porsche."

I exhale heavily, ugh...bringing Deb here could have been a big mistake. She already hates Gabriel with a passion.

The doors of the building open and Alessio comes into view and then Ricardo, and walking behind them is Gabriel.

"Who are they?" Deb asks.

"The two tall guys in front are his brothers Alessio and Ricardo."

"Hmm." Deb wiggles her eyebrows. "I don't mind a bit of Italian suit porn."

"Ricardo lives in London," I reply as my eyes linger on one person only, Gabriel.

Towering above everyone, he's wearing a dark blue suit and a white shirt, his dark hair has a curl to it and damn it, my heart is still on the bottom of his shoe. Seeing him for the first time in two months brings with it a wave of emotion, and I immediately tear up.

I miss him, lord how I miss him.

"Is that him at the back?"

I nod through tears.

His back is ramrod straight, and the way he walks is just so...

male. He's talking to Alessio, and Mark falls in to walk in front of them with Ricardo, the other brother.

How could three brothers all be so genetically blessed?

"Do it."

"What?" My daydream is interrupted.

"Call him."

"Oh shit, I forgot I was supposed to be doing that."

With shaky fingers I dial his number and I hang on the line as I watch.

He digs his phone out of his pocket and looks at the screen.

Thump.

Thump.

Thump goes my heart.

Here it is, the moment of truth...

He looks at the screen and without answering the call puts his phone back into his pocket.

The caustic truth hits me hard in the face.

My vision blurs with tears.

"He's such a fucking prick," Debbie mutters under her breath.

I sit and stare into space, my heartbeat hammering in my ears.

And now I know.

7

Grace

"MAYBE HE'LL CALL BACK when he's alone, I mean...he couldn't really talk when he was with people, could he?" Deb says as her eyes stay glued on the group of men as they disappear around the corner.

I nod, but I know that's not true.

Gabriel doesn't conform for anyone, if he wanted to talk to me then, he would have.

I slump back into my chair, shocked but not surprised.

"This would have been such a great opportunity to get rolling drunk right about now." Deb sighs, she points to my stomach. "Hope the baby's having fun in there...drinking all the drinks he wants to drink."

"It might be a girl." I look over at her and smirk. I stand, feeling somewhat relieved that calling him is over. "Come on then."

"Where are we going?"

"To get you a cocktail."

"We are?" Her eyes widen with excitement. "But you can't have one."

I link my arm with hers. "I get the feeling that you are going to drink enough for the two of us."

"The three of us."

The three of us.

"Yeah, the three of us." I smile. "I kind of like the sound of that."

"And something unexpected happened in the streets of New York today, a giant drone landed in Central Park."

The late-night news is playing in the background. I glance over to see Debbie fast asleep on the couch, I glance at my watch.

12:05 a.m.

I exhale heavily and look at the screen on my phone.

No missed calls

He didn't call, and I don't know why I was expecting him to, but I honestly thought he would.

I'm beginning to wonder if coming here and wanting to tell him is a monumental mistake. He doesn't want *me*, so he definitely won't want to have a baby together.

I really thought we had something.

The harsh reality is that it was only me that had something. The feelings were one-sided.

And I really have to ask myself that what good is the fantasy of him falling in love with me if I always know in the back of my mind that it was only because he was trapped into it?

Sure, a baby will change things.

We may work through this and end up okay, but deep down I will always know that this isn't what he really wanted. That this was a forced union.

I know how strong-willed he is. Nobody tells him what to do,

67

and for me to tell him I'm having a baby with or without his permission is likely to send him into powerhouse overdrive. I think back to how badly he behaved when I resigned, and that was a tiny drop in the ocean compared to this. It's going to go one of two ways, either he accepts it and welcomes it with open arms or he's going to get nasty.

What if he took me to court for custody?

My hand splays protectively over my stomach. If he did decide to fight me, I couldn't afford the legal fees that he could.

He would win.

An Italian child is all he's ever wanted, what if he then took the baby and the two of them lived in Italy somewhere?

He wouldn't do that to me.

Would he?

I honestly have no idea anymore. He's fiery and impossible and an arrogant prick, but I thought that was just the outer shell and that he had a soft spot for me.

But maybe not.

Maybe that's the real him and maybe, actually...probably, I'm just a lovesick fool who was wearing rose-colored glasses the entire time I knew him.

I stand and point the remote to the television to turn it off. I pull a blanket over my too-many-cocktailed friend and kiss her forehead.

"Good night, drunk girl," I whisper.

"Hmm," she mumbles before rolling over in a dead sleep.

I brush my teeth, get into bed and stare at the ceiling.

More thinking, more overanalyzing and damn it, more beating myself up.

I know what I have to do, I don't have a choice. This isn't my decision; I have to tell him.

Tomorrow, I will.

. . .

I take one last look at myself in the mirror, I'm wearing a black pencil skirt and a linen shirt casually tied in the front. I'm trying to be casually irresistible, so that when he sees me he will fall to his knees and beg for my forgiveness.

I'm not as nervous as yesterday and get a feeling everything is going to turn out. Maybe not as I first thought, but I know I'll be okay whatever happens.

"Do you want me to come?"

"Nope." I pick up my handbag and jacket. "I'm fine, you go shopping and I'll call you when I'm done."

"I can wait outside, I don't mind."

"I'm fine, and don't ask me why, but I'm quietly optimistic."

Deb forces a crooked smile. "Call me the minute you're done." She hugs me.

"Yep." I walk out the hotel room door and into the corridor, excited to get this over with.

Let's do this.

The cab pulls into the curb and I peer out the window at the huge glass fortress and read the sign.

FERRARA

Butterflies swirl in my stomach, not feeling quite so brave now.

I hand the money over to the cab driver. "Thank you."

"You have a nice day now, dear." He smiles.

"You too."

I square my shoulders and without hesitation I march through the huge glass doors, and once inside my step falters. New reception staff are near the security scanners. I look around in a panic, I don't know these people and I don't have any of my security badges to get into the building anymore.

Where's Liana and Margery and Tom?

Fuck.

My heart begins to thump as I approach the desk.

"Hello." The girl smiles. "Can I help you?"

"Yes..." I pause as I try to think on my feet. "I'm here to see Gabriel Ferrara."

"Did you have an appointment?"

"Yes," I lie. "But you will have to call him direct, as it was made in his personal calendar and not with his PA."

"Oh." She frowns and glances to her fellow worker. "That's not how..."

"Tell him Grace Porter is here to see him," I cut her off.

"I'm sorry."

"Call him," I snap, I begin to feel my pulse as adrenaline surges through me. "Tell him Grace Porter is here to see him," I repeat.

She exchanges glances with the girl sitting next to her. "Okay." She picks up the phone and dials a number.

As I wait, I bite my bottom lip so hard that I think I taste blood.

"Yes, hello, Mr. Ferrara. This is Violet from reception." She listens for a moment. "I have a Grace Porter here; she says she has an appointment to see you today." Her eyes flick up to me as she listens.

I hold my breath as I listen.

"Yes, sir." She nods. "Thank you." She puts the phone down.

I stare at her as I wait.

"I'm sorry, Mr. Ferrara is booked out back-to-back today. He can't see you. He sends his apologies."

Oh...

The ground moves beneath me as my every fear comes to fruition.

My nostrils flare as I try to hold it together. "He said that?"

She nods, and it's obvious that she knows this visit was of a personal nature. "Let me look through his diary and I'll try to find you another appointment." She brings up the computer and glances over to her co-worker. "Umm, unfortunately, he doesn't have an opening until August." She winces as if she cares. "I'm sorry."

I nod and step back from the desk. I've never been so humiliated in my life.

Not as sorry as he's going to be.

"Thanks."

For nothing.

I turn, and with my heart breaking in my chest, I march toward the front doors, the stupid tears building like a tidal wave.

And now I know, that's it. It's really over forever, he doesn't want to see me.

There goes my happy ending.

I push through the glass doors and into the cold New York air. My heart is hurting.

Did that really just happen?

Oh my god, oh my god.

Oh my fucking god.

I look up and down the street, I need to get out of here. A barrage of familiar feelings comes flooding back and I suddenly remember why I chose to leave.

I need to get as far away from this man as quickly as I can.

This man, this place, is toxic.

I need to go home.

I march out to the street and put my arm up for a cab, one instantly pulls up and I dive into the back seat.

The driver takes one look at my face. "Are you okay, miss?"

I can't act tough any longer, and I screw up my face in tears, the lump in my throat hurts as I try to hold it together. "Not really." I wipe my eyes in a dramatic fashion. "But I will be."

No matter what the conditions, this baby will never be enough for him. He will always despise the fact that it isn't Italian, that he didn't choose to have it.

Imagine growing up knowing that your own father hates you.

I screw up my face in tears.

The car weaves in and out of the New York traffic and I put my hand over my stomach and make a vow.

I failed to protect myself from him, but I will always protect you.

I cry as I take my diamond bracelet off. I will never put this back on again. It's physically hard to take off because I can't see through my tears.

This was my most prized possession and now he's ruined it forever.

This is the last pain he will ever cause.

He will never get the chance to hurt my baby like he has me.

That's it, I'm done.

Gabriel

"And you'll see on page fourteen of the proposal." I point to the graph on the whiteboard with a pen.

The fifteen people sitting around the board table all flick to page fourteen.

"As you can see, the trend is emerging as..."

The intercom buzzes. "Mr. Ferrara."

I exhale heavily. "Yes," I snap, annoyed, why is she interrupting me?

"Yes, hello Mr. Ferrara. This is Violet from reception."

"Yes, Violet, what is it?"

"I have a Grace Porter here; she says she has an appointment to see you today."

What?

"Ahhh..." I look around the room as thirty eyes watch me. "I see..."

Umm... I take the lid off the pen in my hand as I think.

Shit.

I can't stop this meeting midway through, people have flown in internationally to attend. I've got people with me all day and then a function straight from work tonight with my family.

Fuck...

"I'm booked back-to-back today, Violet; can you reschedule her to come back? Tomorrow, perhaps?"

"Yes, sir," she replies.

"Send my apologies."

"Thank you."

I scratch my head in frustration, *damn it.*

I want to see her.

With all eyes on me, I try to bring my mind back to the meeting.

She's here.

"So...these..." I pause as I try to collect my thoughts, "...trends."

She's here.

I refocus my thoughts and carry on with the meeting as I try my hardest to keep a straight face.

She came back.

Tomorrow I get to see her.

The round dinner table is filled with family members. It's my brother Alessio's birthday.

The table chatters on in Italian as my mind wanders off on a tangent.

I've been with a lot of women, many...most, actually, don't speak Italian and it's never mattered before because I knew it wasn't going anywhere. Their ancestry didn't matter to me.

But if I were ever to want something more with a woman who didn't, how would that look?

Tonight, for example...

Would Grace be sitting there, not understanding anything that anyone is saying, would I have to translate or would she just refuse to come at all?

I mean, sure, anyone can learn Italian, but that doesn't change who you are at the core.

My future dreams depend on having a family that's filled with generational traditions, trips to Italy with my siblings and their children and the cousins growing up together and playing the games that we did as children.

A closeness and familiarity.

I envision my life in an American household and how different it would be from the one I have always known and wanted for myself.

If I chose that life, I know for certain that my wife and children would always be on the outside. They would never truly be accepted by their extended family.

Dream girl or dream life.

It's either or, it can't be both.

One life is Italian with my family, the other is with Grace.

I couldn't bear it if they rejected her...*and they would.*

I sip my scotch and slosh it around my mouth before swallowing, the thought is depressing.

Alessio leans in close so that only I can hear him. "Let's go to Atticus. This place is boring as fuck, and I need some ass."

"I'm heading home."

He screws up his face. "Why?"

"Because I want to."

"What the hell is wrong with you lately?"

"Just because I'm not fucking every woman with a pulse does not mean there is something wrong with me."

"You're getting soft," he mutters dryly as he sips his drink.

I roll my eyes, but his comment hits home.

He's right.

What the hell *is* wrong with me lately, I haven't been out in weeks.

I've lost interest in everything; everyone just seems so...average.

I down the last of my drink. "I'm out." I put my hand on his shoulder as I walk past him. "Have a good night."

I kiss my mother and sister as I say my goodbyes and I walk out of the restaurant and onto the street where my car is waiting.

"Good evening." Mark smiles.

"Hi." I get into the back seat and we whiz through the streets of New York as I stare out the window.

At least I get to see her tomorrow.

. . .

The sun slowly sets behind the buildings and I pick up my phone and check it for the hundredth time today.

It's nearly five, where is she?

I call down to reception. "Hello, this is Gabriel Ferrara."

"Oh," the young girl's voice stammers. "Mr. Ferrara, hello."

"May I speak to Violet?"

"Yes, speaking."

"What time did Grace Porter say she would be back today?"

"Ahhh." She has no idea what I'm talking about.

"The woman who came to see me yesterday."

"Oh right, the lady you were too busy to see."

I roll my eyes at her sarcasm. "I was in a board meeting and I asked you to reschedule. When is she coming back?"

"She didn't reschedule."

I frown as I rise to stand. "What do you mean?" I snap.

"I..." She hesitates as if scared to go on.

"Spit it out."

"She left, sir. She didn't want another appointment, seeing the first was weeks away. She seemed upset."

I hang up and immediately dial Grace's number. I pace back and forth as I wait for it to connect.

The number you have called has been disconnected.

Panic runs through me.

No.

I dial the number again.

The number you have called has been disconnected.

"Don't you dare." I continue to pace as my temper rises. "You try this fucking shit on me and that's it!"

I call the number again in the hope that I've dialed the wrong number.

The number you have called has been disconnected.

Infuriated, I throw my phone, and it bounces off my desk and onto the floor.

With my hands on my hips, I pace back and forth. "She thinks she can cut me just like that?"

She thinks that I can't find her if she changes her fucking number.

This is her being a control freak...that's what this is. I scramble for my phone and make another call.

"Hey."

"Mark, I want you to find an address for Grace Porter."

"Well, why don't you just call her?"

"Because her phone has been disconnected."

Silence.

"Well..."

"Don't *well* me," I snap. "Find out where she is." I hang up and continue pacing and my phone rings, it's Mark again. "What?" I snap as I answer.

"What town does she live in?" he snaps back.

"Connecticut."

"Connecticut? Are you sure that's it, because I need a state or at least a town to run the search."

I roll my eyes. "I don't fucking know, I'll check." I hang up and march out into the office to see that Richard is still at his desk. "Where did Grace Porter move to?"

He glances up. "Sorry?"

"Grace Porter," I snap impatiently. "Where is she? Where did she move to?"

"Ahh...Maine. I think?"

"Maine?"

"Surprised she didn't move to Texas actually?"

"Why?"

"Because of Willie."

"Who's Willie?"

"Willie Nelson." He widens his eyes. "You know how much Grace loves Willie Nelson."

"Thankfully not." I pinch the bridge of my nose. "Fuck me dead. That'll do me." I storm back into my office and call Mark.

"Hi."

"She lives in Maine."

"Anything else?"

"She has appalling taste in music."

"Oh...kay." He listens. "So where did you get Connecticut from?"

"I don't know." I shrug. "Just find her."

"What for? You didn't even bother to know where she lived, why would you want to find her?"

"Because I said so...that's why. You need to remember that you work for me, so you will do whatever I fucking say."

"What's the offer?"

"What?" I fume.

"What are you going to offer her? I happen to like Grace and I'm not finding her if you are just going to screw her around. She's left town and changed her number for a reason."

The sky turns red.

"What I do with Grace Porter is none of your fucking business." I sneer. "You're fired." I hang up the phone.

An hour and six scotches later, I collect my briefcase and make my way downstairs. I walk out the front door to see Mark standing beside my car.

Infuriating.

I walk over. "What are you doing here, I fired you."

He rolls his eyes as he opens my door. "Like the other fifty times you've fired me."

I get into the back seat and he slams the door behind me.

Fucker.

We drive through the traffic as I glare out the window. "Did you find her?"

"I'm not looking for her." He casually turns the corner.

"Why not?" I snap.

"Because last time I saw Grace Porter was when you had me stake out her house as her moving truck came, and she was crying and miserable." His eyes meet mine in the rearview mirror. "I thought she was your friend."

"She is."

He raises an eyebrow. "Well?"

"Well, what?"

"What kind of man looks for a woman if he already knows that when he finds her, he won't give her what she needs?"

My eyes hold his.

"I know you're a selfish prick, but you need to think about this because it's not just any old girl, it's Grace Porter."

My heart sinks.

"You already told me you are to marry an Italian woman. Has that changed, has it?" His eyes flick up to meet mine in the rearview mirror again.

"Just drive the car," I yell. "You piss me off. You're fucking fired. For real this time."

We drive in silence for a while as adrenaline surges through my system. "You think you know everything about me, well, I've got news for you. You know nothing. Zero."

"I know a lot more about you than anyone else, that's for sure."

I roll my eyes. "Will you just shut the fuck up? I don't pay for your opinion."

"You want my opinion?"

"No."

"Yeah, well, you're going to get it anyway," he snaps. "Ever since the Christmas Party and that night you spent with Grace."

"I never spent a night with Grace."

"You're lying. I drove her to your house," he barks. "You pulled

78

her out of the car." He grips the steering wheel. "I did think it was strange when you didn't leave the yacht in Italy."

"You weren't even in Italy," I fire back.

"No, but the security boys called me from over there to see if everything was okay because you hadn't left the yacht the entire time you were there."

"I was tired."

"Of being a prick?"

"Shut the fuck up." I punch the back of the seat as I begin to lose control.

"You haven't gone out since Grace left; you haven't had one single date."

"So what?" I yell.

"That's not who you are."

"Shut. Up."

"Are you going to do what you *want* to do, or are you going to do what you *have* to do?"

I clench my jaw as I stare out the window. "You have no idea what you are talking about...or what is expected of me."

"I know more than you. Let's go get her." He shrugs. "I'm ready, you want Grace, so let's go get her."

"So you're my quack now with the reverse psychology?" I pinch the bridge of my nose as my elbow rests on the door. "I fucking hate you, you know that?"

We fall silent as the car pulls up at a set of traffic lights and the sad reality sets in. "I can't have Grace." I sigh.

"So why do you want to find her?" he says in a softer tone.

Because I miss her.

We sit in silence for a long time as my mind goes over the depressing facts.

He's right.

I have to let her go, it's not fair for me to chase her when I can't offer her what I want to.

"Forget I said anything," I reply as I stare out the window. "It doesn't matter."

79

The car whizzes through the security gate and into the underground parking lot of my building as the memory of my Gracie lingers.

So close but so far...I need to forget her.

Grace

I watch the baggage handler throw the last of the bags into the cargo hull. We boarded a plane and are on the tarmac, about to leave New York forever.

It's pouring with rain, the sky is depressed, along with my heart.

I did it, I changed my number. Not that he was ever going to call anyway, but at least now I have finality.

I will never have to see his name pop up on my screen... Or get excited every time it rings, only to be disappointed when it isn't him.

"You okay?" Deb smiles over at me as she takes my hand in hers.

"Uh-huh." I fake a smile back.

But I will never be okay, my heart has been broken beyond repair.

If I never date another man for as long as I live, I will be happy. I don't know what headspace I'm in, but it's like I'm purposely trying to torture myself.

I'm listening to "Someone Like You" from Adele on repeat.

As the plane hurtles down the runway, I silently wipe my tears.

The lyrics about finding someone else hit different this time.

I screw up my face in tears, if only.

8

Grace

I SIT in the waiting room with my handbag on my lap, my knee bouncing up and down with nerves.

Please let everything be okay.

At first, I didn't want to be pregnant, but now that I've got my head around it, having a healthy baby is all that I want. I've got this feeling that because I was so against this in the beginning that now I'm going to be punished. Maybe that's just mom guilt starting early.

I didn't tell Deb that my appointment was today, I wanted to come alone. She can't be at every doctor's visit and I'm sure this first one is just standard practice, and besides, I need to get used to doing things alone.

The doctor walks out of his office with a folder in his hand, he's around forty-five, with salt-and-pepper hair, he has a kind-dad vibe. "Grace Porter?" He looks around and smiles when he sees me stand. "How are you today?"

"Good, thanks." My heart is beating like a drum and I walk past him into the office and take a seat at his desk.

He sits down and opens the file and reads it. "Congratulations.

You are..." he pauses as he reads on, "...twelve weeks and five days pregnant."

I clutch my handbag with white-knuckle force. "Yes."

His eyes rise to meet mine. "A planned pregnancy?"

"Yes," I lie.

He keeps reading. "And what about the father, is he excited?"

"I was artificially inseminated."

His eyes rise to meet mine. "At what clinic?"

"In New York at the Chelsea Fertility Clinic," I reply without missing a beat. I've done my research and that's all he should need to know; he has no legal reason to contact them.

"Fantastic." He smiles. "This baby is a gift."

"Yes." I force a smile, feeling guilty for lying.

"Okay," he replies. "Let's do an ultrasound, hop up onto the bed for me."

I lie down and pull my T-shirt up.

"This will be a little cold." He squirts gel onto the end of the ultrasound wand and holds it over my stomach.

Silence.

He moves it around and pushes the wand deeper into my stomach.

"Is everything okay?" I ask.

"Yes, just finding your baby. It's hiding in here somewhere."

I hold my breath as he pushes and prods me.

Squelch, squelch, squelch...

"There we are, do you hear that?" He smiles. "A perfect heartbeat."

The sound brings a big smile to my face. "I can hear it."

He frowns and then keeps prodding and poking. "Hmm, that's interesting."

"What is?"

"There are two heartbeats."

"What?" My eyes widen. "What do you mean?"

"Do you have twins in your family?"

"No."

"Well, you do now."

My mouth falls open as the bed moves beneath me. "Twins?"

"Uh-huh." He wipes my stomach with a tissue and cleans his wand, he takes my hand and helps me sit up. "Back in your chair."

I stare at him in a daze.

Twins.

Twins.

The word rolls around in my empty head and bounces off the sides.

"There are two babies?" I gasp.

"Uh-huh." He smiles as he swivels his chair from side to side. "You hit the jackpot and got some good strong sperm."

Or not.

"Oh..." I begin to hear my heartbeat in my ears.

Two...there are two. I couldn't deal with one, and now there are two.

Two, two...there are two babies.

"Grace?" the doctor says, interrupting my thoughts. "What do you say to that?"

"Huh?" My eyes rise to meet his. "I beg your pardon."

"It's going to be fine." He smiles reassuringly. "Twins are a gift, and I know you will handle this like a pro. It's completely normal to be apprehensive. But of course, depending on how they are in utero will determine the birthing plan we make moving forward."

I stare at him in horror, I have to push two babies out of my vagina.

It's too small for one.

How the actual hell am I supposed to do two? I get a vision of me dying on the delivery table...

Oh. My. God.

"How does that sound?"

I glance back up at him, having no idea what he just said. "Good," I lie, there is nothing sounding good about this at all.

"Okay then, I'll see you in four weeks." He writes something down on a piece of paper and passes it over. "Take these vitamins and eat a varied diet. Try to have as broad a range of vegetables and fruit as you can and keep up the fluids."

I stare at him, mystified.

That's it? He's going to casually send me home carrying an entire fucking army in my stomach?

"Goodbye, Grace."

"Goodbye." On autopilot, I stumble out of the doctor's surgery and wander to my car. I slump into my seat and stare out through the windscreen.

Too shocked to cry, too panicked to think and unable to speak.

Twins.

Gabriel

The car pulls into the curb and I open the door.

"Have a nice day," Mark says as I climb out of the car.

"You too."

I walk in through the front doors of the Ferrara building and stride to the elevator. Roderick the attendant gives me a polite nod as he pushes the button. "Good morning, Mr. Ferrara."

"Morning."

I stare at the doors as I straighten my tie, I can feel all eyes on me as I wait.

Hurry up.

"Beautiful day today," Roderick says, trying to make polite conversation.

"It is."

Why is this elevator so slow?

"Looking forward to getting to work today, sir?"

My unimpressed eyes rise to meet his. "Why are you so chatty?"

"Oh." He gives me a lopsided smile. "I think it makes things less awkward."

My eyes hold his. "I disagree."

The doors open and I walk past him into it and turn toward the front, I see his face fall as the doors close.

Ugh, every morning he annoys me with his perky can-do attitude.

I don't want to talk to you.

Fuck off.

I push the button and begin the climb to the top floor, the elevator stops on level three and I exhale heavily.

The doors open and two men are waiting to get in, their faces fall when they see me and I raise an eyebrow.

"Sorry, Mr. Ferrara." They stay where they are.

I push the button to close the doors. I need a private elevator to this godforsaken place.

Once upon a time I would get here earlier and train before work, I haven't done that since...

I run at home now before I come, the urge to get into the office early has left along with Miss Porter. It's no fun getting dressed in front of Greg. In fact, it's no fun with Greg at all.

He's the most boring person I've ever met. Actually, the entire office is boring now.

I've always been a workaholic, prided myself for my dedication to Ferrara Media.

But lately... I hate coming here.

I hate walking past her empty desk, I hate that nobody rolls their eyes at me or talks back and gives me cheek. I hate that I can't feel her eyes on me as I get dressed. I hate that I don't feel my dick tingle when she chews the end of her pen.

I hate that she left me.

The doors open and I walk through reception. "Good morning, Mr. Ferrara."

"No visitors today."

"Yes, sir."

I open the doors and walk through the desks, I see a few people standing and talking in the photocopier room and my blood boils, what do they think this is?

I march over, their faces fall when they see me. "This isn't a tea party. Get back to work."

"Yes, sir." They scatter like mice.

I walk into my office, slam the door, throw my briefcase onto the table and fall into my chair.

This place is fucking ruined.

Grace

Debbie's wide eyes hold mine. "Twins?"

"Uh-huh."

"Like *twin* twins, like two babies twins?"

"Yep."

"Hmm." Deb has been shocked to silence, she sips her coffee as she chooses her next words carefully. "Well... This is great," she lies.

I stare at her deadpan. "And how is this great?"

"Well." She holds her hands up all animated like. "Your family is done, you can stop after this if you want."

"I'll be stopping, one hundred percent I'll be stopping." I sip my stupid decaf coffee as I think, even my coffee is ruined now. "A household where the children outnumber the adults is . . ."

"Busy." Deb cuts me off. "You'll be busy."

I nod, not wanting to be a downer.

"Oh my gosh, I saw the cutest thing in the shop on the way here. I'm getting it for you on the way out."

"What is it?"

"A memory box."

"What's that?" I frown.

"You know, like a cute little box that you put memorabilia in for your pregnancy. Your ultrasound pictures and any little notes or cards you get along the way."

"I don't want a memory box."

"Why not?"

"Because the way I'm feeling, all I want to write in it is how this is all so unfair and I don't want my child . . ."

"Children." Deb cuts me off.

"Ugh, *children* to ever find out that I was crushing on my boss. They can never know about Gabriel and our one-night stand."

"You are not fatal attraction." She rolls her eyes. "You're so dramatic."

I sip my coffee, annoyed that she's right, I *am* so overdramatic at the moment, I can feel myself doing it but can't seem to stop.

"Fine, I'll buy you two. One for the kids to find with all the cute fluffy stuff, and the other memory box a dumping ground for your heartbreak crap."

"Why would I want a dumping ground for my heartbreak?"

"It will be therapeutic to write everything down and when you're past this stage of your life and happily in love, you can throw this one out. Nobody will ever know...and the kids will still have their fluffy feel-good memory box to look through."

"Maybe." I sigh, distracted.

"Every time you put something in the happy memory box, you need to put something in the dumpster fire box."

I smile, something about that name tickles my fancy. "We're calling it a dumpster fire box?"

"Why not? Your love life is a complete dumpster fire, let's be honest," she mutters dryly.

I giggle and hold my coffee cup up to cheers her. "You've got that right."

The afternoon glow begins to bounce off the water and I smile. My favorite part of the day is here. I grab my notepad and pen and slide the glass door open. "You coming out, Buds?" I call.

My toffee-colored fluffball comes toddling down the stairs, life is bliss, I have a dog now. Buddy is the cutest thing that I never knew I needed. I went to the shelter to get a puppy and came home with an old man, not that I'm complaining, he's perfect in every way. We wander down the stairs and sit.

The sun setting over the lake is magical and one of the main reasons I bought this house. Although small and quaint, my home is like a fairy tale, filled with character and to-do projects. It's a renovator's delight.

My dream home.

As soon as I saw it I knew that I had to make it mine. Three acres of land situated on a point of the lake with one-hundred-and-eighty-degree water views on three sides. There's a long, sweeping driveway lined with the most beautiful oak trees you have ever seen, and one day I'll save up enough money to do a proper drive; for the moment it's dirt road.

At the front of the house is a sweeping veranda, a separate garage, and a garden, then the back of the house is all glass. It's like a Swiss chalet with the upstairs inside the shingle roof with beautiful arbor windows.

But the real magic of the house is the private wharf.

My very own private piece of paradise. You walk out of my back sliding glass doors and onto the veranda, down six steps, and then I'm on the wharf looking straight over the lake.

I have a deck chair and I sit out here every afternoon and watch the sun set over the water. For now I drink tea, but I can imagine having an afternoon glass of wine while the children play.

I put my hand protectively over my stomach. I'm six months pregnant.

And life is good.

My dumpster fire box has worked a treat and Deb was right, venting on paper and putting it into the box is cathartic. Lately, I've turned my venting into poetry. I just write whatever whenever and none of it makes sense, but somehow it makes me feel better. As if releasing all the negativity from inside makes room for all the joy.

I open my notepad and chew on my pen while I think, what will I write today? I think for a moment.

I can forgive him for not loving me.
What I can't forgive is myself,
for ever believing that he could.

I close the notepad and the evening breeze whips my hair around, the birds begin to chirp as the beautiful pink glow lights up the sky. It really is a sight to behold.

The magic is here...

Gabriel

The sound of the engines roar around the circuit, the car pulls in and the pit crew jump into action.

Monaco, the Grand Prix.

I'm in the marquee that's overlooking the track. "Here you go, sir." The waiter delivers my scotch on a tray.

"Thank you." The atmosphere is electric, the crowd huge with beautiful people everywhere you look.

"So where are you based?" the beautiful blonde asks.

"New York."

"My favorite city in the world."

"We have something in common." I raise my glass.

"I'm sure we have a lot in common." She gives me a sexy smile and I look over her shoulder and see the unmistakable auburn hair.

Is that...

I watch the woman from behind, wearing a red dress and laughing as she talks to someone. My heart skips a beat.

Gracie.

"So what do you..."

"Excuse me." I brush past the woman and walk straight over. "Gracie."

The woman turns and my face falls, it isn't her. "Excuse me, my apologies. I thought you were someone else."

"Sorry to disappoint you." She smiles.

"Not at all." I fake a smile and walk to the bar; I wait in line with a full drink in my hand.

"Everything all right?" Mark asks from beside me.

I glance up. "Why wouldn't it be?"

"You thought that was Grace Porter, didn't you?"

"Who?" I act oblivious.

"You know, I hate seeing your face fall every time you see a redhead."

"Yeah well... There are a lot of things I hate about you." I drain my glass and slosh it around in my mouth before swallowing. "Stop watching me and get back to work."

"Last time I looked, my job is watching you." He winks.

"Fuck off," I mouth.

He saunters back to his place by the wall and I step forward in line to the bar and drag my hand through my hair as I wait.

I hate that he knows me.

Grace

"We're going to get going, sweetheart." Mom kisses my forehead.

"Well done today, Gracie," Dad says as he looks lovingly down at the babies in their crib beside my bed. "You did good, baby."

"Thank you so much for being in the delivery room with me." I kiss my mom as she leans over me and then my dad. "I'm so grateful for you two."

"We'll be back first thing tomorrow." Dad smiles as he adjusts the baby's little blue bonnet. "You be good babies for your momma tonight," he tells them, and with one last smile, they disappear down the corridor.

It's midnight, and the maternity ward has fallen quiet. My room is dark and lit only by the strip lighting in the bathroom.

For the first time I'm left alone with my two babies, fraternal twins, a little boy and a little girl. Wrapped tightly in their little bunny rugs and snugged in together in the one crib.

I'm having this weird out-of-body experience, it's as if I'm hovering way up above and watching the three of us. Together at last...but then so alone.

No dad here to welcome them into the world, to comfort me, or to tell us it's going to be okay. Words that I so desperately need to hear.

Now that they've arrived and are real-life little people, my deception seems all too real.

I'm a bad person, I should have told him.

My nostrils flare as I try to keep it together, the lump in my throat is painful. It's like I've been holding in tears for nine months and the glue that held me together is disintegrating before my eyes.

This is a happy day. *I will not cry.*

A hot tear rolls down my cheek and I swipe it away.

"Hey," a nurse says as she walks through the door. "Are you okay, darling?" She comes and sits on the side of my bed and takes my hand in hers.

"Yes," I whisper.

"Big day, huh?"

I nod.

"Are you in pain?"

"No."

"Don't be a hero, Grace, C-sections are painful, and you need to be rested before you go home alone with these babies."

Home alone.

Hearing it out loud breaks the dam and I screw up my face in tears.

"Oh sweetie, tomorrow will seem a lot brighter. I promise."

I nod, unable to answer through the lump in my throat.

She reads my chart and pulls out some pills from her pocket. "Here's what we're going to do." She passes me the pills. "You're going to have these and try and get some rest, and I'm going to sit in that chair in the corner and watch over you and your babies while you sleep."

"But..."

"But nothing, you won't be alone tonight." She squeezes my hand in hers, the tears rolling down my face. "I won't leave you. I promise."

"Thank you," I whisper. I take the tablets and lie back down and she pulls the blankets up over me and tucks me in.

"What are you going to name your babies?"

I shrug, unsure. "Something Italian."

"Their father is Italian?"

I nod.

She gives me a sad smile, finally understanding why I'm upset.

There was no donor sperm, only a lie covering for an absent dad.

She sits on the side of my bed and rests her hand on my shoulder, such a simple act of kindness that means so much. "What are your favorite names?"

"Dominic and Lucia," I whisper.

She smiles down at me. "They sound like the perfect names."

"You think so?"

"You're going to be fine, darling, and you're going to find the love of your life and he's going to love your babies just as much as you do."

I screw up my face in tears again, damn it. I'm unstable.

"Close your eyes and go to sleep," her loving voice whispers, she brushes her hand over my hair. "Tomorrow's a new day."

9

Gabriel

"Fire him." I sit back in my seat, annoyed.

"You can't fire him," Alessio gasps as the boardroom falls silent.

"Watch me." I push my intercom. "Greg, get Rodney Roberts up here, please."

"Yes, sir."

"Listen, I know this report is not great but he can improve on it, I'm sure." Alessio fights his case.

"I agree with this, he's trying. We need to give him another chance," Victor chips in.

"We've already given him another chance and he didn't come through, he can sponge on someone else's time and money, not mine," I snap.

"But..."

"Why do you soft cocks always feel sorry for people, this isn't a fucking charity organization. If you don't perform, you don't get to keep your job, it's as simple as that. He is at the top end of his game, he doesn't have the privilege to be lazy."

My intercom buzzes. "Yes," I answer.

"Rodney Roberts is off sick today, sir."

"Of course he is. Thank you." My eyes flick to Alessio, and he winces. "The final nail in his coffin."

"Can I take your order?" the waitress asks.

I glance over to Serafina, my date. "Cosa mangi?" *("What are you having?")*

"I'll have what you're having." She smiles over at me.

I stare over the table at her. *Grow a backbone, for fuck's sake.*

Ugh...

"A green salad and the lobster times two, please." I close the menu and hand it over to the waitress.

Serafina is as beautiful as they come, tall, dark and with a body to die for, Italian to the bone, and nothing about her interests me in the slightest.

I think I'm broken.

I subtly glance at my watch, two hours until I can get the hell out of here.

Grace

Laughter and screams sound through my house as I chase two naked toddlers around with nappies. To them, getting out of the bath and having me chase them around with clothes is the funniest thing ever, and I have to admit, even I love it.

My babies are eighteen months old, the biggest blessing and the absolute loves of my life. Our home is filled with laughter and chaos but above all...so much love.

Dominic is the oldest, he has dark wavy hair and olive skin with big brown eyes, he's a mini version of his father. Personality and all, he's feisty and short-tempered, dominant and intelligent and the biggest mommy's boy of all time. And then there's Lucia, we call her Lucy for short. Although she looks like her father, with her dark hair and big brown eyes, she couldn't be more different. Tiny compared to Dominic, she's calm and placid with the sweetest little nature. She idolizes her brother and has a quiet confidence about her. While Dominic wants to sit curled up on my lap, Lucy prefers to sit with Buddy on the couch, she doesn't want to sit on my lap, she's so independent.

"Come on, guys, we need to be on time today," I plead.

Dominic squeals with laughter and runs into my bedroom and dives onto the bed as I chase him. "You're a little nudist, Dom." I tackle him and roll him over to hold him down. "Stop squirming." I put his nappy on as he laughs and tries to escape me. "Come on." I try to act stern as I struggle to fight him. "We don't have time for this today."

I'm not lying, we really don't. I go back to work next month, and today our new nanny arrives. I've concocted up a plan and in my head it makes perfect sense, but in reality, I have no idea how it's actually going to turn out.

Deb and I have spent hours and hours discussing how the future is going to go down and one thing is strikingly clear: I need to prepare for the day they ask who their father is. I can lie to the world about artificial insemination, but I will never lie to them.

When they ask...and they will, I'll tell them the truth.

I need to prepare them the best of my ability, I need them to learn about Italian culture, speak the language and appreciate the difference between our heritages.

I've hired a young Italian nanny, she arrives today.

She's going to study teaching part-time at the college and live here rent free with pay, in exchange for minding the kids while I work three days a week and teaching them how to speak Italian.

They need to learn it along with English, now, in their formative years. And besides, it will kill two birds with one stone: I can go back to work and get a new roommate, the kids will benefit and she gets to live in America for a few years. It's a win-win situation... I hope.

. . .

We stand at the arrival terminal; the children are sitting in their double stroller and are completely preoccupied with their muesli bars, their latest obsession, and I'm about to go into cardiac arrest.

This is a terrible idea, what the hell was I thinking?

A stranger living in my house...she could be a serial killer or anything. Those references could be completely doctored.

I get a vision of how feral the twins can be and my temperature rises. What if she's a princess, I can't deal with perfect princesses.

Our life is chaotic, and Buddy our dog sleeps on the couch when he isn't supposed to and our house isn't always tidy and...I begin to feel sick to my stomach.

What have I done?

My phone beeps a text.

Just getting off the plane now

She's here.

I smile and nervously type back,

We're at the arrival gate.
I'm the one with the double stroller.

The people begin to walk down the ramp and I watch on with my heart in my throat. "Look, here comes Maria," I tell them. "Behave please, no tantrums today." They keep munching on their muesli bars, totally uninterested in anything I say.

I see a young girl with dark hair, and she sees me and smiles and waves.

She's wearing a gray tracksuit and her long dark hair is up in a high ponytail. She bounces over. "Grace?"

"Maria?" I smile awkwardly.

"I'm so glad to be here." She laughs and pulls me into a hug. "Thank you so much for picking me up."

She's normal.

She bends down to lean into the stroller. "And who are you?"

"This is Maria," I tell them. "This is Lucy and Dominic."

"Hello, cuties." She smiles.

Dominic accidently drops his muesli bar on the ground and without missing a beat, Maria bends and picks it up with her bare hands.

"Oh, that's gross, sorry." I wince. "Let me take that."

"No, I've got it." She pulls a tissue out of her pocket and wraps the sloppy muesli bar up. "We'll get another one when we get home," she tells him. "Lick your fingers."

Dominic smiles up at her all awestruck and licks his fingers.

And just like that everything falls into place. Suddenly, I know that this is going to be wonderful. That *she* is going to be wonderful and the world is officially saved.

She gives me a big, friendly smile. "Let's go home."

I pull the car into the parking lot of the mechanic's, damn it, this is a shit fight. I quickly give the car a neaten up and collect the receipts and coffee cups in the front console. Why does my car service always fall on the most chaotic of days? Maria had a college assignment due this morning, so I was up helping her with that until late last night, and then this morning Dominic was running through the house and bumped his head. To top it off, Buddy went out this morning and got completely covered in mud, came back through the doggy door and rubbed it all over the living room rug and couch as if it were a trophy.

Ugh... It's been the morning from hell and I haven't stopped running since the moment I woke up.

I would have canceled the car service if it were not for one small detail.

"Hey, you," a raspy voice calls from inside the office and I smile. "Hi, Russ."

He walks out to greet me, light brown curly hair and olive skin, with the biggest blue eyes you ever saw.

My mechanic Russel is the hottest man in Greenville, not in a handsome bachelor kind of way. In a subtle *the way he smiles* kind of way.

Getting my car serviced is the highlight of my life.

He smiles and our gaze stays locked for a beat longer than it should. "Been too long since I saw you, Grace."

"Well..." I drag my hand through my hair, he makes me giddy. "I can't have my car serviced any more than I do, Russ. I think they call that stalking."

"You can stalk me any day." The air swirls between us.

My eyes drop to the tight blue jeans and his red flannelette check shirt. He has thick quads and ropey veins down his forearms, big broad shoulders.

Everything about Russ screams raw, unfiltered man.

We've had this flirty banter going on for over a year now but it never seems to eventuate to anything. I know he's single and not a player, but that's all I really know; he lives a little out of town and grew up here, but the rest of him is a mystery. From what I gather, nobody seems to know much about him.

He leans his behind on my car and crosses his feet at the ankles. "You know, I've been thinking."

"About what?"

"How . . ." He cuts himself off.

"What?" I ask impatiently. "Go on."

"Do you want to go out some time?"

The floor spins.

"Like on a date?"

"Yeah." He gives me a smile. "I mean...I know you have the twins and it's not—"

"I have a nanny now." I cut him off.

His eyebrows shoot up. "You do?"

"Uh-huh." I shrug. "So, I can go out now..." I shrug again. "I mean, not all the time, but...sometimes. I have a little more freedom."

He smiles and I feel it all the way to my toes. "Saturday night?"

"Uh-huh."

"I'll pick you up around seven?" he asks.

Is this really happening?

"Uh-huh."

He walks over to me. "You know, you're saying uh-huh a lot." He takes my face in his hands and looks down at me.

The air leaves my lungs at his touch, and the only thing that will come out of my mouth is a weak "Uh-huh."

"You should probably kiss me to get me through until Saturday...uh-huh?"

"Uh-huh..."

His lips brush mine, softly but with the perfect amount of pressure.

Oh...

We kiss again and again and he pulls back and licks his lips as he stares down at me. "Your car isn't the only thing I need to service today."

"What?" I giggle, shocked.

"Grease and oil change." He laughs.

"Pervert."

"For me, I meant for me."

"Sure you did." I pull out of his grip and walk backward so I can keep looking at him. "I have to get to work."

"How are you getting there?"

"Mr. Holdsworth, my neighbor, is picking me up from the main road, he's out there waiting."

"Did you forget something?"

"Nope, I think my work is done here this morning."

He gives me a sexy smile. "I'm going to need your keys."

"Oh, right." Embarrassed, I dig through my bag and fetch my keys and hand them over, he grabs me all rough like and kisses me again. "You behave in Mr. Holdsworth's car now."

I burst out laughing. "He's eighty-nine."

"You could bring a petrified rock back to life with that kiss."

I walk off toward the main road and I can feel his eyes

watching me, and I have to concentrate on not jumping in the air and kicking up my heels in excitement.

Finally!

Saturday night, 7:08 p.m.

Headlights shine up the street and a car slowly pulls up in the driveway. "He's here," Maria calls.

"Okay," I call back. Ever since Russ and I kissed last Tuesday, I'm like a little kid at Christmas. He woke something up in me that had been long forgotten, and I don't remember ever being this excited for a date.

I think I've turned a corner and finally realized it's okay to want something for me. It's taken me three years of being a mom and many lectures from Deb and Maria to realize that I don't need to feel guilty every time I do something that doesn't revolve around my kids. I guess I always felt that, because I'm doing this parent thing on my own, that they should get every ounce of me and my time.

Tonight, that changes, no more all or nothing. I need to find a balance, happy home life and a man who...I smirk, who am I kidding?

I want a hot man to fuck me well, to use my body like I want to use his.

It's been way too long.

A knock sounds at the door, and my heart skips a beat. Maria and I purposely wore the kids out today and did every activity on earth so that we could get them to bed before I go out. That way I have no excuse to be preoccupied with worrying about what's going on at home. We both know me too well.

"Hello." I hear Maria's voice as she opens the door.

"Hello, I'm Russel." His deep voice echoes through the house.

I take one last look in the mirror; I'm wearing a black fitted dress that Deb and I bought during the week, my hair is down and I'm wearing makeup and black lingerie.

Lingerie.

With my heart beating hard in my chest, I come down the stairs to see Russel standing at the front door with a homemade bunch of flowers. Our eyes meet and he smiles softly. "Hi." He looks me up and down. "You look beautiful."

"Hi." I beam.

He passes me the flowers and I nearly melt into a puddle.

"I'll put those into some water, you two get going." Maria smiles as she looks between us as we stare at each other.

"Thanks." I pass her the flowers and float out the door and out to Russel's truck. He opens the door for me and then leans in. "Do you have any idea how gorgeous you look?"

"You should kiss me."

He rolls his lips. "Aren't I supposed to wait until the end of the date to do that?"

"Nope." I grab his face and bring it down to mine, our lips touch and the kiss is long, slow, and deep. "Dinner?" I murmur against his lips.

"What?" he pants, overcome with arousal. We kiss again and again and I can feel his erection as it leans up against my leg.

Yesssss...

Arousal screams through my body like a fire truck, we can't go out like this.

"Takeout at your house?" I pant against his lips.

"Works for me." He slams the door shut and nearly runs around to the driver's side.

What the hell? We didn't even make it out of my driveway.

We're like animals.

I don't remember driving to his house, I don't remember getting out of the car or what furniture he has inside.

All I know is that now I'm in Russel's bedroom and his eyes roam up and down my body as he slowly peels my dress off.

The lights are dimmed and the room is quiet, every breath between us is magnified.

Thump, thump, thump goes my heart. It's been a long time

since someone has seen me naked and I've had two children since then. What if he doesn't like what he sees?

Say something.

"You are so gorgeous, Grace," he murmurs as he takes my face in his hands and kisses me deeply. "You're all I think about."

He throws me back onto the bed and spreads my legs, he looks up at me as he licks me there and I nearly jump off the bed.

The first time he touched me was with his tongue. I smile goofily up at the ceiling.

I need this.

Gabriel

I walk out of my building and see Mark standing by the car, he gives me a weak smile that doesn't reach his eyes. "Good morning." He opens the back door for me.

"Hello," I say as I get into the car.

We pull out into the traffic and I watch him in the rearview mirror, his face is etched with worry.

"What is it?" I ask.

His eyes flick up to me. "What's what?"

"What's wrong with you?"

"Nothing." He exhales heavily.

"Don't lie to me, you've been a sad sack of shit all week."

He rolls his eyes and keeps driving, and I can't stand it. "Pull over."

"What?"

"Pull the fucking car over."

"Why?"

"Because I said so."

He pulls the car over to the side and I get out of the car and open his car door. "Get out."

"What are you doing?"

"I'm driving today."

He stares at me, confused. "What the hell am I supposed to do, then?"

"Get in the passenger seat, you idiot. Unless you want to walk home."

He rolls his eyes and walks around to get into the front passenger seat, and I pull back out onto the road.

He looks over at me. "What are you doing?"

"Driving."

"Why?"

"Because when I'm depressive and moody, you drive me, so now it's my turn to drive you."

"I'm not depressive and moody."

"Good, because that's my position around here."

We drive in silence for a while.

"Depressive isn't even a word," he says casually as he looks out the window.

I keep driving.

"And for the record, you're not depressive, you're just moody," he continues.

"Well...for the record." I stop at the traffic lights. "I'm not moody, people are just imbeciles."

"Are you calling me an imbecile?"

"One hundred percent. Tell me what's wrong with you."

Silence.

"I'm driving around this city until you tell me and I don't have time for your bullshit, spit it out."

He drags his hand through his hair. "Zoe gets married this weekend."

My heart sinks.

Zoe was his childhood sweetheart who left him when he was on a deployment. She said she couldn't put her life on hold for a man who goes to war.

"Well..." I grip the steering wheel. "Good riddance to her."

He nods sadly.

"You are seeing someone else, why do you care what Zoe is doing?" I ask as I turn another corner.

Silence.

He shrugs. "I'm not seeing her anymore."

"Oh. Why not?"

"I just... I compare everyone to her, you know?"

I do know.

I listen as I drive.

"And I know we can't be together and I don't even want to be, but..." He hesitates.

"But what?" I ask.

"Thinking of Zoe takes me back to a time in my life when I was happy and everything was simple because she was the only girl in the world that I wanted."

The traffic comes to a standstill.

"Every woman just seems so average."

"Amen to that." I sigh. "I thought it was just me."

We keep driving in silence.

"Maybe we're just getting old and maybe the thrill we used to get from love has lost its luster," he says.

"It's possible." I shrug. "Probable, actually."

I turn another corner as we drive and an idea comes to mind.

I call the office.

"Good morning, Mr. Ferrara," Isabell answers.

"I won't be in today."

"Ahh." She hesitates. "You have a fully booked day, sir."

"Reschedule everything."

"Are you unwell?" she asks.

I hit end call. "Mind your business," I mutter under my breath.

"Why did you call in?" Mark asks. "What are you doing?"

"Taking you to Vegas for the weekend."

"Why?"

"Gambling, alcohol and strippers," I reply as I drive.

"You think playing poker, drinking scotch, and fucking multiple high-end strippers is going to get me over Zoe?"

"No." I shrug. "But it will be fun." I glance over at him and he smirks.

"You owe me four hundred dollars, by the way," I tell him.

"For what?"

"I'm not being your therapist for free, you know?"

He rolls his lips to hide his smile. "What kind of therapist offers gambling, alcohol, and cheap sex as treatment?"

"The fun kind."

Twelve months later.

I follow the two girls down the pier toward my yacht as they totter along in their skin-tight dresses and sky-high stilettos, giggling and tipsy. Giovanna has long dark hair and a body to die for, and Amara is her identical twin. "What happens when we get to your yacht?" Amara smiles sexily over her shoulder.

"You both get on your knees, that's what." I gesture to my yacht. "Keep walking."

They both laugh as they continue to walk, they're going to fucking get it.

We are in St. Tropez in the South of France; I've been in Italy for a month and called in here on my way home. We arrive at the yacht, and Mark is waiting at the end of the gangplank. His eyes roam over the two gorgeous women I'm with. "Evening, sir."

"Good evening, Mark."

He unhooks the black rope to allow access and the two girls laugh and chat as they walk onto my yacht.

"Lucky prick," he mutters under his breath.

I smirk. "I'd ask you to join us…"

He raises his eyebrow, suddenly interested.

"But I don't share."

"Fuck you," he whispers.

I chuckle and walk across the gangplank and onto my yacht. I look around for the girls. "Where are you?" I call.

"Up here."

I take the stairs two at a time and once at the top and into my bedroom, I find them both naked and on their knees, waiting for me.

My cock thumps in appreciation. "Good girls."

Grace

I read the text from Deb.

> *I need to see you*
> *Urgently.*
> *Can we have lunch today?*

Huh?
I text her.

> *What's wrong?*

I wait for her reply.

> *Nothing is wrong but I need to see you.*

Jeez, I wonder if she's fighting with Scott. I reply.

> *I have lunch at 12:30*
> *Meet at usual place?*

A reply bounces straight back.

> *Okay see you then.*

Twelve forty, I walk into Chachi's to see Debbie sitting at the back, and I wave as I make my way to her. "Are you okay?" I ask as I kiss her cheek.

"I'm fine, but you need to sit down."

"What's wrong?" I slump into the seat.

"I could be the worst friend in the world for wrecking this surprise, but I've been thinking about it all night and I want you to be prepared and not ruin this."

"For what?" I frown.

"Russel is going to propose."

My face falls. "What?"

"He called over yesterday to ask me what kind of ring you would want."

I stare at her, horrified.

"And he's going to go all out with a grand proposal, and I just want you to be excited when he does it, you know?"

The walls begin to close in around me.

"Russel is a great guy, Grace." She takes my hand across the table.

My eyes well with tears. "Why would he want to get married?"

"Because he loves you and you've been together for two years now. You guys are great together."

"And you told me because..."

"Because I knew you would react like this and I wanted it to be to me and not him. He doesn't deserve to see your face fall."

Sheer terror begins to run rampant through my body. "I don't want to get married, Deb."

"Why not?"

Her silhouette blurs and I get a lump in my throat, unable to articulate myself.

"Russel is a great guy," she tells me.

"I know he is."

"And you two have great chemistry, and the sex is great."

"I know."

"And he loves you and he's great with the kids. Remember how incredible he was when Buddy died?"

I put my head into my hands.

"You should be jumping from the rooftops in excitement."

"I should."

"The only reason I told you is because deep down, I knew you wouldn't be."

"How?" I ask.

"What?"

"How did you know I wouldn't be excited?"

She stares at me for a beat. "I watch the two of you together and it's obvious that his affection is greater than yours. His commitment to the relationship is stronger than yours. He's one hundred percent all in, and you're...just not."

"I don't know what the hell is wrong with me," I whisper. "Russel is my dream guy, everything about him is perfect. But..." My voice trails off.

"He's not him."

"This has nothing to do with Gabriel," I snap, annoyed.

"Doesn't it?" she snaps back. "I think it does. I think you're still hopelessly in love with Gabriel Ferrara, and no man, no matter how perfect he is will ever live up to him."

"That's complete bullshit. I haven't thought of Gabriel in years."

"Grace." She squeezes my hand in hers. "You need to learn to love what's good for you."

Her silhouette blurs.

"Russel is good for you." She gives me a sad smile. "He loves you."

"I know."

"If you don't love him enough to marry him, you need to stop being selfish and let him go so that he can find someone else."

I screw up my face in tears. "I don't want to lose him."

"Then don't." She smiles. "Marry him, be happy. Because that's what you deserve. A man that worships the ground you walk on."

The thought of marrying Russel rolls my stomach, in fact the thought of marrying anyone rolls my stomach.

"Please, Grace. Think on this, don't mess up a perfect relationship because you're scared."

"I'm not scared, Deb, that isn't it."

"What is it, then?"

"The reality is..." sadness fills me to say this out loud, "...something is missing with Russ."

"Like what?"

"I don't know. If I knew, I would fix it."

Gabriel

I slide the king into place. "Checkmate."

Mark rolls his eyes.

"Beating you is becoming boring." I sigh.

"I only play with you because you pay me to," he replies dryly.

I chuckle and sip my scotch.

"Why are we playing chess on a Saturday night, anyway?" he asks.

My eyes roam over to the wall of windows and the twinkling New York lights way down below. "I don't know." I sip my scotch. "Do you ever get the feeling that there is something missing?"

"How so?"

"I don't know, I have everything...and yet."

"If you want something more when you live the life you do, then the rest of us mere mortals are screwed," he replies.

I sip my drink again as I drift into deep thought. "Maybe I should get married."

"Maybe." He shrugs. "Ariana is . . ."

"Perfect." I cut him off.

He nods.

We start a new game of chess as we both fall into our own thoughts. "I always thought when I met the one, I would be chomping at the bit to make it legal," I say as I think out loud.

"Not sure if I'll ever get married, to be honest," Mark replies.

"I want children."

"You need children to pass all this crap down to." He gestures around my apartment.

"For the record, my eighty-million-dollar penthouse is not crap."

He chuckles. "But does it make you happy?"

"No." My eyes roam around the penthouse. "Doesn't appear to."

"So are you going to marry Ariana?"

"No."

"Who are you going to marry then, if not her?"

"I don't know. Ariana is beautiful and adoring, Italian and everything I should want. We've been together for over a year and I do love her."

"But you're not in love with her?"

"Maybe I'm incapable of it."

"Probably." He thinks for a moment. "You owe me five hundred bucks."

"For what?"

"I'm not being your therapist for free, you know."

"What solution have you given me, you just told me I'm incapable of love," I fire back. "And since when did your price rise?"

He chuckles. "The truth is costly."

I walk into my apartment just on six and see rose petals scattered up the hall.

What the hell is this?

"Ariana?" I call, confused. As I keep walking, more rose petals. "Ariana?" I turn the corner and see a huge love heart on the floor made of rose petals with flickering candles and music and Ariana is on one knee.

No.

"What..."

"I love you." She smiles up at me. "I know you're supposed to be the one to ask, but I can't wait any longer."

No.

"Sweetheart...I just."

"Will you marry me, Gabriel?" she asks hopefully as she looks up at me.

My heart sinks. The very last thing I want to do is hurt this beautiful woman.

"I love you so much," she whispers through tears. "Make me the happiest woman alive and become my husband."

And this is it, the moment where I have to choose what I know is good for me. I drop to my knees in front of her, torn between begging for forgiveness that she has to put up with me and the need to run as far away as I physically can. "Yes." I softly kiss her lips.

"Yes what?"

"Yes, I'll marry you."

Gabriel

Seven years to the day after Grace left Ferrara Media.

I GLANCE up at the sign hanging over the door.

ELEVEN
MADISONPARK

I push through the door and walk right on in. "Good after-noon, Mr. Ferrara, your table is this way, sir." The waiter nods with a smile.

"Thank you." I follow him through the restaurant and see my brother Alessio sitting with my mother at her regular table by the window.

She breaks into a broad smile as she sees me.

"Mama." I kiss her two cheeks.

"Ciao, mio caro Gabriel." *("Hello, my darling Gabriel.")* She smiles.

"Ales." I pat my brother on the shoulder before sitting at the table.

Alessio pours me a glass of wine and passes it over. "Glad you're here, Mom can lecture *you* now." He raises his wineglass before taking a huge gulp.

My eyes flick up to my mother. "Che succede, mamma? Qualcosa non va?" (*"What's wrong, Mama?"*)

"He canceled his date with Arabella." She scowls.

Alessio looks over at me, deadpan, and I chuckle.

"If you like Arabella so much, you should date her yourself," he replies dryly.

"She is the ultimate woman," she replies.

"For Gabriel," Alessio fires back.

"Gabriel is married."

"Not yet." I roll my eyes. "Calm down."

"In five weeks, so same thing."

"There's still time to run." Alessio smirks as he raises his glass to me.

I smile and then drop my face immediately.

My mother's main mission in life is to marry off her children, she's being met with harsh resistance on all counts.

I open the menu, peruse the choices and roll my eyes. "Why do we always come here. I hate vegan food."

"And yet you always eat everything on your plate," Mom replies.

"I want meat." I sigh.

"When you are married, you will want for nothing."

Ugh. I gulp my wine too, Alessio's mood is rubbing off on me.

Nagging is her favorite sport.

"Where is Carina?" I ask.

"Your sister had an appointment."

"What did you say to Arabella?" Mother asks Alessio.

I glance over and see a familiar face, what was his name. I watch him for a moment as I try to place him...*Rodney.*

He worked for me back when Gracie was here.

I wonder...

He stands to go to the bar, and before I can stop myself, I stand

113

too. "Torno tra un attimo." (*"Back in a moment."*) I stride over and stand next to him at the bar. "Rodney." I smile.

His face falls before he catches it, and I roll my lips to hide my smirk. *Soft cock.*

"Mr. Ferrara," he stammers nervously. "Hi."

"Hello." I reply. "How are you?"

"Good, and you?"

"I'm great."

The bartender walks over. "What will it be?"

"Let me buy you a drink, Rodney."

"Oh, I couldn't."

"I insist." I smile as I sit down on the barstool. "Two Blue Label scotches, please?"

Rodney's eyes widen at my order. "I've got to go back to work."

"This will make it more fun, then, won't it." I point to the stool beside me. "Sit."

He nervously falls onto the stool beside me.

"The way we parted, it was nothing personal, you know that, right?"

"Yes." He nods. "It was a bad time for me."

I nod. "Where are you working now?" I ask him.

"Ahhh..." He hesitates.

"Miles Media." My eyes hold his. "Am I right?"

"Ah...well...."

"Relax, it's fine." I smile. "They are lucky to have you."

"Thanks."

The waiter puts the two scotches on the bar in front of us. "Thank you." I pick mine up and lift it to my lips, ahh, perfection.

Rodney sips his and winces. "Strong."

I smirk. "Maybe you're just weak?"

"No doubt about it." He rubs his chest as he feels it go all the way down.

"So..." How do I put this? "Have you seen anyone that we used to work with?" I act casual.

"No." He shrugs. "I run into Geoffrey every now and then, he's still with you, obviously."

I nod and take another sip as I listen. "What about Miss Porter, do you ever see her?"

"No." He twists his lips. "I haven't seen her for years."

"Oh..."

"I ran into her when she was pregnant at a trade show but haven't seen her since."

My stomach drops. "She's married?"

"No, she did it alone. Donor sperm."

"What?" I screw up my face. "What do you mean?"

He shrugs. "I don't know, she said that she wanted a child and didn't have a partner so decided to go down the donor sperm route. That's why she moved away, so that she could bring up her child in the country."

What?

I stare at him as I listen intently. "How pregnant was she when you saw her?"

"Heavily pregnant, like huge."

"When was this?"

"Not long after I left work, actually. Within a year of when she left."

"What do you mean?"

"Yeah." He shrugs. "Shocked me too, if I'm honest."

"What was the date?"

"I have no idea, it was..." He frowns as he thinks. "I saw her at the Apple convention in Vermont."

"When was that?"

"No idea, but it was in the year we both left, I know that because I was still living in Manhattan, I remember I moved the weekend after the show."

Hmm...I sip my scotch as I think.

Rodney keeps talking and I take out my phone and google,

Date of Apple convention in Vermont

The date pops up.

July

July...
We were together in the December of the year before.
Hmm.
Weird...
That's seven months after we slept together, so she was already pregnant at the time...or...

"What do you think?" Rodney says. I glance up, I haven't heard a word he's been saying.

"I'm sorry, I'm here with my mother. It was lovely seeing you again." I cut him off and hold my hand out to shake his.

"Oh..." His face falls. "Of course. Good to see you again."
Liar.

"Goodbye." I march back to my table and sit down; my mind is racing a million miles per minute.

She was seven months pregnant when he saw her, seven months after we spent the night together.

Couldn't be...

"I ordered for you," Alessio says.

"Grazie." I take out my phone and text Mark.

Find Grace Porter

Grace

"Find your ballet shoes, bubba," I call as I spread the peanut butter onto my piece of toast.

"Where are they?" Lucy calls from upstairs.

"They should be in your closet," I call back.

I hear things hitting the wall as she throws things out of her way to look. "They're not."

116

I roll my eyes; it would have been easier to find them myself in the first place because now I'm going to have to walk upstairs and get them anyway plus clean up the mess she made while looking for them.

"I can't find them," she screams, on the edge of a meltdown. "I've looked everywhere."

"Coming," I call.

Ugh, every Saturday it's the same.

Running around like a chicken, getting ready for ballet class.

I swear someone must break into our house and hide shit to make my life difficult.

I'm forever looking for something.

I walk upstairs and from the corner of my eye catch sight of her twirling in my bedroom, she's checking herself out in my full-length mirror. I stand and lean against the doorframe and watch her for a moment.

She's wearing a pastel-pink leotard and tutu, little white stockings. Her long dark hair is up in a bun and she is so stinking cute I can't stand it.

"Wow." I smile. "Fabulous twirling."

"I'm getting really good at these." She holds her hands out all professional like.

"I can see." I nod. "Very impressive."

"Maria says that I might go up to the next class next year."

I smirk. She will go up because she's older but I'll play along. "Wow, I didn't know that. Great."

I walk into her bedroom and look around at the chaos, everything is out of the bottom of her wardrobe and strung all over her bedroom. "What happened in here?"

"What?"

"The mess."

"Oh...I was looking for the ballet shoes."

"Couldn't be bothered to put things back after?" I roll my eyes as I begin to look for these bastard ballet slippers.

"I'm twirling."

I roll my eyes as I look around her room, not in the wardrobe, not in the toybox, not under the bed.

Where are these stupid shoes?

"Maybe you should go barefoot today," I call.

"No," she cries.

"Well, where did you put them?"

"Maria must have touched them."

Ugh, she's probably right.

Maria has moved out and is living with her boyfriend, she's here three days a week while I work and she still knows more about our house than we do.

I walk downstairs and text her.

> *Hi Maria,*
> *Sorry to bother you.*
> *Have you seen Lucy's ballet slippers?*

A text bounces back.

> *Hi.*
> *Mr. Snuffles is wearing them.*

"Oh for god's sake."

> *What would we do without you?*
> *Thanks.*

I trudge back upstairs, and sure enough, Lucy's giant stuffed elephant is wearing the ballet slippers. "Mr. Snuffles was wearing them," I call.

"Oh yeah," she calls, unruffled. "He was too."

"Come on, we have to hurry now. Downstairs and in the car."

I rush down the stairs and glance out the window down to the lake. The morning sun is glistening on the water.

This view will never get old.

"In the car, please," I call.

I hold the piece of toast with my teeth as I collect my bags. Straight after ballet we have Little League, and then this afternoon we have a birthday party. Saturdays are always jam-packed with activities.

I walk out the front door onto the large veranda and see a black car come down the driveway.

"In the car," I call. "Fuck's sake," I mutter under my breath.

The car stops and parks at our place and I frown as I look over. *Who is this?* The back door opens and in slow motion I see a man in a navy suit get out of the car...my heart stops.

Gabriel Ferrara.

He walks toward me, his height towering over mine. Big brown eyes and his perfect square jaw. "Hello, Grace," he says in his deep purr of a voice.

Emotion instantly overwhelms me and I get a lump in my throat, suddenly I'm taken back in time to the girl he didn't want.

I always knew this day would come, but now that it's here...*I'm not ready.*

"Hello, Gabriel." My eyes flick to the house. "What are you doing here?"

His dark eyes hold mine. "I think you know."

The screen door slams shut and Lucy comes sauntering out in her little tutu.

Gabriel's face drops and he watches her walk over to us.

Bang.

Bang.

Bang beats my heart.

No...

"Hi." She smiles happily as she takes my hand in hers and swings it back and forth, damn it, why is she so friendly?

"Hello," Gabriel replies coolly. "What is your name?"

"Lucia."

Gabriel's jaw clenches as he stares at her. With her dark Italian features, she is undeniably nothing like me. My eyes well with tears, knowing that his anger is going to be ruthless.

Fuck.

Don't cry. Don't cry.

"What is your surname?" he replies to her.

Lucy smiles proudly as she swings my hand back and forth. "Porter."

Gabriel's murderous eyes meet mine.

He knows.

My skin crawls with fear...

"Go in the house, baby," I whisper.

"What?" She frowns up at me.

"In the house," I snap more urgently. "Ballet isn't on today, I just found out. Go in the house now."

"But..."

"Lucia. Now."

Lucy shrugs sadly and then waves at Gabriel. "Bye." She turns and walks back into the house, he doesn't take his eyes off her as she disappears. As she walks through the door, his eyes meet mine.

"Is she..."

I swallow the lump in my throat.

"How could you?" he whispers angrily.

"Gabriel..." I whisper through tears. "Please, you need to leave."

"You think you can hide my fucking child from me?" he growls.

My worst nightmare is coming to life.

"You need to leave," I spit.

"I will do no such thing," he yells as he loses all control.

I screw up my face in tears. "Stop it."

"Don't you," a little voice yells as it pushes him away from me. "Leave my mom alone."

Gabriel turns and sees the furious little boy who has seemingly come out of nowhere.

His face falls when he sees the miniature version of himself.

"This is Dominic," I whisper. "Lucia's twin brother."

11

Grace

GABRIEL STUMBLES BACK as Dominic pushes him. "Get away from her," he yells.

"Dominic," I stammer. "Leave it, go inside the house."

"No." He stands between Gabriel and me. "Go away," he demands.

Gabriel's chest rises and falls as he struggles for air, his eyes are locked on Dominic's.

"I. Said. Go. Away." He grabs my hand and tries to pull me into the house. "Mom, come on. Don't cry."

The car door opens and Mark climbs out, my eyes flick to him. I didn't even realize he was in the car. "Hi, Grace." He smiles.

"Mark."

Dominic pushes me toward the house.

"It's fine, Dom, go inside. I know Gabriel. You need to leave us to talk."

"No. He's mean." He stands in between Gabriel and me. "Come inside with me."

Gabriel and Dominic glare at each other in a standoff.

"Gabriel, now is not the time," I stammer nervously. "We'll

organize to meet and talk, but...not here and not now. Please?" I whisper, I gesture to the back of Dominic. "Now is not the time."

"Let's go," Mark says.

Gabriel's furious eyes hold mine, and I wither under his wrath.

"We'll come back later," Mark says as he opens the back door of the car for Gabriel.

Without a word, Gabriel turns.

"Don't come back," Dominic spits.

Gabriel turns and I can feel the thermonuclear energy about to blow, he is livid.

I grab Dominic and push him behind me. "Don't be rude," I warn him. "That's not how we speak to people, you know that."

With one last murderous glance, Gabriel gets into the car and we watch on as it slowly pulls away.

I close my eyes in relief...and then in horror. In all of the nightmare situations I could ever have imagined of how this day would go if it ever happened, that was the absolute worst scenario.

Fuck.

I pace back and forth in my kitchen as panic sets in.

Why did he come here? How did he find out?

My name is Lucia Porter.

Oh my god...he knows, of course he knows, the children are the spitting image of him.

Maybe I should pack up the kids and go on the run?

*He won't do anything, he won't do anything...*I try to tell myself.

The problem is, I know him. Better than he knows himself, and I can bet my life on it that he is in shock right now. But when he recovers and gets himself together...

God help me.

The adult thing to do would be to call him and organize to meet.

And then do what?

Beg him not to take them from me.

Gabriel Ferrara is a powerful man; I know exactly what he is capable of.

He's going to be furious.

Maybe he already has a wife and other children of his own? Maybe he won't want anything to do with Lucy and Dom. Maybe they are just a blip on his radar.

Then why did he come?

Why did he just show up here unannounced if he didn't have an agenda?

He knew... The moment I saw him, I could tell that he knew.

I keep seeing the animosity on his face, the sheer disgust at what I've done.

And who could blame him?

I'm disgusted in myself that I never told him that he fathered my children, regretted it from the day they were born, but in all honesty, how could I have done it any differently?

How could I have told him that I have not one but two children of his when he already told me that he wanted nothing to do with me? He said that we could never be together and that he only wanted an Italian wife and to have Italian children.

This was never in my plan either...I am the victim here... not him.

He had his fun and left without a care in the world. He's been living the high life and I had two little babies while nursing a broken heart.

It's been hard.

My stomach twists in my chest. I've purposely never looked him up because I didn't want to know how wonderful his life was going.

But I have to know what I'm up against here, I enter into Google:

Gabriel Ferrara wife

My heart beats in my chest as I wait for the answer.

Gabriel Ferrara engaged to Ariana Rossi.

I search her name and click on images.

My stomach twists, picture after picture of the most beautiful Italian woman you have ever seen.

Long dark hair, perfect olive complexion, a figure to die for and looking like she's just stepped off a runway. She's everything that I'm not.

Not that I care, I hate him.

I'm so infuriated with myself that I wasted all those years working for him while pining for a man who didn't even know I existed.

What the hell was I thinking?

I hate what he did to me, but damn it, I hate that I'm now the one feeling guilty as if I've done something wrong.

He asked me to stay away and I did just that.

Dominic walks out in his Little League uniform and I smile. "You ready to go?"

He nods in an over exaggerated way. "Uh-huh."

"Lucy," I call. "We're leaving, honey."

"Coming."

I throw our bag of snacks over my shoulder. I just need to get on with it.

I tap my foot as I wait for Deb to answer her phone. *Ring ring, ring ring.*

"Pick up."

The crowd cheers and I pretend to be excited. The very last place I want to be today is at Little League.

I can't get on with it, I'm freaking the hell out.

You've reached Deborah, leave a message.

"Call me urgently," I whisper into the phone. The crowd all

cheers and I push the phone into my ear to try and cancel the noise. "Shit's gone down, bad shit." I hang up in a rush. "Where the hell is she?"

Debbie is the only person who knows the whole story.

"Where is she?" I dial her number again.

"What's wrong?" She answers first ring.

"Thank god." I stand. "Excuse me." I squeeze past the other parents who are sitting in the stand. "Excuse me." I need to get away from everyone so I can talk privately.

"Where are you?" I ask.

"I'm away for the wedding."

"Oh god, I completely forgot." I drag my hand through my hair. "Sorry to interrupt."

"What's wrong?"

"Gabriel turned up at my house."

Silence.

"Did you hear me?" I stammer.

"Gabriel who?"

"Gabriel Ferrara," I snap as my eyes bulge from their sockets. "What other Gabriel is there?"

"Oh...*fuck.*"

"He knows."

"He knows?" she whispers in a panic. "How does he know?"

"I don't know."

"What happened?"

"We were leaving to go to ballet and I had toast hanging out of my mouth and then he turned up and I knew that he knew and I cried and then Dom went into crazy guard dog protection mode and I thought Gabriel was going to kill him."

"Oh...Grace. Shit, this is bad. This is really, really bad."

I pinch the bridge of my nose as I listen. "You think?"

"What are you going to do?"

"I don't know, he was furious and he left and then—"

"And then what?" She cuts me off.

"I googled him and he's getting married soon."

"To who?"

"I don't know, some beautiful Italian bitch."

"Good, good riddance. Fuck off, asshole, and leave us alone."

"Why would he come here when he's getting married?" I whisper angrily.

Silence.

I can almost hear her brain ticking over.

"I mean...it doesn't make sense," I stammer. "Why now?"

"Oh..." She gasps as if having some kind of revelation.

"What?"

"He wants to buy you."

"What?" I frown.

"He wants to ensure you never talk so that his new wife never finds out about his illegitimate children."

That idea rolls around in my brain, that doesn't sound like him. "I don't know..."

"Think about it, why else would he be coming now? How would he have found out now if he didn't know all along?"

My eyes widen. "You think he's known all along?"

"I don't know, but this is fucking suspicious if you ask me."

"What if he tries to take them?" I whisper as I begin to panic. "What if he wants custody?"

"He won't."

"What if he takes me to court, I don't have the money he does to pay for fancy lawyers."

"He won't," she says. "Trust me, he's coming to make sure you never talk."

"You think?"

"I know."

Fear fills me. "Deb..."

"It's okay, Grace. Relax. Panicking is not going to help. You are their mother; he can't show up here and take them, that's not how it works. The courts are not going to give custody to an absent workaholic."

I nod, feeling a little better. "You're right."

"He didn't want to see you again, he told you that point blank. You went to tell him and he refused to see you, you are not in the wrong here."

"I should have called him and let him know I was pregnant. I knew it back then and I still know it now."

"He would have made you terminate the pregnancy," she whispers angrily. "He already told you it was going nowhere and that he wanted nothing more to do with you. You've done the right thing, you told everyone that it was a donor sperm pregnancy. You want nothing from him and you could have taken him for millions. Billions, even."

"You're right." I feel a little more empowered. "I'm overreacting, aren't I?"

"Probably not, but I don't think it's the scenario that you think it is."

I hear someone's voice in the background on Deb's phone. "You go back to your wedding. Sorry to bother you."

"It's going to be fine, Gracie. I'll be home Tuesday."

"Okay." I hang on the line, not wanting to get off the phone.

"Love you, bye." She hangs up and the crowd cheers. I turn back to the game as I feel a little of my equilibrium return.

This is all fine...fine, fine, totally fine.

They say that no news is good news, I only wish that were true.

A storm is coming...

I can feel it brewing all the way from New York.

I glance over to Lucy and Dom as they lie on the couch, watching television.

Happily oblivious to their mother's inner turmoil.

It's Sunday night, and I don't know what to do next. I haven't heard a word from Gabriel since he left here yesterday morning.

Should *I* call *him*...?

I glance over at my two precious babies lying top to toe on the couch, a blanket over them, so oblivious to everything. I need to make sure that's how it stays. They cannot be affected by any of this, I won't drag them through it.

I'll call Gabriel tomorrow and ask him to meet. This needs to be amicable between us. He's getting married soon and he can move on with her and have children of their own and live happily ever after in their penthouse in New York.

But I need to make something absolutely clear with them from the beginning.

These children are mine.

"Come on, guys." I pack up the school lunches and put them into their bags. "Let's roll." Monday mornings are always hectic, but when you haven't slept for two nights, they are especially chaotic. I bundle everyone's backpacks onto their backs and we walk out the front door. I stop on the spot.

A black car is sitting in my driveway.

The driver gives me a stifled smile and gets out of the car and stands beside it.

Fuck.

Acting cool as a cucumber, I walk down the front steps and unlock my car. "Jump in the car, guys."

"Who's that?" Dom asks.

"My friend. Get in the car." I open the backseat door and wait as they climb in. I slam the door shut and walk over to the man. "Can I help you?"

"Hello, Miss Porter." He smiles. "My name is Benson, I'm here..." He seems nervous. "Mr. Ferrara sent me, I have a doctor in the backseat accompanying me."

I glance down and can't see into the car through the blacked-out windows. "What are you doing here?"

"Mr. Ferrara has instructed us to carry out paternity tests." He gives me an awkward smile.

What?

"No."

"What do you mean?"

"I mean no, what else could I possibly mean?"

"Miss Porter, I strongly advise that you go ahead with this."

"And I strongly advise you to keep out of my business. My children have school today and will not be taking any such tests."

"Just one moment." He dials a number on his phone. "Hello." He turns away from me so that I can't hear what he's saying, but I still can. "She said no." He listens for a moment. "I'm not sure..."

"Is that Gabriel on the phone?" I ask.

He nods.

I walk over and snatch the phone from him. "Listen here, you self-centered son of a bitch." I sneer. "You stay the hell away from me and my children. If you dare come to my property again without an appointment, I will call the police quicker than you can say the words *restraining order*." I hang up the phone and pass it back to him. "Goodbye, Benson." I get into my car and pull out of the driveway.

Fuck you.

12

Grace

I SIT in my car for a moment as I try to will my heart rate to drop back down, it's beating so hard in my chest that I feel like I'm about to have a heart attack.

I dropped the kids at school and grabbed a coffee on the way, all the while about to go into cardiac arrest.

It's fine, he doesn't know anything, and knowledge is power. While he doesn't know anything we are safe.

He will, though...

One day soon I'm going to have to tell him, in fact I think I already kind of admitted it. I close my eyes, overwhelmed with fear. I know how postal he is going to be and...damn it. I can't believe I'm living this lie; this was never who I was.

Maybe it's better if he does find out...maybe then I can finally forgive myself for it and move on.

With one last look in my rearview mirror, I drag myself into work.

"Good morning, Ruth," I say as I walk through the front doors.

"Good morning, Grace." She looks up at me over the top of her glasses. "Everything all right? You look frazzled."

"I'm great," I lie with a smile as I walk through the office. "Everything is just great."

I'm a disaster, Ruth, and my children are the spawn of the devil...literally.

Why wouldn't I have just politely declined? What on earth was I thinking that I was going to achieve by screaming down the phone? All I've done is made him angry, and if there's one thing I know, it's that Gabriel Ferrara when angry is a catastrophic force.

Dumb, dumb, dumb.

I get a vision of Gabriel sitting at his desk in New York and I can feel his rage from here. Complete with the red sky, the lightning, the earth splitting in two and swallowing me whole in true horror movie fashion.

I inwardly kick myself. *Shit.*

Why did I curse and carry on like an immature child on the phone?

Damn it, I need to be smarter about this.

Something about that man brings out the absolute worst in me.

Ugh... So stupid.

I storm into my office and dump my briefcase on my desk. Now, to top off my morning from hell, I have to organize home loans all day.

Ugh, I hate my job.

I work at a bank as a loan manager, it's a good position, great pay with hours that I can work around the kids. I should be grateful for the opportunity, and I am...it's just... Mindless, boring, and crappy working out how much debt people can go into all day long.

As much as I hate to admit it, I miss the exotic days in New York of wearing six-inch heels and tight pencil skirts to work and staying back and having drinks with my work friends in cool bars. I get a vision of back then and Gabriel in his black briefs making me coffee every morning while I went through his day.

Stop it.

"Good morning," Mervin calls as he walks past my office.

"Morning, Merv," I reply as I open up my computer.

He sticks his head back around my door. "Do you want to buy some brownie cookies?"

Ugh...

"I guess." I grab my purse. "How many fundraisers do you do exactly? I swear I need to loan myself some cash just to support your kids' sporting activities."

"I know, right, I'm sick of selling this shit too." He walks into my office and puts the box of cookies on my desk.

I pass him over ten dollars. "You know I buy these things from you with the full intent of taking them home and sharing them and then, next thing you know, I've eaten the lot of them."

"Same." He takes the money and looks through his wallet for change.

I scrunch my nose as a waft of something bad surrounds me, and I look around. "What is that god-awful smell?"

"I don't know?" He looks around.

"Oh...it's disgusting." I wince.

"The hell is it?" He shrugs and looks on the bottom of his shoe. "Hopefully my office doesn't smell." He disappears down the hall.

"Ruth," I call. "Do you know what that smell is?"

"Not really," she calls, disinterested. "I smelled it before when I walked in the door, though."

Fuck's sake.

"Oh yuck, it's putrid in my office, I think there must be a dead rat in the ceiling or something," Merv calls down the hall.

"Eww."

This day just keeps getting better.

4 p.m.

An email pops up on my screen,

Your next appointment is here.

Mr. Don Johnston.

Don Johnston, what kind of name is that? I glance at my watch, I hate having appointments with new clients this late in the day. I reply to Ruth.

Send him in please.

I close down my email and take a sip of my water and stand and open the door.

Gabriel Ferrara is striding down the corridor toward me, and my eyes widen in horror.

"Hello, Miss Porter." He sneers as he walks past me into my office.

Shit.

Fake appointment.

Diabolical.

I glance around my office for an escape route before closing the door.

He's towering above me, wearing a perfectly fitted suit; his black hair has a bit of a curl to it and his animosity is encapsulating the room, making everything else feel so small and insignificant.

"What are you doing here?" I ask.

He sits down at my desk. "You told me to make an appointment." He points to my chair. "Sit."

I drop into my chair, my nervous heart hammering. "What do you want?"

He sits back and crosses his legs, arrogance personified, and his dark eyes hold mine. "I would like to know a little bit about you."

I shrug as I act casual. "There's nothing to know."

"Cut the bullshit, Grace," he fires back. "Do you have something to tell me?"

I swallow the bucket of sand in my throat as my eyes hold his. I

133

imagine him flipping the desk and smashing the windows or something equally dramatic.

"Like what?"

"Do. Not. Play. With. Me." He bangs his hand on my desk and I jump.

I swallow the nervous lump in my throat.

"Are they or are they not *my* children?"

His silhouette blurs.

His jaw tics in anger. "Answer. The. Fucking. Question."

I nod. "Yes."

"Yes what?"

"You..." I try to say the words out loud, but my dry mouth betrays me, I can't even form a sentence.

"You what?" he spits angrily.

"Yes. You are their biological father," I say quietly.

His haunted eyes hold mine, and he sits back in his chair.

Silence...

I wait for him to say something, he doesn't. He just sits there, shocked...or perhaps he's just counting the ways to hurt me. He doesn't need to count them, I already know it's an infinite number.

"You...we..." My voice trails off.

He drops his eyes to a spot on the carpet, he can't even look me in the eye.

"You didn't wear protection, Gabriel."

His eyes rise to meet mine, his hatred for me dripping from his every cell.

"I'd been on antibiotics that month, and..." I roll my lips as I try to compose myself, I can hardly see him through the tears. "You told me..."

His eyes drop back to the carpet, his silence is beginning to scare the hell out of me.

"What was I supposed to do?" I stammer. "You told me you didn't want to see me ever again."

Silence...

I watch him, waiting for the explosion, waiting for some type of reaction, even an overreaction is better than this.

"Do they know?" he eventually asks.

"No."

"Who knows?"

"Nobody, I told everyone that they were conceived through IVF using donor sperm."

His eyes drop back to the carpet.

Say something.

Gabriel Ferrara doesn't do silence.

"I don't want anything from you, you don't have to worry," I stammer. "You can live your life as normal; we will never bother you."

His dark eyes rise to meet mine, and this time they flicker with fury. He sits forward in his chair. "Do you honestly think that you can keep *my* children from me?" He sneers.

Fear runs through my system.

"I cannot believe..." His voice trails off as if stopping himself from elaborating.

Why is he not exploding? He's acting weird and out of character, it's very unsettling.

"What were you going to say?"

His eyes hold mine. "You are the most selfish person I have ever met."

What?

"You let your feelings for me betray your own children, preventing them from having access to their father." He swallows the lump in his throat as if overcome with emotion.

"You have a fiancée. You will have more children, Gabriel," I whisper.

"I will." He tilts his chin to the sky in defiance as he sits forward, his anger returning loud and clear. "Did you really think I would never find out?"

The hairs on the back of my neck stand up.

"I thought the day you left me was your biggest betrayal," he whispers.

You forced me away.

"Just because I didn't want you never meant I didn't want them." He sneers.

Oh...

A knife straight through my heart. I stare at him through tears. There's the Gabriel I know. Cold and heartless.

"Here is what is going to happen," he says in a cold and calculating voice. "Today I am sending a medic around to your house, and they are having a paternity test and *you*—" he glares at me, "— are finally going to do the right thing by your children."

I open my mouth to say something.

"If you try to stop me from seeing them...even once. Prepare yourself for the consequences. Do you understand me?" he growls.

"Is that a threat?"

"Push me and find out."

My stupid eyes fill with tears of fear. "You haven't changed, still the self-centered bastard who only thinks of himself."

A trace of a smirk crosses his cold, hard gaze. "I think you know me well enough, Grace, to know why I'm angry."

"You didn't want anything to do with me."

"This has nothing to do with you," he spits. "I have missed six years of my children's life. Six birthdays. Six Christmases, six *fucking* years, Grace."

My stomach twists, I'm on the edge of a full emotional meltdown.

"Do the paternity test," he warns.

"And if I don't?"

"Prepare yourself."

My eyes hold his. "For what?

"Armafuckinggeddon." He stands, and without another word, walks out of my office. I stare at the back of the door he just left through.

Oh no...

Emotion takes over, and I put my head into my hands and cry.

I sit in my car around the corner from my house as I try to pull myself together.

I was so rattled that I had to leave work, I told them that I had just been told an old friend had died.

I'm just a dirty liar now.

My eyes are red and swollen, and damn it, I feel so unstable.

Terrified.

His words come back to me: *"If you try to stop me from seeing them...prepare yourself for the consequences."*

My god, how has it come to this?

Last week, my life was normal, my biggest drama was finding ballet slippers, this week it's like a bad dream.

A living nightmare.

The worst part is, I already know their paternity, there isn't even a need to do the test. There's not one seed of doubt in my mind. Gabriel Ferrara is their biological father and there is nothing I can do about it.

"Just because I didn't want you never meant that I didn't want them."

"Oh." I screw up my face in tears. His words still hurt. I went straight back to being that woman who was madly in love with him, the pitiful woman with my heart on the bottom of his shoe, taking his hits blow by blow.

"Stop it, pull yourself together. You have to go home."

I pull down the sunshield to fix my face in the mirror and I catch sight of a black car pulled over to the side of the road and parked about two hundred meters behind me.

What?

I turn around and my heart sinks for the thousandth time today, he's having me followed so that I can't disappear. And if I were a better person, I would tell you that going on the run with his children has never occurred to me.

But it has...especially today.

"You are the most selfish person I have ever met."

He's right, I am...but it takes one to know one.

And he's the fucking king.

I pick myself up and dust myself off. I wipe my eyes and put my sunglasses on. I know I have to play by the rules, but fuck him. We're doing this on my terms.

I pull out and drive down the road until our house comes into view.

I can do this.

I sit on the couch as the doctor walks the kids through the paternity test. "Just like this." He shows them how he swabs his mouth. "It's easy, see?"

Two security guards are waiting out on the porch, and a doctor and a nurse are inside with us.

I'm remaining silent because, I mean...what is there to say?

They know or at least suspect that I've been hiding his children, and I can only imagine what they must all think of me.

He told me to leave.

I watch on as they swab Lucia's mouth and then Dominic's, they take a strand of each of their hair and put the swabs into test tubes.

"There you go, all done." The doctor smiles.

"How long will the results take to come in?" I ask.

"Around twenty-four hours, tomorrow sometime." He replies.

I nod, and I want to blurt that I already know the result and that I'm not some sleep-around swindler who is trying to take him for millions, but damn it, I will only look like more of a loser.

"Thank you." I open the front door in a cue for them to leave.

"Goodbye." The nurse smiles softly as she walks past me. "Good luck."

Seriously?

I don't need luck, bitch. I glare at the security guard standing outside the door.

"Goodbye." I close the door behind them with a sharp snap.

I look down at my two beautiful babies who are looking up at me through their perfect innocent eyes. "Let's go out for dinner, get something yummy and delicious." I widen my eyes. "Chocolate cake for dessert."

"Yay," they squeal.

"Go get changed." I smile.

They bolt over and disappear up the stairs.

Momma needs a drink.

Gabriel

"You ready for lunch?" Alessio says from the door of my office.

"Yeah." I concentrate on the email in front of me. "Give me a minute."

He flops onto the couch in my office and takes out his phone as he waits. "Did you see the new accountant on level three?"

I keep typing. "No."

"Ridiculously hot," he replies. "Blonde hair and big, fuckable tits."

I raise my eyebrow as my eyes stay glued to the screen. "You think everybody's hot with fuckable tits."

"There's a lot of talent in this building at the moment, let me tell you."

"Keep it in your pants." I sigh, uninterested. "Where is Ricardo?"

"He's meeting us there."

I send the email and read the next one that's marked urgent.

"Hurry up." He looks at his watch. "I have an appointment I have to be back for."

"Fine." I stand and grab my wallet and stuff it into my suit pants. "Let's go."

We walk out into the foyer, get into the elevator, and stand to face the doors.

The elevator stops two floors down and I exhale heavily. "Fuck me, we need a private elevator."

"No way. I do my best talent spotting in these elevators."

I roll my eyes and the doors open. Two girls in their mid-twenties are standing and waiting to get in. Both dressed in pencil skirts that leave nothing to the imagination. One has dark hair and one is a sandy blonde. Their eyes widen when they see us.

"Ladies." Alessio smiles all seductive like. "Going down."

My eyes flick over to him. *You wish.*

He smirks, knowing exactly what I'm thinking.

"Hello, Mr. Ferrara." The brunette smiles shyly up at me as they get in, her eyes linger on my face.

I nod. "Hello." I keep my eyes on the doors as they close.

"Beautiful day outside," Alessio says.

"Isn't it?" The blonde smiles. "I just love the sun, I wish we had a beach in New York so I could work on my tan."

"You could always work on your tan in the park," Alessio replies. "Park tanning is a thing, you know?"

Good grief.

I inwardly roll my eyes; fuck...his pickup lines are so bad.

"Cold weather makes me miserable," the blonde continues.

Who cares?

"Sounds like you need a big injection of vitamin D," Alessio replies as he casually adjusts his cuff links.

I twist my lips; I know what vitamin D he's referring to.

The one in his pants.

The elevator comes to a stop on level ten. "This is us." The blonde smiles up at Alessio. "Nice to see you again, Mr. Ferrara."

"Call me Alessio."

She giggles on cue. "Okay...Alessio." The doors go to close and he puts his hand out to stop them. "What is *your* name?'

"Misha."

They stare at each other for a beat, and I exhale heavily. *Hurry up, fuck it.*

"Nice to meet you, Misha." He dips his head.

The doors close and he smiles, all proud of himself.

"Seriously?" I curl my lip.

"She's going to get it."

"Vitamin D is the best you've got?"

"Works every time." The door opens again and he smiles sexily. "Good afternoon, ladies."

I roll my eyes. Ugh...here we go again.

We walk into the bar and see Ricardo is sitting at a table in the corner on the phone, and we make our way over to him. "Yes." He listens and narrows his eyes at us as we sit down. "This is unsatisfactory."

"Who's that?" I mouth.

He clenches his fist and points it to his phone.

"Can I get you a drink?" the waitress asks as she walks over.

"I'll have a mineral water, please."

"Same," Alessio says.

Ricardo holds his hand up in question and points to his beer.

"Some of us have to work, you know?" Alessio mutters.

Ricardo listens to the person on the other end of the phone. "Okay, I understand that." He listens again. "I don't believe that for a moment."

"Who are you talking to?" I frown.

"Because no parking lot is that big, my speedometer doesn't lie, and when I drop off my Lamborghini for parking, I do not expect your fucking valet driver to go joyriding around New York in it."

Alessio's eyes widen and I chuckle.

"Because there are fifty extra fucking miles on the clock," he snaps. "How do I know?" His eyes nearly bulge from their sockets. "Because this is a collector car worth two million fucking dollars. Of course I know the speedometer reading."

"Holy…" Alessio mouths, wide-eyed. "What the fuck?"

"Here you go, two mineral waters," the waitress says.

Ricardo holds his hand up again when he sees our drinks arrive.

I sip my drink and stare out over the restaurant; I get a vision of Gracie sitting at her desk. Her long hair was in a ponytail and her big pouty lips were…

My heart sinks.

You think you know someone…

I think back to all those years ago and the night we spent together; I see us rolling around in my bed.

On my desk.

In the shower.

A collage of naked skin and orgasms, the uncontrollable fire that burned between us.

The look on her face in the morning…

My stomach twists.

"Earth to Gabe." Alessio waves his hand in front of my face to bring me back to the here and now.

I glance up at him. "Huh?"

"What the hell are you doing?" He frowns.

"Huh?"

"What's wrong with you this week?" Ricardo asks. "You're off with the fairies."

"Nothing," I snap. "I've got a lot on my mind, that's all."

"Like what?"

"Like how many ways there are to break your ugly face," I snap as I open the menu. "Mind your business." My phone vibrates on the table and I answer as the boys go back to their conversation.

"Gabriel Ferrara."

"Hello Mr. Ferrara, this is Dr. Granger."

My heart stops. "Yes."

"The results of the paternity test are in, sir."

I close my eyes as I brace myself.

"It's a positive match, it's confirmed without a doubt that you are the biological father of both children."

Unexpected emotion fills me and I get a lump in my throat.

They're mine.

I sit in the back of the car as Mark drives me home from work.

You could cut the air with a knife; my heart is heavy and we are both silent.

How do you tell someone you are about to marry that you have two illegitimate children?

Ariana is going to be heartbroken.

I'm heartbroken...but not for the same reason.

I've missed out on so much of my children's lives, time I can never get back.

And Grace...

I get a vision of her at her workplace, her auburn hair, and a face that I knew so well. The deep sense of familiarity I got from her, the one person on earth I trusted with my life.

So evil... And yet, still an ethereal creature.

My mind is buzzing with a million scenarios, none of them good.

The car pulls to a stop out the front of my building and we both sit still in the car.

"Good luck," Mark says softly, he knows I'm walking into the gallows to hurt the person who loves me the most.

"If I could change it..." I whisper.

"I know."

I drag myself out of the car and take the elevator to my floor, the double doors open and the scent of something delicious instantly fills my senses.

My heart sinks and I close my eyes.

How is this happening?

I walk into the apartment and put my briefcase in my office

and then I find Ariana in the kitchen. I lean on the doorjamb and watch her for a moment.

She's doing what she loves, the best damn cook in New York city if you ask me.

Wearing an apron, she's putting something in the oven while things are cooking on the hotplates, a million things on the go.

"Hello."

She looks up and sees me and smiles. "I didn't hear you come in."

"But I did." I smile as she kisses me. I see her glass of red wine. "Drinking on a school night?"

"I'm celebrating." She pours me a glass.

"What are we celebrating?"

She passes me my glass of wine and holds hers up to mine. "Thirty-five days until we get married."

I force a smile and clink my glass with hers. "Something smells delicious. What is my chef serving tonight?"

"We have a kingfish ceviche followed by a ragu with creamy polenta and tiramisu for dessert."

"How do you have the energy to cook a three-course meal for me every night?"

"Looking after you is my favorite thing to do."

My heart sinks. "We need to talk."

She smiles and goes up onto her toes to kiss me. "I know, but first the suits." She takes me by the hand and leads me to a stool by the kitchen counter where I sit down. "Now, I know that you wanted the black..."

I stare at her as I pretend to listen, but my mind returns to Gracie in the bank. *Cut the bullshit, Grace. Do you have something to tell me?*

The tears welled in her eyes, and by the look on her face, I instantly knew it was true.

The way it put a hole in my heart.

How could she have done this? How could she have hidden my

own children from me for six years? My mind returns to us in the shower that night, naked and kissing in each other's arms.

The level of intimacy that ran between us was like nothing I've experienced before or since.

I grieved for her for years, and to think that... I get a lump in my throat.

She had my babies the entire time.

"Gabriel?"

I glance up with no idea what Ariana has been saying. "I'm sorry?"

"Are you not listening to me at all?"

"Forgive me, I'm... Busy day."

"What did you have to tell me?" she asks.

She looks up at me with her big brown trusting eyes.

Tell her.

"I..."

Do it.

"I have to go away for work tomorrow."

"Oh," she replies. "How long will you be gone?"

"A few days."

"Okay." She smiles. "Do you want me to come?"

"No." I sip my wine. "I'll be working the whole time," I lie.

"So anyway, back to the suits." She changes the subject and once again my mind goes back to the unfolding catastrophe.

My life is a mess.

Grace

The sound of their cries echoes through the silence, wings flap against the water as they take off.

A bird in flight is a beautiful thing.

I sit on the back porch and stare out over the lake. My life is a mess...and at a time when I should be frantic, I feel eerily calm.

The truth is out and damn it, it feels cathartic.

He knows.

I'm not carrying the secret alone anymore.

I always knew that one day the truth would come to light, and as every year ticked over, I got a little more terrified.

Not only of Gabriel...but of the children hating me for not telling them the truth about the donor sperm and IVF.

I'm glad it's out.

The children are still young, and I haven't had to have the conversation with them about who their father is yet, hopefully they're young enough that they can forgive me.

"Mom," Dom calls from inside. "A car just pulled up."

I close my eyes as I prepare for battle.

"He's here."

13

Grace

I WALK BACK into the house and peer through the window to see Gabriel get out of the car. It's Thursday, he couldn't even wait for the weekend.

He's wearing a charcoal suit with not a hair out of place, chunky watch, and expensive shoes, he looks like a fish out of water here.

"He's back," Lucy says from her place beside me.

"You be nice," I tell her. I glance back to Dominic. "You use your manners today, please."

He stays silent.

"Dominic, do you understand me? Best behavior today."

He nods.

We all watch from our place from the window as Gabriel walks up the front stairs, and I open the door before he knocks.

"Hello."

"Hello." He nods, his eyes find the children behind me and he stares at them for a beat.

I step back to grant him access. "Come in."

He walks past me into the house, and Dom and Lucy look up at him as if he's an alien.

Gabriel looks around our quaint little house and is quiet, for the first time in history I get the feeling he is lost for words.

That makes two of us.

"Please meet..." My voice trails off and I put my hands on Lucy's shoulders. "This is Lucia." I present her to him. "Lucia, this is my friend, Gabriel."

Gabriel's eyes flick to me in question, and I give a subtle shrug. I have no idea how to introduce him.

"Hello," Gabriel says to her.

Lucy stands at his feet and looks up at him. "You're very big."

"Tall," I correct her.

"You're very small," he replies.

"Lucas Marks calls me a mouse because I'm so small," she says matter-of-factly.

"Well..." His eyebrows flick up as if surprised. "You tell Lucas Marks that he has big ears."

What?

"This is Dominic." I cut them off. "Dom, this is Gabriel."

"Hi," Dom says without so much as a glance.

Gabriel's jaw ticks as he stares at him, clearly annoyed by his rude behavior.

Fuck.

"Would you like a cup of coffee?" I ask to change the subject.

Gabriel's eyes come back to me. "Yes," he replies.

"Why don't you guys go outside and play before dinner?" I fake a smile; everything is great here. Nothing to see. Happy, happy, happy.

"I don't want to go outside," Dom replies.

Gabriel's unimpressed eyes flick over to him.

"Go upstairs then, sweetie." I widen my eyes at him. *Not now, fucker.*

Dom stomps up the stairs as if I'm a major inconvenience.

This damn kid will be the death of me.

If there's one thing I've learned over the last six years, it's that sleeping with a dominant man may be hot, but raising one as your son is a lot less desirable.

Lucy stands at Gabriel's feet as she continues to look up at him. "Why are you wearing that?"

"Wearing what?" he asks.

"That..." She gestures to his clothes.

"My suit?"

She nods with a goofy smile. "It's funny."

"You never saw a suit before?" He frowns.

Help.

"Upstairs, sweetie." I cut her off. Please stop telling him how uncultured we are. "Mommy has grown-up things to discuss with Gabriel."

I glance over at him to see that his face is cold and expressionless.

Take the offer, Lucy, trust me...upstairs is a much better option.

She skips upstairs and the room falls silent, ugh... Don't leave me alone with him.

Gabriel sinks into a chair at the dining table and I flick on the coffee machine.

Shit...I search my mind for the next thing to say.

I glance over my shoulder to see him looking around my house, I can't imagine what he's thinking. Everything in his world is opulent and over-the-top luxury and this is a little log cabin on the lake where everything is homemade. Even our cushions on the couch are crocheted, not that I like them. Mavis down the road makes me all kinds of ugly shit. The kids think her creations are marvelous and who am I to be a grinch.

I put Gabriel's coffee down on the table and take a seat beside him.

"So..." I shrug.

"So..."

"You." I swallow the bucket of sand in my throat. "I'm assuming the results are back."

"Yes." His eyes hold mine. "How were you so sure?"

"Because I don't sleep around, and you know that."

He rolls his lips and remains silent.

"So what happens now?"

He sips his coffee and winces. "Ugh. What is this fucking shit?"

"Coffee, Gabriel."

"Christ almighty, you still make the worst fucking cup of coffee." He pushes his cup forward. "That's inedible."

"You drink it, not eat it," I snap.

He raises an eyebrow as a silent warning, and I widen my eyes back. "Don't."

"Don't you."

God, this is never going to work.

We fall silent for a while.

Finally, I ask him what I need to know. "What are you doing here?"

"I came to make the arrangements."

Arrangements?

"For what?"

"You're going to have to move back to New York."

"Sorry...?"

"I'm very busy with a lot on and I don't have time to be coming out here."

What?

"Of course I will cover the costs and get you a nice place, the movers will pack for you and everything will be taken care of."

I stare at him as I have an out-of-body experience.

"I was thinking of my penthouse in Park Avenue, you may decorate it however you wish, I suppose." He thinks for a moment. "But I want to get a say on the interior designer you choose."

I blink in surprise. "No."

"What about my terrace in Manhattan, then? I thought you may prefer that one, it is only four bedrooms, though, and it doesn't have as good a view." He thinks for a moment. "And the commute to my place will take longer in peak hour traffic. No...I think I would prefer you in Park Avenue, it's a two-story penthouse, it's a lot bigger and closer to my place."

"I'm not moving anywhere."

"What do you mean?"

"The kids' lives are here. Their friends and school are here." I shrug. "I'm not moving them anywhere."

"Yes. You are."

"No. I'm not." I feel my temper begin to rise. "You can't just barge in here and demand that I move back to New York. You have no say in where we live."

He narrows his eyes. "I want and *will* be taking fifty percent custody of *my* children. With or without your permission."

"*Your* children?" I cross my arms as my temper prepares to blow. "That's a joke, right?"

"What the fuck is that supposed to mean?" he whispers angrily. "I have the paperwork to prove it."

"You made it very clear the night they were conceived that it was a seminal transfer."

His eyes flicker with fury.

"You are a sperm donor and nothing more."

"How fucking dare you," he hisses. "You walk into my office late at night after a Christmas party and seduce *me* on my desk. Strategically fall pregnant. Carry my child in secret for nine months, give birth to not one but *two* of my children and never once call to let me know." He stands. "Who the fucking hell do you think you are kidding with this Pollyanna act. And while we are at it, how dare you name my son Dominic?"

"What did you want me to call him?"

"Gabriel."

"I know a Gabriel, and it turned me off the name."

"You can talk, you're a deceiving witch who is using my children as a weapon against me."

"Get out."

"No."

"Get the fuck out," I whisper angrily. "We don't want you here."

"They don't even know me."

"And that's how it should stay. Go home to your fiancée, Gabriel. Start again, have a million Italian babies with her."

He glares at me. "I'm organizing the move."

"Go to hell."

"You want to do this?" He raises an eyebrow. "You really want to push me, because I can go for full custody if that suits you better."

"And there it is," I whisper angrily. "I knew it was coming. Get the fuck out right now."

"You cannot stop me from seeing them."

"I never said I was. If you want to build a relationship with them, you come here to do it. *You* are the adult; *you* are the one who needs to make the effort. You have a private jet, for fuck's sake, you can fly in whenever you want."

"I want them closer."

"Get to know them first."

"If you live in New York, you can come back here every weekend."

"What?" I explode. "Can you even hear yourself? You have absolutely no interest in these children and their well-being. Let me get this straight, you want them to live in New York through the week and come back here on the weekends?"

"Yes."

"But you work fourteen-hour days through the week."

He opens his mouth to say something but I cut him off.

"And at the time when you could actually spend some quality time with them on the weekends, you want to pack them up and send them back here to get out of your hair."

"That isn't how it is."

"That's exactly how it is." I march to the door and open it. "Get out."

Gabriel

My blood boils, the audacity of this woman.

"You need to think long and hard about this, Gabriel."

"Think about what, exactly, what's that supposed to mean?"

"It means if you decide you want to be a father, it's a full-time job. Every sporting match, every dance practice. Every vomiting bug and cold, every damn meltdown. You do not get to pick and choose what you are present for in their lives. I will not have my children pine for their absent workaholic father." She shrugs.

"And then what happens when you have more children and you have even less time?" She throws her hands up in the air. "You want to move them away from all of their friends and then your new bride gets pregnant and you and her are super busy doing baby things and she doesn't want them around...what happens to them then?"

My heart drops.

"It's all...or nothing, Gabriel."

I stare at her for a beat, and her demeanor changes from aggressive to empathetic.

"Look, I know this isn't how you wanted things to go, me neither, but it happened, and I'm sorry I didn't tell you back then, but I was only trying to protect them."

"From their own father?" I gasp.

"You need to go home and really think about this," she says sadly. "And if you decide that this is all too hard, I understand. I get it, I really do." She shrugs. "Everybody will be none the wiser, and when the children are old enough to understand the dynamics, we can tell them together then."

I stare at her for a beat.

"You're not the bad guy here, Gabriel, I know I did the wrong thing by not telling you, but I was scared and alone and it hasn't been easy. I've cried myself to sleep more times than I can count, but I have put their needs first every single time, and you coming here with your selfish demands, wanting to upend their entire lives so that you don't feel like a failure, is just not going to cut it. They deserve better than a half-assed father with a point to prove."

I get a lump in my throat.

"Do you know why I didn't want to tell you?"

"Enlighten me."

"Because in the eyes of your family and to the rest of the world, they are and *always will be* the illegitimate children who were conceived on your desk late one night with your PA. They will never fit into your life, Gabriel, don't you see?" Her eyes well with tears. "I don't want them to feel like second-class citizens, and if they go to New York...that's exactly how it will be. Your family will never accept them. They will always be Gabriel Ferrara's bastard children."

My heart sinks.

"If you want them in your life, and I really hope you do, you need to immerse yourself in *their* world and build a relationship with *them*. I cannot allow them into yours until I know for certain that their hearts are safe."

I clench my jaw.

"Gabriel, you need to understand, money means nothing to them. They don't care what your job is or who you are, they just want their dad to love them, they just want a normal dad to love them back. They're happy now, they aren't constantly waiting for a visit from their dad because I know that once we tell them, they will be. They will want your attention all the time. Parenthood isn't a part-time job. If you can't be an engaged and present father, then for god's sake for once in your life put someone else's needs before your own, do the right thing by them and stay away."

Her silhouette blurs, and I quickly turn toward the door. "I'll be in touch."

I walk down the stairs and out to my car.

That is not how I expected that to go. I sit in the car for a moment while I collect my thoughts.

"For once in your life put someone else's needs before your own, do the right thing by them and stay away."

She's right, I really do need to think about this.

I'm being selfish.

On autopilot, I start the car and pull out onto the road. I glance back at the house as it disappears in the rearview mirror.

Fuck.

I didn't even say goodbye to them.

I lie in the darkness and watch the shadows change on the ceiling.

Sleep...the elusive dream, I'm a walking zombie.

I haven't slept in days.

Ariana is asleep beside me, oblivious to everything. Physically, I'm here with her, but the rest of me is not, it's hovering somewhere over Greenville in Maine.

Gracie's words keep going over and over in my head... *For once in your life put someone else's needs before your own, do the right thing by them and stay away.*

I know she's right. This isn't about me; this is about my children and what's best for them, and I know that I have to leave them be. I can't be who they need, and it kills me.

I work so much that I'm hardly present in my own life. How can I be present for two small children who live on the other side of the country?

I have two choices: stay away and abandon my children but keep Ariana or...start a new way of life that involves living between here and Greenville with my children.

Grace...

One moment I'm thinking with my head and staying away and marrying Ariana.

And then like clockwork, my mind returns to Maine... With her. I see a vision of Lucy and Dominic, dark hair, olive skin.

They look like me.

I imagine them at a school concert with no father there to cheer them on, and it brings me such a deep sense of sadness.

Does it affect them?

Grace says it doesn't, but it would have to, if not now then down the track most definitely. I know the situation is impossible, Grace won't move to New York and I can't leave.

Grace is right and I should stay away.

They won't care, they never knew me anyway...the thought of that breaks my heart.

I get a lump in my throat at the situation I find myself in. I feel so cheated.

I'm at a cross roads in my life, and whatever road I choose to go down...I will miss something on the other side.

"I don't give a fuck what he's asking, pay it. Get me that fucking story," I snap as I turn the corner in my car. My eyes flick up to Mark, who is following in the car behind me. I'm so wound up that I can't even sit in the car with him.

Driving is the only thing I seem to be able to control.

"He won't do an interview; he's declined to talk to anyone."

"Do not insult my intelligence, I'm sure Miles Media is in negotiations with him right now. Get the fucking story." I hit end of call and come to a stop at a pedestrian crossing.

Fucking incompetence, I'm sick to death of it.

An old lady walks at a snail's pace across the road. "Hurry up, old bag."

Another lady crosses, and then another. I exhale heavily. "Come the fuck on, what are we waiting for?"

And then I see it...my heart stops.

A man walks out onto street, holding the hands of his two children. They're dressed in uniform, he must be walking them to school. They're chatting and talking as they walk, oblivious to everyone around them.

What are they talking about?

The father says something and the children both laugh and my stomach twists. I watch them keep walking, wondering what school they go to.

Beep, beep. A car horn sounds from behind me, bringing me back to the moment.

I glance up to my rearview mirror and glare at the driver behind me. "Shut the fuck up before I hurt you."

Grace

I sip my coffee as I stare into space. The last week has been a blur, firstly shock and horror that Gabriel found us, and then devastation as my worst fears came true.

He came, he met them, and when I purposely pushed to see how committed he was, he left without a fight.

He doesn't want to be in their lives, and I know I should be grateful that he's at least being honest, but it doesn't make me feel any better.

I'm sad for the kids, it was one thing when he didn't know they existed, but now that he does... How will I explain this to them when they are older?

What a fool.

These two children are a gift, and how he doesn't want to be a part of their life is beyond me.

I put my head into my hands. Maybe everything he said about me is true. Maybe I am the world's most selfish person. He thinks I kept them a secret out of spite...

Did I?

No, I kept it a secret to protect them...if he can't see that, then screw him.

We owe him nothing anyway, and there's no more wondering what if.

At least now I know.

Friday night.

I empty the jar of sauce into the pasta as I stare into space. Lucy is watching television in the living room and Dom is upstairs somewhere.

I've had a shitty day, got abused by an asshole work client whose loan application got declined and it kind of spiraled from there. I came home, had a shower and immediately opened a bottle of wine. There are some benefits to being the only adult living here, I get to do whatever the hell I want to...as long as it doesn't involve leaving the house.

"Mom, someone's at the door," Lucia calls.

"Who is it?" I frown, ugh...who the hell is coming over at this hour?

"I don't know," she calls, uninterested, and returns to watching her show.

I flick my tea towel over my shoulder and walk through the house and open the front door in a rush. Cold dark eyes meet mine. "Gabriel."

Oh no.

"Hello." We stare at each other for a beat.

"What are . . ."

"I'm here to see my children." He cuts me off as he walks past me into the house. "Stay out of my way."

14

Grace

"Stay out of your way?" I gasp as I march after him. "That is..." I widen my eyes, about to explode, "...not happening."

Wearing a navy suit and tie, it's obvious he has come straight from work. He dumps his laptop case onto the floor and looks around as he puts his hands on his hips. "Where are my children?"

Something about him calling *my* children *his* children is like waving a red flag in front of me. "Listen." I pull him by the arm into the kitchen so that they can't hear us. "You do not get to show up here unannounced," I whisper angrily.

"I just did." His cold eyes hold mine, and he steps forward, causing me to step back. "I'm staying here tonight."

Something about his huge body with all its dominance standing over me makes my stupid body react, the air crackles between us and damn it, this hot asshole is infuriating.

"Yeah, well, it's not happening. You'll have to get a hotel or something."

"Everything is booked out."

"*Not* my problem."

"Let's get one thing clear, Grace..." He takes another step

forward, causing me to take another step back. "I am your problem, your only fucking problem. I will be staying here in this house *with my children* tonight."

"No."

"Call the police and have me removed." His eyes flicker with fury. "I dare you."

"I will have no hesitation in doing that, asshole."

"Do you really want to start the war, Grace?"

"Bring it."

He gives me a slow, sarcastic smile.

"What the hell do you want from me?" I spit.

"Equality," he growls. "And god damn it, you are going to fucking give it to me. I am here to say goodbye to my children forever, and I'm staying here."

"I don't have a spare bedroom, there is nowhere for you to sleep."

"I'll sleep in your bed and you can sleep with the kids. It's just one night."

"I am not sleeping with the kids," I scoff.

"Then you share a bed with me." He raises a sarcastic eyebrow.

A million depraved thoughts run naked through my mind...

"That is out of the question," I snap. I stare at him for a beat while I collect my thoughts.

Wait, what did he say?

"You're here to say goodbye to them?" My eyes search his.

"It's for the best." He tilts his chin to the sky in defiance.

Oh...my poor babies.

My heart runs into a puddle on the floor.

"Fine," I whisper, distracted. "You stay in my bed and I'll..." I pause, "...sleep somewhere else."

He stares at me for a beat, and I get the feeling he's collecting his thoughts as well. "Thank you." He looks around the kitchen as if searching for the next thing to say. "What time is dinner?'

Fuck.

FUCK...

I've made Italian, but not just any Italian.

Bad Italian, really bad Italian.

The kind that will turn his stomach. Spaghetti Bolognese complete with pasta sauce that came in a jar and instant pasta, it's not even good instant pasta, it's cheap crap I bought for ninety-nine cents.

Oh, fuck my life...

"I'm sorry, I didn't make enough for you."

He glances at the huge saucepan simmering away and amusement flashes across his face. "There is plenty, I'm sure it will be just as good as my mother's."

That's it!

"Listen here, you . . ."

"Hi." Lucy comes around the corner, cutting me off.

"Hello there." Gabriel smiles down at her. "Do you remember me?"

She nods in an over exaggerated way.

Gabriel looks around the house. "Where is your brother?"

"He's upstairs," Lucy gushes as she swings her arms in glee, ugh...does he have this effect on all women, even children?

"Can you go and get him for me, I have something to tell you."

Lucy skips off, and my eyes widen in horror. "What do you mean, you have something to tell them both?"

"I'm telling them."

"What...now?" I gasp.

"No time like the present." He points to a dining chair. "Sit."

I drop into the chair as all the blood drains from my body. "What are you going to say?"

"Whatever I fucking like," he snaps.

"Gabriel...you can't...they're little children."

"Relax, I'm not going to tell them that Mom got her pussy out on Dad's desk...although I'm positive that would make for a more interesting story."

My eyes nearly bulge from their sockets. "Are you fucking serious... Do not dare tell them and disappear, it isn't fair."

"Here he is." Lucy walks into the kitchen, cutting me off again, Dom trailing behind her.

"Hello." Gabriel smiles at both of them. Lucy smiles and Dominic looks him up and down straight-faced.

For the first time in my life I see fear flash across Gabriel's face.

I need to take over.

"Dom." I put my hands on both of his little shoulders. "This is Gabriel, you remember him, don't you?"

He nods.

"Gabriel is my friend from New York," I tell them.

Dominic's eyes flick up to me and I know he's remembering the last time Gabriel was here and how he made me cry.

Damn it, why did I do that?

"Sit down." I direct them to the dining table. "Let's all eat dinner together while we discuss a few things."

Gabriel opens his mouth to say something and I hold my hand up to stop him.

"Dinner is where we discuss things in this house." I widen my eyes to him in a shut-up gesture.

"Right." He drops into a dining chair and the kids do too.

I turn to refill my glass of wine and take a big gulp. What is he going to say...what the hell is he going to say?

He's completely unmanageable.

Fuck...

"I'll have some of that too, please," Gabriel says.

Good god, this is supermarket wine that cost $7.99.

Please earth, swallow me whole.

"Sure." With sweat dripping down between my breasts, I take another wineglass from the cupboard and fill it and then pass it to him.

"Thanks." He takes a huge gulp and winces before his horrified eyes flash up to meet mine.

"I know." I nod.

"But do you?"

"Yep...pretty much." Tastes like shit, but it's cheap and gets the job done.

I tip my head back and drain my glass. I immediately refill it and get to work on dishing dinner out.

"How was school today?" Gabriel asks.

"It was good." Lucy smiles.

"What class are you in?" he replies.

I look at the pot of spaghetti sauce, I really don't want him to eat it.

Fuck this, why didn't I order pizza tonight like I wanted to?

"What is your teacher's name?" he asks as he tries to continue the conversation.

I dish out the kids' two bowls and then mine, and then I get to his.

What do I do?

He's going to hate it, he's going to really hate it... But what if... I glance over my shoulder to see if he's watching me.

"Are you two in the same class?" He continues trying to make conversation.

If he's going to hate it anyway, I'm going to make him really hate it. I open my fridge and scan the contents, what can I put in it?

I need the ultimate booby trap. *Don't mess with me, fucker.*

My eyes roam over the condiments in the door and take out the mustard, the pickles, jarred chilli, anchovies, and pickled onions.

"And is she nice?" Gabriel asks.

Lucy goes off on a big tangent, telling him all about the school and I get to work.

I turn up the heat on the saucepan and glance over my shoulder again. If he catches me doing this, I'm so dead.

I put in three tablespoons of mustard, pour in the chilies and then the pickles, I add half the jar of anchovies and then throw in some whole pickled onions.

That should do it.

I stir it to heat them through. I wince as I look into the pot, it kind of looks like a fishy eyeball stew.

"Hope you guys are ready for a taste sensation." I dish Gabriel out a huge bowl and roll my lips to hide my smile.

"Did you get this recipe from Becco?" he asks.

"Oh, Becco." I sigh sadly. "I miss Becco." I frown over at him. "How do you remember my favorite restaurant in New York?"

"How could I ever forget, it's all you ever talked about."

Did I really use to always talk about pasta? How odd.

Hmm...

I put everyone's bowls in front of them on the table and Gabriel looks down at his eyeball stew. I quickly turn back to the counter so that he doesn't see my face, and I sip my wine while imagining him choking on it.

I'm brilliant.

I sit down at the table and look over at Dom glaring at Gabriel across the table.

My heart sinks.

I need to fix this, if this is their final goodbye I want it to be nice for both of them.

"Dom." I smile. "Gabriel is Italian, he comes from Italy."

Dom's eyes flick to Gabriel for confirmation.

"I am." Gabriel nods.

"He speaks Italian." I smile as I prompt them.

The children's eyes both widen as they stare at him.

"Tu parli italiano?" Dominic asks him.

Gabriel's mouth drops open, and his eyes come to meet mine. "Who taught them?"

"I had an Italian nanny so that the children could learn in their formative years, she's moved out now but she was incredible."

"I can't..." For the first time ever he's speechless.

"I've prepared them the best I could."

Overcome with emotion, his eyes well with tears and he nods, lost for words. He picks up his fork and shovels in a big mouthful of food. I watch and see the exact moment that he tastes it, he coughs sharply and holds his hand in a fist in front of his mouth as he tries to swallow it.

"Delicious, isn't it?" I smile.

"So yummy, Momma," Lucy says as she takes another mouthful.

Gabriel takes a huge gulp of water as he looks around the table at us all eating.

"Do you like it?" I ask.

"Hmm." He widens his eyes and begins to push a pickled onion around his bowl with his fork as he tries to work out what it is. "It's like nothing I've ever eaten."

"Do you live in Italy?" Lucia asks.

"No, I live in New York," he replies as he takes another bite. He winces and closes his eyes as he tries to silently deal with the horror.

I kind of wish the kids weren't here so that he could say what he really thinks, this is priceless.

Lucy talks and talks, and I glance over at Dominic who has not said a single word, and I know I have to just come out with it.

"Guys, there is a reason I have asked Gabriel to come over to see us," I say. "And it's a very special reason."

"I don't think that's necessary—" Gabriel cuts me off. "Wouldn't want to ruin this..." his eyebrows flick up as he pushes the food around with this fork, "...delicacy."

"Why were you mean to my mother?" Dominic comes straight out with it.

Gabriel shovels a huge forkful into his mouth so he doesn't have to answer and then coughs again. He rolls his lips as he tries to process what's in his mouth. "What kind of pasta sauce is this?" He winces before picking up his water and gulping it.

"Delicious pasta sauce," Lucia answers.

Gabriel's eyebrows flick up in surprise. "You have your mother's tastebuds, that's for certain."

"She doesn't like you," Dominic says as he looks Gabriel dead in the eye. They glare at each other across the table.

Oh fuck, here we go.

"Don't be rude, Dominic," I snap.

Lucy's eyes widen as she looks between the two of them.

"Cerca di mostrare un po' di rispetto a tua madre. Questa è casa sua," Gabriel says. (*"Show some respect to your mother at her dinner table."*)

"No," Dominic says.

"Parlami in italiano," Gabriel fires back. (*"You speak to me in Italian."*)

"No." Dominic gets up and marches upstairs.

"Torna subito qui," Gabriel calls after him. (*"You come back here right now."*)

"No."

The table falls silent and Lucy stares after him before she finally continues to eat.

Gabriel puts his fork down and I gesture to his bowl. "You need to eat it all."

"I want to live."

I exhale heavily, that was a disaster. I should have put arsenic in his food and put us all out of misery.

"Eat. The food." I smile through gritted teeth. "Don't make me force-feed you...because...I will."

Gabriel glares at me and eventually picks up his fork.

My god, that couldn't have gone worse. Dom is a handful, sometimes too much for even me.

"Lucy, why don't you take Dom's dinner up to him."

"Okay." Lucy grabs her brother's bowl and toddles off upstairs.

I wait until she is out of ears' reach. "What did you say to him in Italian?"

"He was being rude, so I pulled him into line."

"What?" I screw up my face. "You do not get to pull him into line on the first day of being a father."

"He doesn't get to be rude to me on the first day of being my son. Not on day one, not ever. He needs to learn straight away that bad behavior will not be tolerated."

I slump back into my chair and look around the empty table. "Eat your food."

"I'm getting you a cook."

"Why?"

"Because no wonder he's in a bad mood. The poor bastard is being poisoned to death." He stirs the food in his bowl. "And for the record, you cut the fucking onions up. Not throw them in whole."

I glance down at the eyeball pickled onions in his spaghetti and I get the giggles.

"There is nothing funny about your cooking, Grace."

"Kind of."

"Not at all," he snaps.

"Well, you need to eat what I cook the children; it tells them that you are like them."

"If they like this..." He gestures to his plate as he searches for the right word. "Then we are nothing alike." He puts his head into his hands and exhales heavily in disappointment.

I watch him for a moment. He really is feeling so out of his depth here. Empathy fills me.

"Dominic is strong-willed."

He sits for a moment as if processing my words. "I wanted tonight to be nice so that they would remember me fondly."

"Well, in that case...don't be yourself."

"What?" He screws up his face. "That's your advice, don't be myself?"

"You're a rude pig. If you want them to like you, act nice."

"I am *not* a rude pig."

"Oh yes you are. And for the record, Dominic is the carbon copy of you and will not back down, he's a lot to handle. If you want his respect, you have to earn it."

"Well, that works both ways."

"No. Don't you dare pull that card."

He stays silent and Lucy comes bouncing back to the table, she sits down and continues to eat.

Gabriel watches her for a while as if having an out-of-body experience.

"Where will I be sleeping?" Gabriel asks.

"In my room."

"I take it that's upstairs?" He pushes out his chair as if about to get up.

"No." I stand in a rush. "I have to straighten things up in there. You finish your dinner and I'll get it ready for you."

He nods, distracted. "Thank you."

I look between him and Lucy, do I leave her here alone with him?

He's her father...

God, I really need to wrap my head around this.

"Are you two okay down here together if I go upstairs and organize a few things?" My eyes linger on Lucy as I wait for her reaction, she smiles goofily with an over exaggerated nod.

Ugh...traitor.

Can't she at least act uninterested in him for my sake?

"I think we are doing just fine, aren't we, Lucia?" Gabriel smiles over at her.

"Yes."

The vision of the two of them blurs as my eyes well with tears. I turn toward the door so that they can't see my face and stumble to the stairs. In the darkness, I sink down to sit on one halfway up.

I can hear my heart beating in my chest as an overwhelming panic runs through me.

He turns up here, says a few pretty words and already she willingly adores him.

Just like that...and he's leaving.

I sit in the darkness for a while and I can hear them talking in the distance. Gabriel is asking her questions and she's loving the attention.

She says something that I can't hear and I hear Gabriel laugh and then she laughs too.

My beautiful little girl, so happy to be talking with her father, I smile softly in the darkness.

Okay, I need to get my act together and try and fix this situation with Dominic, I want him to have a happy memory too. I stand and make my way upstairs and knock on the closed door. "Dom."

Silence...

I open the door to find him sitting on his bed playing with his Nintendo Switch, and I sit down beside him. "Are you okay?"

"Yep." He keeps playing.

"Did Gabriel upset you?"

"Nope," he says, he keeps playing as he acts uninterested.

"What did he say to you in Italian?" I ask.

"Nothing much."

I sit beside him for a moment and I don't want to make this more dramatic than it needs to be, this has to be in his time, not mine. "Is it okay if I sleep in here with you tonight on the trundle bed?"

"Yeah, all right." He keeps playing.

Damn it, this is getting me nowhere and I have to clean my room for Gabriel.

"I'll be back soon, bubba."

He nods and keeps playing the stupid game.

I rush into my bedroom and look around at the chaos. Ahhh... Why aren't I a housewife superstar, it would be so much more convenient at times like this.

I stuff my washing into the clothes hamper, I gather up some clothes that are hanging over the chair in the corner of the room and throw them onto the top shelf of my wardrobe.

I run my eyes over the contents of the wardrobe, unorganized and disorderly.

Oh man, if he looks in there, I'm totally screwed.

Ugh, I don't have time to worry about that now. I slam the door shut.

I pull the covers back on my bed. I should change the sheets.

Damn it, I only changed the sheets yesterday and my other set of sheets is still on the line.

Shit.

These sheets will have to do.

I remake the bed and straighten up the cushions, oh crap, can't forget that...I rustle through my bedside drawer for my vibrator and stuff it into the basket of washing and hide it with some clothes.

I do a quick clean of my dressing table and throw my makeup into my top drawer as I look around the bedroom, what else... have I missed anything?

Is there anything in here that is too personal for him to see?

Who am I kidding, it's my bedroom, everything is personal.

Gabriel

"I'm going to take a look at the lake," I lie.

Lucy smiles up at me with the most beautiful little face I have ever seen. I rush out the door and immediately dial Mark's number.

"Hey," he answers.

"Hi, change of plans."

"What do you mean?"

"I'm going to spend the night here."

"What? I thought you were there to say goodbye."

"I am." I pause as I look over the lake. "It's just...not as easy as I first thought."

"Well...what should I do?" he asks.

"Just stay in the hotel and..." I shrug, "...I'll come and get you in the morning."

"Okay. Enjoy every second, okay?"

We are now counting the time with my children in seconds, I get a lump in my throat at the thought.

I hang up and turn back toward the house. Standing in the darkness, I can see Grace and Lucia washing the dishes as they chat away.

I've never felt so out of control of my life.

. . .

"Lucy, show Gabriel where my bedroom is, please?" Grace tells her.

"This way," Lucia says, she takes my hand in hers as she leads me through the house.

"What cute little hands you have." I smile.

She holds them both up for me to look at and I try to memorize every detail.

I feel sick to my stomach.

Why did I snap at Dominic?

I feel like shit about it, but he will not disrespect me. Not now, not ever.

No, I did the right thing.

We get to the top of the stairs. "And this is my room." Lucia smiles proudly as she shows me her room. It's pink and pretty and has big letters on the wall that spell out her name. Dolls and teddy bears are all perfectly sitting up against her pillow. "It's very nice."

"It is." She smiles as she swings her arms.

My eyes linger up the hallway. "Where is Dominic's room?"

"This way." She skips past me out of the room and down the hall to his. "He's in here."

I stand at the doorway and watch him for a moment, he's sitting on his bed and playing a video game. I look around his bedroom, it's navy blue and boyish. Instead of dolls, there are Lego statues proudly displayed everywhere. "This is a nice room."

He keeps playing his game, completely ignoring me.

"Dominic, don't be rude," Grace tells him from behind me. "Get off your game, please."

He exhales heavily and puts the controller down.

"I said, it's a nice room," I repeat.

Dominic looks me dead in the eye without any emotion. "Is that all?"

He is like me.

I bite the inside of my cheek to stop myself from smirking. "I don't want us to get off on the wrong foot," I tell him.

He rolls his eyes and it's like waving a red flag in front of a bull.

"Did you just roll your eyes at me?"

"Dominic, don't be rude; this is your last warning." Grace pulls me by the hand up the hall. "Your room is this way, Gabriel." She pulls me into her bedroom and slams the door behind us. "Stay away from him and let him cool down."

"What?"

"I told you to give him time, he's processing."

"Processing what...being a rude prick?"

"You being here. He's a child," she spits. "And now you are being one. Stay in here and go to sleep."

"No," I spit. "I will not be sent to my room when I have done nothing wrong."

"For the love of god, do not leave this room. You can talk to him properly in the morning. Sleep is a reset for children, everything is forgotten overnight," she snaps. through gritted teeth. She grabs my two shoulders and walks me over to the bed and then pushes me backward. I bounce onto my back and something about her standing over me sends an unexpected surge through my cock.

I feel myself harden as I stare up at her.

"What?" she snaps.

"What, what?" I splutter, disgusted where my thoughts have gone.

"Why are you looking at me like that?"

"Like what?" An unwelcome smirk flashes across my face.

"The hell is wrong with you, what are you doing?"

"If you throw me onto your bed, expect a damn consequence." I sit up on my elbows.

"Oh my god." She narrows her eyes. "You're perverted."

"Glad we finally agree on something."

"Go to sleep and do not snoop through my bedroom."

"Don't flatter yourself."

"The bathroom is down the hall." She leaves the room in a rush and slams the door behind her.

I flop onto my back and stare up at the ceiling. I grab a pillow and put it under my head.

Grace's scent wafts all around me and I inhale deeply.

I know that smell...

It's the perfume she used to wear that drove me wild.

On more than one occasion I had to tell her not to wear it because on the days she did, I would get nothing done; I'd be too busy wanking in my office bathroom all day.

I close my eyes. Throb...throb...throb...goes my cock.

I pick up another pillow, same scent. I look over to see her dressing gown hanging on the back of her door and I get up and hold it to my nose.

Thump.

Thump.

Thump goes my cock...

Everything in here smells like Grace in Techni-dick-sucking-color.

Damn, that fucking woman pisses me off.

I hold the gown to my face again and inhale deeply.

All I can smell is Gracie. A lingering memory of that night we spent together begins to play in my mind. Her creamy pale skin, how tight she was...how well she took my cock.

How hard I blew.

Throb...throb...throb...

Stop it...you're about to get married to someone else...you fucking sleazebag.

I exhale heavily, disgusted with my dick. Fuck...it's going to be a long night.

I glance at the time on my phone, 2 a.m.

I haven't slept a wink, a rock-hard cock with nowhere to go will do that to you.

Tossing and turning and trying to think of something else.

The reality is that I'm not going to get any sleep until I come, there's no way around this. It's not going down.

I put my hand into my boxer shorts and give myself a slow, long stroke...hmmm.

I need to fuck myself...been a long time since I've done that.

My eyes roam around the darkened bedroom for some lube or tissues. I climb out of bed and turn the flashlight on my phone and walk around, looking for my wanking toolkit.

I go through the contents on the dressing table and nothing.

Hmm...the bathroom.

Surely there will be something in there. I open the door and peer down the darkened hallway, everything is silent. I look left and I look right and then I tiptoe down the hallway, using my phone flashlight to light the way.

Thump, thump, thump goes my cock.

Seriously...shut the hell up, I'm trying my best here.

I walk into the bathroom and quietly close the door behind me. Shining my flashlight onto the bathroom cupboard, I spot a bottle of baby oil.

Yes...

I grab it and the box of tissues and turn to leave when the bathroom door opens.

"Ahh." Grace jumps in fright and flicks the light on. "What the...you scared the crap out of me." Her eyes drop down my body. "What the hell is that?"

I glance down to see what she's talking about to see the tip of my erect cock is sticking out the top of my boxer shorts.

Fuck.

"Oh... That's my cock."

"I can see that," she whispers angrily. "Why is it hard?"

15

Gabriel

"IT'S NOT."

"Yes. It is."

Oh god...

"Why are you even looking at my private business?" I whisper.

"Because your troublemaking private business is hanging out in my bathroom."

"I take offense," I splutter as I feel the situation spiraling out of control. "And for your information, he is not a troublemaker, he's a problem solver."

"There are no problems to solve in this house," she whispers angrily. "Put it away." She rushes out of the bathroom and I hear her stomp up the hall.

I look down at myself, oil in one hand, tissues in the other, with my hard dick half hanging out of my boxer shorts. I've hit the bottom of the barrel.

Fuck.

. . .

Morning light shines through the windows and I sit on the edge of the bed fully dressed. I glance at my watch for the tenth time.

6:54 a.m.

What time does everyone get up in this house?

I'm usually up and dressed and on my way to work long before this.

I walk over to the window and open the curtains and look out at the view.

The sun is just rising, and there is a fog hanging over the lake, the sounds of birds chirp in the distance and trees sway in the wind. The view from up here is something else.

It's beautiful, serene.

Unlike me.

I've spent the night horny and wanking, wondering if Dominic will come around and speak to me today before I leave, and then there's the national disaster of the 2 a.m. bathroom visit... Hell, what a night.

She's right, my dick is a troublemaker, a huge pain in my ass.

One thing is for certain: I'm still physically attracted to Grace.

Which is an absolute nightmare because I'm marrying someone else in four weeks' time.

Creak...go the floorboards from up the hall, someone's awake. I hear the bathroom door, and five minutes later, I hear the toilet flush, and then I hear the stairs go as someone walks down them.

Who was that, was it Grace?

My mind goes back to the horror of being caught with a hard-on and a bottle of oil at 2 a.m.

Ugh, how the hell do I talk myself out of that one?

Pretend it didn't happen.

I'm going with that.

My door opens slightly and I turn to see two little brown eyes staring at me through the crack.

"Good morning, Lucia." I tap the bed beside me. "Come in."

She pushes the door open and smiles up at me. "Good morning." My heart somersaults in my chest.

She's all crumpled and sleepy, the cutest thing I ever saw in her little pink pajamas.

"How did you sleep?" I ask her as she walks in.

"Good." She stands beside me. "How did you sleep?"

"I've had better nights." I shrug.

She puts her little hand on my kneecap as we talk and oh... This day is perfect already.

"Where is your mom?"

"Downstairs." We sit for a moment in silence. "Shall we go see Momma?" she eventually asks. "She likes to hug me good morning."

"I bet she does." I smile, damn if she isn't the sweetest. "Let me get dressed and I'll meet you down there."

She looks me up and down. "But you're already dressed."

The truth is that I don't want to face Grace yet, I'm stalling. This walk of shame is particularly rough. I glance down at myself as I search for an excuse not to come now. "I need to go to the bathroom."

"Oh." She looks at me. "To do a poo?"

What the fuck?

"I don't think that's something you should say to someone."

"A wee, then?"

"Let's not talk about bodily functions, shall we?" I frown.

"A bodily what?"

Jeez-uz.

"I'll meet you downstairs," I say, a little sterner.

"Okay." With her little hand still on my knee, she smiles up at me as if waiting for me to say something.

"Okay..." I widen my eyes at her. What is she waiting for, am I supposed to say something here?

"Okay." She keeps staring up at me all doe-eyed and it dawns on me, she's as unsure what to do now as I am.

"I'm glad I met you," I tell her.

Happiness beams from her smile, and just for a moment I feel my heart leave my chest. I push the hair back from her forehead as I stare at her beautiful little face. "You're a lot like your mom."

She gives a nervous little chuckle. "You look like Dom."

My heart sinks. "Where is he?"

"Still sleeping."

Hmm... Suddenly, I want to get downstairs quickly, I want to be down there before him. "Okay, run along and I'll see you downstairs."

She skips out of the room, and I watch her disappear as I smile after her. That was the best wake-up visit of all time.

I go to the bathroom and wash my face and with trepidation slowly walk down the stairs. I can hear Grace and Lucia talking and I stop midway up to listen to what they are saying.

"Where's Dom?" Grace asks.

"Jupiter."

"What do you mean?"

"The boys went to Jupiter to all get stupider."

"I don't think that's very nice to boys, do you?"

"But it's just a joke, don't you get it?"

"Not a funny one."

I find myself smiling as I listen to them talk, and they chatter on for a good while. It dawns on me that listening in on them is as creepy as all hell, so I step heavily on the bottom step so they hear me coming. "Good morning," I say as I walk into the kitchen.

Lucia smiles broadly. "Good morning."

"Morning," Grace grumbles with her back to me as she makes her coffee.

I pull out a chair at the dining table and take a seat, my eyes linger on her rounded tight ass and my cock twinges in appreciation.

Stop!

"What's happening today?" I ask to take my mind off the situation.

Grace turns toward me, and for the first time I see her face, makeup free and tousled hair.

Oh...she's so lovely.

"You're leaving," she says abruptly.

My dick shrivels.

I nod, ashamed of my moonlight behavior.

She sips her coffee as her eyes hold mine.

I have no idea what's going through her head right now, but I'm sure it's evil.

I should have worn an armored vest.

"Apologies for..." I widen my eyes. "You know."

"Not accepted." She glares at me. "Do you want a coffee?"

"Sure." I fake a smile. This is awkward as fuck. "Thank you."

She turns to the coffee machine and my eyes drop down her body and linger on her ass once again. I feel a rush of blood to my loins.

Lock it up.

What the hell is going on here?

She passes me the cup of coffee. "I'm going out to hang the washing on the line," she tells Lucia. "Are you okay in here with Gabriel?"

Lucia smiles broadly over at me. "Yes."

Pride fills me.

Grace walks out the back door, and I wait until she is out of hearing range. "Does your mom have a boyfriend?" I ask Lucia.

"No."

Hmm...

"Does she have any..." I pause as I try to articulate my words, "...man friends that come over sometimes?"

"Just Jack."

"Jack?"

There's a Jack?

"Who's Jack?"

"Oh, he's Dom's Little League coach."

"Oh...he is, is he?" I narrow my eyes, the old sporting coach

179

lusting after the single mom trick...hey? "Isn't that against some code of ethics or something?"

"Code of what?"

"Never mind." I sip my coffee and the vile taste of burned poison hits my tongue. I cough and nearly choke.

What the...?

"What's wrong?" Lucia frowns.

"This isn't coffee."

"What is it, then?"

"It's a Molotov cocktail." I wince.

This damn woman can't cook for shit.

"A Molotov what...?"

Fuck me.

"You ask a lot of questions." I cut her off.

"You say a lot of weird things..."

"Thank you for pointing that out." I drag my hand down my face. The sooner I get out of here, the better... "That's if I make it out alive before being poisoned to death," I mutter under my breath.

"Who's poisoning to death?"

"Nobody," I snap. Dear lord, I've never wanted to scream *Mind your own business* at someone so much in my life.

I feel someone's eyes on me, and I turn to see Dominic standing at the door, watching us. He's in checked pajamas and his hair is standing on end. "Good morning, Dominic." I force a smile, determined to do better with him today.

"Hi," he grumbles as he walks into the kitchen. "Where's Mom?"

"Out the back," Lucia replies as she eats her cereal.

He walks straight past me and disappears out the back door, and I stand and watch him through the window. He walks out to Grace as she hangs the washing on the line. She gives him a big broad smile and drops to her knee and hugs him tight. They hug while he says something to her and she laughs and says something back.

My stomach twists with jealousy.

Of course he likes her more, she's had him his entire life while I have been hidden and lied to.

Anger surges through me.

Fuck her.

I drop back into the chair and act casual as adrenaline surges through me.

Dominic walks up the stairs and into the house, and I snap out of my daydream. "Where's the clean washing basket?" Dominic asks Lucia.

"Why?" She looks him up and down and chews as she eats.

I inwardly roll my eyes, what's with this kid and the questions?

"I need my Little League uniform."

She shrugs. "I don't know."

Does this house have no organization whatsoever?

He disappears into the laundry and I lower my voice. "Does Jack ever come over at night?" I whisper.

"I don't know."

"How don't you know? You live here?" I whisper.

She shrugs.

I pinch the bridge of my nose in frustration. For a busybody child, she sure is light on useful information.

"What's this?" Dominic says from the door.

I glance over to see him holding a big pink vibrator and my eyes widen. "Where did you get that?"

"It was in the washing basket among the clothes."

I remember Grace carrying a basket of washing out of her room last night, she must have put it in there to hide it from me. I roll my lips to hide my smile.

"What *is* that?" Lucia frowns.

I stand and snatch it from him. "It's a..." I look around the room as I search for an appropriate answer. "It's a massager."

"A massager?" Dominic frowns. "What do you massage with this?"

Pussy.

"Ahhh…" I hesitate while I troll my mind for an answer. "Necks and stuff."

"What kind of massager is it?" Lucia asks.

I don't fucking know…

"Kitty cat massager," I reply.

Dominic frowns. "That's weird."

"I have to agree."

I smile as satisfaction fills me.

Good old Jack is not getting the job done.

Grace

I peg the washing on the line with force. Who the hell does this imbecile think that he is, he barges in here, demands I give him a room and then disrespects me by having a raging erection at 2 a.m.

I get a vision of his hard dick and how beautiful it was.

Ughh…

I peg the clothes on hard. I hate this man and I hate that his dick is just hanging around in my house at night.

All hard and fuckable like. And he knows it, too, he knows how good his dick is and he's just parading it around, and damn it I need to get laid stat.

My blood boils and I peg the last of the clothes on and march inside to find Dominic, Lucia and Gabriel sitting at the table, eating cereal together.

Hmm, this is all very civilized.

I pick up my coffee and take a sip and casually glance over to see something standing on end on the table in front of Gabriel.

Huh.

My vibrator…

I spit my coffee out. *What the fuck?* "What are you…what the hell…what are you doing?" I stammer.

"Eating my cereal." Gabriel's mischievous eyes hold mine. "Dom found your kitty cat massager in the washing basket."

My eyes widen.

Gabriel smirks. "It's a very small massager."

No, no, no...this can't be happening.

"Well..." I wobble my head around as I try to think of a comeback. "I have a very small neck," I spit. "Stay away from my massagers."

I march out of the room and into the hallway and put my head into my hands.

This is single-handedly the most embarrassing moment of my entire life.

How could I forget that it was in the washing basket?

What the hell is wrong with me...and of course he had to be here to see it.

Oh.

My.

God.

I want to die a thousand deaths.

With my heart thumping hard through my chest, I march upstairs.

I hate him, I hate everything about him.

This is all his fault, I was flustered when he showed up here and I stuffed it in that laundry basket and completely forgot about it because I don't even feel comfortable in my own home. How dare he barge himself in here and sleep in my bedroom, that is a private place, my sanctuary.

I can hear Lucia chatting downstairs as I begin to pace back and forth in my bedroom.

With every lap on the carpet, I become more infuriated.

I'm not standing for this.

He needs to get out of this house right fucking now.

He's one of the richest men in America, don't tell me he can't find a hotel.

I'm not buying it.

I storm downstairs and into the kitchen. "Gabriel, can I speak with you for a moment?" I announce.

Gabriel looks up from his cereal as if I am a major inconvenience. "Yes."

"Alone." I gesture to the stairs with my chin.

He rolls his eyes as I imagine myself throwing a full-blown punch to his stupid square jaw. "Back in a moment." He fakes a smile to the kids.

I turn and march upstairs and then into my bedroom and he walks in behind me. "What?"

"Close the door," I growl, and by the sound of my own voice, it's clear the psychotic part of my brain has been well and truly activated.

He closes the door and puts his hands on his hips, arrogance personified. "What do you want?"

"You need to say goodbye to the children and get the hell out of my house."

He narrows his eyes and steps forward. "I'll leave when I am good and ready."

"Listen here, you." I poke him in the chest. "Your little midnight hard-on tells me that you are good and ready now, so..."

"I already apologized for that."

"Not well enough."

"Calm down."

"Calm down!" I shriek. "I will *not* calm down."

A trace of a smile crosses his face. "You're annoyed about the massager."

"I'm not annoyed, I'm fucking infuriated. How dare you invade my privacy."

"Your son found it, what the hell did you want me to tell him, Mom's been flogging her pussy with a fake dick?"

"You're an animal."

"We've already established this," he fires back.

"You need to get out," I spit.

"I'm trying," he growls. "Stop the carry-on, do you think I want to stay here and..."

"And the wanking with the oil and the tissues...just what the fuck, Gabriel?"

"Why are you cursing so much, and come on." He does smile this time. "You have to admit me being caught is pretty funny."

"If you were a thirteen-year-old boy it's funny, a grown man who is engaged to be married, it's horrifying."

"That wasn't my fault," he fires back. "It was yours."

"How the hell is this *my* fault?" I shriek.

"Well..." He's flustered and searching for words. He drags his hands through his dark hair. "Those sheets smell like you and..." He widens his eyes as if searching for divine guidance. "I am only human, you know?"

"What the hell is that supposed to mean?"

"Come off it, Gracie, stop acting naïve." He rolls his eyes.

Gracie...

Hearing him call me Gracie brings back a sea of memories and I stare at him as my brain malfunctions.

"Don't flatter yourself, Gabriel, I have zero attraction to you."

That I'll ever admit to.

"We are very alike," he whispers angrily.

"We are nothing alike," I fire back. "You think you're God and I know you're the devil."

He finds that amusing and gives me a slow sexy smile. "A little difference in religion never hurt anyone."

I feel the heat from his gaze all the way to my toes.

No...

Get him out of here, right now.

"Listen, just..." I throw my hands up in the air in defeat, I have no idea how to deal with this situation. "You really need to stop being so Gabriel Ferrara and start being more goodbye children. Go and say goodbye and leave."

He exhales heavily before marching out of the room, and I hear him stomp down the stairs.

I stare after him to the sound of my heart pumping so hard that it's nearly beating out of my chest.

This is my worst frigging nightmare.

. . .

Twenty minutes and ten panic attacks later, I make my way downstairs.

Calm, keep calm...everything is perfectly fine and I am totally calm.

"Are you coming to Dominic's game?" I hear Lucy ask Gabriel.

No.

"Ahhh..." I hear Gabriel pause. "Would you like me to?"

"Yes," Lucy says excitedly. "We can sit together.

Just fuck off back to New York already.

"Are we ready to go?" I call as I collect my car keys and handbag.

"Ready, Mom."

"Go get in the car, guys." I pass the car keys to Dom. They bounce out the front door and Gabriel appears out of the kitchen. He's dressed in different clothes now, where did he get those? Is Mark in Greenville too, did he bring them? He's wearing a gray T-shirt and jeans; his black hair has a messed-up wave to it and as his dark eyes hold mine, I feel my stomach flutter for the first time in a long time.

Russel and I broke up over a year ago and since then I've been on two dates with two losers. My flutters have been few and far between.

"What are you doing?" he says in his deep voice. "Go and get ready."

"I am ready."

His eyes drop down my body and back up to my face. "You're not going out dressed like that."

I look down at myself, have I got something spilled on me or something? "Like what?"

"You're wearing gym clothes out in public?" He frowns.

"Yes, Gabriel. I am not a catwalk model like your fiancée, nor would I want to be. Go home to her."

He narrows his eyes.

The sky has turned red, this man is the most infuriating sexist pig of all time. I stomp out and dive into the car and start the engine and he knocks on the window.

Adrenaline is pumping through my body and I glare at him through the window.

He knocks again.

"Mom..." Lucy says from the back seat. "What are you doing?"

Be the adult.

"Nothing." I fake a smile and wind down the window as I act calm. "Yes, Gabriel."

"I will come to the game before I leave this afternoon."

"Okay." I grip the steering wheel with white-knuckle force and widen my eyes at him.

Don't push me, fucker...I am about to end you.

"So I will see you all later this afternoon, okay?" he says over me to the children in the backseat.

"Okay." Lucy smiles.

Gabriel turns his attention to Dom. "I'll see you this afternoon, Dominic?"

Dominic shrugs.

Gabriel's cold eyes roam over to me and from the look on his face it's obvious he blames me for Dominic's hatred.

"This has nothing to do with me."

He glares at me and I glare right back.

Screw you.

I pull out and drive down the road before I say something nasty and horrible in front of my children.

I need to be a better person...for them.

The crowd cheers and I sit in the stands and stare into space. I'm here in body, but mentally, I'm a million miles away.

Saturday afternoon at Little League, it's mid-afternoon and the weight of the world is on my shoulders. As the adrenaline from our fight this morning left my body, it's been replaced by a sense of melancholy.

I get a vision of him in his boxers last night, his bare chest and his hard dick...

Ugh...

As impossible as Gabriel is, I cannot deny the physical attraction I have for him. It's deep in my soul and I now know for certain that I will never be rid of this curse.

I hate it, and damn it, I just need him to leave and go and get married.

Leave us the hell alone.

"You're quiet," Deb says from beside me. "You okay?"

I glance over to see Gabriel walk up the stairs and take a seat in the front row of chairs.

"Yeah, I'm okay." I sigh. "I just have the feeling that my whole world is falling apart."

Gabriel turns and looks around for me, our eyes lock and we stare at each other for a beat as something swirls between us.

I can't put my finger on exactly what it is.

"Maybe your world isn't falling apart," Deb replies as her eyes linger on Gabriel, "Maybe it's falling into place."

16

Grace

"ARE YOU SERIOUS?" I snap.

"Stop whining about him being in your house. He's trying to do the right thing and came to say goodbye in person. He could have just gone to court and gotten an order to take them to New York just like you thought he would. You told him it's all or nothing, your words and not his. He's obviously thought long and hard about this and realized the fact that he can't be there for the kids as much as they need him and is graciously stepping aside. I know it's not the decision you hoped for, but you are the one who did the whole ridiculous all-or-nothing scenario."

"Because I don't want my kids to be here waiting for him all the time while he's in New York with his new kids while totally ignoring them. They are happy now; they want for nothing."

"I get it. I really do." Deb sighs as her eyes go back down to him. "And he does too. He's thinking of their needs before his own and trying to do things the right way, at least give him some credit for that."

"What about the invasion of my privacy?" I widen my eyes. "Huh?"

"Don't blame him for you leaving your dildo around." She widens her eyes back.

"Mom." Lucia comes running up the stairs toward me all excited. "Gabriel is here."

My stomach flips with fury at her excitement. "Is he?" My eyes roam down to the front row and I can see the back of him as he sits and watches, his broad shoulders, they stand out from a mile.

"Can I go and sit with him?" she begs as she jumps on the spot.

I fake a smile. "Sure."

"Yay." She skips down to the front row and shimmies along the seats until she gets to him. I watch on as she taps him on the shoulder. He smiles broadly when he sees her and then moves his jacket from the seat to make room for her to sit down beside him. He says something and she smiles goofily up at him, her excitement that he's here is palpable. I watch their interaction with my heart in my throat.

"How could you ever be sad about that?" Deb says. "Look how happy she is."

"He's leaving."

"I know."

"So how is her getting to know him doing anyone any good? This is a disaster waiting to happen."

"Let him have his hour with them. He will be back in New York tonight and they will never see him again."

"True." I sigh. "I just don't get why he wanted to come in person to say goodbye. If he's leaving, just do it by text. Don't put us through it."

Deb raises an unimpressed eyebrow. "They are not just your kids, you do know that, right?"

The game goes on and on, but my mind is a mile away. My gaze keeps dropping down to Gabriel and Lucia talking and laughing as they watch, and I hate to admit it, but I'm livid that Lucia is awestruck by his nice-guy act.

I'm your mom, have some fricken loyalty kid.

. . .

"That was a great game," Deb says.

I glance up, miles away. "Yes." I clap as I pretend to know the game has ended.

What the hell, I've been so lost in thought, I've missed the entire game.

Gabriel and Lucy come up the steps of the grandstand to see us.

"Good lord," Deb mutters under her breath. "Could he be any hotter."

"Looks are deceiving," I whisper through a fake smile.

He holds his hand out to Debbie. "Hello, I'm Gabriel." His voice is deep and husky.

Debbie shakes his hand. "Hi." She smiles mischievously as she stares up at him. "I'm Debbie, Grace's best friend and cousin."

"Oh." His eyes widen. "I didn't realize you were related."

Bang, bang, bang goes the blood through my veins. Why does his close proximity affect me so much?

Cut it out, hormones.

"Do you live here too?" Gabriel asks Debbie.

"Yes, I'm the reason Grace first came to this town."

"Hmm." Gabriel acts grumpy. "I have you to blame for stealing her from me, do I?"

"I guess so." Debbie laughs, and I roll my eyes.

Don't try to charm her...you asshole.

Ugh...go back to New York.

"Oh." Deb's eyes flick to me. If I could say something, I would, I'm too distracted by the adrenaline screaming through my veins.

"Dominic played great," Gabriel says casually.

"He did, didn't he?" Deb agrees.

Did he? I have no idea; I didn't watch one minute of the match. Too busy dissecting the trainwreck.

"Shall we head down?" Gabriel asks.

I nod, unable to push one nice word through my lips.

We walk down the grandstand and over to the side of the pitch and Dominic comes out of the changerooms with his bag; he glances up and sees Gabriel and his face falls.

So does my heart.

Gabriel forces a smile and I die a little inside. For both him and Dom.

"Great game," Gabriel says.

"Thanks," Dom grumbles.

Suddenly it's awkward.

"I'll get going," Deb says. She rubs her hand through Dom's hair. "Great game, buddy."

"Thanks, Aunty Deb."

"Have a great weekend." She kisses my cheek. "Nice to meet you, Gabriel."

"You too." He smiles.

The four of us stand in silence, unsure what to say next.

Gabriel's eyes hold mine. "I've made arrangements for you to be looked after financially, my accountant will be in touch to get your banking details."

"That isn't necessary, we don't want your money."

"Don't be a fool, Grace."

"Don't even..."

"Well." His eyes hold mine. "I guess I should get going."

Emotion crashes over me like a shipwreck as we stare at each other.

"It's for the best," he says as if sensing my inner meltdown. "You're right...about everything."

I nod, unable to push a word past my lips.

"So goodbye." He smiles down at the twins.

They have no idea how significant this goodbye really is.

Don't leave them.

If he doesn't want to be their dad, then I can't change it. It's better he leaves now rather than a long, drawn-out goodbye.

"Gabriel is going back to New York, guys, say goodbye," I tell them.

Lucia looks up at him. "When will you be back?"

A frown flashes across his face. "I...I can't come back."

"Oh." Her little face falls.

"Give him a hug," I prompt them.

Gabriel goes down on one knee and Lucia gives him a big bear hug. He closes his eyes as he holds her close.

"It was so lovely to meet you," he tells her. "I'll never forget you."

Lucy smiles into his hair as he holds her close.

My nostrils flare as I try to keep it together.

They eventually pull out of the hug and he turns to Dominic. "Can I get a hug goodbye?" Gabriel asks him.

Dominic sighs as if he is a major inconvenience.

"Hug Gabriel," I snap as I widen my eyes. Can you stop being a little shit for just once in your life? This could be the only time you will ever get to hug your father, please just do it.

Gabriel grabs Dominic and holds him tight and seeing the two of them together is too much, the dam does burst this time and I quickly wipe a lone tear as it escapes.

I don't even know why I'm crying; I know this really is for the best.

"It was an honor to meet you," Gabriel says as he straightens his son's T-shirt. "You look after your mother."

Dominic nods.

Gabriel stands and his haunted eyes meet mine. "Goodbye."

"Goodbye."

We stare at each other for a beat longer than we should, his eyes drop to the kids and then without another word he turns and walks off.

The earth moves beneath me...

The kids instantly start to chatter as if nothing has happened, and to them it hasn't.

I feel the pain run through me like a tidal wave. Not for me, but for them.

He got to know them, and still he didn't want them.

The lump in my throat hurts as I stare at the ground.

How could he walk away from the two most wonderful things on earth?

What the hell is wrong with him?

Gabriel

I get into the waiting car and slam the door.

Mark turns back to look at me.

"Drive," I snap.

"Are you . . ."

"Yes." I cut him off. "Drive the fucking car."

My elbow is resting on the window and my face leans on my hand and as we pull out of the parking lot, I close my eyes so I don't have to watch them as they disappear.

A deep, dark lead ball sits in the pit of my stomach and I know it will never go away.

That was the hardest thing I've ever done.

I brush my teeth and walk into the bedroom. Ariana is already in bed and reading.

I watch her for a moment, her long dark hair is plaited and her cream silk nightgown stands out against her olive skin. There is no doubt about it, Ariana is one of the most beautiful women on earth. She glances up over the top of her book and gives me a smile. "What are you doing?"

"Looking at you."

She taps the bed beside her. "Come and look at me like that from here."

I climb into bed and take her in my arms. I'm riddled with guilt for a million reasons. I lied to her about where I was last night, I have two children that I haven't told her about, I'm not excited about the wedding in the slightest, but the worst thing of all is...I can't stop thinking about Grace.

I hold her tight in my arms. She deserves so much better.

Her hand slides down my boxer shorts, her engagement ring catches on the fabric and I reach in and pull it out. "I'm tired."

"Since when are you ever too tired for sex?"

"Since tonight."

Since I saw her.

I roll her onto her side facing away from me and I cuddle her back.

"Three weeks until we get married," she whispers into the darkness. "I'm so excited to start our life together." She picks my hand up and kisses it, and I close my eyes in horror.

Fuck...

"Let's circle back to this report next week." I reply to the staff around my board table. "Good work this month, our figures are on fire." They all leave the meeting room with a buzz of chatter. I collect my things and begin to walk back to my office. I pass through reception.

"Mr. Ferrara, your mother and Ariana are in your office, sir," one of the girls tells me.

"Thank you."

I keep walking and roll my eyes, great. What are they doing here, I am way too busy for their wedding crap today.

I walk into the office to find them both with their stilettos kicked off and shopping bags everywhere. They both have a glass of champagne from my bar.

"Ladies," I say as I look around at the disaster zone. "To what do I owe this pleasure?"

Ariana jumps up and wraps her arms around my neck. "We came to show you what's arrived." She kisses me quickly and I pull out of her arms and peck my mother on the cheek. "Mom."

"Hello, darling." She smiles. "Take a seat." She gestures to the couch.

"I don't have time for this today."

"We'll be quick." Mom smiles. "Show him, Ariana."

Ariana digs through the bags and pulls out a box and very slowly opens it.

"Hurry up, this isn't a marathon." I sigh. "I don't have all day, you know."

Mom chuckles as she flops onto the couch beside me for the show.

The box opens and Ariana pulls out two crystal champagne flutes. "These are for all of the tables for the speeches." She passes one to me. "Look at the engraving."

My eyes scan the glass.

Gabriel and Ariana
Eternally bound by love

I curl my lip in disgust. "Bit over the top, don't you think?"

"Nooo," they gasp together.

"Ugh."

"Oh, and there's more." Ariana widens her eyes.

"I can hardly contain my excitement," I mutter under my breath.

"These are the chocolates for the table." She pulls out a silver sample box and unwraps it and presents little chocolate statues of a bride and groom wrapped in foil.

"Look closer," Mom tells me as she passes me a groom.

I look closer. "Why the hell does this chocolate look like me?"

"They digitally remastered our faces onto them."

I cringe. "The last thing I want to see at my wedding is everyone I know sucking me off."

Mom laughs out loud as if this is the best thing that has ever happened. "Those chocolates have made my life complete."

I pass the box back to her. "Your life must be extremely boring. I have to get back to work."

"Show him the surprise." Mom grabs my arm so I can't get up.

"Please don't." I sigh.

Ariana pulls out crystal candlesticks. "Look how perfect these are, and all the guests get to take one home as a souvenir." She points down to the base that's engraved.

Gabriel and Ariana
Eternally bound by love

"If I got this at a wedding and was expected to take it home, I would beat the groom to death with it." I stand and walk over to my desk. "Take your tea party home, girls, I have to work."

"And now for the real showstopper."

I drag my hand down my face. "I wish this show would stop."

Ariana lifts off a cover and there are two white doves in a silver gilded cage.

What the fuck?

"Are they real?" I frown.

"Of course they're real. I've got to take them back this afternoon, but I wanted to bring them to show you. When we're pronounced man and wife, three hundred doves are going to be released into the air as a symbol of our eternal love."

I stare at her horrified, and utterly speechless.

Ariana bats her eyelashes all proud of herself. "Do you love them?"

"No. I do not."

"Why not?"

"When I said you could organize the wedding, I didn't realize you were putting on a circus performance complete with a fucking zoo," I snap. "No doves."

"But..."

"No fucking doves," I snap.

Ariana's face falls in disappointment.

"I'm overruling you, Gabriel. If Ariana wants doves, Ariana is getting doves. Only the best for my new daughter." Mother smiles. "You have all the doves you want, sweetheart, get four hundred just to assert your dominance." Mom winks at me and I clench my jaw.

Don't push it, Mom.

I always wanted a wife that my mother approved of, but these two together is over the top.

"Leave," I snap. "My next appointment is here."

They laugh and chatter as they pack up their bullshit surprises and then slip into the sky-high heels.

I watch them for a moment, beautiful, immaculately groomed, both in designer clothing, perfectly styled dark hair with not a thing out of place, and I have an out-of-body realization that I am marrying my mother's younger twin.

The thought is disturbing, how haven't I seen this before?

Ariana kisses my cheek and my mother kisses the other and then they breeze out of my office just as they entered.

A whirlwind of glamor.

The door closes behind them and my office falls silent. I try to concentrate, but instead I walk to the window and stare out over the view of New York. I slide my hands into my suit pockets and my mind drifts to Greenville...with her.

I think of how different things would have been if we had ended up together.

This wedding would be Gracie's worst nightmare.

Mine too.

Lost between two worlds...

She flicks her tongue over my end and my cock weeps in appreciation. I grab two handfuls of her hair and push my cock between her two lips, it slowly slides down her throat.

A million sensations, my balls contract as they get ready to fire and I feel the heat of her perfect mouth around me. "Suck me," I growl. "Harder."

Suction vibrates through my body and I begin to lose control.

So good, *so fucking good.*

I slam my cock down her throat and begin to ride her mouth hard. She gags and I go deeper. "Suck me dry." We fall into a rhythm. "You swallow every last drop I give you." I go faster, deeper. "Take it all."

Her moans only make me harder, and I'm about to explode, her fingernails dig into my quad muscles and I lose it.

I slam in and hold myself deep as I come down her throat, my breathing is jagged as I struggle for air. Perspiration sheens my body as I look down at her and she opens her eyes.

Long auburn hair, creamy skin, voluptuous breasts, and a body built for sin.

Gracie.

I jerk awake, and as I gasp for air, I look around the darkened bedroom to see Ariana fast asleep beside me.

The room is silent and calm, so unlike the hot place I've just visited.

I can feel that I've just ejaculated, and I drag my hands through my hair.

Fuck...

I pant as I try to catch my breath, it was just a dream.

It's okay, it was just a dream.

Who am I kidding, it was a fucking nightmare.

I wait in the restaurant and sip my scotch, it's my monthly lunch date with my beloved friend Claire.

Claire and I have been close for over ten years, she's cool and calm and hilariously dry. Funnily enough, she married one of my enemies, Tristan Miles. They have kids and it turns out he's actually a good guy, not that I'll ever openly admit it.

I remind myself, whatever you do today, don't say anything about the recent events.

Claire calls a spade a spade and I don't need her getting in my ear about my life.

I already know it's a nightmare, I'm not spending our lunch being lectured.

She waddles through the restaurant and when I see her, I laugh out loud as I stand to greet her.

"What's so funny?" She kisses my cheek.

"Why are you walking like that?"

"Pilates instructor from hell." She laughs and sits down opposite me. "My ass is grass. I'm on a health kick that's about to kill me."

"It's working. You are glowing." I smile.

"Oh, I've got so much to tell you." She jabbers on as she takes her jacket off. "Why didn't you call me back last week, by the way?"

Before I can answer, she talks over me again.

"You won't believe what Patrick has gone and done."

I smile as I listen, something about Claire Anderson brings me a sense of calm. We met not long after her first husband died and for some reason we just clicked. She rants and raves while I listen and she's probably the most normal person I know...apart from Gracie.

"What did he do?" I sip my scotch.

"He thought he would start Tristan's Aston up in the garage..." She looks down at my drink. "Why are you drinking scotch at lunchtime?"

I roll my eyes. "Sorry, Mom."

"Anyway, why he did it, I do not know, and the car jumped out of gear, lurched forward and hit the brick wall."

I chuckle as I imagine the scenario.

"And Tristan is away in Paris and I'm trying to get it fixed before he gets back because he's going to go absolutely postal."

"When does he get back?"

"The day after tomorrow."

"No chance."

"Why, why not?" She puts her hand up to catch the waiter's attention, "All I want is a glass of wine, this healthy crap sucks. Anyway, everyone is saying that they can't fix it at short notice, I mean, it's one little ding and a bumper, how hard can that be to do?"

I lean my face on my hand as I listen to her chaos, and I smile.

"Anyway, I told Patrick he has to pay for it, and then..."

"Does he have a spare thirty thousand dollars?"

"What?"

"It's an Aston Martin, it isn't going to be three hundred bucks, Claire."

"Ugh..." She rolls her eyes. "Why does he have to have such a wanky car, anyway?"

"Because he's a wanker." I sip my drink.

"So..." She finally falls calm as her eyes find mine. "How are *you*?"

My face falls before I can catch it.

"What's wrong?" She frowns.

"Nothing."

"Gabriel," she warns. "Don't lie to me, your face just told me that something is wrong."

I stare at her for a moment.

"Gabe." She takes my hand over the table. "Is it Ariana?"

"No." I shake my head.

"The wedding?"

I drag my hand down my face.

Her face falls. "The wedding...what about the wedding?"

"You cannot tell anybody this."

"It's me, you know I won't."

"So..." I pause while I try to articulate my thoughts. "Last week I saw Grace Porter."

"Oh, Gracie, there's a blast from the past." She smiles. "What's she doing now?"

"Living in Maine with two of my children."

She frowns, not understanding. "What?"

"We..." I stop myself.

"Gabriel, spit it out."

"Before she left me seven years ago, we spent a night together."

"How do I not know this?"

"She fell pregnant and never told me, I recently found out I have six-year-old twins. A boy and a girl. We have the paternity test results; they are definitely mine."

Her eyes widen in horror. "What. The. Hell?" She puts her head into her hands. "How could she not tell you?"

"Exactly." I take a big gulp of my drink. "She did come to see me weeks later, and I wouldn't see her because I was in meetings and..."

"Don't make excuses, she should have told you. That is need-to-know information."

I exhale heavily. "I know."

"Oh my god." Her eyes search mine. "You have children?"

I nod sadly.

"Don't be sad, this is wonderful." She takes my hand over the table. "What did Ariana say?"

"I didn't tell her."

"What?" she snaps. "Why not?"

"Because Grace doesn't want me in their lives."

She stares at me, horrified. "So?"

"She's told everyone that they were conceived using IVF and donor sperm and she asked that if I can't be a devoted father then to step aside and leave them be. She doesn't want them missing an absent father."

"Oh." Her eyes hold mine. "How do you feel about that?"

I shrug. "It's for the best. I'm a workaholic who lives in New York. These children are eight hours away and..." My voice trails off. "They can't miss what they don't know."

She slumps back in her chair and thinks for a moment. "What are they like?"

"I have photos." I open my phone and swipe through to a photo I took of Lucia at the game. "This is Lucia." I pass the phone over and Grace smiles as she looks at it.

"Look at her, she's beautiful," she coos.

"You've never seen a more gorgeous child, Claire." I smile

proudly. "So smart and sweet."

Claire smiles sadly. "And the boy?"

I swipe through my phone again, I took a few photos of photographs that were in frames on the mantle, I knew I would want to look at them later. "This is Dominic." I pass the phone back to her and she gasps and puts her hand over her mouth. Her eyes rise to meet mine. "He's so..."

"Like me." I finish her sentence. "A total little prick."

She giggles. "Really?"

"Ugh." I sip my drink. "Totally unmanageable. We fought the first time we met."

"Oh." She puts her hand over her heart as she swoons. "They are so beautiful."

I sip my drink and put my hand up for another.

"Strong children need strong parents, Gabriel," she says. "If you want to be in their lives, don't let Grace dictate what you can and can't do."

"But..."

"No buts. They can come visit and vice versa. Why do you think it has to be all or nothing?"

"Grace said..."

"Fuck Grace," she spits, "I'm sorry, you are their *father*, this isn't all about her."

"But it is."

"What do you mean?"

I hesitate before letting the next sentence leave my lips. "I can't see Grace and not want her. If I see them, I have to see her, and I can't be married to one woman while wanting another."

Her eyes widen as she finally begins to understand the full complexities of the situation.

"You still have feelings for her?" she whispers.

"It's like she never left. She's all I think about, I'm dreaming of her. I nearly called Ariana by the wrong name while having sex the other day because in my head I was with Grace. I lie in bed beside my sweet, beautiful fiancée while I think about a woman who has been lying to me for seven years, Grace fucking Porter."

"Oh fuck." She stares at me. "Oh hell. This is bad. This is so bad, Gabriel. Your wedding to Ariana is in three weeks."

"Do you think I don't know that?" I whisper angrily. "I'm the worst person on earth. I'm deserting my own children because I know I can't not want their mother."

She holds her temples and then puts her hand up for the waiter. "I need wine for this conversation."

I steeple my hands in front of my mouth as I think. "Why would this happen now when I've been so happy? For the first time in my life, I finally have my shit together."

She twists her lips as she thinks. "Tell me about Grace."

"I don't even know where to start," I fume. "She's insufferable and a liar. A total smart-ass. She hates me, everything that comes out of her mouth is sarcastic and infuriating. Not to mention the worst cook, you have no idea how bad the food is, Claire, it would literally kill a dog. She has this terrible house in the middle of nowhere with knitted cushions and all kinds of random bullshit furnishings and she wears gym clothes around and you can see every single curve of her ass. She smells like a walking wet dream and I had to wank in her bed because I'm perverted and I've never met a more fucking infuriating woman," I blurt out in a rush.

Claire stares at me, horrified. "You're still in love with her."

"I am *not* in love with her," I spit. "I'm attracted to her, big difference."

"You were in love with her when she worked for you."

"No."

"Yes you were. Remember you admitted it to me once, you said that you purposely paraded other women around in front of her so that she hated you."

"I did not."

"Because you knew that if she liked you the same way that you liked her, that you stood no chance of resisting her."

I drag my hand down my face in disgust.

"Tell me about Ariana," she asks.

I shrug sadly. "Ariana is a good person."

She listens.

"She loves me."

"If Ariana hadn't proposed to you, would you have ever proposed to her?"

I clench my jaw, hating my answer. "Probably not."

"Didn't think so." She continues. "If Gracie was Italian and you and her dated back then, would you have proposed to her?"

"Yes, but I don't want to hurt Ariana. She is the nicest person I know; she doesn't deserve this."

"You can't marry someone because they are nice, Gabriel. You can't marry someone to not hurt them. Marrying her while you have feelings for someone else is more painful. How can you possibly think that this marriage is going to work?"

"I get married in three weeks," I whisper angrily. "It is too late to . . ."

"Call it off?" She cuts me off.

"Yes."

I stay silent as I think.

"Tell me this, Gabriel...if you marry Ariana, can you honestly tell me that you will never think of your children and Gracie again? Are you going to regret this for the rest of your life?"

The thought of never seeing Lucia and Dominic again hurts my heart and her silhouette blurs.

We sit for a moment as we ponder over everything.

"If you are calling off this wedding, you need to do it today. Do *not* put Ariana through being stood up in the week of the wedding. She deserves better than that."

"I'm not calling off the wedding," I snap. I tip my head back and drain my glass. "I'm a man of my word. I'm marrying Ariana just like I said I would."

"Fine," she snaps.

"Fine," I fire back.

"I'm not coming to your wedding."

"Why not?"

"Because I can't watch you make the biggest mistake of your life."

Grace

"Oh my god, she's so adorable." I smile at the stage. Lucia twirls in her little bear costume.

"And how about that tree," Deb whispers.

My eyes roam to Dominic standing proudly at the back with his little arms up as branches.

"Best tree I ever saw." I giggle.

We are at the kids' play at school. "There you are, Grace." I turn to see Felicity Fox shimmying through the row of seats to get to me. "I've been looking for you everywhere."

Ugh...the most annoying woman to ever walk the earth. She's the head of the PTA of the kids' school. She's wearing a tight white Adidas tracksuit, and her long dark hair is up in a high ponytail. She's gorgeous and immaculately groomed and the best Stepford wife in Greenville. Except just without the husband, he ran off a few years back and she's been making everyone else's life in town a living hell ever since.

"Ugh," Deb mutters under her breath.

"Hi, Felicity." I force a smile. "How are you?"

"I'm great." She drops into the seat beside me. "I noticed you haven't signed up for the bake sale."

"Yes." I shrug. "I'm just so...busy at the moment."

"We're all busy, Grace," she replies flatly. "But you are going to help on Wednesday, aren't you?"

"I have to work."

"What do you mean?" she gasps. "But you help every year."

And it's the worst day of my life.

"Yes, but this year I'm too swamped."

A total lie, I have Wednesday off, but I can't deal with spending an entire day with this woman. I swore to myself that last year was the last.

"Can't you get the day off?" she snaps.

"No."

"This won't do at all."

"It's a bake sale, Felicity," Deb chips in. "Not the end of the world."

"Yes, but we need Grace because of..." She hesitates. "Well... because of the obvious."

"What obvious?" Deb asks.

"Well...she can't bake, so she has to serve."

"I can bake," I snap.

"Oh, come on, Grace." She rolls her eyes. "We all know you buy your cakes every year."

You do?

"Why else would I be forced to throw your cakes out?"

"You throw my cakes out?" I gasp.

"It's a bake sale." She widens her eyes as if I'm stupid. "Not a buy sale. If we wanted supermarket cakes, we would ask for them." She gives a condescending smile. "But I know what you're like by now."

I begin to hear my angry heartbeat in my ears.

"What am I like?"

"You know." She laughs. "All Grace Porterish."

"Un-fucking-believable," Deb mutters under her breath.

I bite the side of my cheek to stop myself from telling her where to go.

I hate this woman with every fiber of my being, she thinks she's so perfect...it kills me that she is.

"Well, I'm very busy and I can't do the stupid bake sale that you are obviously obsessed with, and now that I know you don't like my cakes, I won't even bother buying them."

"Oh, how sad for your children that their mother won't support them at school."

My blood boils as the sky turns red.

"Are you…"

Deb hits me on the leg to silence me. "Goodbye, Felicity, we're kind of busy right now." She gestures to the stage.

Felicity rolls her eyes and shimmies through the seats again.

"If I ever get that boring, shoot me," Deb whispers as she watches her disappear.

"Gladly."

It's just on 9 p.m., the kids are tucked safely into bed, and after working today, cooking dinner, and then washing up, I've only just showered and sat down for the first time.

I flick through Netflix, looking for a new series to watch.

I've been so preoccupied since Gabriel came back that I've done nothing but worry.

I guess that now he's gone, I can finally relax.

My phone beeps a text in the kitchen, who's texting me at this time of night? I get up and grab it, it's from Gabriel.

Hi

I frown, what does he want?
I text back.

Hi.

My phone instantly rings, and the name *Gabriel* lights up the screen.

What the hell?

"Hello," I answer.

"Hi Gracie." His voice is soft, cajoling. He only ever used this voice with me when we were alone in his office.

"Hi." I frown. "What's up?"

"I just…"

I listen as I wait for him to finish his sentence, he doesn't.

208

A weird feeling comes over me, something is wrong with him.

"Where are you?" I ask softly.

"In my office."

I get a vision of him standing at the window and staring out over the view of twinkling lights as we speak.

"Working late?" I ask.

"Yeah."

I wait for him to elaborate, again he doesn't. I get the feeling he has something to say but for some reason won't.

"The kids are in bed," I tell him.

"Okay...are they alright?"

Him asking if they are all right makes me get a lump in my throat. "Yes."

Silence...

What the hell is going on here?

"They were in a play this week at school. Lucia was a bear and Dom was a tree."

"Yeah?" I can hear the smile in his voice. "What was the play, when a bear shits in the woods?"

I giggle. "Something like that."

We fall into an awkward silence again.

"You know, Gabriel, I've been thinking."

"What about?"

"Maybe..." I pause. "Maybe I was too over the top."

"What do you mean?"

"If you ever want to tell them who you are and come and visit. Just come home and do it."

Silence.

"It's not up to me if you want them in your life. It was selfish of me to think that it was. I just..." I pause as I get another huge lump in my throat.

"You what?"

"Maybe I *am* the most selfish person on earth," I whisper through tears. "I just got scared...you know?"

Silence.

209

We both hang on the line, waiting for the other one to say something, eventually he does.

"Good night, Gracie," he whispers.

"Good night."

The line goes dead and I stare at the phone in my hand.

What the hell was that?

Gabriel

I walk into my penthouse just on 11 p.m.

I've had the worst day in history and it's about to get ten times worse.

I find Ariana sitting on the couch, she looks up at me and smiles. "You must be tired, you work too hard."

I nod and sit down beside her. "We need to talk."

"What about?"

"I can't marry you."

17

Gabriel

"WHAT?" She sits up straight. "What do you mean?"

"Just what I said." I concentrate on keeping my voice calm, the last thing I want is for this to turn into a fight. "Ariana." I take her hand in mine. "You're a beautiful woman. Intelligent and sweet and every man's dream wife."

"But not yours?"

"No. You are." I pause as I try to articulate my thoughts clearly. "This week I've found out some information that has changed the trajectory of my life."

"What's wrong?" she stammers. "Are you sick?" She takes my face in her hands and I pull them down into mine.

"No. It's nothing like that." I swallow the lump in my throat, I really don't know if I can hurt her like this. "Sweetheart." I push the hair back from her face as she stares at me. "I found out this week that I have six-year-old twins from a relationship that I had years ago."

"What?" Her face falls.

"I lied to you last weekend and I went to meet them in Maine."

Her eyes fill with tears. "Who, where...who is the mother?"

Here we go.

"Her name is Grace Porter."

She frowns. "Do I know her?"

"No. She was my PA for seven years."

She flies off the couch. "What?" she screams. "You got your fucking PA pregnant?" She begins to pace. "You got your PA pregnant, am I hearing this right?"

"Yes."

"How could you?"

"It's not something I'm proud of, believe me."

"And you knew nothing of this?"

"No."

"How much money does she want? What is she threatening?" she spits.

"It's nothing like that."

"It's everything like that, Gabriel. You think it's a coincidence that she has come looking for you three weeks before you get married." She throws a cushion at my head; she's flying off the handle and completely losing her temper.

"I went looking for her."

She stills and turns back toward me. "You went looking for her?"

I nod, ashamed.

"Why would you go looking for her?" She drops back to sit down beside me, her eyes filled with tears.

I stare at her, the guilt in my soul feels like it's about to smother me to death.

"I don't know," I whisper.

"Yes you do." A tear escapes and rolls down her cheek. "For god's sake, Gabriel. If you care for me at all, you at least owe me honesty."

I roll my lips, unsure what to say to try to keep this from tipping her over the edge.

"Did you love her?" she whispers.

"I…"

"Back then, did you love her?" she says more sternly.

"Yes."

"So why did you break up?"

"Because she wasn't Italian."

Her face falls as she puts the pieces of the puzzle together. "So you went looking for the woman you loved all those years ago to find that she has two of your children?"

I nod.

Her chest rises and falls as she battles for control. "You want a life with them..."

Her silhouette blurs, the lump in my throat blocking the air.

"Gabriel?" she whispers as her eyes search mine. "Please tell me I'm wrong..."

"No."

"No, you don't want a life with them?" she asks hopefully.

"I mean... You are not wrong." I shrug. "The last thing I want to do is to hurt you, Ariana. I love you. You know I love you."

"But are you in love with me?" she whispers.

I blink to stop the tears.

Slap.

I feel the sting of her hit as it turns my head.

"We are to be married in three weeks," she cries as she loses all control. "How the fuck could you do this to me?" She picks up her wineglass and hurls it at my head, it smashes against the wall. Red wine sprays everywhere.

"Calm down."

"Calm down!" she screams. "I will not fucking calm down. You are leaving me for another woman nineteen days before our wedding. What happened last weekend, did you sleep with her?" she yells. "Is that why we haven't had sex this week, because you still had the taste of your trashy PA on your tongue?"

I stand, my temper beginning to rise. "Enough," I yell.

"The invitations have already gone out, what do you expect me to do. Everything has been paid for."

"Keep everything in credit for when you do marry, you can still have the wedding you want one day. Take your girlfriends on the honeymoon, go and enjoy yourself."

"What?" she explodes. She picks up the television remote and throws it at me. "I don't want a honeymoon with my girlfriends." She's in full-blown hysterics, crying and screaming. "I love you, Gabriel. How could you do this to me?"

"I hate myself for it. But what do you want me to do?" I cry. "I will not lie to you, you know that."

"We work it out," she yells. "Of course you are rattled, you just found out you have children. It's bound to confuse you, but what we have is *real*." She takes my hand in hers. "Don't do this."

"How do we get around it?" I shrug.

"We get married and we work this out like adults. All relationships have exes, Gabriel. Children from a previous relationship shouldn't matter, I will accept them as my own. I promise you. We can be a blended family, your kids, and our kids."

I stare at her heartbroken face and take it in my hands. "Sweetheart." I kiss her forehead. "This isn't just about the children. My affection for Grace is real. I wish that it wasn't there, but I cannot deny it any longer. It has been with me all along, and now...I don't want there to be three people in our marriage, you deserve better."

She cries on my chest and I hold her tight. I can feel how hard her heart is breaking and there isn't a damn thing I can do about it.

I hate myself for doing this to her.

Grace

I make myself a cup of coffee in the lunch room and walk through the office to head back to my desk. "You want to go to the Indian restaurant for lunch?" Marci calls.

"I wish," I call back. "I'm on a budget."

"Ugh, you're so boring."

"Not as boring as the lunch I packed," I call back.

"Ha! Truth."

I walk back into my office and sit down at my desk when I hear my phone ding as a text comes in. I ignore it, I'll check it at lunch.

Another ding, then another.

Who is frigging texting me so much? I take out my phone to see it's Deb.

Omfg Call Me!!!!

I roll my eyes and dial her number; she answers first ring. "Oh my fucking god," she gasps as if the world is collapsing.

"Why are you being so dramatic?"

"He's called off the wedding."

"Who has?"

"Gabriel Ferrara has called off his wedding."

My eyes widen. "What? How do you know?"

"It's all over the news."

"Hang on." I instantly open Google and put in the search bar,

Gabriel Ferrara engagement

It seems the fairy tale is over for Gabriel Ferrara and his fiancée, Ariana Rossi.

Sources tell us that an email was sent out this morning to the wedding guests that the wedding between the glamorous couple has been called off.

Speculation is rife that Mr. Ferrara is the one who ended the union, as the notification to guests came from his personal email. All this only nineteen days before the wedding was due to take place.

Devastated Ariana will no doubt be wiping her tears, almost snagging the world's most eligible billionaire...so close.

No information has been disclosed yet as to why the union ended.

Watch this space.

"What the fuck?" I whisper.

"I know."

"Do you think he's told her about the kids?"

My eyes widen in horror at the thought.

"He did call you the other night and was being weird."

"What....You don't think she left him because of the kids...do you?"

"Maybe."

"If she loved him, she wouldn't care. I mean, it was years before he met her." I chew my thumbnail as I think out loud. "Surely not."

"Maybe she gave him an ultimatum. Them or me."

"No, she wouldn't," I scoff.

"What makes you so sure?"

"Because I'm sure she idolizes him."

"How do you know?"

"Because all women idolize him," I snap impatiently. "My next appointment is here, I have to go."

"I'll call around this afternoon," Deb says.

"Okay."

"So you haven't heard from him at all?" Deb asks.

"Nope." I stare out over the lake; the sun is just setting and we are in my favorite place, my jetty.

"You have to admit this is weird, he finds out about the kids, calls you and then his engagement ends all within a week."

I shrug. "Maybe there was someone else?" I look over to Deb. "Surely he isn't still a womanizer after all these years?"

"Maybe she cheated?" Deb frowns.

"No way."

"Why are you so sure?"

"Trust me, if Gabriel were in love with you, you wouldn't want for anything else."

"I hope she slept with his brother." Deb smirks. "Maybe gang-banged both of his brothers *and* his hot driver and he walked in on them."

I giggle as I imagine the scenario.

"So what happens in this case, would she get a payout from her prenup even though they never married?" Deb frowns. "Would she walk away with nothing or...I mean, were they living together?"

"No idea." I think for a moment. "If he was the one to end it, I know he would look after her."

"What makes you say that?"

"He's a good man."

"He is *not* a good man," Deb scoffs. "He's a douche bag, don't you ever forget that."

"Oh, I know he's a total douche. I mean he wouldn't try and rip her off. Financially, his morals are strong. He looks after his people."

"Except his own kids." Deb raises her eyebrow in a silent dare.

"He did offer but I declined, I already told you that."

"Pathetic half-assed attempt, if you ask me."

My heart sinks. "Yeah..." I sip my wine. "It was."

My gaze rises up at the pink sky, nature is putting on a spectacular show tonight, life is such a contradiction. It's hard to believe, sitting here and looking over such incredible beauty, that I can feel such a deep, overwhelming sadness.

My children didn't want his money, *they need his love.*

"I'll put that paperwork through and we will be in touch." I shake his hand. "It was lovely to meet you, Mr. Thompson." We stand and walk toward the door.

"How long do loan applications usually take to process?" he asks.

"Every case is different, but I think yours will be relatively quick, being so straightforward." I open my office door for him to leave.

"Fantastic. Have a good day." He walks down the hallway and I hear raised voices coming from the reception area.

"I am not leaving until I see her," a woman says.

"She is fully booked today, I'm sorry."

"This is of a personal matter."

I frown as I listen, that voice sounds familiar. What's going on out there? I walk out and my heart stops.

It's Elena Ferrara, Gabriel's mother.

She turns and sees me, her chin tilts to the sky as contempt drips from her every pore.

Fuck...she's not happy.

I drop my shoulders as I prepare for battle. "Are you here to see me?"

"What do you think?" she snaps as she marches past me down the hall and into my office.

"Who is that?" Marci whispers.

"Just...give me ten minutes." I practically run to my office to find Elena sitting calmly at my desk. Her dark hair is swept up in a glamorous up-style, she's wearing a black fitted dress, nude stilettos with a matching nude Chanel bag. Her back is ramrod straight and everything about her screams elegance.

I feel the blood drain out of my body, I look like total crap today and am wearing the oldest shoes I own.

Help...

I close the door and sit down. "Hello, Mrs. Ferrara." I fake a smile.

She glares at me, her face emotionless and cold.

I feel myself begin to perspire as her animosity fills the room. "How can I help you?"

"I think you know." She sits back and crosses her legs.

A bead of sweat runs down between my breasts. "No. Actually, I don't."

Her phone rings and she glances at the screen, she declines the call and puts it down.

My phone rings and she looks down at my screen as it sits on my desk.

Gabriel

218

Oh hell...worst timing. I let it ring out and it immediately rings again.

She raises her eyebrow. "He knows I'm here."

"I don't..."

"He has you under guard," she says almost to herself.

Wait...what?

My phone rings again.

Gabriel

Oh hell, this is an actual nightmare. I pick up the phone.

"Don't you *dare* answer that." She sneers.

"I wasn't going to," I lie. I calmly turn my phone off. I begin to sweat bullets; this woman is such a bitch. "How can I help you, Mrs. Ferrara?" I say more assertively.

Her cold eyes hold mine. "How much do you want?"

"Excuse me?"

"Do not insult my intelligence, Grace, we both know you have an agenda."

I begin to hear the adrenaline as it screams through my body.

"I have no idea what you're talking about."

"Oh please," she scoffs. "Do you really expect me to believe that?"

Knock, knock, knock sounds at the door. I glance over. Who is knocking so urgently?

Knock, knock, knock.

The door busts open and a man walks in, he's wearing a black suit and looks terrified. "Forgive me for intruding, Mrs. Ferrara." He holds a phone out. "Gabriel wants to speak to you as a matter of urgency."

My eyes widen, what the fuck...he *does* know she's here?

I'm being watched...what the...?

She snatches the phone from him and turns it off. "Get out," she orders him.

Please don't.

He scurries out of my office and I glance around for a window to jump through.

"How much?" Her cold eyes hold mine.

"For what?"

"To get out of my son's life," she snaps angrily. "What else could it mean? Do you really think you can seduce my son, get pregnant without telling him, and turn up three weeks before his wedding to the love of his life, ruin everything and get away with it? You are nothing but a manipulative bitch and I won't stand for it."

My mouth falls open in shock...she did not just say that.

"Let me guess... You seduced him on his desk one night after work?" Her eyes hold mine. "I'm assuming you were wearing something sexy, maybe a suspender belt that you purposely let him see?" Her smirk breaks into a sarcastic smile. "And the earth moved for you, but he wanted nothing to do with you after?"

I stare at her, shocked to silence.

"I'll let you in on a little secret, Grace Porter. Gabriel has had sex with most of his PAs. You are nothing special." She looks me up and down. "I mean, look at you."

Boom.

Boom.

Boom...goes my heartbeat in my ears.

She sits forward in her seat. "If you think you can hold my son ransom with your bastard illegitimate children, think again."

I clench my jaw as I imagine tipping my glass of water over her nasty head.

"He'll be over this Brady Bunch fantasy in..." she glances at her watch, "...about two weeks from now, and where will you be then?"

Tears threaten, and I get a lump in my throat as I try to hold them in.

"Ten million dollars."

I stare at her, speechless.

"Fifteen." Her cold eyes hold mine.

Gabriel has had sex with most of his PAs...

"Twenty million dollars. Don't be a fool, Grace, he is going to dump you eventually. There is no way you can hold a man like Gabriel Ferrara. We both know that. Take the money now because, trust me, you will get nothing later."

I pick up a framed photo from my desk and I pass it to her. "The illegitimate bastard children you speak of have names, Lucia and Dominic. They are six."

Her face falls as she looks at them, the resemblance to Gabriel is striking, she can't deny it.

"They are just like their father," I whisper. "Take a long last look at that photo, Mrs. Ferrara, because over my dead body will you ever see them again."

The air swirls between us, a conjuring of evil like you've never felt before.

"Don't underestimate me, Grace," she sneers. "That could be arranged."

"Is that a threat?" I feel a little of my equilibrium return. "Please, threaten me again so I can tape it with my phone. I'm sure Gabriel would love to hear what Mommy dearest has to say to the mother of his children."

You could cut the air with a knife as we glare at each other.

"You're making a big mistake," she whispers.

"Leave." I stand and open the office door. "Security," I call.

The two security guards come into view.

"Escort this woman from my office, please, and call the police. I want a restraining order put on her. She just threatened my life."

She gasps as she stands. "I did nothing of the sort." Her furious eyes come to meet mine. "How dare you?"

"You picked the wrong woman to mess with." I smile at her shocked face. "You...and your twenty million dollars...can go to hell."

18

Gabriel

"So with that in mind, I'll bring it up now for you to see." I talk on speaker as I screen share my computer. I drag up another spreadsheet and my mobile phone rings on my desk, I glance at the screen and see the name Elias.

I frown, Elias is the guard I left in Greenville with Grace.

"I have to take this call; I'll place you on hold for a minute." I hold the call and answer my mobile. "Hi, what's wrong?"

"Well..." He pauses. "I wouldn't say anything is wrong as such, more so peculiar. I'm just calling to check as to why you wouldn't tell me about the visit."

"What are you talking about?"

"Your mother is here."

I frown. "What do you mean, here?"

"Your mother is in Greenville."

"What?" My eyes bulge from their sockets. "What do you fucking mean?" I stand from my chair. "Do not let her near Grace, do you hear me?"

"Too late, she's already in her office."

"What?" I scream. I hang up and immediately dial my mother's number.

No answer.

Fuck.

I call Grace's number as I begin to pace...

Ring ring...ring ring...

Pick up.

The phone number you have called is not
available right now

"Fuck."

I dial my mother's number and she declines the call... "Don't you fucking dare," I explode, rage fills me and I could crumble the phone with my bare hand. I call Elias.

"Hey."

"Where are they?"

"In Grace's office."

"Put my mother on the phone," I growl.

"What..."

"Right. Fucking. Now," I yell.

I hear him knock on the door. *Knock, knock, knock. Knock, knock, knock.* I can feel his panic through the phone.

"Forgive me for intruding, Mrs. Ferrara. Gabriel wants to speak to you as a matter of urgency," he says.

The phone goes dead as she hangs up on me.

"Don't you fucking dare!" I explode.

I frantically scroll through my phone until I get to Frank, my mother's driver, and I dial his number.

"Hell . . ."

"Where the fuck are you?" I scream.

"Ah..."

"Why the hell would you allow my mother to go to Maine?"

"She said you knew."

"I did *not* know. Go into that office and remove her immediately. She's not allowed near Grace Porter under any circumstance, do you understand me?"

"How do I remove her from the office?"

"Drag her out by the fucking hair if you have to," I scream.

"Hang on, they're coming out now."

I listen.

"Oh no," he mutters.

"What?"

"The security guards are escorting your mother out onto the street."

My eyes widen, Grace has had her kicked out. That means they've had a fight.

"Why would she go there!" I yell, I've never been so angry. "You get her the fuck back to New York right now." I hang up and call Mark.

"Hi."

"Organize the jet to go to Greenville."

"When for?"

"As soon as possible. My mother has just been escorted out of Grace's office by security."

"Oh fuck..." he murmurs. "That's not good."

"You think!" I growl. "We need to get there as soon as possible."

"Okay, on it." He hangs up and I pace back and forth as I try to calm myself down. I try to call Grace again and it goes straight to voice mail, her phone is switched off.

If you've fucked this up for me, Mom... I swear to god.

I try to call my mother, again her phone is also switched off.

I'm about to explode.

My phone rings, it's Mark.

"Bad news," he answers.

"What now?"

"We can't get clearance to leave the airport until seven tonight."

"Why not?"

"The airspace is full, that's the earliest we can leave."

"This is the day from hell." I drag my hands through my hair.

"Fine, that will have to do." I hang up in a rush and my intercom buzzes. "What?" I scream as I lose the last of my patience.

"Mr. Ferrara, are you continuing your meeting, the attendees are all waiting online, sir."

Fuck...the meeting, I forgot all about it.

Umm...I try to refocus.

"Get them to break for lunch, restart the meeting in half an hour." I hang up and call my mother again.

The phone number you have called is not
available right now

My blood boils as the sky turns red.

I'm going to kill her with my bare hands.

Grace

I sit in the darkness and stare out over the lake from my back porch. It's 9 p.m. The children are tucked tightly in bed and yet I still can't calm down.

I'm livid, furious beyond belief.

Deb has been over here trying to damage control my heart, but it's impossible.

Mrs. Ferrara's hurtful words keep coming back to me, over and over again like a megaphone on repeat.

If you think you can hold my son ransom with your bastard illegitimate children, think again.

I hate that I let her get to me.

Let me guess... You seduced him on his desk one night after work? I'm assuming you were wearing something sexy, maybe a suspender belt that you purposely let him see? And the earth moved for you...but he wanted nothing to do with you after? I'll let you in on a little secret, Grace Porter. Gabriel has had sex with most of his PAs. You are nothing special...I mean, look at you.

You know what, she hit the nail on the head...that's exactly how it happened. I went to his office late at night and...*oh*, my heart constricts with shame.

I wipe a lone tear that escapes from my eye.

His family are nothing to us, why should I care what they think of me?

My history with Gabriel Ferrara seems to be repeating itself; he's been back for not even two weeks and already I feel like a worthless piece of crap.

Him being around is just not good for me, everything about him reminds me of a time when I felt weak and vulnerable.

Deb thinks I should have taken the twenty million, the Ferrara family would still hate me, of course, but no more than they already do, and at least then I wouldn't have to worry about money. Even if I just put ten million in a trust fund for each child until they reached the age of twenty-one, it would still be beneficial.

I wouldn't have to deal with any of them...but then the down-side is that the kids would never know their father...and how can you put a price on that? And realistically, if he is in their lives, they would get a lot more than ten million each in his will, he's worth billions.

I blow out a defeated breath and stare into space, he already said goodbye last weekend, I don't understand why his mother has come all the way here when he already wiped his hands of them. Deb thinks he was the one who broke up with his fiancée and the old bat is furious about it and blaming me.

Is it my fault?

How could something be my fault when I don't even know what's going on? I turn my phone on and wait for it to light up.

16 missed calls - Gabriel

Ugh...
I turn it back off.

Stay the fuck away from me, asshole, I want nothing to do with you and your toxic family.

I refill my wineglass.

"Got an extra glass for me?" A deep voice startles me, and I glance up to see Gabriel standing in the darkness of the backyard, looking up at me.

"What are you doing here?" I snap.

"I came to see if you're alright." He slowly walks up the steps and takes a seat in the chair beside me.

"I'm fine." I pull my blanket around me tighter as I try to protect myself from this monster. "Go back to New York, Gabriel."

He stays silent as he looks out over the lake.

"I don't want you here."

He nods and leans his elbows on his knees, and we sit in silence for a while, the wind whistles through the trees and the breeze whips my hair around. I want to be anywhere but here alone with him.

"How much did she offer you?" he asks.

I glance over at him, surprised.

"That's what she did...didn't she? Offered to buy you out of my life."

As I stare at him, a new realization washes over me, I know why he's like he is, why he's always in attack mode and on the defensive. His mother is pure evil, I can't imagine being brought up in that environment.

"Twenty million," I whisper.

Hurt flashes across his face before he hides it. "Did you accept it?"

"If you have to ask me that then you don't know me at all." I roll my eyes in disgust. "Honestly, I don't need this crap, Gabriel. Please...just...go away," I whisper.

I'm trying to stay calm and keep my over dramatization to a bare minimum, but I have to ask the question. "Why would she come here?" I ask.

"I broke off my engagement to Ariana."

"What does that have to do with me?"

"Everything."

I frown, confused. "I don't understand."

"Grace..." He pauses as if trying to get the wording right in his head. "Did you ever wonder why I came looking for you?" he asks softly.

"I..." I shrug, unsure what to say. "No."

"I came looking for you because I never..." His eyes search mine. "I would think of you at strange times and random places. For no reason at all you would pop into my head."

"Gabriel..." I cut him off.

"Let me finish," he snaps. He clasps his hands together as if steeling himself. "I came to find you to put to bed this strange..." He frowns as he tries to articulate himself, "...unfinished feeling I have between us."

"It doesn't..."

"I thought you would be married and happy and I could get the closure I needed and start my new life."

I stare at him, horrified.

"But it backfired because as soon as I saw you..." he pauses, "...I knew."

"Knew what?"

"That I was marrying the wrong woman."

What the fuck is happening right now?

"And then I found out about the children... And I was angry. But..."

"Stop."

"We can make this..."

"Stop it," I snap as I jump out of my chair. "What are you saying?"

"I broke up with Ariana because I want to be a father to my children and because...I can't see them without..." He pauses.

"Without what?"

"Without seeing you. How can I be married to someone else while knowing that I still have feelings for you?"

228

This man is the living end.

"What?" I spit angrily. "You don't have feelings for me. You never did then, why the hell would you now?"

"You're angry."

"I'm not angry," I fire back. "I'm disgusted. Poor Ariana. You're a fucking douche bag. That poor girl is three weeks out from her wedding and you are breaking up with her for a cheap fuck you had on your desk seven years ago."

"It was never a cheap fuck," he growls as he begins to lose his temper. "You know damn well it wasn't."

"You're pathetic." I storm inside.

"How am I pathetic?" He's hot on my heels.

"You have cold feet and are looking for an excuse to get out of the wedding." A gust of wind whips around the house. "Close the door," I snap. "Do not bring me into this, you're as bad as your mother."

"Cold feet have nothing to do with this." He shuts the door. "You asked me why my mother is blaming you and I'm telling you why. I never said that I'm in any position to pursue something with you right now, just stating the facts as to what's gone on in my life this week."

"Don't bother *ever* pursuing something with me, Gabriel." I fume as I poke him hard in the chest. "Go back to New York. Man up and marry Ariana."

"I don't want Ariana. I want you."

"Tough shit," I whisper angrily. "I want nothing to do with you. Apart from my babies, that night was a big mistake."

"We had something, and you've been rearing our children all alone..."

"I wasn't alone."

"What does that mean?" He puts his hands on his hips, indignant.

"Is that what you think?" I throw my hands up in disgust, of course it is. "That I've been sitting here alone and brokenhearted, crying over the infamous Gabriel Ferrara all this time."

"What *have* you been doing?"

"I've been in a three-year relationship to a man that I loved deeply."

His face falls. "You're with someone?"

I really want to lie right now, but I know I can't.

"Not anymore...but."

"So..." He goes to take me in his arms.

What the fuck?

I pull out of his grip. "Gabriel...I'm telling you this with all sincerity, so please listen. Go back and marry Ariana. Don't let go of something wonderful for an average night seven years ago that meant nothing."

"You're lying."

"Mom," a little voice sounds from the stairs.

We both look up to see Lucia standing midway up.

Shit.

"Oh, hi, baby." I fake a smile. "I'm sorry, did we wake you?"

She nods as she rubs her eyes all sleepy like and wanders down the stairs.

"Hello Lucia," Gabriel says softly.

"Hi." She smiles up at him and holds her little arms up for a hug.

Ugh...not now.

Gabriel drops to his knee and hugs her. "I'm sorry for waking you, princess."

Why does she have to be so damn cute all the time?

"Are you staying in Mom's bed?" she asks.

"No." "Yes." We answer at the same time.

"I would love to stay, that way I can see you and your brother in the morning." His eyes find mine. "Would that be okay, Grace?"

I glare at him. "No," I mouth behind Lucia's back.

"Thank you," he replies as he totally ignores me. "Why don't you go up to bed, Lucia, and I'll come up and say good night in a moment."

Damn it, why are they so familiar with each other, this is not okay.

Lucia's smile beams through the room. "Okay." She skips up the stairs and disappears.

"You need to go home."

"What I need is to finish our conversation."

"The conversation is *over*. I think you're disgusting being here and saying these things while your poor fiancée is crying at home right now."

"She is not my fiancée anymore, and I cannot be responsible for other people's feelings."

"And that statement right there is exactly why you repulse me," I whisper angrily. "You will always be the selfish prick that I remember you as."

"You can't deny it, Grace. The spark is still there between us." He steps forward, causing me to step back. His close proximity steals my every brain cell and I find myself speechless as I stare up at him. "Gabriel..."

"Yes, Gracie." He raises an eyebrow, all playful.

"This is never happening so get it out of your thick head right now." I turn and march up the stairs, great, now I have to clean my room so the entitled prick can stay over. I look down at him from the top of the stairs. "Tonight is your last night under my roof."

"We'll see."

"Fuck off," I mouth.

"No," he mouths back.

Ugh...this man is infuriating, I stomp into my room and close the door. I look around at the chaos.

I'm not even joking; this *is* the last time.

Gabriel

"Your room is ready," Grace says as she comes back downstairs.

Your room.

"Thanks." My eyes hold hers before she snaps them away.

She can't even look at me.

"Where will you sleep?" I ask.

"In Dom's room."

I nod, unsure what to say next.

"Good night." She disappears up the stairs and leaves me alone. I look around the quiet house. It's empty from people and yet feels full, as if the love they share is a tangible force.

My phone beeps a text and I glance at the screen, Ariana.

I drop to sit on the couch before opening it.

My heart is broken.
Come back to me.
I love you.

I close my eyes in regret. I imagine Ariana heartbroken back in New York.

Grace's words come back to me... *I'm telling you this with all sincerity, so please listen. Go back and marry Ariana. Don't let go of something wonderful for an average night seven years ago that meant nothing.*

Is that what I'm doing?

A lead ball sits in my stomach, my life is a mess.

Fuck...

19

Grace

The sound of Dom's regulated breathing sounds through his bedroom like a drone. The sun is just peeking through the curtains, and I don't think I slept a wink all night.

How can I be married to someone else while knowing that I still have feelings for you.

I exhale heavily. I don't need this drama in my life, and after freaking out all night, I have made a decision. I'm not thinking about it again.

I slowly climb out of bed, put my robe on and go to the bathroom. I catch sight of myself in the mirror and cringe, oh hell...I look like crap. I wash my face, tie my hair up into a bun and make my way downstairs.

"Good morning," I hear his deep voice purr.

Glancing up, I see Gabriel standing at my coffee machine, he's freshly showered and wearing navy suit pants, his white shirt is open and his tanned broad chest and torso are on display.

I am instantly reminded of our mornings back in his office.

"Coffee?" He raises his eyebrow in question.

"What are you doing?" I pull the cords of my robe tighter, suddenly feeling very exposed.

"What does it look like?" He holds his coffee cup up.

"It looks like you are being a poser, that's what."

He gives me a slow sexy smile as he sips his coffee. "I should ask what are you doing."

"What do you mean, what am I doing?"

"Why are you wearing that hideous dressing gown?"

My mouth falls open as I look down at myself. "This is a beautiful dressing gown," I gasp.

"If you're ninety."

"Listen . . ."

"We need to talk." He cuts me off.

"You're damn right we do," I whisper.

"I have to go back to New York, but I'll be back on the weekend." He sips his coffee casually. "We can tell the children then."

"Tell them?"

"I've made the decision and I am staying in their lives; you can't ask me not to. I *am* their father, Grace; I want them to know. My new life with them needs to start, and I'm not putting this off any longer."

My heart sinks and I know he's right, I can't fight this anymore, the writing is already on the wall. I nod in resignation.

"I move into my new place on Saturday," he continues.

"Your new place?" I frown.

"I've rented a property in town."

"Here?"

"There was nothing suitable to buy at the moment, but I'm on the lookout."

I feel faint.

"You're actually...moving here?"

"I'll be splitting my time evenly between here and New York. I'm setting up a second office here and can do everything else by Zoom."

What the hell?

"I have an opening for a PA if you're interested in the position." He winks.

"I'm good."

"I hear the Christmas bonuses are worth it." He smirks.

"Hard pass." I snatch my coffee cup from him. "When are you going back?"

"This morning." His eyes hold mine. "Just waiting for them to wake up so I can see them before I leave."

I sip my coffee, unsure what to say next.

"What are you doing today?" he asks.

I shrug. "I have the week off."

"Oh." He thinks for a moment. "I would ask you all to come to New York with me, but..."

But what?

"I'm in the middle of a situation in New York and now is not a good time."

His mother.

"I wouldn't go anyway. Did you think about what I said last night?" I ask him.

"No."

"Why not?"

"Because I've already made my decision."

"It's not too late, Gabriel. You can still have it all."

"Meaning what?"

"Meaning that I want you to be happy, you can still be a father, see your children *and* marry Ariana."

"That's not the all I want, Grace." His eyes hold mine.

"Gabriel... It's not going to happen between us."

"Not now."

"Not *ever*." I glance down to see the ripples on his stomach, and then, remembering where I am, I snap my eyes back up to his.

A trace of a smile crosses his face.

"What?"

"Do you like what you see?"

"Nope." I pull my gown closed tighter. "Hideous."

"Ah..." He sips his coffee. "You told me I was hideous once before."

"I did?" I frown.

"Yes, right before you told me you fucked my computer mouse."

Oh hell...I'll never live that down.

"Yes, well..." I feel my face flush with embarrassment, "...my stationery intercourse days are well and truly over."

"Shame."

"Or not." I need to change the subject. "Why do you have someone watching me?"

"Because I want you safe."

"I am safe."

"If the press get a hold of this info about you and the children, you will have reporters camping out the front, this is for your protection, not mine."

I don't want him knowing everything I do. "No."

"It's nonnegotiable, Grace, and not up for discussion." His eyes hold mine in a silent dare.

I may be seeing this slightly new and improved version of Gabriel Ferrara for the first time, but his strongest instinct is still to fight. I don't have the energy for more dramatics today, I'm going to let it go for now.

"Go upstairs and wake the kids, they need to get up now anyway," I tell him.

"Okay."

"I'm going to make some breakfast. Do you want some?"

"Ah..." His eyes flick to the kitchen as he hesitates. "Ah..."

He's scared to eat my cooking, I roll my lips to hide my smile. "I'll make you something special."

"That's not necessary."

"It would be nice for you to eat breakfast with the kids, go wake them up."

236

He disappears up the stairs and I open the fridge and peer in.

Now, what's the worst breakfast I can possibly make?

Gabriel

I make my way up the stairs and down the hallway. I catch sight of Lucia sitting up in bed, her hair is all messed and she's in a cute pink nightdress and reading a book.

What child reads a book when they first wake up? She's a literal genius.

"You're such a good girl, no wonder that your mother is so proud of you."

She smiles sweetly over at me and I feel my heart melt. "I bet you were the cutest little baby." I sit down beside her on the edge of the bed.

"I was," she agrees.

I smile at her innocence. "I wish I knew you then."

She nods as she thinks. "Me too."

"Do you have any photos of you when you were a baby?"

"Mom does." She nods. "There are even some when we are still in her belly."

"Really?"

Pregnant Grace.

"Can I see them?" I ask.

"Okay." She smiles, all excited, she takes off and I follow her down the hallway into Grace's bedroom. She bends down and looks under the bed.

"What are you doing?" I frown.

"They're under here." She slides a chest out from under the bed.

"Oh."

She opens the lid and smiles proudly. "These are all our photos."

I stare at the box in awe, a transportation to the past, to all I've missed. "Thanks, Lucia, this is perfect."

"Mom keeps everything special under her bed."

"Does she?"

Hmm...

"Well, this is great. Thank you." I push the hair back from her forehead as I stare down at her. I'm not sure I've ever seen a more perfect child, not that I've ever looked closely at any, I guess. "Is your brother awake yet?"

"Don't know. Where's Mom?"

"Downstairs."

"I'm going to go see her."

"Okay."

She toddles off and I wait until she has gone down the stairs and I quietly close the door.

Let's see what other special things Mom keeps under her bed.

I kneel down and peer under, there are a few boxes and I slowly slide them out.

Photographs mainly.

Hmm, right at the very end is another box that looks identical to the one with the baby pictures. I wonder what's in there. I slide everything out of the way and nearly have to half crawl under the bed to retrieve it.

It's dusty and looks like it hasn't been opened in a long time.

I glance back up at the door. If Grace comes in now, I'm dead. I slowly open the box and frown, it's full of notes and trinkets and random things. I pick up a coaster and turn it over.

Peter's New York

Hmm, that's the bar we used to go to, haven't been there for years, actually.

Why would she have kept this, weird.

I keep digging through the box and pull out a napkin, a note is scribbled on it.

It's not possible to miss someone this much.

Gabriel...where are you?

My stomach twists.
I read it again.

It's not possible to miss someone this much.
Gabriel...where are you?

When did she write this? I turn it over to try to find a date.
She missed me?

But she told me last night that we were just a cheap fuck on a desk...*she lied.*

A little knock sounds at the door. "Gabriel?"

Damn it, Lucia has impeccable timing. "Just a minute," I call.

I slide everything back under the bed and quickly stuff the box I'm holding into my overnight bag and put my clothes on top of it. I'm taking this box home; I need to study that napkin. I'll sneak it back in later.

I open the door and see Lucia standing there, waiting patiently for me. "Yes?"

"Breakfast is ready." She smiles up at me.

"Great." I glance up to see Dominic come out of his room. "Good morning, Dominic," I call.

"Hi," he grumbles as he walks into the bathroom and shuts the door.

Hmm, we need to work on this, damn kid hates me.

"Let's go see Mom." I take Lucia's hand and walk down the hall with a spring in my step.

She wrote about me on a napkin...and she kept it.

Things are looking up.

. . .

"Everything all right?" Mark's eyes flick up to meet mine in the rearview mirror as we drive to the airport. "You're very quiet."

I run my tongue over my teeth. "What are the ingredients in scrambled eggs?"

"Eggs." He frowns. "Milk, maybe cheese." His eyes meet mine again. "Why do you ask?"

"I just ate scrambled eggs that tasted like fish and were laced with eggshells." I wipe my mouth with a tissue as my stomach rolls.

"Really?"

"You have no idea how bad her cooking is." I wipe my mouth again to try to get rid of this vile taste in my mouth.

He smiles to himself in the front seat.

"Not in the least bit funny."

"Actually, it is."

"Yeah well..." I turn my attention out the window. "If I die, tell the police who poisoned me."

"Sure thing."

"I'll be moving out here on the weekend."

"Permanently?"

"Thursday through to Monday morning each week."

"Oh." He continues to drive.

"You have your own house on the property I've rented. Although I understand if you don't want to be here. You can stay in New York, I mean...let's face it, this place is a fucking dump."

"I'll come." His eyes flick up to meet mine. "I kind of like it here." He turns the corner into the airport. "And besides, I go where you go, remember?"

I give him a lopsided smile and nod in a silent thank you.

Mark is the only person who goes wherever I go, whenever that is.

At a time in my life where everything is unknown, his steadfast presence is a calming force.

"How did it go last night, with Grace I mean?" he asks.

"Well…" I run my hand over my stubble as I think. "She told me she hates me."

"Okay." He drives as he listens. "And the kids?"

"We tell them who I am on the weekend."

"How does it feel to have two children?"

I twist my lips. "Terrifying."

"So…what's on today, boss?" He smiles as we pull up at the airport.

"First stop. My mother."

The plane touches down onto the tarmac and I immediately dial Frank's number.

"Hello, Mr. Ferrara."

"Where is my mother?"

"She's at a charity lunch for the Ferrara Institute at Town Hall."

I clench my jaw, annoyed. "What time does that finish?"

"It goes well into the evening, sir."

Fuck's sake.

"Fine, call me tomorrow when she's up and about."

"Yes, sir."

I hang up and glare out the window as I imagine how tomorrow is going to go.

Twenty million dollars is all my happiness is worth.

The city lights twinkle over New York. I pour myself a glass of scotch and place it on my desk beside the box that I got from beneath Grace's bed. I've been anxiously waiting all day to get to this box, what did she mean when she wrote on that napkin?

I take the lid off the box, sit down and slowly begin to sift through it, there's photos and note cards, a weird combination of things that don't really go together but they all seem to be from around the time that Grace was pregnant.

I pick up a piece of paper that has been ripped out of a book.

> The Lord knew that I would miss him so much that
> one baby couldn't fill the hole that he left
> So he gave me two.

For a long time I stare at her handwriting and I don't know what the hell kind of box this is, but it's fucking depressing.

With a big sip of scotch, I dig a little deeper and find a diary, the cover is creased as if it has been taken everywhere. I open it up and read the entry.

> I went to New York to tell him about our baby.
> He refused to see me and I've never been so humiliated in all of my life.
> Or heartbroken.
> I can't see this page for the tears, I don't know if I can do this alone.
> He's given me no choice.
> Alone I am.

I close my eyes in regret.

My heart twists as I think back to that day, if only I had handled things differently. If only I had gone down to see her, would things be different now...would my children know me?

My vision blurs and, feeling like the biggest piece of shit on earth, I keep digging through the box until I get to a pastel pink-and-blue congratulations baby card and I open it up.

> Gracie,
> You were a rock star in birth
> and we are so proud of you.
> Love,

She didn't even tell her mom and dad about me. I picture her with two little babies and nobody knowing who the father is and my heart hurts.

She really has done this all alone.

I can't imagine what it would be like having a child and not being able to tell anyone who the father is. Did they ask her questions, or did she just lie straight from the beginning?

I think back to my mother's offer of twenty million dollars and what an insult that is. If she had wanted the money, she could have taken it years ago.

There's a black velvet box underneath everything and I frown and open it, the diamond tennis bracelet I bought for Grace is inside. Carefully strapped into place, it's sparkling and looks brand new, as if never been worn.

Why would she wear it, she hates you, remember?

My stomach twists some more. I couldn't have fucked this up harder if I tried.

I flick through the diary and read another entry,

Today I start prenatal classes and what should be a day that's exciting and one that I've been looking forward to...all I can feel is dread.

I'm the only single parent in the class, it's bad enough I have to do this alone...but being forced to watch everybody else's husbands and partners be excited feels simply too much to bear.

I get a lump in my throat as I stare at the entry, I hate that she did this alone. I hate what I put her through.

I pick up my phone and scroll through the numbers. *Ring ring...*

ring ring...

"Hello," Grace answers.

"Hi." I smile softly, just hearing her voice makes me feel better.

"Gabriel, hi. I'm sorry but the children are asleep."

"I'm not after the children."

"What's wrong?"

"I just wanted to hear your voice."

Silence...

I close my eyes, filled with regret.

"Grace," I whisper, "I'm so sorry."

"For what?"

"For not being there when you needed me."

"It doesn't . . ."

"It matters to me." I cut her off. "I hate that I wasn't..." I stop myself saying anything more, unsure how to make this better, "... there for you."

We fall silent as we both wait on the line for the other to say something.

"I'll be there Thursday night after work," I tell her. "As soon as I finish, I'll be on my way."

"It's probably going to be too late by the time you get here to see the kids, they have school the next day."

"I know." I think for a moment. "I was hoping that you and the kids could come over to my house on Friday night...and..."

"Are you sure you still want to tell them?"

"Positive."

"It's not too late to change your mind, you know."

"I'm not changing my mind."

"Call me on Friday."

"Okay."

"Good night."

I smile as hope fills me. "Good night, Gracie."

. . .

I walk out to my waiting car to find Mark standing by it. "Good morning, sir."

"Morning."

"How did you sleep?"

"Like a baby."

The drive to the office is relatively short, and my mind is a whirlwind of nervous excitement. I just want to get back to Greenville...to her.

I think about the weekend and moving into the new house and telling the children, and I smile out the window. . . I have so much to look forward to.

I'm more excited about this weekend than I ever was about my upcoming wedding. That in itself says a lot.

I thought that perhaps I was making the biggest mistake of my life by ending it with Ariana, but finding that box has brought with it a sense of relief.

I'm not in this alone, Grace did feel the same, and I know that a lot of time has passed since then...but if she felt it once, she can feel it again.

The car pulls up to the front of the office to a media circus with security guards waiting around. "Fuck's sake."

"Shall I keep driving?"

"No, I have to go in. Pull the car up."

The car comes to a halt and Mark gets out and opens my door, the cameras start to flash and the bodyguards begin to push people. "Get back."

"Mr. Ferrara, are you devastated about the wedding?" someone yells.

"Is it true you're having an affair, Gabriel?" another shouts.

"Who is the other woman, Mr. Ferrara?"

I brush past them as the cameras flash.

"Where is Ariana now? Is it true that she has checked into a mental health clinic?"

I clench my jaw in fury as I push through the crowd.

Fuck this.

I take the elevator and walk through reception. "Good morning, Mr. Ferrara."

"Good morning."

"Mrs. Ferrara is in your office, sir."

Great.

"Thank you." I walk up the corridor and into my office to find my mother sitting at my desk, her back is ramrod straight with not a hair out of place.

I roll my lips to stop myself from outright verbally attacking her, close the door behind me and take a seat at my desk.

I can hardly contain my anger, and animosity swirls through the air. "Yes, Mother?" I say. "Can I help you?"

She crosses her legs and sits back in her chair. "You're angry."

I glare at her as I hold my tongue.

"I went to her to protect you," she stammers as she begins to get nervous. "And I saw her evil firsthand with my own eyes."

The anger in my soul begins to smolder with a new fire.

"You cannot throw away what you have with Ariana for Grace Porter. I cannot allow it."

"Ariana and I are over."

"Don't be ridiculous, you love Ariana."

"And *you* are supposed to love *me*." I slam my hand on the desk, causing her to jump.

"I do love you."

"You tried to buy my own children out of my life," I bellow. "How the fuck is that loving me?" I glare at her, on the verge of a full-on meltdown. "You've gone too far this time, Mother."

Her eyes fill with tears. "Don't say that," she whispers. "She's no good for you, Gabriel."

"*You* are no good for me," I scream. "Get. The. Fuck. Out. Of. My. Office. Right. Now."

The door bursts open and Alessio comes into view, his eyes flick between us. "What's going on?" he asks as he closes the door behind him.

"Get her out of here," I snap as I walk to the window. I drag my hands through my hair, too angry to even look at her.

"What's happened?" He frowns.

"Your mother offered Grace Porter twenty million dollars to leave me."

"I did not," she lies. "I offered her a nondisclosure contract, there's a big difference."

Alessio's eyes widen. "You're with Grace Porter now?"

"No, he's not. He's having a mental breakdown, that's what he's doing," Mother snaps, infuriated. "He's going to patch things up with Ariana...that's if she will even take him back."

"Get out," I whisper as a thermonuclear atomic bomb comes dangerously close to blowing up.

"I will not stand by and watch you ruin your life," she spits.

"Good. You're not invited to, anyway."

"What the hell is that supposed to mean?" she cries.

"It means that I want nothing to do with you." I point to the door. "Get out!"

"You fool," she fires back. "You're ruining everything you worked so hard for."

"I'm warning you. If you dare go near Grace or my children again...there will be *fucking hell to pay*, do you hear me?"

"You do not get to speak to me like this." She picks up her handbag in a huff and marches from my office and slams the door behind her, the office falls silent.

Alessio begins to pace in a panic. "That was way too much."

Adrenaline is surging through my bloodstream, and I'm positive that the whole building just heard that exchange.

So much for keeping it together and being calm.

Fuck.

My phone rings on my desk, the name Elias lights up the screen.

What now?

"Yes," I snap as I answer it.

"Hello. Umm...Mr. Ferrara."

"What is it?"

"I just called to let you know that Grace is having lunch with a man," he says nervously. "He met her at her work and he had his arm around her as they walked into the restaurant."

What?

"Who is it?" I growl.

"I believe it's the man that you told me to watch, Jack Spalding."

The hairs on the back of my neck stand to attention as a fury like never before runs through my blood. "Go inside and sit at the table next to them."

"Inside the restaurant?"

I begin to hear my heartbeat in my ears.

"Do not leave them alone for one fucking second."

20

Grace

"You look so beautiful today, do you know that?" Jack smiles over the table. "I love you wearing blue."

"You said that already." I give him a lopsided smile. "Thank you, though."

Jack is the nicest man I know, and, damn it, I really want to like him. He's fair-haired, blue-eyed and handsome, he's athletic and has every attribute any woman would want, quite the catch really. We've been friends for years and recently started to go out occasionally. I know he likes me in a romantic way...I mean, he doesn't hide it.

I keep waiting for the zing to hit me, for something to happen that will magically make me see him in a different light.

So far, no such luck.

But I'm not a quitter, I know he would be a great partner, I just have to get my body to catch up with my head. I'm pushing through this until the attraction comes...and surely it has to soon, this is our fifth date.

"What are you having?" I ask as I open the menu.

"Hmm." He looks over the choices. "I'll have whatever you're having."

I glance up. "You don't want to choose your own?"

"I'm happy to do whatever you do." He smiles dreamily over me as he leans on his hand.

Ugh...don't.

"Okay, I'm having a salad." I slam the menu shut. "And a glass of wine."

"Sounds good."

We fall into an awkward silence, I'm silent and he's awkward, but honestly who the hell knows anymore, I've lost all sphere of reference as to how I'm supposed to feel on a date anymore.

I look out over the people in the restaurant that are all chatting and laughing, excited to be seeing each other. I feel an over-whelming sense of failure.

What the hell is wrong with me?

For once, can't I just want someone who is good for me? It's not all about butterflies and chemistry, and damn it, where is the waitress?

"I planted some beans today." Jack smiles. "You're going to love them when they're ready for picking, it's a real thrill to get your hands dirty in the garden."

I smile over at dear old Jack, so sweet and kind although utterly clueless about the kind of thrill I'm looking for. "Do you grow all your own vegetables?" I ask.

"Every last one, you can come garden with me on the weekend if you want? I'll show you how to weed properly."

Dear god...

"I'm pretty swamped this weekend, thanks anyway." I force a smile as I look around the restaurant. *Where is the freaking waitress?*

Gabriel arrives on Thursday and we're telling the kids. Nerves swirl in my stomach at just the thought.

"What are you doing?" he asks.

I glance up from my daydream. "I beg your pardon?"

"What are you doing this weekend?"

"I have an old friend visiting."

"Oh great. I'd love to meet them."

Gabriel would eat you alive and pick his teeth with your bones.

"Sure." I fake a smile. "I'll let you know."

From the corner of my eye, I see the clock tick over. 2:19 a.m.

I thought my sleepless nights of worrying about Gabriel Ferrara were long over.

And yet, here I am.

Lying in the dark, staring at the ceiling like a zombie, hovering somewhere between heaven and hell.

In the highs of heaven, my children will be reunited with their father, no longer will I carry the burden of guilt of denying them the truth. The hell part isn't so cut-and-dry, I'm terrified of Gabriel coming back into my life.

Of the power he has over me, of the love I'm not sure I'll ever shake.

The hurt and destruction to my heart I know he will bring.

It's weird, like I have this disattachment to all things love, to all the men who have tried to love me over the years and the thought of marriage and a happy ever after.

Like a disease creeping in the dark, waiting to strike. My attachment to the pain he caused grows stronger than ever, and what does that say about me?

I loved him, but more than that, I love to hate him.

It's easier to blame someone else for things gone wrong.

Sure, the attraction between us is still there, but that's all it is.

A physical attraction will never win a war or spin the world on its axis.

Only love can do that, and this is as far from that as it gets.

I hope he looks after my babies.

I can think of only one thing worse than him not loving me...

Him not loving them...

Friday afternoon, I grab the four cartons of milk and put them into the fridge. The worst part of grocery shopping is unpacking it when you get home.

My phone dings and I read the text as it comes through, it's from Gabriel.

Finally here and settled.
I'll see you tonight.
My address is.

I read the address and frown, ugh, he's so predictable. Of course he got a house on the most exclusive street in town.

My stomach flips. *He's here.*

"Guys," I call as I act unexcited. "We're going to have dinner tonight with our friend Gabriel from New York, remember him?"

"Really?" Lucia gushes with excitement.

Dominic looks up from his place on the couch. "Can I stay home?"

"No, baby." My heart sinks, damn it I hate that Dom saw Gabriel and me fight that first visit, definitely not my finest hour. "Gabriel's a nice man and you'll like him if you just give him a chance."

Dominic curls his lip, unimpressed.

"What will you wear?" I ask him to change the subject.

"Can't I wear this?" He looks down at himself.

"Why don't you wear something nice?"

"Like what?"

"I don't know, dress up with some nice pants and a shirt or something."

"Can I wear my new yellow dress?" Lucia butts in.

"Of course you can."

"Can you braid my hair?"

"Yep." I smile.

Dom goes back to watching television and I know I have to move him along or else he will sit there procrastinating forever. "Dominic, go upstairs and have a shower and wash your hair, sweetheart," I tell him.

"Now?"

"Yes, now." I widen my eyes. "Turn the television off, please."

He grumbles his way up the stairs and I hear the bathroom door close behind him.

Nerves dance around in my stomach. Tonight is the night. Up until now they've never really asked questions about their biological father, they've been too young to really understand it all.

Please let this go well.

Lucia takes off up the stairs all excited, and then another thought hits me, what the hell will *I* wear?

An hour and a half later, we drive up the road as I glance at maps on my phone. "It should be just up here on the left." I keep driving. "And remember, we are using our best manners here tonight. It was very nice of Gabriel to ask us to dinner."

I just want tonight to run smoothly without the drama of Dominic's cheeky shenanigans.

"What will we be eating?" Dominic sighs.

"You will eat whatever he serves up."

"What if it's brains?" Dom replies.

"Then you eat the brains."

"What if it's caterpillars?" He smiles darkly as Lucia frowns in horror.

"Then you eat the damn caterpillars."

Turn right.

Google notifies me of the driveway and I peer at the lights disappearing up and over the hill.

Jeez.

253

The sweeping driveway is huge and grand with big white ball lights on both sides, it looks more like a main road than it does a driveway.

"This is it," I say as I turn right.

"This is his house?" Lucia gasps. "Is he rich or something?"

"He must be," Dom agrees. "Only rich people have driveways like this. I bet he has a pool too."

"Who cares if he's rich or not?" I snap. "It's rude to talk about money, guys. Please never do that."

Oh hell, these kids are going to sound so uncultured and country bumpkinish.

Well...they are.

We continue up the hill for miles and the car is silent as we look around at the beautiful surroundings, okay...this driveway is swish, it's like the botanical gardens, even I'm in awe.

Ugh...so typically him.

What a wanker.

My palms begin to sweat as I hold the steering wheel, the magnitude of tonight is really beginning to freak me out. "Guys... just please, promise me that tonight you will be nice to Gabriel, okay?"

"Yes, Momma." Lucia smiles from the backseat.

My eyes flick to Dominic in the rearview mirror for confirmation. "Dom?"

"Yes." He huffs. "I told you already."

We come over the top of the hill and my eyes widen at the sight. The house is white and huge, three stories tall and lit up with the same fancy big ball lights. It has a sweeping veranda and beautiful gardens.

"Woooooah," the children gasp from the back seat.

I swallow the lump of sand in my throat as I park the car. "This is it."

The front door opens and Gabriel comes into view, he waves and smiles as he walks down to greet us. "Hello." He opens my car door.

Be nice for the children.

I look up at him and smile awkwardly. "Hello."

Tall with dark hair and a jaw that could cut glass. He's wearing blue jeans that fit snug in all the right places and a white T-shirt. I've only seen him in casual clothes a handful of times, luckily for me...because he looks damn well delicious.

"Ahem."

I clear my throat as I try to clear my mind of its pornographic thoughts.

"Lucia." He smiles as he bends and hugs her. "You look lovely." He straightens the ruffles on her dress.

Dominic gets out of the car and Gabriel smiles down at him. "Hello, Dominic."

Dominic fakes a smile but doesn't offer his hand or a hug or anything. "Hi."

Fuck's sake, kid...be nice.

"Please...come inside." Gabriel gestures to the house and we follow him up the stairs. We walk through the huge double front doors and are instantly hit in the face with opulence.

The foyer has a double timber staircase, and the floor is black and white marble tiles laid in a pattern. "Wow...this is...." I grip my handbag with white-knuckle force. "Nice."

"It's okay." He walks us through to the oversized kitchen and living area and my mouth nearly falls open. The kitchen is the size of a restaurant and all white marble, and the living area has over-sized white couches and a white rug.

How do they keep all this white stuff clean?

"Wooooah," Lucia gasps as she runs to the back glass concertina doors. "Is that a boat?"

"Holy..." Dom gasps.

I peer out to see an infinity pool overlooking a flawless mountain view, there's black-and-white striped deck chairs lined up alongside of it and a swim-up bar.

What the hell?

"There *is* a boat," Dominic cries.

I look past the pool to see a lake with a floating rowboat tied up to the pier.

My horrified eyes meet Gabriel's and he winces, knowing exactly what I'm thinking. "The boat on the lake is overkill, I must admit." He shrugs.

"Can we go look? Can we go look?" Lucia bounces on the spot.

"Can we, Mom?" Dominic chimes in.

"Is it safe out there?" I ask.

"Sure." Gabriel opens the glass doors and the kids go running out into the back garden.

I look over to the left of the property and see a house, smoke is coming out of the chimney. "Is someone living there?" I ask.

"Mark."

"*Mark* Mark?" My eyes widen in surprise. "Your driver from New York Mark?"

Gabriel chuckles. "Yes, *Mark* Mark."

"Oh..."

"He was looking forward to getting out of New York and wanted to start over with me."

"Oh..." I shrug. "I can't believe..."

"That I moved here?"

The smell of his aftershave wafts around me, and I hold my breath so I don't know how good he smells, it's a pity that I already do.

"Part-time," I say as I walk out to the edge of the stairs to look out over the children down by the lake.

"I'll be here four days a week, that's more time here than I'll be in New York."

I spin toward him. "Are you *sure* about this?"

He holds his hand up at our surroundings. "Does this house look uncertain?"

My stomach flips with nerves as we stare at each other.

"I'm going to tell them over dinner," he says.

"What are you going to say?"

"I've gone over the conversation in my head a million times and I keep coming back to one thing."

"What's that?"

"The truth."

"The truth?" I frown. "What do you mean, the truth? The truth between us is ugly."

"I'm going to tell them that we were friends and we kissed and... We had sex."

What?

"They're too young for the sex part," I whisper in a panic.

"Okay...not the sex on the desk part."

I nod.

"I'll tell them we did it in a bed." He gives me a playful wink.

"No sex talk at all," I stammer. "You can tell them all about the birds and the bees in five years."

"Deal," he replies without hesitation.

Five years.

We stare at each other and it's weird... Something's different tonight. We aren't hating each other, or maybe I'm just sick and tired of hating him. Either way...it feels nice to not want to stab him.

"So...what's for dinner?" I ask.

"Well..." He shrugs. "I was going to cook, but..."

"But you can't cook?"

"Coming from you, that's an insulting question," he fires back. "I've ordered pizza to make the night run smoother."

"Okay."

"I wasn't sure what they liked, so I ordered one of everything."

"How many pizzas did you order?"

"Ten."

"Ten," I gasp.

"Nutella pizza for dessert. I got two of them."

"Good, one for me and one for you."

"Or both for me and none for you."

"That too." I smile at the return of the friendly banter we always shared.

His eyes twinkle with a certain something as we stare at each other.

Stop it.

"I've made up the guest rooms for you," he says.

"What do you mean?"

"I thought you would want to stay too if they are? You know, until they settle in with me."

"I didn't plan on them staying. I haven't packed them an overnight bag or anything."

His face falls.

"You can't rush this, Gabriel, let's just get through tonight first. Who knows how they're going to react."

He nods, disheartened.

"They *will* stay, they'll stay all the time. Just not tonight," I tell him.

"Right."

I can feel his disappointment. "Did you order wine with the pizza?" I ask to change the subject.

"I brought my own from New York. I tasted your local wine last weekend, remember?"

I smile. "Ahh...of course you did. Smart choice."

"Would you like a glass?"

"Maybe just one."

His eyes hold mine for an extended beat as if he's waiting for me to say something, and the air swirls between us. I snap my gaze away.

Maybe I shouldn't drink at all tonight.

Gabriel carries the pizzas into the dining room. "We'll eat in here; I've set the table."

I look into the formal dining room, the sixteen-seat antique table is perfectly set with fancy silverware and linen napkins, there are fresh flowers in the middle of the table and it looks like something out of a movie set or something.

"Maybe we should eat in the kitchen around the kitchen counter," I suggest.

"Why?"

"It's less formal and more relaxed, it will lighten the mood."

He thinks for a moment as he looks around the table. "Maybe you're right." He runs his hands through his hair as if in a complete panic.

"You're nervous?"

"I'm not nervous," he snaps. "I'm freaking out."

"It's going to be fine."

"How do you know? Dominic hates me."

I puff air into my cheeks. "Well, we just have to work on it. Rome wasn't built in a day. He'll come around, he's a lot like you."

"That doesn't help me, I know how I think."

I stare up at him, this is the first time since I've known Gabriel that he has openly discussed a weakness. "Let's just get this over with."

"What are you going to say again?" I whisper as I follow him into the kitchen.

"The truth." He puts the ten pizza boxes on the counter.

The truth sucks. "Maybe I should tell them?"

"No. I want to do it."

"Are you sure?"

"Sit down," he snaps, he fills our glasses of wine, passes me one and tips his head back and drains it. He immediately refills his glass and gestures to mine. "Keep up."

I roll my lips to hide my smile. "Kids," I call. "Dinner is here."

They come barreling in from the other room and climb up onto the stools.

"Oh my god," Lucia gasps. "Why are there so many?"

"Because we're hungry, that's why," Dominic replies as he opens the first box. "Eww, onion." He scrunches his nose up in disgust.

"This one over here, pepperoni, your favorite." I pass them both a slice. I didn't have the heart to tell Gabriel that they will only eat one of his ten pizzas.

"Thank you," Dom says as he takes a big bite.

"Yum." Lucia smiles, all excited. I glance over to Gabriel and he's white as a ghost.

"So, guys, we have something to tell you," I say.

They keep eating, totally engrossed in their pizza.

"Gabriel..." I widen my eyes at him. "Now," I mouth.

"Well." Gabriel pauses as if articulating his words. "Your mom and I have just recently found out some very exciting information."

They keep eating, totally uninterested.

"As you know, your mom and I have been friends for a long time..." He takes a huge gulp of his wine.

"Are you guys listening to Gabriel?" I ask.

They nod as they eat, they are so not listening.

"Anyway," he continues. "Your mom and I worked together and we were once in love."

What?

They both stop eating to look at him.

"I mean, I didn't realize it at the time, and..." He swallows the lump in his throat. "Anyway, one day when your mom was leaving New York to move here to Greenville, we shared a very special kiss goodbye."

My heart twists as I remember that night.

Dominic frowns, his eyes flick to me for confirmation and I nervously smile and take his hand under the table.

"And your mom moved here and I stayed in New York and I was very sad for a very long time."

Huh...

What the fuck is he doing?

"Then one day your mom found out that she was pregnant, and she was so excited to have two little babies in her stomach." He smiles softly over at me.

I begin to hear my heartbeat in my ears.

"You know when the doctors came over to your house and they had those swabs that you put into your mouth and they cut a little piece of your hair?"

Lucia nods in an overdramatic way.

"Well, that test told us that..." He looks around at us all again as if searching for divine guidance. "I'm your father."

Dominic stares at him, emotionless.

"What did you say?" Lucia frowns.

"I'm your father." He gives a lopsided smile. "I'm very excited about it and I hope you are too."

Lucia's eyes widen. "Father...like a dad?" she gasps.

"Yes." He smiles. "Like a dad."

Dominic drops his pizza onto his plate.

"Yay." I smile awkwardly as my eyes flick around to everyone at the table. "Isn't this exciting?"

"Yes." Lucia jumps up and bounces over to Gabriel and he gives her a hug.

"I thought you were my dad," she lies.

Gabriel chuckles as he pushes the hair back from her face. "Did you, now?"

My heart melts at the sight of the two of them, and then I glance over to see Dominic glaring at me. "What have you got to say, baby?"

"I don't want a father," he says flatly. "Can we go home now? I'm tired."

Gabriel's face falls.

Little shit.

"No, we're staying here and having pizza like we planned. Gabriel has moved here all the way from New York to get to know you, and you *will* be polite."

There's no treading lightly with Dominic, I have to be blunt with him about this from the get-go.

He pushes his plate forward in protest. "I'm not hungry anymore and I want to go home."

Gabriel's unimpressed eyes flick over to him and I know I have to defuse the situation before it turns into a full-blown argument.

"No, Dominic, you will not spoil this moment," I say sternly. "If you can't be nice, go and wait in the living room and watch the television. You do not get to dictate how this night goes. This is very exciting news for you and Lucia."

He's as stubborn as a mule and Lucia deserves better than for him to ruin this. He stomps off out of the room, Gabriel's hurt eyes follow him and then come to meet mine.

"That's why we both have black hair." Lucia smiles up at Gabriel, totally unfazed. She reaches up and touches his hair.

"Yes."

"And we both have brown eyes."

"We do." He smirks down at her.

I glance into the living room to see Dom pointing the remote at the television.

Damn it, why did he have to react the way he did, perhaps I should have told him in private before we came.

Lucia bounces back over, sits down and begins to eat her pizza while Gabriel and I sit in silence, every now and then his eyes roam into the living room back to Dominic.

The mood is heavy, and I have no idea what's going through Gabriel's head, but I can't even begin to imagine how he'd feel.

Hearing his only son say that he doesn't want a father... Ouch.
What a mess.

This is my fault; it was too much too soon. We should have told them at our house, where Dominic felt comfortable and safe in his own environment.

Ugh, you idiot.

Gabriel chews his pizza, and disgust flashes across his face.

"What's wrong?" I ask.

"I don't know what kind of pizza this is, but good god, it's bad." He curls his lip and drops it back onto his plate.

Poor bastard can't even get a decent pizza in this place. I think of all the things I've served him up to eat over the last few weeks and I can't hide my smile.

"What's so funny?" he asks dryly.

"*You* are a food snob."

"I..." his eyebrows flick up as he searches for a comeback, "... openly admit that I prefer edible food."

I get the giggles.

"Glad you find this amusing." He opens another pizza box and peers in, he narrows his eyes as he focuses on something. "Is that pineapple?" He picks a piece off and flicks it onto the plate. "What the..."

"Just eat it."

He takes a bite and winces as he chews in slow motion.

"Well?"

"This one is a little better...I guess." He shrugs.

"I've finished," Lucia announces. "May I be excused from the table?"

"You may," I tell her. She bounces off into the living room to sit with her brother.

"Pay no attention to Dominic, this is my fault," I whisper.

He raises an eyebrow as if agreeing with me.

"I just meant that we should have told him at my house."

"What's not to like about this house?" he whispers angrily.

"I'm just saying... Maybe we should hang at our house for a while until he comes around."

"So you're going home just like that? I've been looking forward to this night all fucking week."

"Then come with us," I whisper.

"I'm not kicking you out of your bed for one more night."

"Then you can sleep on the couch."

"There are seven bedrooms here," he gasps.

"Not yet," I whisper. "This is a lot to take on for a little boy, put yourself in his shoes for a minute."

He exhales heavily.

"Let's finish dinner and then go back to my place."

A trace of a smile crosses his face.

"What?"

"Nothing." He twists his lips. "I just like the sound of you saying that."

"Gabriel..."

"Yes, Gracie?" He smiles sweetly.

"Stop playing games, I'm telling you right now that this is for their sake only, I have no interest in you whatsoever and you are sleeping on the couch."

"Of course I am." He smirks as if knowing a secret.

Damn it, playful Gabriel Ferrara is very attractive.

"I mean it." I widen my eyes to accentuate my point.

"You're the boss, Gracie." He holds his two hands up in surrender.

Gracie.

"Let's go back to our house," I call out to the kids.

"Oh no," Lucia calls.

"I'm coming too," Gabriel calls back. "We're bringing the Nutella pizzas for dessert."

"Yay," Lucia calls back.

No reply from Dom.

"How long are we going to pander to King Dominic?" He curls his lip, unimpressed.

"Until you get him to like you."

"And if that day never comes?"

"It better." I stand and start packing up the pizza. "He's not like Lucia, he won't just like you. You started off on the wrong foot when you upset me, that's all. He will come around when he sees me and you getting on."

"Define getting on."

"Not getting on, you idiot," I whisper. "Getting along."

"Together?"

"Oh my god," I whisper. "Get in the car before I run you over."

. . .

Fifteen minutes later, we pull into my driveway, Gabriel in his car behind me.

"The ducks are out," Lucia gasps. "Can we go see them?"

"Yes, okay."

They both jump out of the car and disappear around the side of the house.

We walk up onto the porch and go to open the front door. Gabriel comes up behind me and stands way too close, I feel his breath on my neck and every cell in my body stands to attention.

"Do you mind standing back a little?" I ask him.

He takes an overexaggerated two steps back.

"You know, you're getting a little too comfortable with me," I warn him.

"You said we could be friends."

"Yes but..."

"But what, Gracie? This is me being friendly."

Am I being overdramatic? "Okay, but...just so you know."

"Trust me, I know." He rolls his eyes as he stuffs his hands in his pockets. "You're like Mother fucking Teresa now."

"No shit."

You have no idea.

I open the door and we walk inside and I look around our home, it seems so tiny and insignificant now that I've seen his new place.

"Home sweet home," Gabriel sighs sarcastically.

"He feels comfortable here."

Dominic walks in the back door with a basket of kindling and goes to the fireplace, he bends down and begins to scrunch up the paper.

Gabriel watches him. "Do you light the fire all by yourself?"

Dominic nods as he keeps loading the kindling in.

"Dominic is the fire man of our house," I say proudly.

"Impressive." Gabriel nods. "I'm not sure I could light a fire all by myself, you'll have to teach me one day."

Dominic doesn't acknowledge him and keeps doing what he's doing.

"Dominic..." Gabriel says. "I know that you're angry that I haven't been around for you and your sister...but I want you to know that...I'm angry too."

Dominic glances up at him and then catches himself and acts uninterested, he goes back to his task.

"I feel cheated that I've missed out on so much of your life so far," Gabriel continues.

Guilt runs through me like a freight train.

"But I want you to know that I'm here now and I'm not going anywhere."

Dominic gets the lighter and lights the paper up, the orange flames flicker.

"And just because we got off to a bad start, it doesn't mean we won't have a wonderful relationship going forward."

Dominic pauses as he stokes the fire and I know he's listening.

"I'm going to make this up to you and Lucia...and your mom."

All those nights I lay in bed and cried myself to sleep because I wanted my children to have a father, and now, hearing this, it's...

I get a lump in my throat as I watch on.

"Dom," Lucia calls from the back deck. "The brown duck is back. Quick."

Dominic glances up at me for approval to leave. "You can go out if you want," I tell him.

He runs out through the back door and Gabriel slumps to sit on the arm of the couch. Empathy fills me, and I put my hand on his shoulder. "He's going to come around."

Gabriel puts his hand on top of mine. "I wish I were so sure."

The warm, strong muscles under my hand suddenly come into focus and I remove my hand only to have Gabriel hold it in his. "I wasn't lying, Gracie. I'm not going anywhere. I promise you."

"This has nothing to do with me, Gabriel, the only thing that matters is your relationship with the twins. Leave me out of it."

We stare at each other as emotion wells between us, memories of a horrible past that my heart won't let me forgive.

His face flickers with red and golden shadows of the fire. "I'm just asking you to leave the door open for us."

"That door has been closed for many years, Gabriel."

He runs his hand up my leg as he stares up at me, and I know that look, once upon a time I dreamed of it every night. "I'm not the boy I was back then."

"Then who are you?" I ask.

"I'm the man who wants to right his wrongs." His hand slides around to my behind. "A man who knows what he wants."

"We are never having sex. Get it out of your head right now."

"I'm not after sex, I'm after a connection." His eyes search mine. "I want to feel your heartbeat from the inside, I want to show you mine."

Oh...

He stands, bringing us millimeters apart, and he takes my face in his hands. I stare up at him as my heart completely stops.

"Put me out of my misery." He bends and his lips softly brush against mine. "Tell me there's a chance for us."

21

Grace

HIS TONGUE slowly swipes through my open lips and my knees nearly give way beneath me. My eyes flutter closed as the moment takes me over.

Oh...

We kiss again, and this time his tongue slowly slides into my mouth, awakening every female instinct that I've suppressed for years.

This man...the physical reaction I have to him...it's carnal, primal, and damn well addictive.

Wait...what the hell am I doing?

I pull out of the kiss and step back. "Gabriel, you need to stop."

"What's wrong?" He reaches for me again and pulls my body against his. "Get back here."

"No." I take a further step back. "This isn't about you and me, this is about the children and your relationship with them."

"What the children need is for us to be together."

"That's not true at all, and besides..." I troll my mind for a get-out-of-jail card. "I'm already seeing someone."

His eyes narrow and he steps toward me, forcing me to step

back. "Who is he?" he growls. The dominance of his action sends a wildfire through my body. I feel my pulse between my legs.

Just throw me across the table already.

"A very nice man," I reply in an overly high-pitched voice. "You can't come barging in here with a few pretty words and expect me to drop everything."

His eyes hold mine and then, as if sensing that I'm lying through my teeth, he breaks into a slow, sexy smile. "And are you getting everything you need from him?"

Not even close.

"Yep," I squeak.

"Well." His dark eyes hold mine as he lifts his hand to my face and cups my jaw, his thumb swipes over my bottom lip. "I hope he fucks you just as deep as I want to."

Thump.

Thump...goes my heart.

I feel faint...

He turns and without another word walks out the back door and down to the lake to the children. I go to the window and watch him, my body screaming for more of his touch, aching like never before. My skin tingles with excitement and every hair on the back of my neck stands to attention.

But I can't go there, not now.

Not ever.

It's late and the children are going up to bed, Gabriel has insisted on sleeping on the couch.

I want to stay up and watch television but I don't trust my slutty self.

All I can think about is his dick and how badly I want it.

I'm disgusted with myself.

I put the pile of blankets on the end of the couch. "Are you sure you don't want to sleep in my bed?"

His dark eyes hold mine and I know he's as hot for it as I am. "If I sleep in your bed, we are one hundred percent fucking."

I feel myself melt into a puddle.

What position?

"Well." I act uninterested. "That's not happening, so the couch it is." I turn and practically run upstairs without looking back. I march down the hall and into my bedroom and close the door behind me.

I glance down at the lock. *Should I leave it open?* I imagine him sneaking in while everyone sleeps, I get a vision of looking down at his face between my legs, his lips wet with my arousal, his cock hard, throbbing, and ready to ride.

The fuck is wrong with you?

I flick the lock and begin to pace. I need to get rid of some of this X-rated energy.

This is bad, bad, bad.

I wake feeling exhausted. I hardly slept a wink last night. Tossed and turned until the wee hours, and I honestly don't think I fell asleep until six this morning.

Ugh, and I have a million things on today.

I drag myself out of bed and go to the bathroom. I stare at myself in the bathroom mirror and wipe under my eyes and fix my hair.

It shouldn't matter how I look, but somehow it does.

I throw my robe on and make my way downstairs to find that Dominic is already watching television. I glance over to the couch to see the blankets folded neatly on the end of it.

"Where's Gabriel?" I ask.

Dominic shrugs, his eyes glued to the television.

I look around the house and peer out into the backyard. "Did he go home?"

He shrugs again, oh my god, this child is infuriating. "Dom, listen to me, please."

"I don't know, he was gone when I got up," he groans as if I'm a major inconvenience.

"Oh." I go to the front to see that his car is gone. "Well."

Once less problem to worry about, I guess. I feel the weight of my world lift from my shoulders. Damn it, that man stresses me out.

"We've got ballet this morning and then your game, a big day ahead of us. Who wants pancakes?"

My eyes roam over the grandstand.

"He's not here," Debbie says into her coffee.

"I thought he would be," I mutter, distracted. "Why move all the way here if you aren't even going to the game, you know?"

"Well." She sips her coffee as she thinks. "Maybe you hurt his feelings last night when you rejected him."

"I hurt his plans for his dick, that's all." I roll my eyes. "What does he think, he's going to say a few pretty things and I lie on my back and open my legs for him?"

"I totally would, he's fucking hot," Deb replies, her eyes glued to the field.

"Um, excuse me." I giggle in surprise. "You're married."

"I know." She sighs. "Happily, but man...the way he looks at you."

"What do you mean?"

"You can feel his testosterone pumping through his body." She fakes a shiver. "What I wouldn't give to have a man want me like that."

That's an odd thing to say. I frown as I watch her. "Is everything okay with you and Scott?"

"Yeah." She sighs. "I don't know, I guess we never had that fire between us."

"Not even in the beginning?"

"Nope." She exhales heavily. "We are best friends who have sex, we always have been best friends who have sex. It was never a carnal attraction. I mean, we only have sex once a fortnight now, and it's more a closeness thing rather than a sexual thing."

"Are you still in love with each other?" I ask.

"I guess." She keeps watching the game as if uninterested in this conversation. "Lately he's been distant, but I can't imagine a life without him. I just mean that..." She pauses, as if searching for the words. "Physical attractions like that are not the everyday thing. If you have one with someone and he has it back, it's worth exploring."

"But our history . . ."

"Is history." She cuts me off. "Let it go."

Jack walks down along the front of the grandstand and we both watch him. He's wearing his uniform and has his super-white socks pulled three-quarters up his shins.

"You have been on how many dates with Jack?" she asks.

"Five."

"And you haven't even kissed yet?" She raises an unimpressed eyebrow.

I shake my head.

"That's weird, don't you think?"

"I'm just not feeling it." I roll my eyes, knowing she's right. "There's something wrong with me, I'm sure of it."

Jack looks up and sees us, his face lights up and he waves.

"I'm going to go down and see him." I stand.

"And do what?"

Ugh, I hate it when Deb gets all sensible and hard-hitting on me.

"Talk to him, what do you think?" I shimmy across the row of seats and make my way down the stairs to meet him on the concourse at the side of the stadium.

"Hey you." He smiles. "Beautiful day, isn't it?"

"Hi, Jack." This is why I like Jack, he's so uncomplicated... talking about the weather and stuff, this is what I need in my life.

Good, supportive, weather-loving people.

"You didn't call me back last night?" He frowns.

Oh crap, I didn't even know he called.

"I didn't have my phone on me," I tell him. "I'm sorry."

Fuck.

"Hello," a deep voice purrs from beside me. I look up to see Gabriel towering over us. His dark hair has a wave to it, he's wearing sunglasses and the heavenly scent of his aftershave wafts around me. Wearing black jeans and a gray sweater, he looks like a walking orgasm.

Damn it.

"Gabriel." I swallow a nervous lump in my throat as I look between the two men. "Hi," I stammer in my high voice.

What the hell is going on with my voice box when I'm around him?

He holds his hand out to Jack. "Gabriel Ferrara."

"Hello, I'm Jack Spalding." Jack smiles and shakes his hand, I nervously glance between them. "Isn't it a great day today?" Jack continues. "The sun is shining and life is good."

Amusement flashes across Gabriel's face as he looks him up and down. "Okily dokily."

Oh hell... What does that mean? It's a Ned Flanders reference, Gabriel is calling him Ned Flanders. Ahhh... Abort mission...

I widen my eyes at Gabriel. *Behave fucker.*

Gabriel stands tall, his feet wide, back straight and dominance oozing from every cell.

"Gabriel is an old friend from New York," I splutter.

"Not quite a friend, though," Gabriel replies. "Am I?"

"Who are you?" Jack smiles all excited like.

"I'm the twins' father."

Jack stares at him as he does the math. "What...what brings you to Greenville?"

"My family."

"Your children," Jack corrects him.

"My children *and* Grace."

"But Grace is with me."

"Not for long." Gabriel's eyes hold his in a silent dare.

Jacks face falls.

"I've moved to Greenville to get my girl back," Gabriel announces.

"You've moved here?" Jack whispers, unable to hide his dismay.

"Stop it, Gabriel," I snap. "Be nice."

"Oh...but I am being nice. I'm letting Jack know of my intentions. Being underhanded is not my style, you know that, Gracie."

Jack stares at Gabriel, horrified. He's probably never met someone as aggressive in real life before, not many people have.

Gabriel's eyes hold Jack's. "All's fair in love and war...right, Jack?"

Jack stares at him, speechless.

"May the best man win." Gabriel gives me a slow sexy smile and then he glances at Jack. "Good luck, Jack...you're going to need it." He turns and saunters off into the crowd as we both stare after him.

That was the most egotistical display of power tripping in the history of the universe.

And it was fucking hot.

Oh god...my face is fuchsia red, my pits are sweaty, and damn it, why is that man's ego so out of control?

Poor Jack.

"I'm so sorry. Ignore him," I stammer. "He's...a, Gabriel is a different kind of man."

Jack is still staring after him, if I'm being honest I think it turned him on too.

He drags his eyes back to meet mine. "Can I see you tonight?"

"Ahh..." I look around for divine guidance, rip the Band-Aid off, don't let this go on. "I've got a lot on at the moment," I reply. "The twins are settling in with Gabriel and I need to be there for them."

"He's already won, hasn't he?"

"No. He hasn't, and I won't be getting back with Gabriel. Not now, not ever. I'm sorry you had to deal with him today, that wasn't fair."

His eyes search mine and empathy wins, I can't end it under these circumstances.

Not today, anyway.

I mean, not that we have anything to end, we haven't even kissed.

"Let's meet up for lunch through the week, shall we?"

"Okay." He gives me a lopsided smile. "I really like you, Grace. I think we have a future."

My heart sinks, how I only wish that were true.

"I'll call you during the week?" I ask.

He nods, seemingly mollified for the moment, and with a wave I make my way back up to the grandstand.

"Oh my god," I whisper as I sit down beside Deb.

"What was that about?"

"Gabriel is a literal nightmare."

"Why?"

"He just told Jack that he's in town to get his girl back."

Deb's eyes light up with excitement. "How very caveman."

"This is not funny," I whisper angrily.

"No, but it's hot."

"Shut up." All of these years all I wanted was for him to fight for me and the kids, but now that he's finally decided to, it's the last thing I need or want.

I take out my phone and text Gabriel.

How dare you!

A reply bounces straight back.

Nobody gets in the way of what I want.

My eyes bulge as I fume.

You can't have me!

His reply bounces in.

But I will.

"Ugh, this man is infuriating." I show Deb the texts and she reads them.

"Seriously, can I watch you two have sex? It's going to be fucking fire." She smirks. "Open an OnlyFans account, you'll make bank."

I snatch my phone from her. "We are not having sex." That came out louder than expected, and we both cringe as we both look around. An old lady gives us a judgy side eye.

"Seriously, though." I lean into Deb and whisper, "What should I do now?"

"Go to the shop. Buy. Lube."

4 p.m., and not a peep from Gabriel since I saw him at the game this morning.

The sky has turned red, and I've ranted and raved all damn day.

This isn't okay, his behavior is totally unacceptable. He can't just turn up here and be an arrogant prick to try to rattle my boyfriend. Well, he didn't just try, he excelled at it. Poor Jack is rattled to the bone...and who could blame him?

Not that Jack and I are star-crossed lovers or anything...but Gabriel doesn't know that. What if we were?

What if I loved Jack with all of my heart and Gabriel just planted a seed of poison into our relationship?

What then...huh?

I stir the chocolate brownie mix in the bowl as I mutter out loud to myself. "If he thinks my cooking was bad before, just wait until he tastes my next meal. I'm putting full-blown dog shit in it."

I stir the mix with vigor. "And if he thinks for one fucking second I'm putting up with his bullshit, he can think again."

"What's bullshit?" Dominic asks from the doorway.

Crap...can't I even mutter to myself in peace?

"Nothing, bubba, sorry, that's an inappropriate word." I smile sweetly. "Just thinking about a show I'm watching on Netflix," I lie. One thing I've learned over the last three weeks about this whole shared-parenting thing is to not let my feelings seep in and poison the kids. Once you say something in passing about the other parent, they hold on to it forever.

"Gabriel is here," Lucia yells excitedly from upstairs. "Yay." She comes screaming down the stairs and runs out the front door to greet him.

Dominic walks to the front window and peers through the side of the curtains, quietly watching.

"Why don't you go out and meet him too, baby?" I tell him. "That would be nice."

Dominic shrugs, unsure what to do.

He's warming to him.

My anger momentarily dissipates and I smile. "It was nice he came to your game today, wasn't it?"

He stays silent.

"Do you like Gabriel coming to see you all the time?"

He shrugs again.

I walk over and stand behind him as I put my hands on his shoulders, we both watch out the window as Lucia talks a million miles per minute, she's being all animated and he's laughing as he listens and talks to her. They're getting something out of the trunk of his car and loading it onto the grass in a pile. I smile as I watch them, and then I remember something, something very important.

Gabriel Ferrara's a fuckface...who I hate.

I go back to the kitchen to continue making my brownies. "They're carrying something big in, Mom," Dominic calls.

I hope it's a coffin, he's going to need it.

"Why don't you go and help them?" I call back.

"I don't know if..." He contemplates.

Ugh, why is this child such an over thinker?

"They're walking around the side of the house with the stuff," Dominic calls as he runs to the back door.

"Just go out and see what they're doing." I roll my eyes as I pour the brownie mix into the cake pan.

"Will you come?" Dominic asks hopefully.

Ugh...

"Sure." I open the back door and Dominic comes to stand beside me.

"Hi there, you two." Gabriel smiles up at us as he and Lucia carry something down to the water's edge.

"Hello." I smile through gritted teeth.

Fucker.

Dom holds my hand and bites his bottom lip as if to hide his smile.

He's so cute, I can't stand it.

"What have you got there?" I call out to them.

"I bought us a new card table and chairs and a firepit."

Us.

I narrow my eyes. "Why?"

"Because I thought we'd play cards out here tonight."

I clench my teeth.

You thought wrong, I'm drowning you in the lake and burying your body in the woods tonight.

"Oh," I reply flatly. "Great."

I go back inside. I really don't have the capacity to deal with him today, this is a nightmare.

Gabriel begins to set up the card table and fold out the chairs and Dominic wanders down to the water's edge to watch them.

"Can you sort the kindling for the fire, Dom?" Gabriel asks him. "I need a man around here to get this firepit under control. Do you think you can do that?"

"Okay," Dom replies enthusiastically, he runs inside to collect the things. He begins collecting the kindling and throwing it into the basket.

Ugh... I roll my eyes. He's now using Dom's pyromaniac tendencies to bond.

Well played.

I peer into the oven at my brownies as I imagine Gabriel choking on them.

"Mom, we're making a fire out the back," Dominic calls. "And we're playing Uno."

Oh...

He's excited.

"That sounds so fun, baby," I call back. "Maybe we could take some blankets out there too," I suggest.

Dom's eyes light up. "The checked ones in the linen press?"

"Uh-huh."

He runs and takes the stairs two at a time.

"Mind if I come through your back door?" Gabriel's deep voice purrs.

I glance up to see him standing in the doorway, he's giving me the look, and I know exactly which back door he's talking about.

"You will never be coming in my back door," I mutter dryly.

"Famous last words." He peers into the oven to see what I'm cooking.

"Listen, don't talk to me," I whisper as I look around to see if I can talk without anyone hearing. "You are in the doghouse."

"Excellent."

"How is that excellent?"

"Doggy style is when I'm at my best."

What?

"Mom." Lucia walks in, interrupting us. "We're playing Uno and having a fire outside."

"Great," I say over enthusiastically. "Oh joy. This is the best night of my life."

Lucia turns her back and I cross my eyes and stick my finger down my throat. Gabriel's eyes dance with mischief. He puts a shopping bag on the kitchen counter. "And look...I bought snacks."

"Funny you say that, I was just about to cook you up something extra special."

"Please don't."

"Ha-ha, you're so funny," I mutter as I turn back to check on the brownies.

Kill me now.

This is a nightmare, but the kids are so excited, I can't ruin this for them.

And he knows it.

The master manipulator.

Infuriating.

Half an hour later, we are sitting around the little card table on the lake's edge and Gabriel is reading the instructions to Uno out loud while the children listen intently.

For fuck's sake, this isn't rocket science. Just deal the cards already, I don't have time for this shit.

"Each player gets seven cards," he reads.

"We know." I sigh.

He glances up. "You know?" He looks around, disappointed. "You've all played this game before?"

"Not this exact one," Dominic lies. "This is a different sort."

Huh?

"Oh, good." Gabriel smiles in relief.

Why did Dom say that? We have played this game ten million times before.

Lucia smiles over at me. "This is so fun, isn't it, Mom?"

"Best night of my life." I sip my wine, unimpressed. I'm sure gardening with Jack would be more fun than this.

Gabriel deals out the cards and we all pick them up and begin to organize them in our hand. I glance over to the kids, who are smiling goofily, they're so happy.

I have a momentary out-of-body experience as I remember dreaming of a night just like this for them.

Simple fun with their father.

Emotion overwhelms me and I unexpectedly tear up. I blink to hide my tears and then glance up to see Gabriel watching me. As if knowing exactly how I feel, he gives me a soft smile and a subtle nod, and I smile too.

I need to take me and my feelings out of the equation. This night means everything to the twins and Gabriel and that's all that matters.

Two hours later.

The burning wood cracks, and Gabriel and Dominic hold their sticks in the flickering flame. Night has fallen and along with it has come the peaceful serenity of the lake.

It's beautiful out here.

"I can't wait to taste these toasted marshmallows." Lucia beams, she and I are sitting at the card table, waiting for the boys to serve us our dessert.

"I can't believe you've never had this before?" Gabriel smiles proudly as he twists his stick.

I think we did have them years ago and someone burned the bejesus out of their lip so I never got them again, not that I'm telling them that.

"Just about done," Gabriel tells Dominic. "Turn it over again."

Dominic turns the stick again, he's concentrating as if this is brain surgery. He hasn't said anything much directly to Gabriel tonight but he's hanging off every word he says.

I'm happy and sad and overwhelmed, and damn it, seeing them with him makes me realize how much they've missed out on.

"All done," Gabriel tells Dominic. They walk over and proudly hand over our sticks with the melted marshmallows on the end. "Careful, they're hot," he warns us. "Blow on it to cool them down."

His words are gospel, and the children begin to blow on their marshmallows in an over exaggerated way.

He takes a nibble and smiles. "Ah, davvero delizioso." *("Ah delicious.")*

Dominic tastes it. "È la cosa più deliziosa che abbia mai assaggiato." *("This is the best thing I ever tasted.")*

Gabriel smiles.

"Lo mangeremo quando andremo in Italia, non è vero, Mamma?" *("When we move to Italy we will eat this, won't we, Mom?")*

"Speak English, Dom, I don't understand," I tell him.

"When we move to Italy we will eat this, won't we, Mom?" he repeats himself.

"We will." I smile.

Gabriel's face falls as he stares at Dominic. "You want to live in Italy?"

Dominic nods. "Lo stesso vale per Lucia."" *("Lucia does too.")* "Mamma ha detto che non appena compiremo sedici anni ci trasferiremo lì per un paio di anni per imparare la lingua e le tradizioni." *("Mom said when we are sixteen, we are moving there for two years to learn the culture.")*

Gabriel's eyes search mine.

"I want them to know who they truly are." I smile sadly.

His eyes well with tears as he stares at me across the table.

This is one of those moments where the planets align and you know that all the decisions and hard work that you put in years ago have paid off.

"I wanted to prepare them for your world as best as I could."

"Our world, Gracie," he whispers. "It's our world."

Oh...

His tears do break the dam this time, and he wipes them away as they roll down his cheeks.

This is the first time I've ever seen him like this, beautifully vulnerable.

"Why are you sad?" Lucia asks.

"I'm happy." He stands and pulls me out of my chair and hugs me tight. "Thank you. Thank you," he whispers as he holds me close. "You have no idea how much this means to me."

I let myself relax into his hug, and then, like clockwork, his large, strong body begins to talk to mine, and I feel the twinge of arousal surge between us. I pull out of his grip.

His eyes hold mine, and I know that he felt it too.

"Let's get back to this game," I announce to change the subject. "I'm about to kick your butt, Mr. Ferrara."

"Yeah," Dominic growls.

"Me too," Lucia chimes in. "I'm winning this time."

He sits back down and smiles through tears as he looks around the table, and for the first time in his life, he's utterly speechless.

And for the first time in a long time, I feel proud of myself.

"Into bed." I kiss Dominic's head as he walks up the stairs. "I'll be up in a moment to say good night."

"Okay."

"Buona note," Gabriel says from beside me.

"Buona note," Dom says as he walks up the stairs. "Night, Mom."

I walk into the kitchen to straighten things up and Gabriel lingers by the door; it's as if he wants to say something but is holding his tongue.

"Thank you for tonight," I say. "It meant a lot to the kids."

"It's me who should be thanking you." His eyes hold mine and like a tide in the ocean the mood changes, electricity crackles between us. "I can't . . ."

"You take my bed tonight." I cut him off, I don't know what he's going to say but I really don't need to hear it.

"No, no."

"I'm fine on the trundle, you are twice the length of the couch. Take my bed."

"Gracie, I . . ."

"Let's not ruin a good night, shall we?" I cut him off. "Whatever you are going to say...please don't."

His eyes hold mine and I know that deep down, he knows I'm right.

"Good night."

A low and deep throb has been brewing between my legs, and damn it, I really need to get over this stupid attraction. Whatever my body thinks it needs, it isn't happening...

Not now, not ever.

I take the stairs two at a time. I wish it were tomorrow already, it's going to be a long night.

I flick the blankets back and stare at the ceiling, it's a blazing inferno in here. Is there any air in the bedroom at all?

Why is it so damn hot?

Dominic is fast asleep up on his bed while I lie down below on the trundle. My thoughts go to Gabriel and how emotional he was when he found out we planned to go to Italy one day. It was a great memory, one that I will always remember.

He was so shocked; he didn't have a clue that it was coming, and that's what made it all the more special. I see his tears and I smile into the darkness.

Throb...

Throb...

Hell, I need to get laid, or at the very least have an intimate three-hour date with Bob my vibrator. I'm feeling hot and bothered and overly sexual and I know it's only because he's around again. Which is stupid, because he is the last person I want to have sex with.

If only my body would keep up with the logical grudge that I hold.

Unfortunately, my human and very female primal instinct to mate with a dominant male has been triggered.

Just being around him is...hard.

Hard...

I bet he'd be hard... A vision of him naked and looking down at me runs through my mind. A vision I've never forgotten because it's burned into my brain.

One night with him in the flesh has given me years of fantasies in my mind.

Stop it!

Ugh. I drag my hand through my hair and roll over and punch my pillow.

I stare at the ceiling for over an hour until I can't stand it any longer, maybe I need to go to the bathroom? Maybe that's why I'm not sleeping.

I climb out of bed and pull my white nightdress down. No wonder I can't sleep, I'm all twisted in this stupid thing. I'm not used to sleeping in pajamas.

I tiptoe down to the bathroom. The little red nightlight that plugs into the power point throws a warm glow across the room. I do my business and am standing at the basin, washing my hands when I feel my hair being swiped to the side, soft lips open-kiss my neck.

He's here.

Goose bumps scatter up my spine as my knees weaken beneath me.

He kisses my neck again; this time his teeth graze my skin and I feel a surge of arousal scream through my blood. His hand wraps around my body dragging me back onto his erection.

Our eyes meet in the mirror, and he bites my earlobe as he holds me tight, his hand comes to aggressively cup my breast. He's wearing only boxer shorts, his broad, muscular body shadowed in a beautiful shade of red.

"Gabriel..." I whimper. "I don't think..."

"Stop thinking," he breathes into my ear. "Just feel." His hand slides down the front of my panties and he circles his fingers through the lips of my sex as he opens me up.

Fire blazes in his eyes as he feels how wet I am.

Fuck...

He turns my head and kisses me, his tongue takes no prisoners as his fingers slide deep into my sex. My body contracts around him and he moans into my mouth in appreciation.

Something snaps.

Suddenly, we're desperate.

He lifts my knee to rest on the counter, bringing me wide open and then he plunges his fingers deep inside of me, stretching me out. I whimper as his body takes mine over. I can feel his engorged length sitting snug up against my ass.

He begins to fuck me with his hand as he kisses me deeply, the sound of my arousal sucking him in echoes through the room. Our kiss is animalistic, our teeth clashing, his grip on my jaw is nearly painful.

But I can't stop...

I need him, even if it's only physically, even if it's only for one night. In this moment, right now. My body needs what only his can give me.

He turns me and sits me up on the bathroom cabinet and brings my legs up so that my feet are on the counter. I'm in a seated squatting position and like this I'm totally at his mercy.

His dark eyes hold mine as his thick fingers slowly slide into my sex.

First two, then three...then four. Deep, powerful movements where he's nearly breaking the counter. I grip his forearm and feel it flex as he curls his fingers deep inside my body.

Gabriel Ferrara is a legend for a reason, nobody can make a woman come harder than he does. He hits the spot.

Every.

Damn.

Time.

This is too good, I can't speak...I can't even breathe.

The floor moves beneath us as I see stars.

I let out a deep moan as my body does exactly what nature

intended. I shudder hard and cling to him as a freight train of an orgasm rips through me.

He kisses me through it as my body quivers, his tongue diving deep into my mouth, and I know he's holding on to his control by a thread.

"Get into my fucking bed," he growls into my mouth as he holds my face in his hands.

I...there are no thoughts in my head, none that make sense, anyway.

Next thing, I'm getting dragged down the hall toward my bedroom by the hand, and he closes the door behind me and flicks the lock.

I look around the room, confused. "Why is the mattress on the floor?"

"Because you're about to fucking get it." He pushes me down onto it.

"You knew this was going to happen?" I frown up at him.

"Of course I did. Your pheromones have been sucking my cock all day." He pulls his dick out of the top of his boxers and slides it over my mouth, pre-ejaculate smears across my lips.

Fuck...

I take him deep into my mouth and swirl my tongue, he tips his head back and moans as he holds my head in his hands. "Suck. My. Cock." He pushes himself deep down my throat until I gag.

His eyes are ablaze with fire as he holds himself too deep for me to take.

I pull off. "Too much." I cough.

"You're right." He pushes me onto my back and comes over my body, bringing my legs up over his forearms as he holds himself up. "You are too fucking much." He slowly slides in deep, and every muscle in my body contracts around him.

We stare at each other as our bodies exchange power.

A magic swirls between us, a spell that once cast cannot be broken. My body giving him the softness that his hardness needs and vice versa.

His eyes flutter closed as if totally overwhelmed.

I stare up at him in awe.

Never has there been a more addictive lover, Gabriel Ferrara is the ultimate.

Hung, experienced and intense.

The power oozing from his body is all-consuming.

Every woman's fantasy.

He slowly pulls out and slides back in. "Okay?" he whispers.

I nod, grateful that even when this aroused, he's aware of his size and the damage his body could do. He slides in again and circles his hips, first one way and then the other, to open and stretch me out for him.

My feet are up around his shoulders and like this I'm completely at his mercy.

He leans down and kisses me with the perfect amount of suction. My eyes close in pleasure.

"Tell me if I get too rough," he whispers in my ear as his lips roam down to graze my neck.

"I'm okay," I breathe. Better than okay. This is fucking perfect.

He pulls out and then slams in deep.

"Oh..." I whimper as I cling to him.

I glance over to the mirror to catch sight of him, his thick quad muscles contract as he pumps me. His body is covered in a sheen of perspiration and his broad shoulder muscles are popping as he holds himself up.

His hips delivering deep punishing hits where he drives me through the mattress.

Dear god, I may not survive this.

He begins to moan, and the slapping of our skin echoes through the room.

I glance at the door; did he lock it?

If a child walks in right now, they will be scarred for life, hell, who am I kidding...I will be anyway.

No sex is this good.

We fall into a rhythm, his deep punishing hits welcomed by the softness of my body.

"Gracie," he whispers as he looks down at me.

I smile softly up at him and take his face in my hands. I half sit up so I can kiss him.

Him being inside of me isn't enough, I need to be closer.

He falls still as we kiss; his eyes are closed, completely lost in the moment. My orgasm is so close that I can feel it, and I clench around him, he moans in pleasure.

A thrill runs through me and I do it again, he grips me tighter.

He's close.

"Fuck me," I breathe. "Just fuck me. Give me everything."

He slams into me, knocking the air from my lungs. We both cry out as he comes deep inside of me.

Hearts pounding, breathless and totally overcome, we kiss tenderly, holding each other through the heavenly high.

Time seemingly stands still.

Eventually, he falls onto the mattress beside me and pulls me close. Still kissing me over and over again. His tongue tenderly worshiping me, his body weeping out of mine, his flaccid cock resting against my open thigh.

There's a beautiful tenderness swimming between us, something that I've never felt from him before.

"Dreams do come true," he whispers in the darkness. "I'm never letting you go, Gracie." He kisses me again and then falls onto his back, totally spent.

The ceiling blurs as I stare up at it through tears.

What have I done?

I jump as I wake...did I dream... I glance over to see Gabriel fast asleep flat on his back and I close my eyes in horror.

Oh no...*fuck.*

His regulated breathing tells me he's still in a deep sleep. I slowly climb out of bed, and as I swing my legs, I get a sharp sting between my legs.

Oww...I'm sore, the man's an animal.

I throw on my robe and sneak out of the room. I hold my breath as I ever so quietly close the door behind me. I don't want him to wake yet, I need to get myself together before I have to face him.

I rush down the hall and catch sight of myself in the mirror, my hair is all over the place and my face is flushed. I look thoroughly well and truly fucked; I am, on all counts, so that's...fitting.

Ugh...

I rush down the stairs and flick the coffee machine on, then pace back and forth while I wait.

This is a disaster.

The colossal fuckup of all fuckups.

He broke me so hard that it took years to recover...and one sniff of his manhood and I turned into a stray cat on heat.

The machine pings, and I get a vision of us last night.

Damn...that was some good sex.

Stop it!

I make my coffee and go out to sit by the lake. I immediately call Deb.

"You slept with him, didn't you?" she answers.

"How do you know?"

"Why else would you be ringing me at seven a.m.?"

"This is a fucking disaster," I whisper.

"Well...your girlie likes him."

"My girlie's a ho."

"Obviously."

"God." I drag my hand through my hair in disgust at myself.

"So..."

"So what?"

"How was it?"

"It was porn sex." I pinch the bridge of my nose. "Stupidly good."

"Hmm." She thinks for a moment. "It might work out."

"It's not going to work out, Deb," I whisper angrily. "I don't even want it to work out. Yes, he's hot, but he's a controlling, power-hungry asshole who is going to break my heart, and that's after he's stripped every piece of confidence I ever had from me."

"You don't know that."

"Yes. I do."

"Mom," calls a voice from the back door. I turn to see Dom standing by the back stairs, his hair all messed up, and he's in his striped pajamas.

"Got to go."

"What are you going to do?" Deb asks.

"Fake my death is sounding good." I hang up and walk to Dominic and take him in my arms. "Good morning, my special little guy." He holds me close for an extended time.

My favorite thing in the world is the morning hugs that my children both give me, it's as if they haven't seen me for a year.

Lucia walks out sleepily; she's carrying her teddy and is all crumpled and sleepy. I bend and hug her next. "Where's Dad?" she asks casually.

My world spins on its axis.

Dad.

Suddenly, I feel overemotional. I'm going to screw this up for them. This is going to go bad between us and he's going to leave them and it's going to be all my fault.

"He's still sleeping."

"Can we watch cartoons?" Dom asks.

"Sure."

"Can we have Pop-Tarts for breakfast?"

I'm having tequila.

"Why not?"

They settle in on the couch and begin to watch their shows as I try to come up with a crisis-management plan.

Okay...I think long and hard as I stand at the sink, looking out the window over the lake.

What now?

This doesn't feel right. I don't feel elated or on a high or even remotely excited.

All I can sense is dread. A weighted heavy blanket of oncoming doom.

"Good morning." I hear Gabriel's smooth voice from behind me.

"Hello," Lucia calls.

"Hi," Dominic grumbles.

I close my eyes as I feel his two hands slink around my waist from behind, his lips drop to my neck. "Good morning." He pumps his hips into me and I feel his erection underneath his clothes.

"Stop." I pull out of his grip.

"What's wrong, hard night?" He chuckles. "Bit tired and grumpy today, are we, angel?"

"Oh my god." I make two more cups of coffee. "Can you...not?"

"Not what?" he teases, he has that naughty twinkle in his eye.

"Be so..." I widen my eyes as I search for the right word... "overbearing."

"Impossible." He pulls me close and kisses my lips. "I just had the best night of my life and am officially walking on air."

"Drink your coffee," I mutter dryly. "You're creepy like this."

"That was so..." His eyebrows flick up as if he's imagining something. "Insanely hot last night. Wasn't it?" He puts his lips to my ear. "My mouth waters just thinking about it."

"Stop it," I whisper as I pull away from him. "We need to talk."

He sips his coffee as he gives me the look. "Are you sore, because my cock is."

"I doubt that, your dick is as match fit as they come." I look around guiltily. "Listen...that can't happen again."

"What do you mean?" He smiles, thinking this is some little play-hard-to-get act.

"You and me, it has to end...it's no good."

He chuckles and grabs me roughly by the behind and pulls me

close. "This is just the beginning, and you're a bad liar, because it was so fucking good."

Knock, knock, knock, sounds at the door.

"Someone's at the door," Dominic calls just as he opens it.

"Hello," a woman's voice says.

"Hi," Dominic replies.

Gabriel's face falls and he rushes into the living room.

Huh?

I walk out to see a beautiful woman, she has long dark hair and perfect bone structure. Her face screws up in tears when she sees Gabriel across the room in only boxer shorts and my heart stops.

Oh fuck...

Ariana.

22

Grace

"Hello, Ariana," Gabriel says calmly. "What is going on?" His voice is cajoling and gentle, the same one he uses with children.

"I was waiting at your house all night." She screws up her face in tears. "And you didn't come home."

I can feel her heart breaking from here.

"Come, let's..." He holds his arm out to her. "We should go outside and talk."

Lucia and Dominic are watching on with great interest.

He opens the front door and gestures to it. "This way."

"I'm not going anywhere," she screams like a maniac.

Uh-oh.

Gabriel rolls his lips, clearly angered. "Grace...take the children to Debbie's, please?"

"No," Ariana screams. "They should know what you've done."

Gabriel's eyes flick to meet mine with an urgency. "Now."

Ahh...

"Come on, kids." I grab my keys. "Your father needs to talk in private."

"You stay right where you are!" she yells at me.

The children freeze on the spot.

"Grace!" Gabriel demands.

"Now," I yell. I grab Dominic's and Lucia's hands and drag them out the back door and we race down the steps, we rush out the front to the car and I hear glass smash inside.

Argh, she's trashing my house now.

"What's happening?" Dominic demands.

I have no idea how to respond. "Umm..." I open the door of the car with force. "We'll talk on the way."

Ariana starts screaming and yelling inside, and it echoes through the neighborhood.

Oh man...she's completely losing it now, and who could blame her. She found her newly ex in his silk boxer shorts with another woman and his kids. If only she knew what actually happened last night...*she does.*

That poor, poor girl.

"But we're still wearing our pajamas," Dom protests.

"That's fine," I splutter as I push him in the car.

Another thing smashes from inside. Shit...is he safe? Should I call the police or something?

We bundle into the car and take off down the road like maniacs.

"Who was that?" Dominic demands.

"Your father's friend."

"Why was she crying?"

I grip the steering wheel with white-knuckle force. How the hell do you answer that question? I can't lie, he saw it with his own eyes. "She and your father used to date and he broke up with her and she's clearly upset." My eyes flick to meet his in the rearview mirror. "It's okay, these things happen sometimes between adults."

His eyes hold mine, and I can see his little mind running a million miles per hour. "He always makes girls cry, doesn't he?"

My heart sinks.

The children have never seen any of this; without a full-time father or man in the house, they've been blissfully protected from any kind of disturbance or fight.

"No, he doesn't always make girls cry. Adult relationships are complicated, Dom," I reply. "Luckily for you guys, children's stuff is way easier to handle."

"Why did we leave?"

"Gabriel didn't want you around her when she was being angry and upset, that's all. She will be okay, don't worry."

My mind flicks to Gabriel back at the house. I hope he's okay. Maybe I should drop the kids at Deb's and go back to check on him?

My presence will surely only escalate the situation. No...I need to stay away.

We pull into Deb's driveway and she's out with a cup of coffee, watering her garden, she frowns as we all get out of the car in our pajamas. "What's going on?"

"Gabriel's girlfriend came over and was crying and smashing glass things," Dominic replies as he walks past her into the house. "She's going crazy and wrecking our house."

Deb's eyes widen as they meet mine. "Are you serious?"

"Deadly." I sigh. "I need coffee."

Deb and I sit at her kitchen, bench deep in thought. "I think you should go back and check on him," Deb says. "What if she..."

I drag my hand down my face as I think. "He'll be fine."

"How did she know where you live?"

"No idea."

"And she sat outside his house all night waiting for him to come home?"

"Apparently." My heart sinks. "I've been exactly where she is and I feel sick knowing how hurt she would be."

"But he's yours now." Deb sips her coffee.

"Ugh, so not mine." I shake my head in disgust. "Don't get excited, it was a one-time event."

"Are you sure about that?"

"Positive."

Gabriel

Grace rushes the children through the back door and my heart sinks, the last thing I would ever want is for them to have to deal with this. I turn my attention to Ariana; she's crying hysterically and out of control.

"Calm down," I tell her.

"Calm down?" she gasps. "Calm down?" she cries again. "Did you fuck her?"

I stay silent, unsure what to say.

"Tell me the truth, Gabriel. Did you sleep with her on what was to be *our* wedding night?"

Fuck.

I've been so carried away with Grace and the children that I completely lost track of time. Yesterday *was* supposed to be our wedding day.

I'm such a fucking asshole.

"Did you even remember?" she whispers through tears, her voice cracks, betraying her hurt.

"Of course I remembered," I lie. I need to defuse this situation and get her out of here, she's completely unstable. "I'm here to see my children."

"Do *not* lie to me." She picks up a glass and hurls it at my head; it smashes against the wall.

"Hey," I say sternly. "You do not break anything in this house."

She picks up another glass and hurls it, glass flies everywhere as it explodes against the wall. "I'll burn down her entire fucking house, she's nothing but a trashy homewrecker."

Ugh...she's been speaking to my mother.

"Let's go back to my house."

Where the fuck is Mark?

297

"No. I want to wait for her to get back." She folds her arms and begins to pace. "I have a few things I want to ask her."

"Such as?"

"That's for me to know and for you to find out."

My anger simmers dangerously close to the surface, and I grab her by the hand. "Out. Now."

"No," she screams, and begins to hit me hard in the chest. "How could you?" she cries hysterically. "How could you do this to me?" She keeps hitting me over and over. "You said you loved me. We were just starting our life together, how could you walk away from something so beautiful?" She pummels my chest and it's official, I am the worst kind of human.

She's completely broken.

"Baby, I'm sorry. I'm so, so sorry." I pull her close to try to calm her down, and I hold her in my arms as she cries against my chest.

We stand in each other's arms for a long time, and I don't know how to make this better. There's no way I can. I'm utterly and irrevocably in love with Gracie, and if I'm honest, I always have been. My feelings for Ariana only scratch the surface on what I feel for Grace...and now with the children in the mix, everything else pales in comparison.

What kind of man am I?

Ariana's body wracks with tears as I hold her. "Shh." I try to calm her down. "It's okay," I whisper. "It's going to be okay."

"How can anything ever be okay again if I don't have you?" Her tearful eyes hold mine.

I want to give it to her straight, tell her that she's better off without me because even if we were together, I would still love another woman from afar.

But I can't.

Not now, not when she's like this.

I owe her better than this, I have to care for her. "Come on, I'm taking you back to New York," I say softly as I hold her.

She looks up at me. "You're coming back to New York with me?"

"Yes."

She smiles through hopeful tears.

Fuck.

"Come on." I put my arm around her and gently usher her out of the house and put her into my car. She's like a broken child, sobbing uncontrollably. I can't bear to see her like this.

Look what you've done.

We drive in silence back to my house as my mind races a million miles per minute.

What's Grace going to think of me leaving with Ariana?

This looks bad even to me, but how can I help it? What kind of person would I be if I didn't care for Ariana when she's like this?

We pull into my driveway and make our way up to the house; Mark is in the driveway and he looks up puzzled as I park the car.

I glare at him. *Where the fuck were you?*

His face falls as he connects the dots and he rushes to open my door. "Hello?" he stammers.

I get out of the car and slam the door; my fury is palpable.

"What's going on?"

"Ariana came to Grace's this morning. Apparently, she sat out the front of this house all night."

Mark's eyes widen in horror. "I didn't see her," he stammers, "I swear I didn't see a thing."

"Organize the plane, I need to take her home."

"Yes, sir."

I walk around to Ariana's side of the car and she's crumpled up in a ball, still crying. I reach in and lift her out of the car and Mark's eyes widen as he sees her state. He rushes ahead and unlocks the front door for us and I carry her in and place her carefully down on the couch. "Get me a blanket."

"Yes, of course." Mark runs up the stairs.

"Ariana, I'm going to make you something to eat," I say softly as I swipe her hair back from her forehead.

"I'm not hungry," she whispers.

"You are eating, you've lost a lot of weight since I last saw you. You need something in your stomach."

Mark reappears with a blanket and I carefully place it over her. I put a pillow under her head and snuggle her in. "I'll be back in a moment, okay?" I turn to Mark. "Do not take your eyes off her," I growl.

I'm so furious that I can barely look him in the eye. What's the point of having guards at this house and Grace's if not one of them does their fucking job?

Heads are going to roll over this.

"Yes, sir." He drops to sit on the opposite couch as if scared for his life.

He should be.

I walk out into the kitchen and open the refrigerator, what the hell will I get her?

I take out my phone and text Grace.

I'm sorry
Ariana is distraught,
I'm taking her home to New York.
Call you as soon as I can.

I press send.

I get to making Ariana a grilled cheese sandwich and a hot chocolate and I check my phone, no reply from Grace.

Fuck.

I text her again.

This isn't how it looks,
I can't let her go home alone,
she's too upset.

I pause as I think what to write next.

I'm physically going with Ariana,

but I'm leaving my heart with you.
I'll be back as soon as I can.
I love you

I think for a moment, I can't say I love you for the first time in a fucking text message, and certainly not in these circumstances.

I delete the words *I love you* from the message and I read it again.

This isn't how it looks,
I can't let her go home alone,
she's too upset.
I'm physically going with Ariana,
but I'm leaving my heart with you.
I'll be back as soon as I can.
Xox

I press send and walk out into the living room with the grilled cheese and hot chocolate.

Mark is sitting deathly still and Ariana is asleep. The poor thing is exhausted; she obviously hasn't slept all night. I put the food down on the coffee table. "A word in my office."

Mark follows me down the hall and I close the door behind us. "Where the fuck were you?" I growl.

"I don't...I didn't know...she wasn't." He's tripping over his words as he searches for an answer.

"Where the hell were the guards on Grace's house this morning?" I'm livid, how could this happen?

"I texted them and they weren't starting until nine today because you weren't out and about yet."

"What?" I explode. "My ex-fiancée bombarded me in a house with my children in it. Do you think this is fucking acceptable?"

"No, sir."

"So tell me how was Ariana sitting at the front door here all night and you didn't see her?"

"After you left yesterday afternoon, I watched a few movies and then went to bed. There was no sign of anyone here at all. I thought the guards over at Grace's had taken over the shift."

"You thought wrong, get the fucking plane organized." I storm out my office and up the stairs to pack my bag.

I throw the things into my bag with force. After the best twenty-four hours in history...this happens. I check my phone to see if Grace has replied.

She hasn't.

I begin to pace as I dial her number, *ring ring...ring ring...ring ring.*

You've reached Grace Porter, leave a message.

I hang up.

I'll deal with Grace later; I have to get Ariana safely home to her family before anything else.

Mark arrives at the door. "The plane is ready whenever you are."

I put a T-shirt into the bag. "We'll leave in twenty minutes."

Four hours later.

The plane touches down on the runway at JFK as I stare out the window.

Ariana has slept on my shoulder the whole way home, and I'm beginning to wonder if she's had some kind of breakdown. She isn't acting like herself at all, she's usually so strong and proud, and I don't know what to say that won't just upset her even more.

Keeping my mouth shut is the best option.

Get her home safe. I've already called her parents. I get a vision of her crying and hitting my chest as I held her and my heart sinks.

The most horrible core memory that will forever be burned into my brain, I don't even want to imagine that it might happen again when I leave. I feel physically sick over it.

I glance at my phone, no missed calls.

My attention turns to stare out the window. I didn't even say goodbye to the kids.

What must they think?

A strange woman turns up screaming and crying and then they're rushed out of their own home and suddenly I've gone with her.

Maybe I should drop Ariana home and then fly back to Greenville...but then I have to present to the board tomorrow here in New York.

Fuck's sake, this is a logistical nightmare, them living so far away.

I'm going to call Grace and see if she can fly out here for the week. The kids can have one week off school, surely, these are extenuating circumstances. Dominic and I had just started to turn the corner, I don't want this morning to be in his little brain. He's an overthinker like me, I know how he would be reading into this. He'll think that I've chosen to be with her over them, that I've left of my own free will.

I need to be with them.

Ariana's hand slides up my thigh and she takes my hand in hers. "Thank you."

I glance down at her. "For what?"

"Coming home with me."

I didn't come home with you. I stare at her for a moment as I do an internal risk assessment. I can't upset her again before I get her home safely.

I squeeze her hand in mine and give her a sad smile. "Let's get you home, hey?"

She smiles hopefully up at me and kisses my shoulder. "I love you."

I give her a stifled smile as my heart breaks all over again for her.

This is possibly the worst day of all time.

The plane comes to a stop and I stand and grab the bags. Mark takes our bags down and I help her out of her seat. I grab her handbag and take her hand and lead her out of the plane and down the stairs to the waiting car on the tarmac.

I open the door and wait while she climbs in and I get in behind her.

Almost there.

Ariana holds my hand in her lap as we drive through New York City, and I sit silently with my heart in my throat. What happens when we get there?

It kills me to hurt her, how do I do this?

I think of all the men and women who leave a marriage and effectively walk out on their children. How do you walk out one day for another person and never go back?

I feel sick for leaving my kids today just to take Ariana home...

My phone vibrates in my pocket, *Grace.*

The urge to read the text takes me every inch of control to fight. I can't open my phone in front of Ariana, she'll go postal.

With my elbow leaning on the door, I pinch the bridge of my nose.

I'm caught in a nightmare.

Living between two places, trying to win the love and respect of my children. I have zero interest in work or being in New York anymore and I'm hopelessly in love with one woman while breaking another woman's heart.

We drive into the underground parking lot and Ariana smiles up at me, grateful that I've brought her to my house.

My heart sinks as we turn the corner and I see her parents' car parked in my bays.

She sits forward. "Why are my parents here?" Her panicked eyes flick to me. "You called my parents?"

I grip her hand in mine. "I'm worried about you," I tell her softly.

"Then don't leave me," she cries.

Mark's eyes flick up to meet mine in the rearview mirror.

Fuck...here we go.

Mark pulls the car up alongside her parents and I open the door.

"No," she cries as she clings to me. "You can't do this, we love each other, Gabriel." Her mother and father walk over to the car and look over me in at her.

"Thank you for coming," I say sadly. I climb out of the car as she clings to me.

"Ariana, darling. You're coming home with us," her mother says.

"No, Gabriel, don't you leave me."

Her father reaches into the car and she begins to fight him.

Their silhouettes blur as the lump in my throat nearly cuts off my air.

He drags her from my car, and to the sound of her cries, he puts her in his.

I stand to the side, helpless.

This is devastating.

Her mother gets into the backseat beside her and her father slams the door shut and then turns to me. "I'll never forgive you for this."

My nostrils flare as I try to hold it together. "Deservedly so."

I watch the car slowly disappear.

I've never felt so guilty and sad. Ariana doesn't deserve any of this.

Mark and Andrew stand silently near the elevator and I march past them. "You're all on fucking notice," I growl. "When I pay a fortune for security, I want fucking security."

Their faces fall, and I hit the elevator button with force and close the door on them.

I'm so over this fucking day, I can't stand it.

I ride to the top; the elevator doors open up directly into my penthouse, and I step out and walk straight to my bar. With shaky hands, I pour myself a glass of scotch and drink it straight; it burns all the way down. And so it should, I deserve it.

I pour another one and go and flop on my couch. I stare into space for a long time. I picture Ariana and don't even want to imagine what's happening at her parents' right now.

I dig into my pocket to see that Grace has texted me.

It's fine, I hope she's okay.
Do what you need to do.

I exhale in relief, thank fuck for that.

I lift my glass to my lips, my hand shaking like a leaf. I honestly don't know if I've ever been so stressed. I go to the medicine cabinet and rattle through the meds, finally I find some Xanax and pop two and wash them down with more scotch.

I breathe deep and pace back and forth as I try to will my nervous system to calm down.

Slowly and surely, I feel the Xanax take hold, my heartbeat slows and the shaking begins to subside.

I lie on the couch and stare at the wall. My penthouse is quiet and as the shadows of daylight leave, I'm left alone in the dark with my conscience.

It's lonely here.

"And this here." I point to the whiteboard. "Is..." I click my fingers as I try to remember. "Fuck, what is it, his name has escaped me."

"John?" Alessio cuts in.

"Yeah." I clench my jaw, fuck... "John will be looking after the . . ."

"Program?" Alessio cuts me off.

The board members glance at each other and I want to sink through the floor.

"Can we break for five minutes?" Alessio interrupts me. "I need to take a very important call."

"Of course, meet back here in fifteen," I tell everyone. I march out of the boardroom and into my office. I wash my face in my bathroom and feel someone standing beside me. I glance up to see Alessio leaning on the doorjamb.

"You all right, man?"

"Yep." I dry my face and walk past him back into my office.

"The story about Ariana today in the newspaper has rattled you?"

"You mean the picture of me and her getting off my jet, holding hands, with the headline 'Ferrara and Ariana reunite on romantic getaway'?"

He winces. "Pretty much."

"I just need to get through this meeting before I can even think about that dumpster fire."

"Have you spoken to Grace?"

"No, I zonked myself out last night and fell asleep. I'll call her tonight."

"Go home," he says. "You're not on your game, and you're doing more harm than good in there."

Fuck.

"I'm going to tell them you have a migraine and take over the meeting."

My eyes search his. "I won't go home, but if you could take over the meeting, I'd be grateful. I'm sorry."

"Don't be." He pulls me into a hug. "That's why you have a brother, to catch you when you fall."

"Thanks." I hug him a little longer than normal.

"You okay?" He frowns.

I nod. "Yep, tough week."

At five pm, I walk out of the Ferrara building to a crowd of photographers.

"Mr. Ferrara, is the wedding back on?" Security pushes me through the crowd.

"Ariana and you make a beautiful couple. Can you tell us about your romantic getaway?" someone else calls. I'm bundled into the back of the car and we pull out into the traffic, we whiz through the streets of New York and I glance at my phone to see five missed calls from Elias, Grace's security guard.

I frown and dial his number. "Hello, Mr. Ferrara," he says nervously.

"What?"

"Just letting you know that Grace had lunch again with Jack Spalding today."

Adrenaline surges through my system and my eyes flicker red. "Is that so."

Grace

I sip my tea as I hold the remote up to the television to turn the channel. I probably should go to bed, it's after 10 p.m., but I'm not in the least bit tired.

I hear the front step go and then a soft knock on the door. Who in the world?

I open the door in a rush to see Gabriel, he's in a navy suit and his dark cold eyes hold mine. Animosity drips from his every cell, and a frisson of fear runs through me. "Gabriel?"

"Where the *fuck* did you go today?" he growls.

23

Grace

BEFORE I CAN EVEN process what he just said he brushes past me into the house and begins to pace. He's beyond furious.

"What?" I frown.

"You heard me, don't act fucking stupid," he fumes. "Where did you have lunch today?" he sneers.

Oh shit, my lunch with Jack, I completely forgot all about that.

Right...I open my mouth to reply but he cuts me off.

"I've blown my entire fucking life to smithereens...to be with you...and here you are, going on lunch dates with another man," he growls. "What happened after lunch is what I want to know." He begins to pace with his hands on his hips, his fury palpable.

"I'm having the worst week of my entire life, and I have to worry about Ariana and work and the children, and now, to top it all off, I've had to rush all the way here to rein in my out-of-control girlfriend."

I begin to hear my angry heartbeat in my ears and I put my weight onto my back foot. "First, I'm not your girlfriend. Don't ever call me that again."

"Oh yes you fucking are." The veins in his forehead are sticking out so far, I can almost see his pulse.

"Since when?" I put my hands on my hips in disgust.

"Since Saturday night."

"What? There was no being-exclusive conversation." I screw up my face. "We had sex, Gabriel, that's it."

"That's it?" he explodes. "*That is not fucking it?*"

"Calm down."

"I will not *fucking* calm down," he yells.

"You're going to wake up the children," I whisper angrily.

"Good, go wake them up." He points upstairs like a madman. "Go tell them that I've thrown away my entire life to be with their mother, who just told me that she used me for sex. I'm sure they would love to hear all about it."

He's beginning to really piss me off now.

"I never asked you to leave anything, in fact." I throw my hands up. "Go back to your entire life, Gabriel." I walk out into the kitchen and he's hot on my heels. "Marry your everything and leave me the hell alone, I don't have time for your dramatics."

"You will not see him again. Do you understand me?"

"You can't tell me what to do."

"Watch me!" he explodes. "You will do what I say."

"I'm never going to do what you say," I spit.

"You can and you *will*."

"Listen... You can't come back here being all holier than God and assume that I'm the devil. Seriously, Gabriel..." I puff air into my cheeks, this is a no-win situation. "I'm not Ariana," I snap. "I'm not what you want and nor would I ever want to be."

"You are what I want."

"I know you still love her."

"Not in the way I'm supposed to," he fires back. "I love *you*."

What?

We stare at each other. His chest rises and falls as he struggles for air.

"I love you, Grace," he whispers. "I've always loved you."

310

Oh no...

My eyes well with tears because damn it, life is cruel. For so many years all I wanted was to hear those words, and yet, now that I do, I feel nothing.

"I'm sorry."

"What does that mean?" He frowns.

"I never wanted you to throw your life away," I whisper, unexpected emotion overwhelms me and tears well in my eyes. "I never wanted you to feel a one-sided love. I wouldn't wish it on my worst enemy."

His face falls as his eyes search mine.

"Gabriel... You broke something between us, and I don't..." I screw up my face in tears. "I wish I did love you...it would be so wonderful for the kids to have their parents together."

He turns away from me as the tears break the dam and run down my face. I hate that I can't do this even for them.

"When you broke my heart, I thought I would never recover," I whisper.

I stare at his back; he can't even look at me.

"And then I did, but when I healed, I healed different. I'm not the same girl anymore, Gabriel, and I don't know how to get her back, it's like I'm dead inside."

His head drops.

"I'm sorry," I whisper. "Don't hate me..."

His head rises as if angered. "Touché."

I screw up my face in tears and he walks through the back door without looking back.

The door clicks shut with a sharp snap. "I'm sorry," I whisper to the empty room. "But you have no one to blame but yourself."

The alarm goes off seemingly two minutes after I finally fell asleep, and I turn it off with force. I lie for a moment and stare at the ceiling as I try to collect my bearings.

Did that actually happen last night, or did I dream the whole thing?

Ugh...I drag myself out of bed and walk into the bathroom to see the wild monster staring back at me.

The homewrecker.

I'm not proud of myself or my actions on Saturday night, I should never have slept with him when I knew he had hopes for us. But in my defense I had told him time and again that I didn't want anything with him going forward, he just didn't listen.

Saturday night was never planned, it just happened...when he accosted me in the bathroom in the middle of the night.

It wasn't exactly fucking romantic.

He knew exactly what he was doing, he used my physical attraction to him against me, made it impossible for me to stop. His fingers were already deep inside me before I could even think of a protest, by then my body had taken over from my brain. I will not take the blame for this.

No...this is on him.

I tie up my hair and turn on the shower. It's going to be a long day. I'm exhausted already.

I put the lunchboxes into the schoolbags. "Come on, guys, we have to leave," I call. "We're going to be late."

Lucia takes her schoolbag from the counter.

"Go and wait out the front, I'll be out in a second."

She walks out the front door. "Hi," she gasps excitedly. "Mom, Dad's here."

What?

I stick my head around the corner and can see him standing on the front porch.

Dominic comes bounding down the stairs and runs to the front door.

"Hello, my man," Gabriel says to him.

Dom gives him a lopsided smile. "Hi."

"I've come to take you to school today if that's okay. I hate that I didn't get to say goodbye to you both on the weekend."

Dominic bites his bottom lip to hide his smile, and his eyes flick to mine. "Is that okay, Mom?"

I walk out onto the front porch and am greeted with Gabriel Ferrara in all his masculine glory. Gray power suit with crisp white shirt, dark freshly washed hair, and a jaw so square that it could cut glass. His aftershave has been sent straight from Aphrodite herself.

"Hi," I say awkwardly.

He rolls his lips and nods. "I'd like to take the children to school."

"Of course."

"And I'll be picking them up and going back to my house for an early dinner. I'll have them home around seven thirty."

I open my mouth to protest.

"I return to New York tonight and won't see them again until Friday when I return."

The kids' eyes flick to meet mine. "Can we go, Mom?" Lucia begs.

Even Dom seems excited.

"Sure."

Dom runs inside to get his schoolbag and Lucia kisses me goodbye and then walks down to Gabriel's car to wait.

"Are you okay?" I ask him. "I know last night was awkward, but we really are better off as friends."

"Don't talk to me."

My face falls. "What, why?"

"Because I'm not interested in anything you have to say." He turns and walks down the steps to his car.

Dominic comes out with his little backpack on and kisses me goodbye. "Have a good day, sweetheart." I fake a smile.

I watch them get into the car and drive away, and just like that they're gone...with him. He's going to get nasty, I can just feel it.

This could be the beginning of the end.

Gabriel

We drive down the road and my eyes flick to watch Grace disappear in the rearview mirror. My heart is in my throat, I was hoping that after thinking on it all night she would have had a change of heart.

Obviously not.

Ouch...

"So." I fake a smile to the children. "Tell me where your school is."

"You go up here and turn that way," Dom says as he puts his little hand up.

"You mean right?"

He frowns.

"That's your right hand, so that direction is right."

"Oh yes." He nods.

"I'm left-handed," Lucia announces.

"You are?" I frown.

"Me too," Dominic replies.

"You take after me." I smile proudly. "*I'm* left-handed."

Their eyes both widen. "You are?"

"Whoa..." Lucia whispers in astonishment. "We're left-handed like our dad."

And just like that, my day is better.

We arrive at the school and I park the car.

"What are you doing?" Dominic asks.

"Well..." I pause, unsure what he's asking.

"Mom just drops us and drives away."

"Can I come in and see your classroom?" I ask. "I'd like to see it."

"Oh yes," Lucia gasps. "I'll show you all around the school. The library is the best part."

"Okay, great." I smile. I glance at my watch—I have a Zoom meeting at nine fifteen but they'll have to wait.

We get out of the car, Lucia takes my hand and we walk down

toward the school. The moms who are all standing around the front gate all turn to watch us as we approach, they are in gym clothes and have strollers with younger children.

It's a ponytail brigade, not one woman is made up or has makeup on.

Weird.

We walk past them and I give an awkward smile and nod. "Morning."

"Morning," a few reply.

"Who *is* that?" I hear them whisper.

Lucia turns back to them. "This is our dad," she calls, totally unfazed.

Their eyes widen, and I bite my lip to hide my smile.

"Did you see his shoes?" someone whispers.

We keep walking. "What's wrong with my shoes?" I whisper to Dom.

He looks down at them. "Nobody wears shoes like that."

"Then they should," I reply.

"Our classroom is just up here," Dominic tells me. We make our way up the stairs, and Lucia leads me inside by the hand. It's like I've stepped into an artwork wonderland. There are things hanging from hoops suspended from the ceiling, the walls are covered in art and drawings, and I look around in awe. "This is... spectacular." I smile.

"We put our bags in here," Lucia tells me, she shows me the bag stand with little shelves. "I'm the apple and Dominic is the giraffe." She points to the little tiles on top of each bag spot.

"I see." I watch on as they put their bags into their spot. "And where do you sit?"

"I sit over here." Lucia runs to her seat.

"And this is my seat." Dominic shows me his seat. "I have to sit next to Maryanne."

"Is she nice?" I ask.

"No, she tries to boss me around all day."

I chuckle and look to the back wall, there's a big heading above a heap of drawings.

Our weekend

"What's that?" I ask.

"Oh, on Mondays we draw pictures of our weekend and they hang on the wall for the week," Lucia tells me.

I walk to the back wall and my eyes scan the pictures, and then I see it and my heart stops.

The name *Dominic* in the top right corner, the picture is of a campfire and four people sitting around it. They're holding sticks with marshmallows on them. The teacher has written a comment across the bottom.

My dad came over and we played Uno and had a campfire.
It was the best

Emotion overwhelms me, and the picture blurs.

What is it with me lately, these kids have made me an emotional basket case.

"This is the best thing I have ever seen." I smile as I stare at it. "When it gets taken down from the wall, can I please have this? I'd like to hang it in my office so I can look at it every day."

Dominic smiles up at me, and I push the hair back from his forehead as I stare down at him.

This kid.

"And where is your picture, Lucia?" My eyes return to scan the wall, and I see the name *Lucia* in the bottom row. It's a picture of a girl with dark hair. Huh?

My dad's girlfriend came over and was angry.
She smashed our glasses

"Oh..." My eyes widen in horror.

"Do you want my picture for my office too?" She smiles hopefully.

Not so much.

"Ahh... Sure."

Dominic smirks up at me and I know that he knows.

Some things are not supposed to be on the damn classroom wall, Lucia.

Ugh... That's a conversation for another day.

"Well, I have to get going," I tell them. "I'll pick you up this afternoon?"

They both smile as if this is the best day in their life, and who am I kidding...it most definitely is mine.

They walk me out to the gate; Lucia proudly holds my hand as Dominic walks beside us. He's not touchy and affectionate like her, and as much as I want to hold his hand or hug him, I know that I can't overstep, I have to wait until he's ready. This isn't about me.

"See you this afternoon." I smile as I bend and hug Lucia, my eyes go to Dominic and he stands with his hands firmly in his pockets.

"Bye." He gives me a lopsided smile.

"Will I meet you at the gate this afternoon?" I ask.

They both nod.

"Okay then."

I watch them as they skip off into the distance and I smile broadly, they're officially the cutest kids of all time.

"Hello," a voice says from behind me. I turn to see a woman. "I don't think we've met before." She has long dark hair and is immaculately groomed, attractive, and different from the other women here.

More New York and less Country bumpkin.

"Hello." I put my hand out to shake hers. "I'm Gabriel."

"Hello, Gabriel, lovely to meet you. I'm Felicity Fox." She holds my hand in hers a beat longer than necessary. "I haven't seen you around before?"

"I live in New York. Well, I've just moved here and will be living between the two. I'm Dominic and Lucia's father."

"Really?" Her eyes widen as she stares up at me. "Are you back with Grace, or did you move with your wife or…"

"No, I live alone."

"Oh…" She pulls her hand through her long black ponytail as her eyes hold mine.

Don't even.

"Nice to meet you, Felicity." I cut the conversation short. "I have to get going."

"Bye." She smiles, all sexy like.

I turn to walk away.

"Oh Gabriel," she calls.

"Yes?"

"I didn't catch your surname?"

She wants to google me.

"Porter."

"Oh…" She thinks for a moment. "I…" She shakes her head as if confused.

"You what?"

"I thought that was Grace's family name."

"It is," I reply flatly,

"Oh, so you two were married?"

Go away, pest.

"I have to get going, nice to meet you. Goodbye." I purposely don't answer the question and turn and walk through the school gates as all mom eyes are on me, I feel them watch me all the way to the car.

Ha, country women are horndogs…figures, I guess, what else is there to do around here but fuck, and if Jack is anything to go by on what the local men are like…

Anyway…

I get in and pull out of the parking lot. Now…where do I get a decent cup of coffee in this godforsaken place?

. . .

I drive down to the main street and spot a coffee shop, people are sitting out the front at quaint little tables and chairs. "This will do."

I park the car and walk in, and once again everyone stops to watch me. Has nobody ever seen a suit before?

Seriously...what is this godforsaken place?

I walk past them and in through the front door of the café, a little bell dings over the door and I walk up to the counter. A young man is serving and he smiles an over-the-top smile. "Hello, how can I help you?"

"Hello, I'll have a kopi luwak please?"

"A...what?" He frowns.

"A kopi luwak?"

"I don't know what that is."

"Right." Ugh...I look at the board over the register and I don't know what any of this is. "Okay, give me a Jamaica Blue Mountain."

"A what, what?"

I exhale. What the fuck do they drink in this place? I need to buy a coffee machine as a matter of urgency.

"Okay just...give me whatever coffee you have." I sigh.

"Americano?"

"I guess."

"What was the name?"

"Gabriel."

He smiles. "That will be three dollars twenty, Gabriel."

Hell, at that price, it's probably dishwater. I pay him and go and stand to the side of the café as I wait.

The bell dings and two women walk in. "Hey, Thomas." They greet the cashier by name.

"Hi, Greer, hi, Sadie," he says. "The usual?"

"Yes, please." They take a seat by the window.

"Hey, Thomas," a man calls from his table. "Your brother must be happy with his game last night, scored in the last five minutes."

Thomas smiles as he types in the order. "Loving himself more than usual today."

They all chatter and talk between themselves and I look around at the people in this weird café. Do they honestly all know each other?

And why is everyone being so pathetically nice? It's like *The Twilight Zone*.

"Mr. Gabriel," Thomas calls.

I walk to the counter and he passes me my coffee. "Have a great day, sir."

"Thanks." I take the coffee and walk out and back to my car; I take a sip and twist my lips.

Rough...but palatable, I guess.

This place is weird.

9:10 a.m.

I log onto my computer and click on the Zoom meeting link. I sit and wait for the others in the meeting to join.

I look around the office I'm sitting in, so unlike my taste, with the worst furnishings of all time. I'm going to have to bring some creature comforts from home, I can't live here for half of the time without the things I need.

I begin to make a list in my diary.

Coffee machine.

Office furniture.

Bed.

Linen.

I glance down at my suit. *More casual clothes.*

Gym, I need a gym here. I haven't trained for a week now. I feel like shit.

My mind flicks to Gracie. *I never wanted you to feel a one-sided love.*

My heart sinks, there's a lot of reasons I feel like shit.

The other faces begin to pop up on my screen, and I take a deep breath.

My new normal starts now.

. . .

School pickup is hectic, by the time they came out, it's taken us half an hour to get home. I had to finish work early, but this week was somewhat of an emergency.

"And what else happened today?" I ask as the kids and I walk into the house.

"Barbara fell off the monkey bars at lunch and hurt her arm."

"Is she okay?" I ask.

Dom shrugs. "She's probably acting."

"She wasn't acting, Dominic," Lucia says, outraged. "You don't even know her."

"I don't want to."

I smirk as I listen to them squabble, such a simple conversation but somehow I find it fascinating.

Every day I peel back a little more of their different personalities and learn something more. We walk into the kitchen and the children both stop on the spot.

"This is Mark," I introduce them.

Mark is at the oven and he's cooking something on the cook top. "Hello." He smiles, he's wearing an apron and looks every bit the part of a chef.

"These are my children, Lucia and Dominic." I smile proudly.

"Wow." He smiles as he flicks a tea towel over his shoulder. "You guys sure look like your dad."

"Mark is my friend from New York," I tell them. "He comes wherever I go. He lives in the house out by the pool when we're here."

"Oh." Lucia nods.

Dominic stares at him with the same blank look he used to give me.

"I've made you some brownies," Mark says. "Hope you're hungry." He presents a tray of brownies and they both take one.

"Thank you," Dominic mumbles.

"I had to work today, so Mark has been helping cook us

321

dinner." I smile as I watch them down the brownies. I really need to learn how to cook; it kills me that I can't cook for them myself.

"Do you guys like hamburgers?" Mark asks.

They both nod.

"Mark makes the best hamburgers in all of New York," I reply.

Lucia's eyes widen. "You do?"

"Just you wait until you taste them." He wiggles his eyebrows and they both smile.

"Let's go upstairs, I've got something to show you. Bring your brownies."

They follow me upstairs and down the hall, and I take them to the bedroom next to mine. "What do you think?" I present the bedroom; it's pale blue and has a fireplace and an ornate ceiling. It has two single beds with ottomans at the end of each, one has a pale blue quilt and the other has a pale pink quilt. Each bed has a stuffed animal sitting up on the pillow. There's a rocking chair in the corner and a toybox, no toys in it yet though.

"I had some new beds delivered for you guys."

They both look around the bedroom.

"I thought..." I hesitate. "I thought you might want to stay over one time and I know you like to be together, so..."

"Can we stay over tonight?" Lucia asks excitedly.

"Not tonight, but maybe...if Dom wants to...maybe Saturday night?"

Dom looks around the room as if assessing every detail.

"I could sleep on the floor in here if... I mean, if you wanted to have a campout," I offer hopefully.

Dom gives me a half-hearted smile and nods. "Okay."

"Okay?" Excitement runs through me.

Lucia goes to the box in the corner that the stuffed animals came in and reads the address written on it.

"What's Ferr...ar...?"

"Ferrara. That's my surname."

They both stare at me blankly.

"Look." I scroll through my phone, bring up a photo of my office, and show them the sign written across the building.

FERRARA

"See, that's my surname. This is my work."

"Oh."

"Woooah, that looks cool," Lucia says.

"Do you like it, Dominic?"

He studies the picture and nods.

"My dad has the name Ferrara, and his dad has the name Ferrara. Way back in history, my family all had the name Ferrara."

I stare at them for a moment and I was going to have this conversation much later, but I feel like the universe has given me an opening.

"Would you like to add Ferrara to your name?" I ask. "Because you know, you're my kids, and kids have their dad's name on the end."

Lucia smiles broadly.

"What would it be?" Dominic asks.

"It would be Dominic Porter Ferrara. That way you would have Mom's name *and* my name." I smile softly as I look between them. "Wouldn't it be wonderful if we had the same name?"

Grace

I sit in the clean house and watch the clock.

It's been a weird day, no school dropoff, no school pickup, no dinner to cook, no kids to watch.

Just me...and all this horrible spare time.

I've been for a walk, vented for an hour to Deb on the phone, folded all the washing and cleaned the house, not sure what to do next.

I see the headlights shine up the driveway. *They're home.*

I jump up and open the door in a rush and walk down to meet them. Gabriel gets out first and I smile. "Hello."

He looks right through me and doesn't respond before opening the back door of the car.

Great.

"Here we go. Home time." He smiles to the children.

The kids bound out of the car and he bends and hugs Lucia. "I'll see you Friday," he tells her, he turns to Dom and messes up his hair. "I'll see you Friday, buddy."

Dominic smiles up at him all starstruck.

Gabriel turns back to the car.

He's completely ignoring me...*of course he is.*

"Goodbye," I say hopefully, surely we can at least be civil.

He waves without looking and gets into the car and pulls out. The kids bounce happily inside, and I watch the car as it pulls away.

Ugh... I follow the kids inside.

"Mom, we had the best time." Lucia beams.

"Upstairs and into the shower, it's pretty late," I say. We walk up the stairs with her talking a million miles per minute.

"We had brownies and then we played baseball and then we played catch."

"I helped light the fire," Dominic chimes in. "And we got new beds and are staying over on the weekend," he says as he begins to undress.

"That sounds..." I smile sadly, I hate that they're making plans that don't involve me, "...great."

"Oh, and we have stuffed toys," Dom says.

"And we had hamburgers for dinner and fries, Mark made them he's a good cook and he's very funny," Lucia tells me as she brushes her hair.

"Oh...and we're changing our name to Ferrara," Dominic says casually.

"What?" I frown.

"We're changing our name to be the same as our dad's." Lucia smiles as she steps into the shower. "Isn't it great?"

I see red.

"Back in a moment." I storm down the stairs like a woman possessed.

Oh no he didn't...

I dial his number and he answers first ring. "What the hell do you think you're doing?" I spit.

"Whatever the *fuck* I like."

24

Grace

THE PHONE CLICKS as he hangs up on me. My blood boils. "You did not just hang up on me." I dial his number immediately. *Ring ring... ring ring...*

> *You've reached Gabriel Ferrara.*
> *Leave a message.*

"Ahh." I hang up in a rush, the asshole has declined the call. I try again.

> *You've reached Gabriel Ferrara.*
> *Leave a message*

"That's it!" I explode. "You've gone too far this time, asshole."

"Mom, am I washing my hair?" Lucia calls from upstairs.

I close my eyes and take a deep steadying breath; I have to be calm until they go to bed. "Yes, I'm coming," I call sweetly. I trudge upstairs. I'm so sick of this egomaniac thinking he can just do whatever he wants with the kids without even consulting me.

Change their name. Ha...he's kidding himself. That is not how this works.

I sit on the toilet as the kids shower and bathe while I go over my choices.

There are none.

Tomorrow, I have to go and see a lawyer. This stops now.

I run into my office at 9:05, running late as usual.

Another sleepless night followed by a chaotic morning. My phone rings and I glance down at the number.

School

Oh no, what's happened?

"Hello," I answer.

"Hello, Grace, this is Shelby from the school reception."

"Hi, Shelby, is everything all right?"

"Yes, yes, no emergency or anything. I'm just letting you know that we have had a request from the children's father, a Mr. Gabriel Ferrara, to be included in all school correspondence from now on."

Thump, thump, thump goes my heartbeat in my ears.

"Did you, now?"

"That's fine, isn't it? It's protocol to check with you that this is okay."

I close my eyes and I really want to scream no, but I know I have to pick my battles; this isn't one of them. "That's fine, Shelby."

"Okay, have a nice day."

"You too."

She hangs up, and I stare at the wall for a moment; in fact, I stare at the wall all day.

I have this deep sense of dread that everything's changing and there's not a thing I can do about it.

Why did I sleep with him, what the hell was I thinking?

327

I sit in my car as I dial the number. I had to wait for my lunch break to call Gabriel, and now, because I don't want my nosy colleagues to hear what I have to say, I'm hiding in my car.

Ring ring...ring ring...

"Yes," he answers.

Instantly, my hackles rise, why does he think it's okay to answer the phone like that?

"I believe you are meant to answer the phone with hello."

"What is it, Grace? I'm very busy."

I feel my temperature rise. Honestly, I've never meant someone so infuriating.

"I need to talk to you."

"About?"

"Don't act cute, Gabriel. You know damn well what I'm calling about."

He exhales in an overdramatic fashion. "Oh, let's see, Grace...it could be a plethora of reasons why you called me. What I served the children for dinner, the joke I told them over the table, the fact that I want them to have my name as well as yours, or perhaps it's the school...or maybe you just want to use my dick again to get off."

My blood boils.

"Don't be vulgar," I whisper angrily.

"If the shoe fits."

"Can we just be civil?"

"That doesn't work for me."

Silence...

"I don't have time to sit here and listen to you breathe down the phone, Grace. What. Do. You. Want."

"The kids said you want them to change their name to Ferrara."

"Nope."

"You didn't say that?" I ask hopefully.

"I said I would like to add my name to the end of Porter."

"Oh..." I frown, that isn't what they told me.

"Is that it?"

"Well...can we talk about this?"

"We just did. Goodbye." The phone clicks as he hangs up on me.

I wait in my car in the line outside the school, at least I'm early enough today to even make the line. Some days I have to park ages away and am forced to walk in.

I feel like my head is literally about to explode, he's right, there is a plethora of things, the name thing, the school calling, and then him hanging up on me.

I can't wait to get home and have a glass of wine; I may even have chip and dip.

All bets are off even if it's a school night, and the rules are... there are no rules.

Survival today is key.

The school bell has rung, and I can see Dom standing at the gate, waiting for his sister, he's such a good boy.

I'd go stand with him except Felicity Fox and her coven of witches are there standing around, chatting, and judging everyone like they own the school...ugh.

Felicity is in tight blue jeans and a cute pink cashmere sweater; her long dark hair is in a high ponytail and her perky boobs are high in the air.

What kind of bra does she wear, anyway?

Eventually, Lucia comes into view, and she and Dom make their way down to the car, and get into the backseat. "Hi, guys." I smile.

"Hi, Mom."

"How was your day?" I pull out into the traffic.

"Good," they reply.

"Arnold pooed his pants. He had a stomach bug."

"Oh." I wince. "Poor Arnold. Is he okay?"

"That kid's got real problems," Dominic says as he looks out the window.

"Mom, you wouldn't believe what happened to my lunch today," Lucia says.

My eyes flick up to hers in the mirror. "What?"

"My egg sandwich exploded in my lunch box."

"Oh."

"And her bag smelled like fart gas." Dominic sighs. "Was disgusting. What's a dilf?"

"A what?" I frown.

"A dilf."

My eyes widen in horror. "Where did you hear that word?"

"When I was standing at the gate, I heard Zoe's mom tell her friends that our dad is a real dilf."

"Zoe who?"

"Zoe Fox."

Felicity Fox...AHHHHHHH.

I grip the steering wheel so tight that it's a wonder it doesn't disintegrate in my bare hands.

"What is it?" he asks again.

"It's a..." I search for the right lie. "It's a zoo animal."

"A what?"

"Because he's big, she must think he looks like an ape." I fake a smile. "It's a funny joke, isn't it? Ha-ha."

Dom curls his top lip, unimpressed. "He doesn't look like an ape at all."

That fucking wench, if she thinks for one minute that she is going to get her claws into him, she can think again. As if my life isn't hard enough at the moment, I don't need perky-boobed Barbie to complicate things further.

"Mom!" Lucia yells, interrupting my murder plans. "Are you listening to me at all?"

No, actually, I'm not, Lucia.

"Of course I am." I grit my teeth.

"My big toe ripped out of my sock today," she continues. "It was poking out and rubbing on my shoe all day."

I pinch the bridge of my nose. I need a drink, and I need it now.

"And now we have to clean my bag because it smells like egg," she raves on.

Fuck my life...

"I can hardly wait."

We arrive at home and I park the car, we amble inside and I go straight to the fridge and get a bottle of wine. I open it and as I look for a glass, I take a swig out of the bottle.

I'm beginning to understand how people become alcoholics.

A knock sounds at the door and I hear it open. "Hello, I'm looking for Dominic and Lucia Porter?" a man's voice asks.

"That's me," Dom replies.

Who is that?

I come flying around the corner from the kitchen to see a delivery man. "I have two packages. One for Dominic and one for Lucia," he says.

"Who is it from?" I ask.

"Gabriel Ferrara, their father."

I stare at the delivery man flatly, this is no normal delivery driver, how does he know who their father is? Has he flown all the way here to hand deliver these packages?

The kids' eyes widen, and Lucia begins to bounce on the spot.

Ugh... Don't even.

"I have special instructions that both Grace and the children have to sign for each package."

I walk over and sign for Dominic's and he does too, and his package is handed over to him, then I do the same for Lucia. "Thank you." I close the door in the delivery man's face.

They both take their packages and run to grab the scissors.

I walk back to the kitchen with my heart in my throat, what's he bought them...a pencil case, a pony, an island...fuck, it literally could be anything.

I sit on the couch with my bottle of wine as they take forever to unwrap their presents.

Hurry up already.

Dom gets his open first and he gasps with wide eyes.

"What is it?" I snap.

He holds it up proudly. "It's a phone." A blue iPhone with a postcard handwritten by Gabriel.

"What?" I snatch the card from him.

> *My dearest Dominic*
>
> *I've bought you a phone so that you can call me whenever you want to.*
>
> *It's for calls only and doesn't have internet and has been locked for Wi-Fi (you are too young just yet).*
>
> *Please keep it in the kitchen where Mom can see it at all times.*
>
> *My phone number is programmed in, you just have to press the name Dad and it will connect straight through to me.*
>
> *All my love,*
> *Dad, xx*

Dominic swipes it open and a picture of him and Gabriel posing together lights up the screen. "Wooow." Dominic's eyes are nearly popping from their sockets. "This is sick."

"Oh my god," Lucia yells as she finally gets hers unwrapped. "Mine is pink."

Oh, this just keeps getting better and better. I go and fill my wineglass back up.

This is the day from hell.

It begins to ring in Dominic's hand, and their eyes widen. "What do I do?"

"Who is it?" I play along.

He holds the phone up and a picture of Gabriel comes up, he's in his suit sitting at his desk in New York, smiling and looking all charismatic and punchable.

"Swipe across to answer it."

"Hello," he answers excitedly and then listens for a bit. "Uh-huh." He's smiling goofily. "Uh-huh. It just arrived." His eyes flick up to me. "She's drinking wine out the bottle."

"No," I mouth as I shake my hand around. "Don't say that."

"It was good." He smiles. "Nothing much."

I listen intently.

"Oh, Zoe's mom said you're an ape."

My eyes widen in horror and I begin to shake my hand around again. "No, no."

He stops talking. "What, Mom? Why can't I tell him that?"

For fuck's sake, Dominic.

"Tell him you'll call him back later," I say.

"I'll call you back later, Dad." He smiles, he's so excited that even my frozen heart feels it. He hangs up and Lucia's phone immediately rings.

"He's calling me now," Lucia gasps as if this is a total surprise.

"Answer it," Dom instructs her. He snatches the phone from her and swipes it before handing it back.

"Hi, Dad." Lucia beams.

"Uh-huh." She takes the phone and walks out the back and down to the lake, she paces as she talks to him with a huge smile it's obvious that she wants him and their conversation all to herself.

I watch her through the window, she's probably down there telling him every sordid DILF detail.

This is just great, I'm on the outside in my own house.

Gabriel

I pull into the school parking lot just at three. I made it in time; the bell hasn't gone yet.

I get out of the car and stride up to the gate, I want to be there when they come out. I left work early. I really wanted to pick them up today. Don't ask me why this felt so important, it just did.

I arrive to the gate to see a group of women standing around.

Ugh...

I glance around for Grace. I purposely didn't tell her I was coming in, hoping I would see her too.

Where is she?

"Gabriel," I hear a voice call me from behind, and I turn. It's that woman, the hot annoying one...what *was* her name? "Hello." I smile.

She looks me up and down as if I'm her next meal. "Wow, what a beautiful suit. Is it cashmere?" She runs her hand up my arm, and from the corner of my eye I see Grace's ponytail swing as she swiftly walks past us.

Fuck it.

"Who knows," I snap as I watch the back of Grace disappear into the school. "Great to see you..." I frown as I try to remember her name.

"Felicity." She smiles. "Are you here for the weekend?"

I look in the direction of Grace. "Yes."

"Let's have a coffee tomorrow?"

"Sorry, I can't. Very busy." I look between the women she's standing with but never introduced me to and I nod. "Goodbye."

"Bye," they all call.

I stride after Grace to the kids' classroom; I find her standing to the side. With her arms crossed, she glares at me and snaps her eyes away.

Great, I'm ignoring you first...you can't ignore me. I go and stand beside her. "I didn't see you walk in."

"You were too busy flirting." She raises an unimpressed eyebrow.

She's jealous.

I bite the inside of my cheek to stop myself from smiling.

"Yes, well...my cock is an amusement park, what can I say?"

Her eyes flick to me and she's about to blow.

"Country towns need a new bike to ride every now and then," I reply as I stare ahead. I adjust my cuff links. "You know... For amusement."

Her eyes flicker with fury.

She leans closer so that only I can hear. "So help me god," she whispers angrily. "If you sleep with anyone in this fucking town, I'm going to cut off your dick and stick it up your entitled ass."

"You had your chance, Grace." My eyes hold hers. "And I'm not cold-blooded."

"Is that a threat?"

I remain silent.

"So because I don't want you...you're going to sleep with everyone in town to teach me a lesson, is that it?"

I don't want you.

Hearing those words triggers something in my brain, and I lose all control of my actions. I lean in close. "I'll fuck whoever I want." I watch my words cut her like a knife. "And instead of you sticking my cock up my ass...I'm going to stick it up theirs."

Her eyes hold mine.

"And they'll moan on every *fucking* inch of it."

25

Gabriel

SHE SWALLOWS a lump in her throat, and instead of hitting a return serve like I'm expecting, she storms off toward the parking lot.

I watch her disappear and feel regret in the pit of my stomach. I begin to perspire and the school bell goes. The kids come out of the classroom as I stand patiently to the side.

"Dad," Lucia yells excitedly. She runs and practically jumps into my arms.

Dominic sees me and breaks into a broad smile. He rushes over, and I can tell that he wants to hug me, but he hesitates. Instead, he looks me up and down. "Why are you wearing that?"

"What?" I glance down at myself. "My suit?"

He nods.

"You don't like it?"

He shrugs, not wanting to answer.

This is a twenty-two-thousand-dollar suit, have you got taste in your ass, kid...what the hell's wrong with it? "Let's walk out to the car." I direct them toward the gate.

"Are we coming to your house today?" Lucia asks.

"Tomorrow is our sleepover." I glance up and can see Grace sitting in her car. "Let's go and see Mom."

Lucia holds my hand, and we walk through the parking lot to Grace's car. "Mom, Dad's here," Lucia tells her excitedly.

I lean down to look into the car, and she's wearing sunglasses and staring straight ahead.

"Are you coming over to our house?" Dominic asks me.

"No, I have to work for a few more hours. Tomorrow is our sleepover." I lean down to talk to Grace through the window. "That's still okay, isn't it, Grace?"

She nods but doesn't reply. *Has she been crying?*

"So we won't see you tonight?" Lucia says, disappointed.

"I'll see you tomorrow, guys, keep Mom company tonight." I open the car door and the kids climb in. "Bye." I wave.

Grace drives off without even looking at me. I march over and get into the passenger seat of my car. Mark is behind the wheel.

"Did you see her?" he asks.

"Yep." I pull my seat belt on, disgusted with myself. "I told her I was going to fuck all the women in town...up the ass."

"Nice..." Mark purses his lips. "How did that go down?"

I pinch the bridge of my nose. "Not great."

Grace

I lie on the couch like a zombie, the carbohydrate coma is in full swing, and I have no fucks to give about anything anymore.

Every nightmare of mine has come true.

He's done it, done exactly what I thought he was going to do.

Weaseled his way into the kids' lives and is now going to make living here in my little sleepy town a literal hell by sleeping with every female on heat.

I'm so done with him that I can't even be upset, at this point I'm just numb.

The kids are playing video games and lying all over the floor.

We had pizza for dinner. Well, I had pizza *and* pasta, but who's counting calories on a day like today.

Deb's name lights up the screen of my phone. "Hi," I answer.

"Just checking in on you."

"I'm fine." I sigh, not a drill, I really am fine. I've cried all the tears I have over this man; I will never shed another one.

Fuck him.

"While the kids are having their sleepover, do you want to go out tomorrow night?"

"Where to?"

"We could go to that new cocktail place and, you know, have a bender."

"I do need a bender."

"Okay, it's on."

"Benderville tomorrow night." I smile.

"I'll pick you up at seven, dinner first. Wear heels, we're dressing up."

"I love you." I smile gratefully. "What would I do without you, Deb?"

"Hmm...probably live in a much more exotic place than you do."

"Facts." I smile.

I hang up feeling better. A night with my bestie is just what the doctor ordered.

I sit and stare at the field. I haven't watched a second of the game, but damn it, I will not take my eyes off it.

I don't know what the hell this fool is playing at, but he's really winding me up.

It's one thing to piss me off so badly that I imagine his grisly death, but to come and sit on the other side of Lucia, who is next to me for the entire game today...is unforgiveable.

He has his arm over the back of her chair and every now and then it grazes my arm.

Each time, I pull away as if I've been burned. They're chatting and laughing and I'm listening to him schmooze her in.

No wonder the kids are in awe of him, he's going all out to impress them.

"Would you like a hot dog?" he asks Lucia.

"Yes, please."

"And a drink?"

"Coke please."

"Are you allowed to have soda?"

"Yes."

His eyes flick over to me for confirmation, and I stare at the field as I continue to ignore him.

"Mom, I can have Coke on special occasions, can't I?" Lucia asks.

"Yes," I reply without looking at them.

"Would you like a hot dog, Grace?" he asks.

"No, thanks."

"What would you like?" he asks.

I would like to scratch your eyes out.

"Nothing from you." I clench my jaw, damn it, I hate having to be civil in front of Lucia. I want to scream and kick and tantrum, burn him at the stake and throw him to the wolves.

"Ha, Mom's grumpy today, isn't she, Lucia?"

Lucia laughs on cue. "Sure is."

I wonder why.

I bite the inside of my cheek to stop myself from spitting venom all over him.

He wanders down the stairs of the grandstand and without turning my head, I watch him beneath my sunglasses.

Fuckface, thinks he's so irresistible to all female kind.

I hate that he is.

And how dare he be so good-looking, why isn't he getting uglier with age like the rest of humanity?

He stands in line at the snack bar, and sure enough, Felicity

Fox goes to stand in the line behind him; she's been waiting for this opening all day, no doubt.

She begins to chat and he talks back but keeps facing forward, every now and then I see him glance up to see if I'm watching.

I turn my head away from them in an exaggerated way. I'm still spying, of course...tearing my retinas with all the side eye, I'm sure.

Ten minutes later, he returns with a box of food. He passes Lucia her hot dog and drink and then holds out a hot dog and drink out for me. "Here you are, Gracie."

Gracie.

"I said I didn't want anything."

"Sometimes I'm forced to serve you things that you think you don't want but obviously need. It's for the better good of the outcome."

He's talking about his little outburst yesterday.

My eyes meet his, and he gives me a slow sexy smile before raising an eyebrow. He holds the hot dog up.

I can feel Lucia's eyes watching me, so I snatch the hot dog and Coke from him.

"You didn't say thank you." He smirks.

"So help me," I mutter under my breath.

"Mom," Lucia says. "Say thank you."

"Thank you," I say through gritted teeth.

He gives me a broad smile and taps his hot dog against mine before taking a huge bite, totally unfazed. "Hmm, so good."

Fucker.

Gabriel

I listen to the children chat about their day and I smile up at the ceiling in the dark.

Their first sleepover at my house.

It's been the best night, we had a campfire and cooked on the grill. We played Uno, they showered and we had ice cream, and now it's bedtime.

Who knew such innocent fun would be the best time of my life?

They're in their single beds and I am on the floor of their room on couch cushions laid out in a makeshift bed. I told them that I had to stay in here so that they didn't get scared...but really it's for me. I just want to be closer, it's as if now that my heart has been opened to theirs, I can't bear to be away from them; not even the next room will do.

I've missed out on so much time with them that every second counts.

"What was Mom doing tonight?" I ask casually.

"She went to Benderville," Dominic replies.

I frown. "Where's that?"

"I don't know."

"Who did she go with?"

"Debbie."

Benderville... Benderville... Oh, she's gone on a bender with Deb.

My stomach twists. I hate the thought of her out on the town while she's angry with me.

The kids fall silent as they drift off to sleep, but my mind has gone into overdrive.

I've fucked it, I've fucked everything about it.

I get up and sneak out of the bedroom and go downstairs and get a glass of water.

Don't call her.

Don't call her.

Don't call her.

Too late. I find myself dialing her number.

Ring ring...ring ring...ring ring...

You've called Grace, leave me a message.

I frown, not what I wanted.

"This voice mail is full," her phone tells me.

341

Beeeeep.

Shit.

Dejected, I hang up and call Mark.

"Hey," he answers.

"Where is Grace?"

"Let me find out. I'll call you back."

With my behind resting on the counter, I wait in the kitchen, the room lit only by the overhead fan light. My phone rings almost immediately.

"Yes."

"She's in a cocktail bar called Mimosas. She's with her friend Debbie."

"Who's on tonight?" I reply.

"Tommy and Pearce."

I think for a moment. "Has she seen them before?"

"Not that I know of."

"Send them in."

"Do..." He hesitates. "Do you think that's a good idea?"

"Don't question me. Just fucking do it. I want to know every detail of her night."

"Okay."

"They're to stay out of sight...unless."

"Unless what?"

"Unless she's talking to another man."

"Then what?"

"Then they move in and await my instruction."

"Okay."

I hang up and glare at the wall.

If she's talking to someone else tonight, *it's fucking on.*

3 a.m., I sit on the couch, my feet up on the ottoman, a scotch in my hand.

Anger in my soul.

I'm playing nice and letting her have her night out, I'm not

342

moving in even though Grace has been approached by five men tonight.

Five.

Luckily for her, she's waved them away...lucky for them too.

My phone vibrates in my hand. "Yes," I snap as my heart races.

"Grace has just arrived home in a taxi; she's safely inside."

"Alone?"

"Yes, sir."

I close my eyes in relief.

"Good." I hang up and inhale sharply.

This woman's got me crazy.

I pull into the driveway just on 4 p.m.

The kids are happily chattering on in the backseat, but my mood is somber.

I feel like I'm dropping my heart off at the bus stop and I won't be able to pick it up again until Thursday when I come back.

The more time I spend with them, the harder it is to leave.

It's like I have this ache in my heart for all the time I've lost. When I first found out about the children, the time that had passed seemed irrelevant.

They were six, it was what it was.

But now I know how much joy spending twenty-four hours with them brings me.

Six years is insurmountable.

I turn the car off and drag myself from the car, the kids slowly get out and I hear the front door open. I glance up to see Grace standing on the front veranda.

Are you tired...because I fucking am.

"See you on Friday." I force a smile.

I bend on one knee and Lucia hugs me tight. "Goodbye, baby," I whisper as I hold her longer than I should.

She steps back, and my eyes search Dominic's. "Can I have a hug?"

He steps forward and gives me a rigid weird arm hug and immediately pulls out of it.

My heart sinks, and I force a smile.

"See you Friday."

"Okay." He puts his backpack on and turns to go inside. I glance up and Grace has gone.

She didn't even say goodbye.

I wait for them to walk inside with my heart in my throat.

Don't go.

I open my emails and exhale heavily. The days go slow in New York, the nights go slower.

I've got a sore heart and a thumping dick.

The highlight of my day is at 8 p.m. when I call the kids to say good night.

Alessio pops his head around the corner. "We getting lunch?"

"Yeah." I close down my computer. "I need to grab a few things while we're out."

"Like what?"

"Clothes."

"You never shop in stores." He frowns. "Where's your stylist?"

"Long story." I roll my eyes. "Let's go."

Half an hour later, we walk through the department store in the men's section.

Alessio looks around at the clothes. "Why are we here?"

"I need to buy some new clothes."

"From here?" He winces. "Why?"

"I need to get some clothes that are less designer and more..." I twist my lips as I try to think of the right word. "Lumberjack."

"What?" He screws up his face in disgust.

"Dominic doesn't like my designer suits."

His eyes flick up in surprise. "Are you *sure* he's a Ferrara?"

"Don't you remember what it was like being six, you just want your dad to fit in and be like all the other dads."

"You have never fitted in," he mutters dryly. "Trust me, you don't fit in with the lumberjacks either."

I chuckle as I hold up a checked shirt and eye it suspiciously.

"That's fucking hideous, man."

"True." I put it back on the hanger and keep looking.

"So what is this town actually like?" he asks as we keep looking.

"It's..." I shrug. "I hate to say it, but it's kind of growing on me."

"Why?"

"Grace and the kids are there." I pull off another checked shirt and hold it out to look at it.

"Can I come this weekend to meet them?"

"No, not yet."

"You say that every week." He takes it off me and puts it back. "What's happening with Grace, anyway?"

"She hates me."

His eyes flick to meet mine. "I thought you were all in love."

"It's one-sided."

"Your side?" He frowns.

"Yep." I hold out another shirt. "Maybe I should get a belt with a big fuck-off cowboy buckle?"

"Maybe you shouldn't." He holds up a T-shirt, screws up his face and puts it back. "How's Ariana?"

"I called her yesterday to check on her."

"And?"

"And...I'm officially the worst human in the world. While I'm breaking her heart, someone else is breaking mine."

"Karma." He nods all knowingly.

I fake a smile and drop it immediately.

"So what do they wear in this town?"

"I don't know." I shrug. "Average dad stuff."

"Do you mean to tell me we're shopping to try and make you look like an average dad?"

345

"Yeah." I nod. "Exactly."

"Why would you want to do that?"

"All my kid's life he's been different because he didn't have a dad." I pick up a shirt and throw it over my arm. "I just want him to feel normal. With a normal dad who does normal things."

"Except...you're not normal, you will never be normal. You're one of the wealthiest men in the world."

"Yeah, well..." I pick up another shirt. "That means jack shit to him." I throw another shirt over my arm. "You want to come over to my place for dinner tonight?"

"Yeah, okay." He takes a shirt off me and puts it back. "This one is better." He passes me another shirt from the rack.

"So what's the plan, long term I mean?" he asks.

I think for a moment. "Convince Grace to love me."

7 p.m.

"Chop the onions into thin slices." I watch the woman intently and follow her directions. I carefully chop the onions.

"Now what?" I ask.

"You know you're speaking to an iPad, right?" Mark says from his stool at the kitchen counter.

"Shut up."

"Pour the olive oil into the pan and sauté the onions until they become fragrant."

"How the hell does an onion turn into fragrance?" I frown. "What the fuck is the fragrance, onion juice?"

Mark rolls his eyes and sips his beer. My door buzzes.

"Go let Alessio in, will you?"

Mark disappears to answer the door.

"While the onions are cooking, get the breadcrumbs ready." I watch what she does intently, how does she do so many things at the same time? Alessio arrives in the kitchen and frowns when he sees me in my apron. "What the hell are you doing?"

"Cooking."

346

"Why, where is your chef?"

"Night off. I'm learning to cook from YouTube," I reply.

"This is going too far now." Alessio rolls his eyes. "Who are you and what have you done with my brother?"

"I want to cook for my children."

"So ask Mom to teach you."

"I'm not talking to Mom."

Alessio drags his hand down his face. "I'll stay...but only if you call Mom tomorrow."

"Get out, then."

"Marinate the meat in a closed container," she instructs.

Alessio opens a beer and the boys start chatting while I go to grab a container. I look in one drawer, then another, then another. I can find the bottom...hmm.

The onions sizzle. "They're burning," Alessio calls.

"Shit." I grab the pan with my bare hand. "Ahhh, its hot!" I flick it away and it nearly all tips out.

"You are *so* bad at this."

"Shut up."

I keep searching. "I know why it's called Tupperware," I snap. "It's Tupper, where is the lid."

"So am I going home, or are you calling Mom tomorrow?"

"I'm not apologizing to her, she was in the wrong." The onions are smoking. "Stop distracting me, shit's burning over here."

"You just have to call her."

"I don't care if you don't stay. Fuck off home, then."

"And I don't care for food poisoning. Deal or no deal?"

"No deal," I snap. "Leave my mother to me and stay out of my business."

Alessio sips his beer. "If this tastes like shit, we're going out to eat."

I peer into the pan at the burned onions. "High possibility."

Grace

I take one last look in the mirror; my hair is out and curled, and I'm wearing a pretty cream dress. Brown high-heeled sandals and matching bag.

It's the school dance tonight and I've made an effort and dressed up to try to make myself feel better.

I don't know why I'm so flat at the moment, it's like every time Gabriel calls the children to speak to them on their phones, I die a little inside. Maybe I'm just a selfish cow who liked having the children all to myself.

Not maybe, probably... I'm kind of disgusted with myself, if I'm honest.

Ugh...stop thinking about him.

Who cares what he does?

Not me.

"You guys ready?" I call.

"I look so pretty, I can't stand it," Lucia calls.

I giggle, this girl's got spunk, I'll give it to her.

"Do I have to wear this dumb button-up shirt?" Dom calls from his room.

"Yes. It looks amazing."

"I hate these pants," he calls.

"You're wearing them," Lucia and I call back in unison.

"Come on, let's go."

The lightning crashes, the rain comes down as we pull into the school parking lot.

"Lucky we brought our umbrellas, Mom," Lucia says from the backseat.

"I know, I'm going to drop you guys off close to the door and then go and park the car, no use all of us running in the rain and risking getting wet."

I pull up under the awning that leads to the stairs, and the kids pile out. "See you in five minutes."

"Okay."

I drive over and around the corner and park the car, the rain really hammering down now. "Fuck's sake." I grab the umbrella and rush to get out of the weather. People are running and scrambling everywhere, why does it have to rain on tonight of all nights? I make my way up the stairs to get to the school hall and see the kids waiting by the door. The indoor basketball court has been transformed into a full winter wonderland.

Hand-painted trees in beautiful reds and golds hang from the ceiling, and fairy lights twinkle in the sky.

"Whoa." The kids' eyes light up when they see it. "This is so awesome."

My heart soars as I look around. It's so fun watching them experience everything for the first time, this is their first school disco.

"Shall we sit over here?" I point to the grandstand, and we make our way over and sit on the bottom row of seats. The music starts and the kids all begin to run to the dance floor. "Oh my god." Lucia's eyes are about to pop out of her head.

"Mom," Dominic screams. "Look, Dad's here."

Huh?

I glance over to see Gabriel walking through the crowd to us, he's wearing blue jeans and a navy checked shirt. He looks different tonight, casual and warm.

How did he even know about tonight...oh, the school newsletter.

His dark hair has a bit of length and a wave to it, and his big brown eyes come to meet mine, it's like he's walking toward me in slow motion and I feel his presence in the pit of my stomach. Tall, dark and overpowering.

I swallow the lump in my throat as the kids run to meet him.

Felicity Fox may be onto something here... The dilfiest DILF that ever did DILF.

He scoops Lucia up into his arms and picks her up. "What are you doing here?" Lucia laughs.

"Couldn't miss your first school dance." He laughs, he turns to Dominic and smiles down at him. "Hello, Son." He puts his hand on his shoulder and Dom smiles up at him.

Son.

Something about him calling him that makes me feel emotional.

Gabriel's eyes come to meet mine. "Gracie."

"Hi."

"You look beautiful." He smiles softly.

My stomach flutters.

You hate him...remember.

"Thanks."

He sits down beside me. Lucia dives onto his lap and Dominic sits beside him. "I missed you this week," his deep voice tells them.

"You did?" Lucia beams.

Dominic bites his bottom lip to hide his smile.

I smile too because, no matter how much of a dick Gabriel Ferrara is, he's turning into a pretty great dad.

His sleeves are rolled up to his elbows, and my eyes linger on his strong forearms. His veins are ropelike, and as he moves his hand, every muscle contracts.

It's like a hot wire to my hormones...*cut it out.*

Another song starts, and the kids' friends run over to get them. "Can we go?" Lucia asks.

"Yes. Go have fun." They run off, and Gabriel and I are left alone.

We watch them dance and twirl and laugh. Gabriel is in awe and doesn't take his eyes off them.

While all I can think about is the visceral reaction my body is having to his.

It's like there's this invisible electrical current running between us.

"How was your week?" he asks.

"It was okay."

His eyes search mine. "Apologies for..." he shrugs, "...being..."

"Yourself." I finish his sentence.

"I was going to say *asshole,* but *yourself* is the same thing, I guess."

I nod, unsure how to reply.

"When you told me you didn't want me..." he hesitates, "...I don't know what came over me...it...it made me nasty."

I don't want to get into a forgiveness conversation, I want to stay mad at him.

Mad is safe, mad keeps him away...so I choose to stay silent instead.

We sit for a while and watch the kids; it seems so weird having him sitting here beside me...watching his kids too.

Another couple sit beside him and he begins to chat with the dad, and I look over and the drink table needs help. "I'm going to go and help them," I whisper, trying not to interrupt his conversation.

"Sure, babe." His eyes flick to meet mine. He seems as surprised as I am by his comment and some kind of moment passes between us.

It feels...I don't even know.

Fuck.

I rush to the drink table and begin pouring drinks, it's busy and hectic but it gives me an excuse not to sit beside him.

I'm going to stay here all night.

The night is coming to an end, and the DJ comes onto the microphone. "Can I have all the parents on the dance floor, please. If you don't have a partner here, grab somebody."

I stay standing by the drink table. Someone may be thirsty, after all.

Parents begin to pile onto the dance floor and I watch on with my arms folded.

351

"Gracie," his deep voice purrs from behind me. "This is us. We're dancing."

"I'm good." I fake a smile. "Really." He takes my hand and drags me onto the dance floor.

Willie Nelson's "You Were Always on My Mind" begins to play.

Not this song...anything but this song.

Gabriel pulls me into his arms and holds me tight.

He stares down at me as we begin to sway to the music.

I awkwardly look anywhere but at him.

He smiles softly. "It's fitting."

"What is?"

"That this song is playing." He pulls me closer and an electrical current runs between us. "It's about us."

"Stop it."

"You *were* always on my mind, Grace," he whispers. "Never once were you far from my thoughts."

We stare at each other, an ocean of regret swimming between us.

"I need you to forgive me."

I stare up at him as we sway to the music.

"Tell me how to fix this?" he says softly. "Tell me and I'll do it."

"I wish I knew..."

His lips drop to my temple as he holds me tight, we sway to the music, both lost to our own thoughts.

You were always on my mind.

Oh, this song...so sad and so relevant.

My favorite singer singing one of my favorite songs and I'm dancing with someone I previously thought was the love of my life.

But that was before he broke me. Before I turned cold and heartless.

This is too much. I hate who he turned me into. Tears well in my eyes and as the song ends, I need to get away from him. "I'm going to go and freshen up."

"Grace."

I march out of the hall and out into the cold air, the rain has stopped now.

"Grace," I hear him call from behind me.

"Just leave it, Gabe." I want to get away, I don't trust myself to be with him right now. I go to go down to the quad, and as I tread onto the first step, my footing slips from underneath me.

I fall and hear the crack of my head hitting the concrete stairs on the way down. I roll and roll and tumble and fall down the entire flight of stairs.

Pain, blood...darkness...nothing.

26

Gabriel

BEEP...BEEP...BEEP...BEEP.

Grace's heartbeat monitor sounds softly through the darkened room, and I sit beside her with mine in my throat.

If they hooked me up to the machine, I'm not sure my heart would sound so steady.

She has a tube and pipes coming out of her and two black eyes, the lump on the front of her forehead so big and already purple.

Grace fell down twenty-two concrete steps tonight...running from me.

She has a badly broken wrist that needs surgery, perhaps also her ankle, although it's too swollen to tell at this stage, but it's her head that they're worried about.

She was knocked out cold, the swelling on her brain so bad that they had to put her into an induced coma.

What if she has a critical brain injury and never recovers?

It's 3 a.m., and intensive care is a lonely place where people are fighting to survive, not only the ones in the beds, the people sitting beside them are fighting too.

For me...it's demons.

"Instead of you sticking my cock up my ass...I'm going to stick it up theirs, and they'll moan on every fucking inch of it."

I'm filled with disgust.

What is wrong with me. If I hadn't chased her...she wouldn't have slipped.

My phone lights up.

Graham Messing

Ahh, the neurosurgeon who I got to look at her scans.

"Hello."

"Hi, is that Gabriel?"

"Yes."

"This is Graham Messing. Sorry I took so long to get back to you. I've just gotten out of surgery."

"It's okay," I stammer. "Did you look at the scans?"

"Yeah, I did. She's taken a nasty hit."

I close my eyes as I wait for his next comment.

"Look, as far as I can see, what the local doctors there are telling you is on the money."

I listen intently.

"There's substantial swelling, but it appears that she hasn't suffered a subarachnoid hemorrhage or a stroke. Her brain activity is normal."

"What does that mean?"

"It means that at this stage, all signs point to the fact that there appears to be no significant long-term damage. However, as you know, she didn't respond to the medication last night, and as there was no evidence of a bleed, the doctors chose to put her into an induced coma. All brains recover differently, and given the information the doctors had at hand, I believe they did the right thing."

"Why hasn't she woken up yet?"

"It takes time. I'll call her doctor and suggest that they start to reduce the coma induction in another six to eight hours. We need that swelling to go down to give her the best chance."

"Okay." I swallow the lump in my throat. "What about her ankle and wrist?"

"Don't worry about them, she's not moving, so she can't do more damage there. They both pale in comparison to a brain injury. That is our only concern at this stage."

"Right."

"She's in no immediate danger and in good hands. The induced coma is giving her time to rest and heal, but as you know, every case is different, so the times and outcomes will vary."

I nod as I try to process what he's telling me. "Okay."

"I'll check back in with you in the morning. I suggest you go home and get some sleep."

"Okay, thank you, Doctor." I hang on the line for a beat. "I appreciate you looking over things for me."

"Speak tomorrow." He hangs up, and I immediately text Debbie.

Hi Debbie,
the specialist neurosurgeon just called.
He confirmed what the doctors here said,
she hasn't had a bleed on her brain and
activity looks normal.
He thinks once the swelling goes down she will be okay.

A message bounces straight in.

Thank god
Why isn't she awake then?

I reply.

He said that the induced coma gives her brain a chance to rest and
recover.
That they will reduce it in the morning.

I watch the dots as she types.

Fingers crossed

I reply.

Are the kids okay?

Yes, sleeping sound.
I'm glad they didn't see her after the fall.

Me too.
Thanks so much for having them.
I'll call you as soon as I know something.

Try and get some sleep
Xox

I let out a low, steadying breath as I stare at my love.

I brush her hair back from her forehead. Her bruised and beaten-up face feels so broken. Did she hit every fucking step on the way down?

She must have.

"When you wake up, I'm going to kill you for being so clumsy," I whisper. "You didn't have to be all dramatic and throw yourself down the stairs to get out of an argument." I keep stroking her hair. "We both know you would have won, anyway."

Beep...beep...beep...beep.

Her silhouette blurs. "Please wake up."

. . .

"What's wrong with my hand?" a sleepy voice whispers.

I wake with a start, my head resting on the bed as I sit beside it. "Grace."

She frowns as she looks me over.

"You're awake, baby." I smile. I reach over and buzz for the nurses. "Oh, thank god you're awake." I push the hair back from her bruised face and hold her to me. "I've been panicking all night." I pull back to look her over and she frowns at me.

"Who are you?"

My world stops spinning...

"What?" My eyes widen in horror. "You don't remember me?"

"I wish I didn't," she mutters dryly. "What are you doing, Gabriel ...and why the hell is my hand hurting so much?"

I pull her into a hug and smile into her hair. "Never been so happy to hear you be a smart-ass, Gracie."

The nurse appears at the door. "Hello, Grace. How are you feeling?"

I step back out of their way and she begins to check her vitals. I message Debbie.

She's awake
And so far okay.

My phone immediately rings. "Hi, Deb," I answer.

"She's awake?"

"Yes," I whisper as I walk out into the corridor. "She's being a smart-ass and everything." The doctor walks past me into the room.

"Thank god. Can I bring the kids up?"

"Let me find out what's happening, she's still hooked up to a lot of machines, and I'm assuming there will be further testing. I'll call you as soon as I know anything."

"Okay, thank you."

358

I hang up and walk back into the room to see the nurse looking into her eyes with a flashlight The doctor is talking to her.

"You took a nasty fall; you're in the hospital. Do you remember what happened, Grace?"

"Um." She frowns, and her eyes find mine across the room. "We were dancing."

"Yes." I nod in excitement. "We *were* dancing."

"And then." She frowns as she thinks. "Where are the kids?"

"They're at Debbie's."

She nods.

"You have a broken wrist that needs surgery and an ankle we need to do some more x-rays on. How is your pain? On a level of one to ten, how would you rate it?"

"Twelve," she grumbles. "My head hurts."

"We'll get some pain relief organized, and once you've had your x-rays, you can have something to eat and drink, how does that sound?"

"Thank you."

They both leave the room and I sit down beside her on the bed and take her good hand in mine. "You scared the hell out of me."

"Hmm." She frowns.

I lift her hand to my lips and softly kiss the back of it. "You think *I'm* dramatic, only *you* could hit every step on the way down."

She looks me over...

"What?" I ask.

"You look like shit."

I break into a broad smile, there she is. "You don't look so hot yourself."

Over the next hour, they unhook her machines and get her pain under control as I sit in the corner and watch on. "X-ray will be up soon to take you down, okay?"

She nods. "Thanks." The nurse disappears and she looks around.

"What's wrong?"

"I need to go to the bathroom."

"Umm. I'll call the nurse back."

"No. I'm not using a pan, I'll wait."

"I'll carry you in."

"No."

"Grace." I widen my eyes. "You need to let me help you." I reach down and pick her up like a bride. I carry her into the bathroom and carefully sit her down on the toilet.

"Okay, go out now."

"What?"

"You're not standing there watching me pee."

"Grace...I've licked your asshole, I'm pretty sure I'm good with a tinkle on the toilet."

"Eww." She screws up her face. "Get out."

I go and wait outside the door and look around the hospital room. What's taking so long? "You okay in there?"

"Yes."

"Can I come in?" I wait some more. "Are you ready?"

"Ugh...yes."

I walk back in and pick her up, her cotton hospital gown is gathered on her lap. "I need to wash my hand."

I carry her to the sink and she catches sight of her face in the mirror and gasps at the bruising. "Oh my god."

"Did a good job of it, you clumsy oaf."

I turn the tap on and she holds her hand under the water. "Can you go and get the kids?"

"Deb's bringing them up this afternoon, let's just get you sorted first, okay?"

I carry her back to the bed and carefully lay her down, and she winces. "What's wrong with my hand?"

"Your wrist is broken and you need it pinned, we'll know more after the x-rays."

Her eyes well with tears, her injuries obviously overwhelming her.

"Hey." I sit down on the bed beside her. "Don't worry. You're

360

going to be okay." I cup her face in my hand. "It's all going to be over soon and you'll be all better."

"I don't have time for a broken wrist, Gabe."

"Shh. Let's just be grateful that a broken wrist is the extent of it." I lower her bed. "Why don't you try and get some rest?"

Grace

The battle to keep my eyelids from closing is steep.

These pain meds are good, but boy, do I feel zonked. Gabriel is sitting on the chair in the corner; he hasn't left my side. And as much as I'm telling him to go home, I'm kind of glad he's ignoring me. It's nice to have someone here with me because I'm beginning to realize what a wimp I am. I feel teary, weak, and vulnerable.

"Where are the kids?" I whisper.

"They'll be here this afternoon," he replies softly.

"Poor things, they must be so scared."

He gets up and comes and sits beside me on the bed. "They're okay, Debbie is taking good care of them. You should rest, you need to sleep to be able to heal."

He puts his hand on my shoulder, and the warm contact instantly relaxes me and my heavy eyelids win.

"You like that?" he asks softly.

I nod sleepily.

"I'll sit here while you sleep, my love."

"Mmm."

I turn my face to the side so that it's resting up against his arm.

His presence is comforting; it dulls the pain and calms my nerves.

I feel heavy and heavier... Floating... Peaceful.

"Mom!"

"Sshh," Gabriel's hushed voice whispers. "Mommy's sleeping."

"Oh no, look at her face," Debbie whispers. "Poor thing, it looks so sore."

"She's okay," Gabriel's calming voice replies. "She's going to be good as new soon."

It's like my body's asleep but my mind is awake. I can hear what they're saying but am too tired to open my eyes or reply.

"Grandma," I hear Lucia call, a commotion, and hugs.

"Oh, you sneaky devils." Debbie laughs.

"We were on the first flight this morning."

Mom and Dad are here. I battle to open my eyes.

"Gabriel," my mother's voice says in surprise. "What are *you* doing here?"

"Ahhh. Kids, why don't you go out to the vending machine and grab us all a snack." I hear him handing over coins.

"Yay." The kids run down the corridor.

"Hello, Mr. and Mrs. Porter," Gabriel says. "It's been years since I saw you both, I believe you visited the office a few times while visiting Grace back in the day."

"I'm confused," my father says. "What are *you* doing here?"

"So..." He pauses. "There's no easy way to say this, so I'm just going to come out with it. I'm the twins' biological father."

"What?" Mom snaps. "That's not true, the children were conceived through donor sperm."

"Ahh," Deb's voice interrupts.

"Grace and I dated in secret while she worked for me."

"For how long?" my father snaps.

"Over a year. We were in love."

What?

"She didn't want to stay in New York and I didn't want to leave. We broke up and she moved here. Not long after, she found out she was pregnant."

"She would have told us," Mom replies. "There is no way she would have lied to us for all these years. Grace would never lie to us, you're lying."

"I made her swear to secrecy," he says. "It was against company policy for us to date, and I begged her not to tell."

"It's true," Debbie says softly.

Mom gasps.

"We've recently reconnected and have been trying to work things out."

"What?" Mom replies. "Why wouldn't she have told us?"

"She was protecting me," he says.

"Oh my god," Mom whispers. "I can't believe this."

"She was going to tell you this week, but now...with the accident," he continues.

The kids come bustling back into the room.

"Shh, Mommy is sleeping," Debbie says.

"We'll take them down to the playground," Mom says. "Let her sleep." I hear the door close and I battle to open my eyes.

"Why did you tell them that?" Debbie whispers.

"You think Grace wants her parents to know that we had a one-night stand and that she lied to them for all these years?"

"But . . ."

"But nothing, I'll take the blame. I'm used to being the bad guy, it's fine."

"Why would you do that?"

"Because...I love her."

Silence...

They keep talking, but their voices begin to blend into each other.

I struggle with my eyelids, wake up...just open.

The voices slur, the darkness gets darker.

Blah...blah...blah blah blah.

Slumberland drags me back under.

The sun is just setting over the park outside my hospital window. A gentle knock sounds at the door and Gabriel gets up and answers it. "Hello, yes. She's hungry."

He stands to the side and the lady wheels in the dinner trolley. "Dinnertime." She smiles.

I sit up, excited, and Gabriel wheels the table over the bed to sit in front of me.

"We have chicken soup, followed by meat loaf and vegetables, and a bread roll." She places it all down in front of me. "And fruit salad for dessert."

Gabriel looks over the food suspiciously. "Can she have something else other than meat loaf?"

"That's the only option."

"Hmm," he replies, unimpressed.

"Meat loaf is fine." I widen my eyes at him. *Stop.*

"Would you like water, or lemonade?"

"Lemonade."

"We'll take some waters too." Gabriel gives me the side eye.

She loads it onto the tray and leaves us alone. Gabriel takes the lid off my meal and gets my knife and fork ready.

"You know, you can go home. You don't need to babysit me."

"Oh yeah?"

"Yeah."

"How you going to cut up that horse meat loaf with one hand?"

I stare down at the meat loaf. "Horse?"

"It's dubious for certain." He leans over me and cuts up my food. "How you going to take the lid off your water?" He unscrews the bottle of water and pours it into the glass.

"I've never felt so useless." I sigh.

"Hmm," he says, uninterested. "I feel like you've been a lot more useless than this before."

"When?"

"When you used to work for me."

"Are you kidding me?"

His eyes dance with mischief. "See...if I wasn't here, who would annoy you?"

I twist my lips to hide my smile and I take a big bite of my meat loaf.

"Appaloosa or stallion?" he asks.

"You're gross, you know that?"

A knock sounds at the door and Gabriel ducks around the curtain to answer it, he blocks the view so I can't see.

"Hello," a man's voice says.

Jack.

"What are you doing here?" Gabriel replies flatly.

"I came to see Grace."

"She's not accepting visitors."

"I don't think that's up to you."

"I'll tell her you came by."

"Is she okay?"

"She will be."

"You're really not going to let me in to see her?"

"No, I'm not. Goodbye, Jack." He closes the door in his face and then comes back in and sits down, totally unfazed.

"Are you serious?" I ask.

"About what?"

"Gabriel..."

"Look, I get that you don't want to go out with me." He points to the door with his thumb. "But you've got to be fucking kidding me with him."

I smirk, such an asshole.

An hour later.

"So your wrist surgery is tomorrow, and thankfully your ankle is just ligament damage, so nothing needed there." The doctor reads my chart.

"Uh-huh."

"Hopefully you'll be out in a few days."

"Yep."

My parents and Gabriel all listen intently, it's visiting hours at the zoo.

"Nothing to eat after midnight," he reminds me.

"Uh-huh."

"The orthopedic surgeon will be around later tonight to talk about the operation in the morning."

"Thank you."

He leaves us alone.

"I'll organize to take some time off work," Mom says.

"What for?" Gabriel asks.

"Well, I'll have to stay and help out. Clearly she can't live alone and look after the kids."

"*I'll* be staying with her to help," Gabriel replies.

"I don't think..."

"You don't need to think, Mrs. Porter. I'm staying with Grace and helping her with our children."

"She won't be able to shower herself or anything."

"And..." Gabriel glares at my mother. "I'm not sure if you realize how children are conceived."

"Listen, you two..." I sigh, they're both getting wound up.

"I just don't think it's a good idea." My mom keeps going.

To be honest, I'm not actually sure I could deal with my mom living with me for a few weeks...and Dad has to work.

"I can assure you that I'm more than capable of caring for Grace," Gabriel snaps. "I will reorganize my schedule and work from here."

"I think this is a family matter," my dad says.

"Exactly, and *I'm* Grace's direct family. Our two children need both their mother and father," he snaps. "I can carry her up and down the stairs to her bedroom. You can't."

"No," my mom interrupts.

"I'm right here, you know." I snap. "Maybe someone could consult me?"

"Grace. Tell your parents that I'm staying with you until you're better."

It is true, Mom can't carry me up and down the stairs...maybe I could sleep on the couch.

Gabriel raises an impatient eyebrow in a silent warning.

Fine...

"Gabriel will stay with me, Mom, it's okay, thanks for the offer, though."

"Are you sure?"

Not really.

Five days later.

Knock, knock.

"Come in," I call.

The door bangs open and Gabriel and the kids all smile broadly. Gabriel is pushing an empty wheelchair and the two kids are bouncing on the spot.

It's been the longest nine days of my life.

"Let's go home."

27

Gabriel

I PULL the car into the driveway and stop the car; the kids barrel out and I glance over to Grace, she forces a smile and I can tell she thinks this is a bad idea.

"Are you ready to be waited on hand and foot, my dear Gracie?" I ask.

"Let's just try and survive, shall we?"

"What are you talking about, I've got this in the bag." I get out of the car and go around to her side. This is a piece of cake.

Not a drill, I do have this in the bag. Unbeknownst to Grace, Mark has already cooked us dinner and it's in the fridge waiting for me to heat up. I had too many meetings and didn't have time today.

I reach in and lift Gracie out of the car, she's torn the ligaments on her left foot as well as broken her left wrist, her hand and forearm are in plaster. It's a bit of a nightmare, she can't walk on her foot but then can't use crutches because of her hand. For the next few weeks, she needs to be carried around...not that I'm complaining. I'll take any excuse to pick her up and hold her in my arms.

I carry her in through the front door. "Home sweet home, babes." I look around. "Where do you want to sit?"

"On the couch?"

I gently put her down. "Here you go."

"Thank you."

"Watch something." I hand her the remote. "I'll grab your stuff out of the car."

This is my chance to show her how great I am around the house, she's going to be madly in love with me very soon, I'm going to make sure of it.

I race out to the car and grab her things and a large plastic bag of medication. Her wrist is giving her grief and aching at night, the hospital gave me strict instructions that she is to have medication every four hours. I'm going to set my alarm so I keep on top of it.

I walk back in and take her bags upstairs and straighten up the quilt. I unpack her bag and take the things down to the laundry and throw everything in the washing machine and turn it on.

I'm nailing this domestic shit to the wall.

My phone beeps a text, it's from Mark.

Put the stroganoff into the oven on 325.

I reply.

On it

I walk back out through the living room. She's snuggled up with the kids on either side of her. "You okay, Gracie?"

"Uh-huh."

"Good, I'm just going to throw some dinner together."

A frown flashes across her face. "You're cooking."

"Yes," I reply casually. "Of course I'm cooking, I thought you would want a home-cooked meal?"

"Oh." She smiles, impressed. "I do."

Ha!

369

She's half in love with me already.

I go into the kitchen and carefully take the pre-prepared beef stroganoff out of the fridge and put it into the oven. I turn the dial on to 325 and hold my breath as the light goes on.

It's working... Yes!

"What are you cooking?" she calls.

"An old family recipe, beef stroganoff," I call. "You'll love it."

"Oh, wow." I hear her and the kids chatting about dinner.

Ha, this is brilliant...I text Mark.

What time do I heat up the mash?

His reply bounces back in.

Half an hour
Three minutes in microwave,
stir and then another three minutes.

Right...what next?

I walk back out into the living room. "You guys going to have a bath before dinner?" I ask the kids.

"I'll shower first," Dom says. He bounces up the stairs.

Grace's eyes find mine across the room and I smile proudly, things are going wonderfully.

An hour later, we sit around the dining table. "That was absolutely delicious." Grace smiles. "Thank you."

"I love to cook for my family." I smile as I begin to collect the dinner plates. "You guys go and chill while I clean up the kitchen." The kids disappear, and Grace looks up at me.

"Do you need Fabio to carry you to bed?"

"Fabio?"

"You know, Fabio...the sex god?"

"No, I don't know Fabio." She gives me a crooked smile. "But I would like to go upstairs if that's okay...without the sex god."

"Your wish is my command." I pick her up and she puts her arm around my neck. I feel her touch all the way to the tip of my dick.

Stop it.

We begin to walk up the stairs and my legs burn, my chest hurts, and damn it...I haven't done enough exercise lately.

"You okay?" she asks.

"Yes, of course. You're as light as feather."

You weigh a fucking ton, woman.

We get to the top of the stairs and I struggle down the hall, fully perspiring now and I sit her on the bed. "Do you need a shower?"

"No, I had one this afternoon at the hospital." She looks around the room. "I do need some pain meds, though."

"Yes." I rush into the bathroom and carefully get her pills. "I'm going to send the kids in to say good night and then I'll come and help you get your pajamas on."

"Okay."

I rush back down the stairs. "Guys, go say good night to Mom, I'm going to quickly straighten up the kitchen."

"Already?" they grumble.

I practically throw the dishes into the sink and wipe the benches down. I need to help her undress and get ready for bed.

The urgency is real. Undressing Grace is my favorite thing in the world. I take the stairs two at a time and walk in to find the kids hugging Grace good night, and I smile as I watch them from the door.

She's such a good mom. They absolutely adore her.

Sadness falls over me. How has she done this alone for so long?

I have so much to make up to her...and them.

"Into bed." Grace smiles.

They both go to their rooms. I tuck in Lucia first. "You happy to have Mom home?" I ask.

"Yeah." She puts her little arms up and hugs me. I hold her in my arms for a moment. "You're such a good girl." She lies down all happy with herself, and I pull the blanket up over her and kiss her forehead. "Good night, angel."

"Good night, Daddy."

Daddy.

I walk into Dominic's room and he's already in bed. I sit on the edge and pull the blankets up over him. "You happy Mom's home?"

He nods. "Thanks for taking care of us," he mumbles.

My heart.

"I'll always take care of you."

He gives me a stifled smile, and I bend down and kiss his forehead. "Good night, Son."

"Good night, Dad."

This could be the very best day of my life.

I turn the light off and walk up to Grace's bedroom, "Where's your nightgown, babe?"

"It's in the top drawer."

I look through the drawer. "I'm not going to come face-to-face with that dildo in here, am I?"

She smiles sleepily. "He's gone into hiding after the last time he met you."

"So he should." I grab the nightdress and sit down beside her. "And when I say come face-to-face. I mean...you...come on my face."

"Stop." She smirks. "I am in no mood for your sexual inuendo."

"I know, I know." I take her shirt off over her head. "Just making sure you're listening."

I go to unfasten her bra. "Just put my nightie on first, thanks."

"I've seen your boobs before."

"This is...different."

372

I roll my eyes and pull her nightie over her head and then reach around and undo her bra underneath it.

"How can you undo a bra from underneath clothes around the back of me?"

"I don't know, it's a fluke, I've never done it before in my life." I pull the blankets back and slide her pants down.

Don't look.

The last thing I need when I'm being Mother Theresa is a raging hard-on.

"Do you need to go to the bathroom?"

"Yes, please."

I lift her and carry her in to sit on the toilet.

She widens her eyes. "Can you go out?"

"Ugh." I go out and wait for a minute and hear the toilet flush.

"Okay." I collect her and help her wash her hands and lay her back in bed. I put her on her side and arrange a pillow under her wrist and ankle. "You okay?"

"Yes, thank you."

I turn the side lamp on and turn off the main light. "I'm going to have a shower," I say.

"Okay." She smiles sleepily. Those meds are working great.

I shower and soap myself up. Is it wrong that I'm beyond excited to be here looking after her? I feel like I won the lottery or something. Eventually, I walk into the bedroom in a towel to find Gracie sleeping like a baby and I smile as I watch her.

I throw on my boxer shorts and slink into bed. I lie on my side and watch her for the longest time.

Bruising is not her best look, I have to admit, but to me...she is perfect. Her long hair is splayed across her pillow and her dark lashes flutter as she breathes.

A real-life angel...my angel.

To her regulated breathing, I feel myself drifting into the abyss.

Beside her at last.

. . .

373

"Oww," Grace cries.

I jump awake. "What?"

"You hit my arm when you rolled over."

"Oh." I wince. "Sorry."

"What are you doing in this bed?"

"I..." I rub my eyes as I try to wake up. "I thought you might need something."

"I don't need you hurting me."

"Sorry, sorry," I mumble. "Go back to sleep."

She exhales in frustration, and we lie in the darkness for a while. "Now my hand is aching."

I roll over and look at my phone. "You can probably have some painkillers now, you were meant to have them in half an hour anyway." I get up and grab the pills. She sits up and takes them.

"I need to go to the bathroom."

I lift her and take her to the bathroom. Fuck...I was in the deepest sleep then. I wait for her and then carry her back to bed and lie back down and close my eyes.

"Gabriel," she whispers.

"Huh?" I jump awake.

"You're breathing too loud."

"What?" I screw up my face.

"Roll over, you are keeping me awake."

"But I can't sleep on that side."

"Go to the couch, then," she growls in an *Exorcist* voice.

"Fuck's sake, calm down." I roll over and put my back to her and I'm so uncomfortable, this is not my sleeping position at all. I try to lie as still as I can so as to not disturb her.

Eventually, I close my heavy eyes.

Beep.

Beep.

Beep.

I jump awake. "What the fuck is going on?"

"Your phone alarm is going off."

"Oh." I forgot to turn it off. I switch it off.

"How could you forget that?"

"If I knew, I wouldn't have forgotten." I close my heavy eyelids.

"Mom," someone yells from a distance. "Mom."

I keep dreaming. *Shut up, kid.*

"Mom..."

I jerk awake. "Fuck." I stumble out of bed; Lucia is full crying now and I kick my toe on the bedpost and go hurtling toward the wall.

Ahhh...my toe has been dislocated.

"Stop being so fucking noisy," Grace grumbles. "You've woken up Lucia."

"She woke me up." I hop around. "My toe is not okay."

"I don't give a fuck about your toe."

"Obviously." I limp into Lucia's room. "What's wrong, baby?" She's crying, and I sit beside her. "Did you have a bad dream?"

"Yeah."

"It's okay." I stroke her hair.

"Can you lie with me, Daddy?"

"Okay." I scooch up on the side of her tiny single bed and smile as I close my eyes.

"Gabriel!" Grace yells from the other room. I jump awake.

"What now?"

"I need you."

I throw the blankets back. This is the worst night's sleep of my life.

I go to step and my toe radiates pain... "Ahh, fuck." I limp back to Grace's bed. "What?"

"Don't *what* me," she snaps, "You said you were looking after me, don't *what* me."

I imagine myself throwing her out the window. "What is it, Grace?"

"I'm thirsty."

"So drink your water."

"It's all gone. I need some cold water."

"From the fridge downstairs?"

"Do you mind?"

I do, actually...

"Fine." I limp down the hall and stairs in the darkness. The room glows from the refrigerator light as I open it. I glance over and see my keys sitting on the counter.

Maybe I could sleep in my car?

I fill the glass with water and make my way back upstairs. I pass Grace her water, she gulps...and gulps...and gulps...and gulps...jeez.

"Thirsty?"

"Don't try me," she snarls.

I grit my teeth and get back into bed. She's testing my last nerve. I close my eyes.

"I need to go to the toilet again," she whispers into the darkness.

I slap my hands over my eyes. This can't be happening.

"That's what happens when you drink like a fucking camel, Grace."

"That's it. Go home."

Don't tempt me, woman.

I flick the blankets back and pick her up. "Perhaps I should put a catheter in."

"Perhaps you should shut your mouth."

"You're not a great patient."

"Yeah, well... You're not a great nurse."

I hobble with her back to bed and lay her down, then stumble into bed.

Grace

The throb in my arm wakes me from my slumber, and I screw up my face in pain. The sun is peeking through the crack in the curtains, and I look over to see Gabriel is not in bed with me. He must be downstairs.

Zzzzz.

I sit up. "Huh?" I can hear him breathing. I lean down and look under the bed to see him sleeping flat on his back on the hard floor with not even a blanket.

I glance at the clock. 8:20 a.m.

Shit.

"Gabriel," I stammer. "Gabriel."

His eyes slowly open before closing again.

"We've slept in," I tell him.

"Ironic, seeing as how I didn't sleep at all." He keeps his eyes closed.

"Seriously, you have to get the kids up."

"They can have the day off."

"They can't, it's photo day."

"I'll take a photo of them with my phone."

"Gabriel," I snap.

He drags himself up onto his elbow and forces his weary eyes open. I burst out laughing. His hair is standing on end and his eyes are red and bloodshot.

"You look bad," I whisper.

"I feel worse." He pulls his hand down his face as he sits up.

"You have to go and pack the lunches and get the kids ready."

He nods and climbs to his feet. He limps out of the bedroom.

"What happened to your foot?" I call after him.

"I broke my toe in the middle of the night...not that anyone fucking cares."

I lie in bed and listen to him walk down each stair. "Ahh... Ohhh... Fuck... Ahh."

"Kids," I call. "You need to wake up. We slept in."

My phone beeps a text.

Do you want coffee?

I reply.

You don't have time for coffee.

I smile to myself as I wait for his reply.

I don't have time for your negativity.

"Kids," I call again. "You need to wake up."

My phone beeps a text.

What do I pack them for lunch?

I reply.

A sandwich and some fruit.
A bottle of water and a few cookies or something.
Their lunch boxes are in their bags.

Dominic appears at my door. "Hey, buddy." I smile and hold my arms out for him, he comes and cuddles me for a moment. "You need to wake your sister up and go down and check on your father."

"What's he doing?"

"He's making your lunch and might need a hand."

"Oh no!" we hear Gabriel yell from downstairs. "What the hell do you call this?"

"What's he doing?" Dominic asks.

"I have no idea, go down and check on him, please." Dominic gets up and walks downstairs.

"Oh my god!" Gabriel cries. I hear a sound and I listen to try to make out what it is...wait...is he dry heaving?

"There will be no school today," he bellows through the house. I hear the front door open and slam.

I hear a shuffle up the stairs and Dom appears; he's panting and looks panicked.

"What's going on down there?" I ask.

"A banana has gone rotten and smashed all through Lucy's bag, it's all on her pencils and everything. Dad is heaving and threw the bag out the front door."

"Oh."

Gabriel appears at the door; his eyes are wild. "In what universe do you put a banana in a school bag without a container?"

I stare at him.

"It's all slimy and...it stinks and..." He dry retches as he thinks of it. "I'll never eat a banana again."

"You're going to have to clean it."

"How?"

"With a wet cloth?"

He dry retches at just the thought of it.

"Okay, she can use another bag. You need to wake her up first."

He limps off, and I listen to him talking to her. "Wake up, baby girl."

"No. Go away," she snaps. "I'm tired."

"Join the club." I hear him hobble down the stairs. "Get up."

Lucia walks into my room and crawls into bed with me. "You need to get ready, honey, we're late today."

She disappears, and I hear more things slamming around downstairs.

What *is* he doing down there?

"I hate Tupperware," he cries. A cupboard door slams and I

smile to myself. I wish I had a camera down there so I could watch this firsthand.

Eventually, the three of them appear at my door. "We've come to say goodbye."

I hug Dominic and then turn to Lucia. "You need your hair done, bubba."

Gabriel's face falls. "Oh."

"Get the brush." I point to the dresser. "Just brush her hair and tie it up. Quickly, though, you're going to be late."

Gabriel grabs the brush and then looks over Lucia's hair, he picks up the top layer to find a mass of knots lying underneath. His eyes widen in horror. "What in the rat's nest is this?"

"Just brush it."

"What?"

"Pull the brush through the knots."

"I don't know if you've seen these knots, Grace, but this isn't a simple brush-through kind of situation."

"Give me the brush." I hold out my good hand, and he passes it over. I begin to quickly brush through the knots. Lucia screws up her face as her head pulls back with each stroke.

"Enough." Gabriel snatches the brush from me. "That's barbaric." He begins to brush through her hair slowly and carefully.

"You're going to be late."

"I don't give a flying..." He looks around and remembers where he is. "That's fine." He continues brushing at a snail's pace.

Dominic rolls his eyes and snatches the brush from Gabriel. "Let me do it." He grabs the scrunchie and puts her hair into a ponytail, it's messy but it will do.

God help the photos today; they are going to be a disaster.

"Off you go," I tell them.

"When I get back, we have to go to my house. I have a Zoom meeting at eleven and I need an office," he tells me.

"Okay."

I get a quick kiss on the cheek and the three of them run down the stairs and I hear the car take off. I smile into the silence.

First morning down...

28

Grace

"Your coffee, madam." Gabriel smiles as he reappears after the school drop. He passes me a cup of coffee and sits on the bed beside me. The morning sunlight is beaming on his face, and today seems much brighter. I give him the once-over, his hair is wild, the two cords are hanging out of his track pants, and he has his T-shirt on inside out. "Did you..."

"Did I what?"

"Go into the coffee shop like that?"

"Yeah, why?" He frowns.

"Your shirt is on inside out."

"No, it's not." He glances down to look at himself and his face falls. "Oh my god. It's happening."

I giggle at his horror. "What's happening?"

"I'm turning into one of them..."

"You mean an exhausted parent who is trying their best to survive each day?"

His eyes search mine. "Last night was a disaster, wasn't it?"

"Not at all."

He sips coffee with a defeated demeanor.

"What's wrong?"

"I thought I'd be better at this."

I smile at his delusion. "Every parent thinks they'll be better at this, until you're in the trenches you have no idea how hard it is."

"I know why you let me come here and look after you." He sips his coffee.

"You do?"

"You thought this would push me away and I'd run for the hills, didn't you?" His eyes hold mine. "Am I right?"

We stare at each other as silent confirmation runs between us. "It's not over yet, you still have time to run." I smile, and then a thought comes to me. "Why did you offer to do this? I know how busy you are."

"Because you and the children are my responsibility now. I want to be the one who cares for you."

"The children are your responsibility, not me."

"Grace."

I don't answer him.

"Look at me." I drag my eyes to meet his. "I'm here for you, not the children. I can have a relationship with them from wherever I am...it's a relationship with you that I want."

"Why would you want a relationship with me?"

"Because I love you."

My eyes search his.

"And I need you to love me back," he whispers. "So we can get past this and be happy."

"It's not that easy, Gabriel."

"Then tell me how to make it easy. I can't fix it if you won't even let me in to talk about it."

I fidget with a cushion on my bed as I search for the right wording,

"Do you even want to try to fix us?" he asks.

I nod.

"Then talk to me."

"I can't explain it. I guess..."

"Yes, I'm listening."

"Last night was a million times easier than when I came home from the hospital with two babies. You have no idea how hard it's been and what I've been through and I'm angry and resentful at you."

He sits back. "Fair call."

"And sometimes I just really want to stab you or something."

"Slightly sinister serial killer aspirations...but okay, I'm listening."

"And you've just turned up here, snapped your fingers and expect me to jump into your arms, and it doesn't work like that."

He listens intently.

"And you use your dick against me and that isn't fair."

"My dick?" He frowns in surprise. "What's my dick got to with anything, are you angry we slept together?"

"Yes. Furious with myself."

"Why?" he says softly as he tucks a strand of hair behind my ear. "That night was perfect, how could you regret it?"

"Because it wasn't a conscious decision for me, it was a spur-of-the-moment physical act."

He stares at me for a beat. "You're angry that we did it on my desk all those years ago, aren't you? You're angry because you think it just happened."

"It *did* just happen."

"After I wanted it for seven years. It did not just happen, Grace. In fact, it was the best sexual experience of my life, and now that I know what came from it, it's even more special. It was premeditated in my mind for years before."

I twist my lips as I think.

"Did it just happen for you?" He frowns. "You mean...you didn't want it to happen at all?"

"Not like that." I hesitate before I say the next thing. "The thing is, I don't blame your mother for hating me. If Dominic was three weeks before his wedding and his secretary turned up with two of his children that were conceived on his desk, I'd be devastated too."

"Do not defend her, that is different."

"How is it different?"

"Because we were meant to be together," he snaps angrily. "And don't you dare bring my mother into this. I blame her for my misery for the last seven years. If she hadn't demanded her expectations for me to be with an Italian woman, I would have married you back then."

Married me?

His eyes widen as he realizes what he's just revealed.

"So you're angry with your mother for past things...not just that she came to my office that day?"

"My issues with my mother run way deeper than you could ever imagine, Grace. Let's just leave it at that." He gets up and begins to organize clothes and I watch him for a moment. "What do you mean?" I ask him.

"Let's just say my mother's love has always been conditional."

"Meaning what?"

"Meaning this conversation is over." He marches out of the room and I stare after him, confused and perplexed.

He would have married me back then...what?

Gabriel carries me through the front door of his house just on ten thirty. We don't have an office at my house to do his Zoom from so we needed to come here. I'm feeling a little bit better after our talk this morning and I want to try to make this as easy for him as I can. I have no idea what I'm going to do while he's working, but I do know that I can't stay home by myself yet.

"I've got to get into my suit, do you want to come upstairs?" he asks.

I haven't seen his bedroom here.

"I'm heavy to take up the stairs."

"No, you're not. Come talk to me while I get ready." He carries me up the stairs, down the hall, and into the grand bedroom, then lays me on the four-poster bed.

"I have to shower. Do you need anything?" He passes me my phone.

"Nope. I'm good."

He disappears into the bathroom and I hear the shower running. Although I can't see him in the bathroom, I can see his reflection in a mirror in the bedroom. He takes his shirt off over his head and his broad, muscular back comes into view.

My heart stops as I stave off excitement.

He drops his pants, and although I can't see below his waist, my breath falters anyway. Just knowing he's naked in there does things to me. I drag my eyes back to my phone.

Stop it.

"You hungry?" he calls.

I glance up and see him in the shower washing his hair, his eyes closed and the soap running down his wet body. His biceps bulge as he moves his hands.

Jeez.

"Not really."

Focus.

I keep scrolling through Instagram, and I couldn't tell you what I'm looking at because my mind is in the shower. I hear it turn off and pretend not to notice.

Don't look up.

Gabriel walks back out into the bedroom with a white towel around his waist, his body a ripple of muscle and water beads on his olive skin. I swallow the lump in my throat. "What do you want for dinner?" he asks as he walks into his wardrobe.

"Anything," I reply, distracted.

He reappears with a suit and shirt and lays them on the bed beside me, he grabs some briefs from the drawer and then drops his towel, I'm hit in the face with thick quad muscles, short well-kept pubic hair and his huge dick that hangs heavily between his legs. It's half erect, not fully...but damn...

My eyes linger before I drag them up to his eyes. Satisfaction flashes across his face.

"I don't think you need to get dressed in front of me," I mutter, embarrassed he's caught me ogling.

"You've seen me naked before."

"We're friends for the moment."

"Yeah, well." He dries his crotch with the towel. "Happy to dress in front of my friends too." Standing at the end of the bed, he pulls his black Calvin Klein underpants up and then puts his white shirt on. His eyes hold mine as he does the buttons up in slow motion.

My sex clenches in appreciation...

"Maybe we should just get something easy for dinner tonight." I try to change the subject.

"Like what?" He pulls his suit pants on and zips them up, then walks over to the dresser and sprays his aftershave on.

Leg-opener cologne.

It 100 percent works, because my legs are literally opening against my will.

"I don't know..." I breathe, his scent intoxicating me by the second. "Something easy after a hard night."

His dark eyes rise to meet mine, and he pulls his tie around his neck. "I like the way you say hard night." He does his tie, and I have to wonder...is there anything hotter than a man standing at the end of your bed, tying up his tie?

"Thank you for looking after me." I breathe, distracted. I'm officially drunk on his aftershave; visions of sexual favors are running naked through my mind.

This man is the devil, even though I have a broken wrist, he turns me into a hornbag.

He pulls his suit coat on and checks himself in the mirror, he straightens his tie and turns toward me. "I like looking after you." He picks me up, and I tentatively put my arm around his neck.

Something about him in a suit does things to me...brings back memories of a time when I worshiped the ground that he

387

walked on. He carries me downstairs. "Where do you want to go, babe?"

"Can you stop calling me babe?"

"No." He kisses my shoulder as if it's the most natural thing in the world. "You are my babe."

"Gabriel, we are just friends."

"Okay." He holds me in his arms as he looks at me.

"What do you mean, okay?" I frown.

"If that's what you want, okay."

"Oh."

"Just so you know...even though this is just a friend-looking-after-a-friend arrangement." He kisses my shoulder again. "I'm not giving up on us."

"Why not?"

"Because we belong together."

He holds me in his arms as we stare at each other. He's so strong in his power suit, and I'm a broken, fragile version of myself in pajamas.

He gives me a slow, sexy smile and kisses my shoulder again. "Now...I have to work, stop distracting me." He carries me into the living room. Mark is out in the backyard cleaning the pool, and Gabriel opens the sliding door. "Hi."

"Hello," he calls as he walks up to the house.

"I have to work, so can you help Grace with anything that she needs, please?"

"Sure." Mark smiles over at me. "Hi, Grace."

"Hi." I give an awkward smile. Damn it, he's getting me babysat now. "I'm fine, really."

"No, no," Gabriel says as he organizes me on the couch. "She'll need lunch and snacks."

"Done," Mark replies.

"And if she needs to be moved, come and get me, you're not to touch her."

What the hell?

"I wouldn't dare." Mark smirks.

388

I feel my cheeks turn a bright shade of red.

"Look after her," Gabriel says. He bends and kisses my forehead. "I'll just be in my office. Call if you need me."

He strides down the hall to his office and closes the door behind him.

I'm left alone in the awkward silence with Mark.

"I really don't need to be babysat, Mark, thanks anyway."

"I'm going to get to making you some lunch. Any requests?"

"Got any leftovers from the beef stroganoff you made last night?" I smirk.

His eyes widen and then flick down the hall to where Gabriel is. "I—"

"Was just helping." I shrug. "I get it, I won't tell him that I know."

"What gave it away?"

"Seeing he doesn't know how to turn on my oven and he somehow miraculously cooked everything in record time, it wasn't rocket science to work it out."

"Oh." He smiles. "He's trying."

"I know."

"Do you, though?"

I frown. What does he mean by that?

Mark has something to say, I want to hear what it is.

"Why don't you make us a cup of coffee and we go sit by the pool?" I say.

His eyes drift down the hall.

"I'll get Gabriel to help me out."

"Okay." He disappears into the kitchen and I text Gabriel.

Sorry to bother you.
Can you give me a quick lift out to the pool?
I want to sit in the sun.

The office door opens and Gabriel comes striding out, he has his AirPods in and is talking on the phone. "I don't think that's a good idea," he says, he bends and lifts me into his arms and kisses my arm.

All these arm kisses today...

We stride to the back door and he opens it as he carries me. "No, that won't do. I want the report by Monday." He listens as he walks me down the steps. I can hear a man talking on the other end but not well enough to know what's being said. He carries me down to the pool and sits me down on the deck chair, he kisses my shoulder and smiles. "You okay?" he mouths.

I nod as my stomach flutters.

Without another word, he turns and marches back inside.

Five minutes later, Mark appears with two cups of coffee. He sits down beside me on the deck chair and passes me my cup. "Thank you."

"How hungry are you? You feel like a cooked meal for lunch?"

"I'd kill for a grilled cheese sandwich."

He smiles. "I can do that."

I sip my cup of coffee as I try to work out what to say next. "So...you cook for him?"

He chuckles. "Not usually. He has a chef at home."

"A chef." I frown. "I forget how exotic his life is in New York."

"I know," he replies.

My eyes shoot up in question.

"I didn't mean..."

"No, no, please go on. This is a private conversation; I would never tell him what we talk about if you agree to never tell him that I know he didn't cook last night."

He chuckles.

"You've been with him a long time?"

"Nine years."

"I bet you've seen a lot in that time."

"Yes and no."

"What does that mean?"

"Just that...Gabriel's a creature of habit, not much has changed with him at all...that is, until the last seven weeks."

"Since he came here, you mean?"

He nods.

"I guess it was very different when he was going to marry Ariana too."

"No, not at all." He goes to open his mouth and then stops himself from saying something.

"What?"

"It's not my place to say."

"No, please. Say it. Your perspective would be very helpful; you know him better than anyone. Lord knows I need some help working this all out."

"I just...I don't believe he was ever going to marry Ariana."

"Why not?"

He frowns as he looks over the pool. "I'm not sure how much he's told you about..." His voice trails off.

"About what?"

"About the period of time after you and he were together in New York?"

"When he broke my heart?"

"When he broke his."

My eyes flick to him. "What do you mean?"

"He was never the same after you left."

"I wish I could believe you." I sigh.

He sips his coffee. "Have you ever wondered why he came looking for you?"

My eyes hold his.

"All I'm saying is..."

"What *are* you saying?"

"He always said that you were his one that got away, you were the girl he was supposed to live happily ever after with."

I get a lump in my throat as I listen.

"Pride ruins a lot of relationships, Grace."

"You think I'm going to ruin this?" I whisper.

"Look...it's..." He shrugs. "He deserves to be happy." He gives me a stifled smile. "And so do you and the kids."

"Mark." My eyes search his. "What if... He terrifies me."

"Yeah, well..." He smiles sadly. "Grand love always does."

"That sounds like you're speaking from experience."

"Mine didn't work out so good."

"Why not?"

"Pride."

"Yours?" I frown.

The back door opens and we look up to see Gabriel standing on the porch, he's on phone and looking down at us. He holds his hand up in question at the two of us sitting together by the pool.

"What's he doing?" I ask.

"Being a jealous prick." He stands. "Got to go before I get my head ripped off."

I giggle and watch him walk into the house. Gabriel says something as he passes him by and pretends to swing a punch, Mark laughs and keeps walking.

I sit alone by the pool...just me and my confused thoughts.

Four hours later, I lie on the couch, channel surfing as I listen to Gabriel rule the world through Zoom. He's demanding and bossy, cantankerous and angry. I've come to the conclusion that he hasn't changed at work at all since I left as his PA.

Still the biggest bastard in New York.

Weird.

He's so mellow with the kids...and even me now.

A text pops in.

Do you need to go to the bathroom?

I reply.

Only if you have time

I listen to him wrap up his meeting, and he appears. "You okay?"

"Uh-huh." I smile.

"Bathroom?"

"Uh-huh." He picks me up and carries me down the hallway and sits me on the toilet.

"You know, I thought you'd changed," I tell him.

"What do you mean?"

"You're still so angry at work?"

"I'm assertive, there's a difference, and what would make you think I've changed?"

"Well...you're a big pussy cat with the kids."

"I'm no different, Grace. I'm exactly the same person I've always been." He frowns at me as if having an epiphany. "Has it ever occurred to you that you didn't know the real me back then?"

I stare at him, confused.

No. It hadn't.

"Do you want me to pull down your pants?" He raises a suggestive eyebrow.

"No." I smirk. "I've got it."

The pink glow lights up the lake, and I smile into the sunset. The kids are chattering away as Gabriel cooks steak on the grill, and a new sense of calm has fallen over me.

It's like...the unknown has begun to reveal itself to me...to us.

Seeing the children with him... Everything has changed. Maybe it's my talk with Mark today, maybe it's the drugs, maybe I'm just really fucking high.

But for the entirety of my pregnancy and the children's lives, I have lived in fear, that Gabriel would find out about them...that the children would find out I lied to them...that my parents would discover who the father is. That he would take the kids from me.

Suddenly, the only thing surrounding me is truth, and it isn't half as horrendous as I'd envisaged. In fact, it's been cathartic.

A huge weight of anger, regret and fear has been lifted from my shoulders, and for the first time in seven years, I feel free.

"Like this," Gabriel says. He uses the tongs and flips the steak over and then passes them to Dominic. I watch on as Dom carefully flips the steak, concentrating so hard that his little tongue is sticking out.

Gabriel's hand rests on Dom's shoulder as he watches on. "Good, yes, like that."

Dom smiles proudly, feeling so grown up.

Tonight has been pretty uneventful. After last night, we're all exhausted, and quite honestly, I just can't wait to get some sleep.

Gabriel and Dominic carry the tray of meat over and sit it on the table, Lucia dishes me some salad out onto my plate and Gabriel puts a piece of steak on.

"Well..." I look around proudly. "Look at us being all civilized."

Gabriel smiles proudly, he has a certain twinkle in his eyes whenever things run smooth.

We sit together as we eat, the four of us on the lake as the sun goes down.

And even in a cast, I have a lot to be grateful for.

"Good night. I love you."

"Love you too, Mom."

I kiss the kids and Gabriel disappears with them to tuck them into bed.

I hop into the bathroom and go to the toilet. I'm getting the hang of this hopping thing. I need a shower, but...

Gabriel appears with a plastic bag and electrical tape. "Let's get your cast wrapped so you can shower."

I exhale heavily. "I feel like such a burden."

He stands me up and puts the bag over my arm and thinks for a moment. "You need to undress first."

"This is awkward."

"Why?"

"Because you have to help me in the shower and…"

"I've seen you naked, you know?"

"I know, but it's just weird in this context." Without the pounding body of arousal between us, this all feels a little too…raw and intimate.

"Arms up."

I hold my arms up and Gabriel slowly lifts my shirt over my head.

My pink bra comes into view. He slides my pants down my legs and suddenly I'm standing before him in my underwear.

His eyes roam over my skin, and he smiles softly.

I can't breathe.

"Turn around," he instructs.

I turn to face away from him and he undoes my bra. My breasts fall free.

Thump, thump, thump goes my heart.

"Give me your hand." I put my hand out, and from behind he carefully wraps it in the plastic bag and tapes it up. He then slides my panties down my legs and takes them off.

I can feel his eyes burning my skin as they roam over my naked body. He steps forward, turns the shower on and holds his hand under the water as he gets the temperature right. He may have seen my body before, but he's never seen me this naked.

Raw as it comes.

For the first time, his eyes drop down my front, drinking every inch of me in.

I swallow the lump in my throat, waiting for his reaction.

He runs his finger over the large scar across the bottom of my stomach and his eyes rise to meet mine. "What is this?"

"My C-section scar."

A trace of a frown crosses his face. "Did it hurt?"

I nod.

His face falls as he stares at it. "I'm sorry, Grace," he whispers. "I should have been there."

"Don't." I hop past him and he takes my hand and helps me under the water.

I could cry, not sniffles and tears. Howl-to-the-moon emotions.

Tonight's too real, a little close to the surface. It's like the last seven years are suddenly here and hitting me in the face.

I stand under the hot water with my back to him, unable to look him in the eye,

because if I do, who knows what's going to come out of my mouth.

He leans up against the tiles.

"Can I have some privacy, please?" I ask.

"I don't want you to fall."

"I'm fine, I'm just standing here. I'm not going to fall."

He walks into the bedroom and I put my face under the water. It runs over the top of my head, wetting my hair.

I need to get off this medication. It's making me weak.

I stand under the water for a long time and it's the weirdest thing, such a simple thing as him seeing my C-section scar has cut me wide open.

I'm back there, my heart feels just as broken as the day that he kicked me to the curb.

Eventually, I turn the shower off and he appears with a towel, as if he knows what's going on inside my head. He wraps me in it and softly dries me. He ties it around my chest and I hop to the sink and brush my teeth, and he helps me out into the bedroom. I see he has my nightdress laid out on the bed.

"Arms up." I put my arms up and he slides it over my head. "Sit on the bed and let me dry your hair." I sit down and he towels my hair, he does it rougher and rougher. "You call me barbaric." I wince.

He chuckles. "Let me brush it." He softly brushes my hair and I stare at the wall, again overcome with emotion.

Why is brushing my hair a big deal?

It's the meds...it has to be the meds.

Eventually, he folds the blankets back and I lie down. "Pillow under your arm and leg on the edge tonight, I can't sleep like I did last night," he says. "Oddly enough, I need to breathe."

I smile at my dramatics about his breathing last night. I lie down and he turns off the light and slides in behind me. He puts his hand on my hip bone and I can hear his mind ticking over a million times a minute as he thinks.

"Did you love me?" he whispers. "Back then."

"It doesn't matter."

"It does to me."

I hesitate. I don't want to answer that while I'm feeling like this. "Good night, Gabriel."

He stays silent, his hand tightening around my hip.

"It's a yes or no question, did you ever love me?"

"Yes."

"Do you still love me...even a little?"

I don't answer...because I can't. Because once I give him an inch, he's going to take a mile and I can't deal with losing myself all over again.

"I'm taking that as a yes." He grips my hip bone and pulls me back against his body. "We're going to make it, Grace," he whispers. "I'm going to make sure of it."

"Good night," I whisper into the darkness.

"I'll make a deal with you."

"What's that?"

"We take sex out of the equation."

"What?"

"We try to make this work...without sex."

I stay silent as I think.

"Don't answer me now, think about it overnight." He kisses the back of my shoulder blade. "Good night, my love."

My love.

Maybe...just maybe.

. . .

I wake to the feeling of lips dusting my neck. Gabriel's arm is under my head and his body is snug up against mine, I'm warm and toasty. "Good morning, my Gracie," he whispers in my ear. "How's your hand?"

"It's okay."

His hard length is up against my behind, he flexes it and I feel it move. "Your breakfast is ready," he breathes.

"You know, for someone who took sex off the table, there's a lot of hard dick in my back," I whisper.

"Yeah, well...it's morning." He rolls me onto my back and looks down at me. "Did you think about it?"

All night long.

"I did."

"And?"

Am I a masochist? One hundred percent.

"I can't make any promises."

He gives me a slow sexy smile. "Is that a yes?"

I smile up at him as my hopeful heart thumps in my chest. "That's a let's see what happens."

29

Grace

HE SMILES, and his lips dust mine.

Bang. The door opens and we jump back from each other.

"Why are you sleeping together?" Dominic demands.

Gabriel rolls onto his back and hides his face from him with the pillow. "Mom needed help with her wrist."

"Oh." He sits on the side of the bed and leans down and hugs me for an extended time.

Gabriel widens his eyes in a get-rid-of-him symbol.

"Come on." I get out of bed and take Dominic's hand. "Let's go make breakfast."

I put my weight onto my foot and wince. "I keep forgetting about this stupid ankle." I hop into the bathroom. "Go start getting ready, Dom, I'll be down in a moment."

"Okay." He disappears, and Gabriel almost flies into the bathroom and takes me into his arms as he pins me against the sink. He kisses me softly; his lips linger over mine as we share a moment.

"Today is starting out very, very well," he whispers as he kisses me again.

"No sex," I breathe.

"Relax, it's just a kiss." His lips dust mine.

Jeez...

"Dad," Lucia yells from her bedroom.

His tongue swipes through my lips as he lingers. "Later..." He turns and walks out of the bedroom as if unfazed.

Oh...

My heart pounds hard in my chest as I stare after him.

Just a kiss...it wasn't just a kiss; my whole body is thumping.

Half an hour later, we sit in the kitchen and the morning rush is well underway.

Gabriel is making sandwiches and rushing around in his suit while I sit on the couch. We've had some progress today, my brace finally fits on my foot, so I can get around on my own now.

"Lucia," he calls. "Are you dressed?"

No answer...

He keeps making the sandwiches, and Dominic comes around the corner. "Eww..."

"What's eww?" Gabriel frowns.

"We don't eat lettuce."

"Why not?" he mutters dryly. "Lucia, are you ready?" he calls again. "We're going to be late."

"My teacher wasn't happy that we were late yesterday."

"Yeah, well, tell your teacher to call me if she has a problem," Gabriel fires back.

I smirk into my coffee as I listen to the theatrics.

"Are you taking the lettuce off the sandwich?" Dominic asks.

"Not a chance."

"If we don't like it, we don't like it."

"Sometimes you have to do things that you don't like; exhibit A...do you think I like being heckled while I make your lunch? The answer is no. I do not."

"Lucia," he bellows through the house and I turn my head away so that he can't see me laugh.

"For god's sake, go and check on your sister, what *is* she doing up there?"

Dominic skips up the stairs while I continue to sit on the couch like a queen.

"Having a nice relaxing morning out there, are you?" Gabriel grumbles.

"I am, actually."

Dom calls from upstairs. "We've got a real problem up here."

"What now?" Gabriel calls back. "I don't have time for this shit," he mutters under his breath.

Lucia walks down the stairs and my eyes widen. Her hair is one big knot, and a round hairbrush is sticking out of it.

I drop my head to hide my giggles.

She walks into the kitchen and Gabriel frowns and goes to pull the hairbrush out. His eyes widen as he realizes it's tangled in her hair. "What's going on here?" he snaps.

"The brush is stuck in her hair," Dominic replies.

"I can see that. I mean, how the hell did it get there?" He tugs on it and she wails in pain.

"She was brushing her hair, how do you think?" Dominic replies sarcastically.

Gabriel closes his eyes as he tries to control himself. "Dominic, now is not the time for your smart-ass cracks. Go sit on the couch with your mother."

Dominic skips past me and disappears out the front door.

"Ahhh," cries Lucia. "You're pulling it."

"How else am I getting this out," Gabriel grumbles. "Hold still." He struggles and struggles while she wails and yells.

I'm in full giggles on the couch.

"What the hell do you do in your sleep?" He gets the big scissors out of the drawer.

"What are you doing?" she yells.

"There's no saving this situation, I have to cut the bristles off the brush, what does it look like." Tongue out, he concentrates. "If this doesn't work, next I'm cutting your hair off."

"No." Lucia half laughs.

The front door opens. "I stepped in dog poo," Dominic calls.

"Fuck me dead," Gabriel mutters. "We don't even have a dog."

I burst out laughing.

"Glad you find this so amusing, Grace," he whispers angrily.

"Hilarious, actually."

"Throw the shoes in the bin," Gabriel calls. "Go get another pair from upstairs."

"What?" Dominic calls.

"Do it," he bellows through the house.

Dominic disappears outside.

"This morning routine is not working," Gabriel yells. "We need to streamline our behaviors."

"It runs smooth for me." I sip my coffee. Gabriel comes barreling out of the kitchen and takes my coffee from me. "No more talking. You're officially in time-out for being a know-it-all."

I burst out laughing.

"Don't, this morning is catastrophic."

I laugh harder and eventually he breaks into a smile too.

"Dad," Lucia calls from the kitchen. "Are you fixing my hair or what?"

He pinches the bridge of his nose and closes his eyes and it's the funniest thing I've ever seen in my life.

"Coming."

We pull into his driveway just after nine, and he helps me out of the car. I hobble inside as he holds my hand. Mark is watering the garden as we walk past.

"Good morning," he calls.

"Not really," Gabriel mutters as we walk past.

"School morning not running so smoothly, big daddy?" Mark's eyes dance with mischief.

"Fuck off," Gabriel replies.

Oh...Mark's a smart-ass.

I've never seen this dynamic between them before.

I like it.

"I'm in meetings all day," Gabriel tells him. "Can you help Grace again today, please."

"For sure."

"And . . ."

"I know, no touching her." Mark cuts him off.

Gabriel curls his lip and I laugh. Mark winks cheekily at me.

I hobble inside and Gabriel sets me up on the couch and gives me the remote. "Text me if you need anything." He kisses me softly, his lips lingering over mine.

"Okay," I breathe up against him.

Without another word, he strides down the hall and his office door closes. I smile at the television.

Who is he kidding, this morning was kind of perfect.

1:30 p.m. and boredom has set in.

I've watched television, I've scrolled on my phone, I've even played solitaire.

Mark is out in the back garden doing something. I'm going to go for a walk. I hobble down the hall and slowly open Gabriel's office door. He's on a Zoom. "Yes, that's right," he says as his eyes rise up to me. He flicks his camera off and pats his knee.

I don't know who he's in a meeting with, but there are a few different voices. I frown in question and he pats his knee again.

"I like that strategy," he says. "Let's go with that."

I quietly hobble over and sit on his knee; his lips immediately find mine as his hand runs up my thigh under my dress.

He kisses me, his tongue slowly sliding between my lips as my eyes close.

The voices keep on talking in the background, but all I can focus on is him...and his hand as it slides down my panties.

His eyes flutter as he feels how wet I am, the urgency in his kiss strengthens.

"I do wonder what the percentage of loss would be if we went down that route," someone says.

He pushes his thick finger inside of me and I clench around him. He gives me a slow sexy smile and adds another finger and begins to fuck me with them.

Slow and measured pumps as my body sucks him in.

Our kiss becomes desperate.

His hard cock underneath me begs for attention.

"Gabriel," a voice says, snapping us back to the present. "What are your thoughts on this?"

He turns his head away from me. "It all depends on the network," he replies without hesitation.

Wait...he's been listening to what they're saying?

I stand. He needs to work.

His dark eyes hold mine, and he puts his two fingers in his mouth and sucks them.

Oh...

He licks his lips in appreciation and then rearranges his cock in his suit pants.

"Later," he mouths.

I nod and, drunk on arousal, I hobble back to the couch.

Meow... I need a cold shower.

"Not again," Gabriel's voice screams through the house. "This *cannot* be happening."

I jump awake from my place on the couch.

"Mark," he bellows. "What the hell is going on here?"

Mark walks up to the office and opens the door. "What seems to be the problem?"

"This internet keeps dropping out, this is the third time this meeting."

"And?"

"Do something about it," he bellows. "I'm closing a major fucking deal here."

"Okay." Mark ambles back up the hall and into the kitchen. He casually gets himself a glass of water.

"What are you going to do?" I ask Mark.

Mark rolls his eyes and shrugs. "Pretend to do something about it." He holds his hands up. "Even if I owned the telecommunications company, I still wouldn't be able to do something about it."

I giggle as a full picture of Mark and Gabriel's relationship becomes crystal clear.

"That's a very good point."

"Knock, knock." I hear Deb's voice call from the front. "Anybody home?"

Mark frowns. "You expecting someone?"

"That's my bestie." I smile excitedly. "Come in, Deb," I call.

Debbie walks through the house. "Where's my..." Her voice trails off as she sets eyes on Mark.

From across the room, he stares at her too...

I look between the two of them as they stare at each other.

Wait...what?

"Do you two know each other?" I ask.

"No," Deb replies, all breathy.

Mark rushes forward and picks up her hand. "I'm Mark."

"Goodness." Deb lets out a flustered giggle. "Hello, Mark. I'm Deb."

"Hello, Deb." He smiles all sexy like, her hand still in his.

What the...?

"Ahem...." I clear my throat. "Don't want to interrupt your little moment here."

They step back from each other guiltily.

"Apologies," Mark stammers. "I have to get back to work." He goes to walk out the front door and then stops halfway there and turns and walks out the back door.

Debbie stares after him as if she's just seen a ghost.

"What in the world?" I whisper.

"That was bizarre." She looks at me. "Right?"

"Did you forget that you're married?"

"Fuck, for a second there, I did." She holds her temples. "Good god, he's ridiculously hot." She shakes her head as she tries to reclaim her focus. "I've never had a physical reaction to anyone like that before."

I widen my eyes. "Married," I mouth.

"I know, I know." She hugs me. "How are you, anyway?"

"I have so much to tell you," I whisper, excited.

"Great." She puts her arm around me and we walk toward the kitchen. "Let's put some coffee on."

"You are *fucking* kidding me!" Gabriel's voice bellows through the house.

"What's going on?" Deb panics.

"Internet keeps dropping out." I roll my eyes as I get the cups out. "Ignore him. We certainly do."

"And then Colin said that she told on him but she didn't tell on him," Lucia says as she sits on the kitchen counter.

"Right," Gabriel replies. "Then what did you do?" This is multitasking at its best, he's taking a YouTube cooking lesson on his iPad, talking to Lucia and cooking dinner at the same time.

"So I told him to go away."

"Uh-huh." He pretends to listen as he focuses on his cooking lesson and chops the chicken.

I smile as I watch the two of them.

"Anyway, so Colin was so cross that he pushed Benjamin over."

"What happened then?" Gabriel picks up the iPad to watch closer, I'm sure he has no idea what Lucia is even saying.

"Well, we didn't play with him."

"I see. Listen, I've been thinking about your morning hair situation."

Lucia rolls her eyes.

"I'm going to braid your hair tonight so we don't have knots tomorrow morning."

"Why?"

"Because I googled it and that's what you do."

"Do you know how to braid?" she asks.

"No, but how hard can it be?"

Okay, what the hell?

Who is this man, and what has he done with Gabriel Ferrara?

"No way he's going to be able to braid hair," Dominic mutters under his breath as he plays his game.

"No," I agree. "But it's going to be fun to watch him try."

It's nine thirty before everyone is asleep.

I sit on my bed and pretend to scroll through my phone as I wait for Gabriel to come upstairs. He's already wrapped my plaster in plastic and gone down to check the doors are locked. For someone who put no sex on the table, I'm overly excited about showering and going to bed tonight. Every time I close my eyes, I see Gabriel sucking his fingers in his office today and I nearly orgasm on the spot.

I'm aching like never before.

Gabriel walks in and past me into the bathroom. The shower turns on and my breath catches. Moments later, Gabriel comes into view completely naked.

My eyes roam down his body, his hard thick cock stands erect between his legs.

He's aching too.

"Shower time, my Gracie," he mouths.

Goose bumps scatter up my spine as we stare at each other. His dark hair hangs in curls and his ripped olive skin glows as the steam swirls in the air.

He lifts my dress over my head, and in one quick movement has my bra and panties off too. We stare at each other, our naked bodies betraying what we need from each other.

He holds my face in his hands as he kisses me deeply, pulling me under the water as his tongue works its magic. His strong body pins me to the wall as his lips drop to my neck. Unable to stop myself, I reach down and wrap my fingers around his girthy length and stroke it.

"Hmm," he moans into my mouth. "We are so fucking good together." His fingers knead my breasts, his teeth graze my jawline, and I have an out-of-body experience, looking down at us from way above.

Naked and writhing, kissing like our lives depend on it.

He slides his finger deep into my sex, and I tip my head back in ecstasy as he begins to fuck me with his hand. Deep and hard. I grip his forearm and feel the muscles in it flex as he moves. He adds another finger and another, and my grip on his cock tightens. I work him at a piston pace, and this is it.

The epitome of primal instinct.

No longer in control of ourselves...but being controlled by *it*.

A force way bigger than either of us.

I stroke him and he tips his head back and cries out as he comes in a rush. "Fuck it," he pants, annoyed at himself for blowing so fast.

He lifts my leg as he works me, knowing exactly where to touch me, how to touch me.

I see stars.

The orgasm is so strong that I lose my breath. I nearly pass out with the pleasure.

I shudder into his mouth as he kisses me. He's as lost to this as I am.

No matter what mistakes we've made in the past, no matter how much we've hurt.

The physical part of us...is and always has been.

Perfect.

Thursday morning.

Gabriel kisses me softly. "Text me if you need anything." He disappears up the hall and into his office. I lie back on the couch of his living room and smile up at the ceiling.

It's been the most incredible week; every day things get a little more real.

This is actually happening; *we* are actually happening.

I scroll through my phone as I drink my coffee.

"That is it!" he yells. "This is the final fucking straw." I hear his office door bang open and he strides out. "We're leaving," he announces.

"Do you want to go to my house?"

"No. We're going to New York."

My face falls. "What?"

"The children are on school holidays as of tomorrow, and I have too much on next week. Until this internet is sorted, I can't work from here. I'll get a technician out next week."

"Me and the kids will just wait here until you get back."

"I'm not going without you!" he bellows at the top of his voice.

"But..."

"But nothing," he snaps. "I cannot do what I have to do without the appropriate equipment...and *you* are going to support me."

Mark walks through the back door. "Hey." He sees Gabriel's furious face. "What's up?"

"We leave for New York in the morning."

The kids stare out of the back windows in awe as the car pulls onto the tarmac.

Gabriel is dressed in his navy blue suit, a crisp white shirt and tie. Looking every bit as New York CEO as they come.

Mark is in the front seat, and there's another car of men behind us.

Nerves dance deep in the pit of my stomach.

I'm excited to go to New York, but deep down, I have a bad feeling about this.

It's just two weeks, what could possibly go wrong in two weeks?

The car comes to a halt. Gabriel gets out and opens the door for us. The kids and I climb out and are suddenly stunned to silence.

A sleek jet sits on the tarmac, it has gold detailing around the windows and on the nose. It's so exotic and luxurious looking that I've never seen one like it before.

Not even in magazines...

The scared kids shuffle to stand behind my and Gabriel's legs.

Gabriel kisses the back of my hand and gives me a slow, sexy smile. "Home time, my love."

30

Gabriel

Dominic and Lucia stand behind my legs, scared of the jet, and I smile down at them. "Come." I hold my hand out and Lucia takes it, and to my surprise, Dominic takes the other one.

He's holding my hand.

I want to jump in the air and scream it out loud, but I won't... I'll pretend magical things like this happen to me every day.

"Up the stairs." I lead them onto the plane and we walk down the aisle. "Sit here."

"I want to sit next to you." Lucia beams excitedly.

"Me too," Dom says softly, almost to himself.

Oh...

"I'll go get Mom and be back in a moment." I walk back down the stairs, pick up Grace and bring her onto the plane, and put her into her seat, then move back to the children. "For takeoff, we need to sit in these seats, and then we can move to the couch so that you can both sit beside me, okay?"

They nod.

"You sit here, Lucia, and you here, Dom." I bend and do the seat belts up on the large cream leather seats. "It opens and closes like this." I show them. "Mom and I will sit opposite you." I glance over to Grace to see she has this worried look on her face, and I raise my eyebrow in question.

She smiles and gives a subtle shake of her head.

The stewardess comes out. "Hello, I'm Nala. I'll be looking after you today," she says.

"Hello, Nala. This is my partner, Grace, and these are my children, Dominic and Lucia." I smile proudly.

"Hello." The kids beam.

"Can I get you any drinks for takeoff, sir?"

"You get drinks and everything," Lucia whispers, wide-eyed. "What even is this place?"

I chuckle and glance over to see Grace once again looking like she just swallowed a fly.

I take her hand and hold it in mine.

What's wrong?

"We'll have two glasses of Moët and two glasses of fizzy drink please?"

"Fizzy drink?" Nala frowns.

"Sprite," I correct myself.

Grace smiles at me calling it fizzy drink, and I do too. The children bounce in their seats with excitement. This is a special day. Bringing my children and Grace home to New York means a lot to me.

My eyes roam over Gracie's beautiful face and a sense of calm falls over me, never have I been so under the spell of a woman before. Her calm resolve and inner strength. The way she loves our children, the way she makes me feel. It's as if all my pent-up feelings for her over the years have boiled over and I no longer have any control over them.

I am irrevocably hers.

There's not a doubt in my mind now that she is the love of my life. She has always been the love of my life, long before I even realized it.

My aim is to convince her to move to New York so that we are never apart. The more I settle into my new role as a father, the more I realize that I can't be without them for four days every week.

Nala brings our drinks, and I hold my glass up. The kids smile as they raise theirs to meet mine. "To the Big Apple."

Mark throws the Uno card down onto the table. We're playing with the kids...again. We've converted Mark into a long-suffering Uno champ too.

I glance over to my beautiful Gracie sitting alone on the other side of the plane, she's looking out the window with her book in her hand and then I notice something. She's wearing her diamond tennis bracelet I bought her all those years ago.

She put it back on.

Gracie glances up and catches me staring at her. I wink and she smiles softly.

I feel it all the way to my bones.

I need her, I need us to be officially together, and while we haven't had sex, she's going to hold me at arm's length...she already is.

Tonight, I fix it. Tonight...she's mine.

Grace

The sun is just beginning to set as the car pulls into the underground parking lot, and the kids stare out the window in awe. Gabriel chats away, happily explaining everything to them, all the while I feel myself spiraling.

The last two times I was in New York were so traumatic for me that somehow it's triggered a million emotions. I feel unexpectedly angry with him, I feel scared for me, but more than anything, I feel terrified for my children.

What have I done?

If we don't work out... We're here already.

The thought of going home with the two children alone is more than I can bear.

Gabriel's warm hand squeezes mine and I glance up. "Are you okay? You're very quiet."

I force a smile. "Just tired."

He pulls me close and kisses my temple and I ease out of his grip. "Stop," I whisper.

We're not telling the children we are together yet...remember?

Ugh, this is so like him to assume control.

He gives me the side eye and I turn to stare out the window. I don't know what the fuck is going on with me right now, but I need to snap out of it.

And quick.

It was me who said we could try again. I can't say that I forgive him and then drag things up and throw them in his face forever. The relationship will be doomed before it even begins.

New York is just a place, it's not a behavior, I remind myself.

I know what I've got to do...but realistically, how do you pretend that you aren't so terrified of being hurt again that you can hardly breathe?

The car pulls to a stop, and as they all climb out, I know I have to make a decision right here and now.

Forget the past and live in the present or end this relationship before it turns toxic.

It's either or; it can't be both.

Gabriel leans into the car to help me out. "Let's go, babe," he says softly.

My eyes search his, and this is it, the moment I know I have to decide.

Past or present...

He kisses my fingertips and smiles in at me and I melt into his gaze.

I have to try...

Present.

I climb out of the car and the kids grab both my hands. "Are we actually underground now?" Dominic whispers.

"Uh-huh." I look around nervously. I feel like a little kid again too, everything in New York is in IMAX, even the underground parking lots.

"The elevator is this way," Gabriel tells us as he walks ahead and pushes the button.

The kids' eyes widen, and they balk at the door. "What's this?" Lucia whispers.

Gabriel frowns. "You've never been in an elevator before?"

They both shake their heads and I smile at their innocence. Maybe I should be horrified.

"Hop in." Gabriel smiles. "This will take us up to our house."

"There's a house here?" Dominic whispers.

"Yes."

"On top of the parking lot?" Lucia scrunches up her face in question. "That's weird."

Good grief, these children are country bumpkins.

"Isn't this fun." I pull them by the hands into the elevator, and Lucia cowers behind me.

Gabriel bends and picks her up. "It's okay." He smiles and pushes the button and the doors close. "It's like a rocket ship."

As we ride up, Dom squeezes my hand so tight that he nearly cuts off the circulation.

The numbers over the door rise, and with every floor we go up, I feel a little more of my excitement return.

We're actually doing this.

The doors open to a foyer, on one side it has floor-to-ceiling windows overlooking New York and the other side has big, black double doors.

"Look at New York." Gabriel walks over to the window with Lucia in his arms, they stare out over the twinkling lights way down below. "Isn't she beautiful?"

Dom pulls me back by the hand, he's scared.

"It's okay, baby." I smile. I edge us closer to the window. "Look at the lights, isn't it pretty."

His little eyes roam over the view, and he frowns. "Well...where is it?"

"Where's what?" Gabriel asks.

"The big apple."

Gabriel lets out a deep belly laugh, and it brings with it a tingle to my spine. He has the most beautiful laugh; I don't hear it often enough.

"There isn't actually an apple here." He smiles, his eyes twinkle with delight.

"Well...why do you call it the big apple?" Dominic replies.

"It's just a nickname."

Dominic's eyebrows flick up. "That's dumb, what has this place got anything to do with apples?"

Gabriel laughs again, and I giggle too. "You do have a fair point." Gabriel goes to the big black doors and scans his finger and then presses in a code on the PIN pad. The door clicks in release and he pushes it open.

We are hit in the face with the opulent luxury of a huge living room. The furniture is all cream with black trimmings, a gigantic black-and-cream rug is on the floor, and behind it are floor-to-ceiling windows looking over New York.

"Whoa." Dominic's and Lucia's eyes widen as they peer in.

Holy fuck.

Holy fucking fuck.

This penthouse is new. I thought his last one was over-the-top beautiful.

This one is astronomical.

There are big cream floor lamps and a black square coffee table in the center that is adorned with beautiful ornaments. I get a vision of a ball being kicked and smashing everything to smithereens.

Oh hell...those need to be packed away stat.

"Come this way." He bends down and picks up Dominic too

and walks ahead of me. "Out here is our kitchen." We walk through to a huge cream marble kitchen, what the hell...the island bench must be seven meters long. "And over here is our living room." He brings us through to another living room, and my eyes widen; this living room is as big as the entire bottom floor of my house. "And this is our garden." He pushes a button and the glass doors all begin to slide open.

"What the...?" I frown.

There's a great big yard complete with a swimming pool. A full garden at the top of a skyscraper with grass and everything? Just... what the hell?

I'm flabbergasted.

"A pool?" Dominic yells.

"And it's heated, you can go for a swim now if you like."

Lucia's eyes are the size of saucers as she looks around.

"Down here is the theater room and the gym, my office and a guest bedroom and bathroom," he says casually as he walks down the corridor. "There's a bar room."

"Whoa." Dominic's eyes are bulging from his head. "This is..." His eyes flick to me, and I nod. "I know, bubba."

It really is unbelievable; no wonder Gabriel has been struggling so hard in my tiny ramshackle of a house.

"Let me show you our bedrooms." Gabriel carries the twins inside and I hobble along behind them. He goes to walk up the grand double staircase and looks back at me limping. "We will catch the elevator upstairs for Mom."

"There's an elevator in here?" I squeak.

Gabriel smiles over at me, realizing I'm a country bumpkin too. "Yes." We get into the elevator and he pushes the button.

"You guys take the stairs if you are on your own, okay?" I get an image of one of them getting stuck in here or squashing the other one or something. The doors open and my eyes widen again, we're in another living room. Giant-sized with big slouchy couches and cushions everywhere. "I had all this furniture ordered in for you guys, I thought this could be your living room." He puts the kids down on the floor and opens the television cabinet. "I bought you an Xbox and I got Disney Plus and stuff."

I smile that his sales pitch contains Xbox and Disney Plus.

"Whoa." Dominic begins to bounce on the spot.

"And down here are the bedrooms." He leads us down the grand hallway. "There are six bedrooms, and the end three are ours." He points down to the end. "On the left is Dominic's room." We peer in and see a huge bedroom, it's blue and beautifully furnished, there are floor-to-ceiling windows and big heavy curtains. "Wow." We all gasp.

"On the right is Lucia's room." We all peer in to see the exact same version of Dominic's room, only in pinks. "This is incredible," I whisper.

"And here is Mom's and my room." He presents the room as if he's the best real estate agent in town. "This is all new furniture and stuff for Mom."

I look around, and my eyes widen...

What the...

The room is cream and coffee colors, beautiful velvet bedding and a big duck shell–blue rug. Crystal lamps and oh... "Gabe," I whisper. "This is the most beautiful room I've ever seen."

He kisses my temple. "Do you like it?"

"I love it."

"Oh, and look." He walks to a door and opens it. "This is your wardrobe." I walk into a full other room; the entire walls are shelves and racks, and in the middle is a huge marble set of drawers.

It looks like a Kardashian wardrobe.

"I bought you a few things...it's colder here."

I look around, and there are designer clothes all hanging with the price tags still on them.

My eyes flick to him in question. "You bought me clothes?"

"Just a few things." He shrugs. "You can return anything you don't like."

"Thanks," I whisper, distracted.

"This is our bathroom." He opens another door and I see a sunken circular bath and shower in apricot marble.

My eyes roam around, and I honestly don't know what to look at first. This is ridiculous wealth, how much did this place cost?

"What do you think?" Gabriel whispers nervously. "Do you like it?"

"It'll do...I guess."

He chuckles and pulls me into a hug and kisses my temple. "Thanks for coming, it means a lot."

"Mom." Lucia tugs on my shirt.

Gabriel holds me tight, not letting me go.

"Yes?" I smile, unable to take my eyes off my beautiful man.

"I need to poo?"

Gabriel closes his eyes and I giggle; kids have impeccable timing.

The bedroom is dark, lit only by the television as it drones in the background.

After swimming in the pool and then in the hot tub, dinner and showers and the whole damn rigmarole, we are in bed watching *Home Alone*, the children between us and seemingly settling in for the night.

"Why don't we get you into your own rooms?" Gabriel suggests.

"No," Lucia snaps as she snuggles closer into him. "We want to sleep with you tonight, our bedrooms are scary."

"They're right next door," he mutters dryly.

I smile into my pillow. He wants alone time, and the kids are being super clingy because they're in a new environment.

"We want to sleep with you tonight," Dominic announces. "The bed is big enough."

Gabriel rolls his eyes and pinches the bridge of his nose.

"Great," he mouths across their heads at me. He puts his arms along the pillow and brushes the backs of his fingers across my

419

face. I smile. A simple act to tell me what he's wishing we were doing.

Me too.

Dominic snuggles into me and Lucia snuggles into him, and he smiles lovingly over at me. "I love you," he says softly.

"Love you too," Lucia says all sleepily.

I glance down to see that Dominic is already asleep, and I smile over at Gabriel, he blows me a kiss good night before he turns off the bedside lamp.

I know it's not the night he wanted...but it's pretty perfect anyway.

I wake with a start and look around, disoriented. Darkness, but Gabriel isn't in bed with the three of us.

I sit up onto my elbow and look around, I grab my phone from the side table.

4:30 a.m.

Where is he?

I sneak out of bed and, using the light on my phone, go in search of him. I pad down the hall and check the bedrooms as I pass. Down the stairs and through the house.

No sign of him...is he even here? Where would he have gone...

Ariana.

Panic sets in, and I begin to look more urgently.

Did she call him? Did he rush to her side? I hobble up the hall to his gym, the only room I haven't checked, and I burst open the door. To my surprise and utter relief, I find Gabriel running on the treadmill.

"Thank god." I put my hand over my heart.

He slows the treadmill down, his T-shirt wet with perspiration, his skin covered with a wet shine. His chest is heaving as he struggles for air.

"Hey," he pants as the treadmill comes to a standstill. "What's wrong?"

"I thought you weren't here."

"Where would I go?"

Before I put my brain-to-mouth filter on, I reply, "To her."

He frowns as he stares at me. "To who?"

I wrap my dressing gown around me. What the hell did I say that for? "Never mind."

"No." His chest is still struggling for air. "What did you mean by that?" He pulls me by the hand down the hall and into the kitchen, sits me up on the large island bench and puts his hands on either side of my legs. "Now, I'm going to ask you again...*what* did you mean by that?"

"I just..." My eyes well with tears.

Damn it, I don't want to be this insecure crazy person.

"You mean Ariana?" he pants.

I nod.

"Gracie." He brushes the hair back from my forehead. "I'm one hundred percent with you."

My eyes search his.

"I have called to check on her but haven't seen Ariana since I brought her back to New York. I would never..." He frowns as if shocked by my insecurity. "You think I would go to her?"

"You loved her."

"I did. But not in the way I love you." Empathy fills his face, and he cups my cheek in his hand. "Gracie...is this what's been bothering you today?"

"I just feel like you have unfinished business with her," I whisper. "And coming back here has just..."

"Just what?"

"I have a bad feeling that something is going to happen to ruin this for us."

"Sweetheart." He kisses me softly. "I know this has happened very fast, and yes, it's true, I was with Ariana. But I came looking for you for a reason...because deep down, I knew you were the woman I was supposed to be with."

A tear rolls down my cheek.

"I swear on my life, you have nothing to worry about. I'll never leave you again."

I screw up my face in tears.

"Gracie," he whispers as he holds my face in his hands. "I know I've given you no reason to trust me. But we need to get past this."

"I want to believe you... I'm trying so hard, I just..."

"Tell me." His eyes search mine. "Just tell me how you feel."

His silhouette blurs as the final wall comes down. "I love you," I blurt out. "I've always loved you. From the first day I met you...it's always been you."

He kisses me.

"I left New York because I couldn't bear to see you and not have you. I was dying a little every day in your office."

"You have all of me now." His lips dust mine.

My tears, his sweat...a million regrets.

"I just..." I screw up my face because damn it, now I've opened my mouth, I can't seem to stop it running.

"You just what?"

"We never even went on a first date," I sob.

His face falls as he realizes I'm right. "Gracie..." he whispers. "Will you go on a date with me?"

I shrug, embarrassed that I had to ask for one, more embarrassed that it matters.

It shouldn't, I know it's childish...but somehow, the child in me still believes in fairy tales.

"Not just any date," he says to sweeten the deal. "The date of all dates. My A game of dates. This date is going to be in the Guinness Book of Records, it's going to be so fucking good."

I smile through tears.

"What do you say?" He holds my hands in his.

"I'll think about it." I smile bashfully.

He gives me a slow, sexy smile. "And I want to give you something else to think about...before our date." He lays me back onto the island bench, his hand slides up my bare thighs and he spreads my legs. He dips his head and softly kisses me between my legs through my panties.

Oh...

His dark eyes hold mine as he pulls my panties to the side, and I hold my breath as his tongue slides through the lips of my sex.

My back arches off the counter at his touch.

Fuck...

Arousal flickers in his eyes, and he slides my panties down my legs and throws them over his shoulder. Then, as if losing control, he lifts my knees and holds my legs back.

He spreads me wide with his fingers as his thick tongue licks me deep, right through the middle of my swollen flesh.

I whimper as I squirm. "Get up here," I whimper. "Gabriel...get up here."

He really begins to eat me, his head thrashing from side to side, my arousal all over his stubble.

"Fuck me," I beg. "I need you to fuck me."

But he's lost, too far deep into his desire. Teetering on the edge between heaven and ecstasy. He really lets me have it, and I shudder. "I need you to..."

Oh...good fucking lord.

"You'll wait." He licks his lips.

"What?" I pant. "I can't. Please..."

He pulls his erect cock out of his shorts; it's pulsing and angry, beading on the end, and he swipes it through my creamy flesh.

The anticipation of him being inside of me is too much, I shudder hard and cry out, the orgasm so strong, it sits me up.

With his eyes focused between my legs, he strokes himself once, twice, three times... I watch the moment he ejaculates through the lips of my sex.

Never have I seen something so hot...so ridiculously fucking hot.

He lifts his fingers and slowly slides them through my pulsing body.

Rubbing himself into me, making sure I feel every drop of his semen.

Fucking...hell.

I feel the hot cream of his seed as he smears it through my sex.

He pants as he watches me, the darkness behind his eyes sends a shiver up my spine.

A perspiration sheen is all over his skin, and honestly...I've never seen anything so beautiful.

"I wanted you then," I pant as I pull him down to kiss me. "Why couldn't we...?"

"I'm waiting for our date," he whispers in my ear. "I want it to be special. I'm a virgin, you know."

I giggle as I hold him close. "Virgins don't know how to do what you just did."

"You'd be surprised." I feel him smile into my hair. "Porn is very educational."

Gabriel walks out of his wardrobe in his dark gray suit with a crisp white shirt and I smile. Now that the cat is out of the bag, I can't even pretend to act casual about him. I'm fangirling like a pro.

He walks back into his wardrobe and sprays his aftershave on, and I walk in and grab him by the tie. "Seeing you in your suit makes me want to drop to my knees...Mr. Ferrara."

His eyes hold mine, and he unzips his trousers. "Do it."

We've had the best weekend.

On Saturday morning, we went to the market and wandered around, then we went out for lunch, followed by bike riding around Central Park. Well, the four of them, the kids, Gabriel and Mark, rode a bike, and Gabriel pulled me along in a buggy.

Mark crashed his bike and Gabriel was laughing so hard that he nearly ran us into a lake, it was so fun.

Saturday night we had a dreamy dinner on the terrace and

then the kids played in the hot tub while Gabriel and I drank too much red wine while lying on the deck chairs.

Yesterday we had a lazy day, we unpacked our suitcases and did online grocery shopping to get ready for the week.

Seeing everything fresh through the kids' eyes, seeing the love in his.

I'd forgotten how much I love New York.

This weekend reminded me.

He slams the wardrobe door shut and pushes me down to my knees, in one sharp movement he slides his thick cock down my throat until I gag. He smiles down at me as he tenderly brushes my hair back from my face. "If you're going to talk the talk." He drives himself farther down my throat, and I giggle around him. "Behave."

What must we look like, him in a full power suit, with everything to perfection, and me with wild hair and still in my pajamas.

He grabs my head with two hands and begins to fuck my mouth.

"Suck. My. Cock."

Monday, 2 p.m.

I sit in the park as the kids play on the playground, Mark is hovering around somewhere but won't come and sit with me. Gabriel has obviously warned him to keep his distance from me whenever he's not around.

Jealous prick.

I sip my to-go coffee and smile as I watch Lucia and Dominic talk to a group of kids. I can hear them telling them where we're from and the kids asking questions back.

My phone rings and the name *Gabriel* lights up the screen.

"Hello." I smile.

"Hello, is this Mrs. Cock Sucker?" he breathes, and I can tell he's smiling.

"This is Miss Cock Sucker."

"Hmm, well, with a performance like this morning, you won't be unmarried for long," he whispers darkly. "My cock tingles every time I think of it...well done."

I giggle and look around guiltily. "Did you call me at the kids' playground to discuss my culinary skills, Mr. Ferrara?"

"Absolutely," he whispers. "What are you wearing?"

"What am I wearing?" I glance up into the hard, cold stare of Gabriel's mother, she's standing over me. I glance around for Mark; he's nowhere to be seen.

Fuck.

"Hang up," she mouths. "Now."

31

Grace

"I'LL CALL YOU BACK LATER." I end the call and stand; I need to be eye to eye for this conversation. "Hello."

She's completely fitted out in designer clothes and her hair is swept up into an up style. Her cold eyes hold mine, and she lifts her chin to the sky in defiance.

She's here to fight.

"Before you say anything, I have a few things I want to say to you...preferably before Mark gets back from wherever he is," I tell her.

She goes to say something and I cut her off.

"Firstly, I would like to apologize for telling you that you will never see the children. It's not okay under any circumstances to threaten you with that." I shrug. "I don't know why I said it, and it's not something I would ever do. I regretted it the moment the words left my lips. They are your grandchildren, and you can see them whenever you want to."

"Listen..."

"Secondly." I cut her off again. "I don't blame you for hating me. In fact, I've thought long and hard about this and I put myself in your position, and if Dominic did what Gabriel has done, I wouldn't handle it well either. I probably would have gone more postal, if I'm being honest."

A frown flashes across her face.

Dominic runs over and her eyes roam over him, her face falls when she sees the resemblance to his father. "This is Dominic," I say. "Dominic, this is your dad's mother."

"Nonna," she whispers.

Dominic smiles up at her. "Hello."

I wave Lucia over and she skips over with a big smile. "Lucia, this is your grandmother, Nonna."

"Hi." Lucia frowns up at her.

"Your dad's mom."

"Oh." She smiles up at her, all starstruck.

"Mrs. Ferrara," Mark snaps urgently. "What are you...?"

"It's fine, Mark," I tell him.

"I have strict instructions from Mr. Ferrara," he stammers.

"Mr. Ferrara isn't here," I reply sternly.

"You need to leave," Mark says to a man who is standing close by. My eyes flick to him, I didn't see him standing there before...the penny drops, oh, he's her bodyguard.

"È ora di andare," he says to her. *("We should go".)*

"Dammi un minuto," she replies. *("Give me a minute.")*

Dominic looks between them. "Dove vai?" *("Where are you going?")*

Her mouth falls open and she steps forward. "Parli italiano?" *("You speak Italian?")*

"Sì." *("Yes.")*

Her eyes rise to search mine.

"I tried to prepare them the best that I could." I shrug. "I wanted them to know and appreciate their heritage."

Her chest rises and falls as if she's struggling to breathe.

"Grace, I must insist," Mark says as he holds his hand out for me.

"Say goodbye to Nonna," I tell the children.

"Arrivederci, Nonna," Dominic says.

"Bye." Lucia smiles with a little wave.

She smiles through tears. "Arrivederci," she whispers.

Mark rushes us to the car. "It's fine, Mark," I say.

"Nothing about this is fine, he's going to go crazy, I could lose my job over this."

"What?" I stop on the spot.

"He's warned me again and again to keep her away from you."

"I'm fine, stop being so dramatic." He bustles us into the car and the driver pulls out with haste, I roll my eyes as we drive along. Talk about overreacting. Although the fear on Mark's face in the front seat is unsettling, he's genuinely really concerned. He and the driver keep exchanging worried looks. I don't want them to get into trouble with Gabriel for a two-minute slip.

"I asked her to meet me there," I lie.

"What?" His eyes flick back to me.

"I wanted the children to meet her."

He drags his hand down his face as if this is the worst thing that has ever happened. "Why would you go against his wishes?" he whispers.

"Relax. It's fine."

"Nothing about this is fine."

I gesture to the children who are completely oblivious and staring out the window.

"We'll talk later."

It's just past 5 p.m. when I hear the door click. "Dad's home," I call.

"Daddy," Lucia squeals in excitement, they both come tearing down the stairs and run to greet him.

"Hello, my darlings." He smiles as they both jump into his arms. He's had to learn to pick them both up at once now that Dominic wants a piece of the action too. "How was your day?" He smiles as he holds them.

"Good," Lucia says.

"We went to the park," Dominic tells him.

"I heard." His cold eyes rise to meet mine, and I wince. *He's angry.*

He puts them down and then without saying a word to me, he walks into the other room as they follow him, chatting away.

Okay...

I'm in trouble, why is he always so dramatic?

"What's that drink?" I hear Lucia ask.

"Scotch," he replies. I hear the ice fall into the tumbler.

Hmm...not a good sign.

I go to the refrigerator and pour myself a glass of wine, I keep my drinks in the kitchen like a normal person.

I hear him talking to the children as they walk past me out to the garden.

Still not a word to me. I take a swig as I stand at the sink.

"Why don't you two get in the hot tub," he asks them.

"Yes." They both run upstairs to get their swimming costumes on, and I walk out to the garden. "Hello." I widen my eyes.

Did you forget I'm here?

His cold eyes hold mine and he sips his scotch, contempt drips from his every cell.

"What's your problem?" I raise my eyebrow.

Silence.

He bends and turns the hot tub on, and it begins to bubble.

I swallow the lump in my throat, angry Gabriel Ferrara is someone I wouldn't wish on my worst enemy.

The kids run downstairs and jump into the hot tub. He clicks the safety net on. "Stay on the step," he tells them. "I have to go inside for a moment, I'll watch you through the window." He turns and walks past me into the house.

Great.

He's put them in the hot tub so we can fight without them hearing.

I walk in and he shuts the glass door behind us. "How fucking dare you!" he yells.

430

I jump, startled. "What?"

"I know what you did today," he screams, the veins in his neck sticking out.

"Calm down."

"I will not fucking calm down."

"What did I do?"

"Arranging for my mother to meet my children?" He steps forward and I step back. "When you *knew* that I did not want her anywhere near them."

Oh fuck...he thinks I called her. I did say that, didn't I?

Dumb, dumb, dumb.

"It went well," I say softly.

"I don't give a flying fuck how it went," he bellows so loud that the windows nearly shake. "You." His jaw flexes as he clenches his teeth. "You have no idea what you have done."

"Then tell me," I spit. "How can I make an informed decision if I don't know why they can't see her?"

"Because I fucking said so!" he screams.

My eyes flick out to the kids in the hot tub, happily playing away, oblivious to their drama queen father.

"I've made the decision that she is never to see these children and *YOU*...purposely went against my wishes."

"She's your mother!" I yell back, I'm getting pissed now. "What was I supposed to do?"

He narrows his eyes and his chin tilts to the sky as if having a realization.

"Show me your phone," he says.

"What?"

"I want to see where you called her to arrange this meeting."

Fuck.

"You need to calm down, she was nice to the children, that's all that matters, isn't it?" I stammer.

"Show. Me. Your. Fucking. Phone," he growls.

My eyes hold his.

"You didn't call her at all, did you...?"

I swallow the lump in my throat, staying silent.

"She ambushed you."

"Gabriel..."

"Did. You. Or. Did. You. Not. Call. Her?" he yells as he loses all control.

"No. I did not."

His eyes flicker with fury and he storms toward the front door; I run after him. "Where are you going?"

He grabs his keys.

"I don't want you going anywhere when you're like this."

He brushes past me and into the foyer, he gets into the waiting elevator.

"Gabriel..."

His eyes are murderous as the doors close in my face.

I feel like I should ring ahead and warn his mother that he's coming...but I don't even have her number.

Fuck...

Gabriel

I march through the underground parking lot toward my car and Mark comes running out. "What are you doing?"

"You're fired," I snap as I march past him.

"Grace called her," he stammers as he follows me.

"Grace did nothing of the sort," I fire back. "She was covering for you."

"What?" He runs to walk beside me. "Where are you going?"

My car unlocks as I approach it.

"I'll drive you," Mark says. "You are not driving like this." He steps in front of my car. "I won't allow it."

"Get out of my fucking way." I push him to the side.

"I'm coming with you."

I turn toward him like the devil himself. "I ask you one thing. One fucking thing and you can't even do that. Keep my mother away from my family...how fucking hard can it be?" I explode.

432

"I went to the bathroom," he stammers. "I was gone two minutes."

"So why lie?"

"It's what Grace told me, I thought it was true."

I roll my eyes in disgust as I get into my car. "You get upstairs and you watch over Grace, and so help me god, if you take your eyes off her for one fucking second...I'll kill you myself."

He steps back from the car and I scream out of the parking lot, my black Ferrari roars like a tiger as I pull out into the traffic.

I've never been so angry; years and years of my mother's toxic behavior have finally tipped me over the edge.

I pull up to the lights and my two hands grip the steering wheel. I get a vision of my mother walking up to Grace and the kids today at the park, I can only imagine what she said to them. The audacity.

And Grace was prepared to take the blame...

I inhale deeply as rage simmers deep in the pit of my stomach. I'm so furious that I can't see straight. I can feel my pulse as adrenaline surges through my blood stream. A ticking timebomb about to blow.

Calm down.

Fifteen minutes later, I pull into the parking bay of my mother's building and I storm through the foyer. The doorman nods as he opens the door. "Good evening, Mr. Ferrara."

I walk to the elevator and the doors open, the elevator attendant smiles. "Mr. Ferrara." I walk in and turn to face the front; I readjust my tie as we rise floor by floor to the penthouse.

The doors open straight into her apartment and I step out. Ivan, my mother's bodyguard, is waiting there.

"Mr. Ferrara." He smiles awkwardly. "We weren't expecting you, sir."

"Get out."

My eyes find my mother across the room.

"I—"

"Get. The. Fuck. Out," I yell.

My mother's cold eyes hold mine. "If you're going to speak to my staff like that, you can leave."

"Call it as it is." I sneer. "He's your lover."

Ivan's face falls, and my mother gestures to the elevator. "Leave us," she whispers.

"I don't . . ."

"Get into the elevator by choice, or I'll throw you over the fucking balcony," I growl.

Ivan begrudgingly gets into the elevator and I'm left alone with her.

She goes to her bar and pours amber fluid into a crystal tumbler. "What do you want, Gabriel?" She raises an eyebrow.

"What do I want?" I whisper, I begin to pace as her words roll around in my head. "What do I want... I want a mother who isn't a fucking monster!"

"And I want a son who isn't a control freak." She rolls her eyes. "Did you come here to insult me?"

"I told you to stay away from Grace."

"I wanted to see my grandchildren."

"Lies. You want to set me up to fail. Planting poison into Grace's head is the only reason you would ever go looking for her...we both know that."

She smiles as she sips her drink. "It's charming that you still think the world revolves around you, tell me, does she know that you still love Ariana?"

I clench my hands at my sides.

"That you are with her out of pity and to be closer to your children."

My chest rises and falls as I struggle for control.

"She's poisonous, Gabriel."

"You want to talk about poisonous?" I whisper. "Let's talk about Dad, shall we?"

Her eyes hold mine.

"What kind of woman lets a man beg her for a divorce for fifteen years?"

She smirks, proud of her actions. "The kind that retains control."

"Control over her reputation, control over her social status... control over the money... Tell the truth, Mother, you won't divorce Dad because it will mean you lost...to her."

Her face falls.

"We both know why you hate Grace...she reminds you of someone, doesn't she?"

"Stop it," she snaps. "Get out."

"I'm not finished. I recently came across some very interesting information," I snarl. "I went to our lawyer to add my children to our family trust."

Her eyes widen.

"You can imagine my disbelief when I found out it was already under review, that somebody had recently tried to amend it."

"I had to do it," she splutters.

Fire flickers in my eyes, I feel it deep in my soul. "You cut your own daughter from our family trust?"

She tilts her chin to the sky in defiance. "I warned her."

"To what...to toe the line, to do things your way. To not marry Helena?"

"Helena is no good for Carina."

"Because she's a woman?" I yell.

"Because she's American. I have told you all again and again, I will not tolerate this behavior," she yells at the top of her voice.

"You do not get to dictate who we love. You racist bigot!" I bellow. "Carina is the backbone of Ferrara Media; she has worked her guts out for years and you had the audacity to cut *her* from her inheritance without telling any of us?"

"I stand by it."

"What have you ever done for Ferrara Media other than to drive our father away?" I scream.

"He left of his own free will," she spits more of her venom. "If he loved any of you, he would have stayed."

"Let me make something crystal clear, Mother. I have blocked

435

the amendment; I've told Dad what you tried to do and he's fucking furious. I will spend every last fucking penny I have to protect Carina and fight this...*and you*..." I whisper, "...will get nothing."

She stares at me, guilt written all over her face.

I had hoped I was wrong; I'd hoped it was an error.

The truth hurts.

"How does it feel to betray your own children?" I whisper. "To cut your only daughter out of her inheritance because you don't like her fiancée?"

Her eyes well with tears. "I'm protecting her, I'm protecting you all."

"The only person we have ever needed protection from...was you."

Her silhouette blurs. I can't do this. I can't be here; I can't fight for her to be a good person any longer.

I turn and stumble out of her apartment.

That's it, I'm done.

She's broken my trust for the last time.

Grace

I hear the front door click and I rush to the foyer. Gabriel is standing there; his tie is off and his hair is messed.

Pain is written all over his face.

"Babe," I whisper as I take him into my arms, he drops his head into my neck and I hold him.

I don't know what just happened, but it's upset him deeply, I can feel it oozing out of his soul. We stand in each other's arms for a long time, and eventually he whispers, "I'm sorry I yelled at you."

"It's okay." He needs a soft place to fall.

He hugs me tighter.

"Your children want ice cream for dinner."

I feel him smile into my hair. "Me too."

I take his hand and lead him out into the back garden, where the children are painting on easels. "Daddy," they call in excitement. "We're painting pictures for you with our new paints."

"Great." He smiles softly, and with his arm around me, he kisses my temple. "I'm so grateful that you're here."

Suddenly, the world is right again.

We lie in the darkness in the cocoon of our bed.

Gabriel's head is on my chest, and I aimlessly run my fingers through his hair. Tonight we've hit a new level of intimacy. It's not sexual or romantic, it's a closeness that only family can provide.

He's quiet.

And as much as I want to know what went on tonight, I'm not asking. He will tell me when he's good and ready.

"I don't know why she's like this..." he whispers.

I keep my fingers running through his hair, I'm enjoying it as much as he is.

"She changed when he left."

Who left?

"And the worst part is, I knew he was going to leave and I never told her."

I frown as I try to keep up with the conversation.

"I started working at Ferrara straight out of school, and there was no training period. I went straight to the top floor, straight into management."

I smile as I listen, he's so good at his job, I'm not surprised.

"At the time, I thought it was because he believed in me...but now I know he was just..." He pauses. "He was training me to take over from him when he left. He had planned what was going to happen long before it ever did."

I kiss his forehead as I listen.

"At first, he would go to Italy for a few weeks at a time...the visits became more frequent and longer.

"I ran the company while he was gone, the staff and processes were all in place, I could handle it." He falls quiet for a moment as if thinking back. "Then the fighting between him and Mom began and I could see what was happening."

What the hell is he talking about now?

"I was right there...I saw everything. Then he went to Italy for a month. He was helping his brother run Ferrara Industries over there, but the truth was...he could be who he wanted to be over there...with her."

Okay, I'm lost...

"I hated her, I hated everything about her and what she had done to our family. That he chose her over us."

My heart sinks, his father had an affair.

"I swore I'd never be him; I would never be that weak and give in to temptation."

I hold him in my arms just a little bit tighter.

"But then...it happened," he whispers. "When you started."

"What happened?" I ask softly.

"I'm not the first Ferrara man who wanted his PA."

My eyes widen...oh, fuck.

His father had an affair with his PA and left the family for her.

"And I fought it with everything I had, I was mean and horrible to you. I blamed you for making me feel weak and out of control."

My heart sinks as I remember the time I worked for him.

"I paraded other women, did everything in my power to show you the worst of me. To make you hate me so that I could hold my mother's honor and be the man to head my family, the one thing my father couldn't do."

I get a lump in my throat as I listen, my heart hurts just remembering it.

"And through every one of my flaws...you loved me anyway."

32

Grace

I FLUFF the pillows as I make the bed, I can't stop thinking about what Gabriel told me last night about his father. When I started at Ferrara all those years ago, I knew his father had gone to Italy and that Gabriel had recently taken over from him, but I never knew that he had taken off and left his family for his PA.

Just what the hell, how wasn't I aware of this? Did *anyone* know, or was it an in-house secret? A million scenarios are running through my head as I remember the things Gabriel did and said to me back then.

The women he paraded, the hurtful dismissive comments.

The pain I felt.

All this time I thought he was the devil, when all he was trying to do was not follow in his father's footsteps.

It's literally a miracle that we found our way back to each other.

Gabriel is in the shower and I pull the quilt up and turn it down. After dumping all this information on me last night, he fell fast asleep, and while he slept like a baby, my mind went into overdrive.

His poor mother, I know he's telling me she's evil, but how can I believe that? I saw the way she looked at the kids yesterday and I can't imagine living through the horror she has. I didn't blame her for hating me before, but now...

Now the context has a whole other meaning, a worse meaning.

Lucia walks into my bedroom, all crumpled and sleepy with wild hair, and not far behind her is her brother. "Where's Dad?" Dominic asks.

"He's in the shower." I continue to put the cushions on the bed and draw the curtains, the expansive New York skyline comes into view, the sun is just coming up over the city and I smile as I look out over it.

I love this city... A deep sense of closure on a horrible part of my life has come to fruition. The sun coming up over the city has a deeper beauty to me today.

A peace that I haven't felt in such a long time.

I get it now, the puzzle has clicked together as to why it transpired the way it did, and to be honest, I don't blame him anymore. How could I?

Falling for his PA was the very worst thing in his mind that he could ever do.

It's time.

"Hey," I hear Gabriel call. "You can't be in here, I'm naked."

I glance around to see the two kids standing in the bathroom, trying to talk to him, he's all soaped up with his hand over his privates.

"Why?" Dominic frowns.

"Because..." he splutters.

"We see Mom in the nude all the time," Lucia replies.

"Yeah, well...your mom's a freak," Gabriel says.

I giggle and lean on the doorjamb as I watch them.

"Grace..." Gabriel says, his two hands now covering himself, self-conscious.

"It's okay, Gabe, it's normal for kids see you naked and talk to you while you're in the shower."

"Is it, though?" He widens his eyes. "This is a little more junk than they're used to."

I giggle.

No shit.

It's a little more junk than anyone is used to.

"Okay, guys, let Dad shower in peace." I usher them out of the bathroom and out into the kitchen. "I'm making some breakfast."

The kids flop onto the couch and turn the TV on to watch their shows and I get to making pancakes while I think.

If we're going to do this, I need to go all in.

Twenty minutes later, Gabriel appears, he's wearing a navy suit with a pale blue shirt, his leg-opener cologne, and is simply irresistible. He takes me into his arms, his lips drop to my neck. "I love it when my whorebag is barefoot in my kitchen." He grabs my behind roughly and I giggle.

"You mean the whorebag who doesn't put out?"

"Come to think of it—" he kisses my neck, "—she's terrible at her job."

"I made you breakfast."

"I don't have time."

"Sit," I snap. "You're not going anywhere until you eat pancakes. Kids, breakfast is ready," I call.

He rolls his eyes and sits down and the kids join us too. He serves out the pancakes. "What are you guys doing today?" he asks.

"Well..." I sip my coffee. *Am I really going to say this?* "I thought the kids and I might do the rounds and look at some schools."

Gabriel's eyes flick up.

"What do you say, kids, do you want to stay here with Dad in New York through the week and we go home to Greenville on the weekends?"

The twins' eyes are wide.

"We could have the best of both worlds." I smile to try and sweeten the deal. "You could play sports at home on the weekends with your friends and then you could make new friends here at school through the week."

Gabriel takes my hand over the table and lifts it to his lips and kisses it softly.

I smile as I look around at the kids. "We can't leave Dad here by himself, we have to stay together. So it's all of us here, or all of us at Greenville."

"We would be at both places," Gabriel says as he looks between them. "It will be so fun living here all together."

"Could I get a new pink backpack?" Lucia says seriously.

"Yes. Without a doubt," Gabriel answers.

Seriously...that's her demand?

Dominic twists his lips. "But what about Tommy?"

"Tommy could come and stay here sometimes," I offer. "And we could take him to Central Park and go bike riding. You'll see him every weekend too, he will still be your best friend, nothing will change."

Dominic smiles as he imagines it.

"But only if we find a good school." I pretend it's not already decided in my mind.

Gabriel smiles broadly, knowing it's a done deal. He gets up and gets the ice cream from the freezer and puts a scoop on everyone's pancakes.

"What are you doing?" I smirk.

"Celebrating."

Gabriel

I have so much work to do that it's not even funny and yet I sit here in my office, rolling my fingers on the desk, staring into space. A date... A date...

My A game date.

Where the fuck am I taking Gracie for our first date?

I don't want a three-hour date either, I want a full night alone with her...blow-her-fucking-mind style.

But then, who do I get to babysit, I know she won't leave the children with just anyone.

Maybe Mark...hmm, she won't be happy with that.

I mean, I could ask Carina or one of my brothers, but I've not even let them meet yet because I wanted to sort the stuff out with Mom first...not that there's anything remotely sortable now.

No, I want to do the family meeting with inviting them over to our place for dinner, make a real effort in bringing everyone together for the first time.

Maybe I'll call Deb and ask her to come for the weekend.

I open my computer and type into Google.

Best first date locations

I read through the options and roll my eyes. "Fuck off, that's cringey." I twist my lips as I think some more.

Most romantic restaurants in New York

No. No. No... "Who writes this bullshit?"

Hmm...where is going to put us in the mood? I think about getting Gracie naked and my cock begins to pump between my legs.

I need to fuck.

Hard.

This date has to be a deal-breaker.

I type into Google.

Love songs

My door opens and Alessio sticks his head around it. "Hey."

"Hi."

"You going home today or what?" he asks.

I glance up to see it's getting dark outside, the New York lights

443

have begun to light up the sky. "Come in here for a moment," I say. "Close the door behind you."

"Yeah." He flops onto the couch. "What?"

"Where can I take Gracie for our first date?"

"Huh?" He frowns. "I thought she was already here."

"She is."

"Isn't she already in love with you?"

"Yeah, but..." I exhale. "Focus on the question...what is the best date I can take her on...like of all time." I lean back on my chair. "Like blow-her-mind kind of dating."

He thinks for a moment. "Blow her mind...or your mind?"

"Huh?"

"Well, if it's blow her mind, take her to a sex club and let five hung dudes rail her."

I screw up my face. "What?"

"I guarantee she'll never forget it." He smirks.

I pinch the bridge of my nose. "Why are you such an idiot?"

"If a woman took me on a first date and lined up five hot women for me to nail...I'd marry her on the spot." He shrugs. "Just saying."

"Out." I point to the door. "Imbecile."

He chuckles as he leaves, and I slowly pack up my desk while I keep thinking.

Paris...maybe Prague. Thailand is nice this time of year.

What about Aspen?

Hmm....

Fuck this, I've been tearing my hair out all day, trying to think of something.

All I know is that it needs to be in the next two days, because my balls are literally about to explode, and not in the good way.

All this family shit is great, but fuck me...I need some pussy love.

I walk into the bathroom and eye the shower...maybe just a quick wank to get me through until bedtime.

No...behave. Go home.

I take the elevator to the ground floor and walk out to Mark standing beside the car. "Hello." He smiles.

"I still hate you, remember?"

"I prefer to forget." He opens the car door for me and I get into the backseat. I stare out the window as we drive along.

What about Antarctica?

It's white, cold, and not much else to do but fuck in bed...that would work.

That would work great.

I exhale heavily and stare out the window.

"Tough day, boss?"

"Yeah." I sigh. "I'm trying to think of the perfect first date to take Gracie on."

His eyes meet mine in the rearview mirror. "That's easy."

"Enlighten me."

"Take her to your favorite place on earth...and just be you."

"Just me isn't good enough for Gracie."

He smiles as he turns the corner.

"What?"

"Have you seen the way she looks at you, man?"

"How does she look at me?" I frown.

"Like you walk on water."

"Yeah well, she can talk..." I smile at the warm fuzzy feeling that only my Gracie can give me. "She hung the moon."

Twenty minutes later, we pull into the underground parking lot and Mark pulls the car up to a halt, I climb out and lean in to get out my briefcase.

"Daddy!" squeals through the parking lot. "Daddy!"

I look up to see the twins bolting toward me, so excited to see me that they jump into my arms. I pick them both up and their little hands wrap around my neck.

Oh...

I get a lump in my throat.

I glance over and see Mark and the boys have the biggest smiles too.

And then I see her, my love.

Standing by the elevator, how long has she been waiting down here with them to give me that surprise welcome home?

With the twins in my arms, I walk toward her and kiss her softly, my lips lingering over hers. "You're going to get it," I whisper.

She giggles as she hits the elevator button.

"What's she going to get?" Lucia asks. "Can we all have one?"

"No," I mutter. "This is for Mom only."

Suddenly, I know exactly the date that I want to take Gracie on... I'm taking her to my favorite place on earth and I'm going to be myself.

We get into the elevator. As we ride to the top, I hitch the kids up as they begin to slip off my hips. "I have a surprise for you."

Grace raises an eyebrow, thinking she knows what it is.

"Debbie is coming to New York for the weekend to stay with you guys while Mom and I go away for grown-up time."

"She is?" they gasp, excited.

"Yes, she and Mark are going to stay with you. It's going to be so fun." My eyes find Gracie's. "How does that sound?"

She smiles softly. "That sounds perfect."

I walk down the sidewalk with Mark, I have a suit fitting a couple of blocks away and it's quicker to walk.

"So...Debbie," Mark says.

I give him the side eye. "What about her?"

Mark and Debbie seem to have become familiar with each other through us, and I wish I could say I haven't been suspicious, but I have.

"What's her husband like?" he asks.

"I don't really know him, seems a bit boring if you ask me."

He nods as he listens, and I get the feeling he has something to say.

"Why do you ask?"

He shrugs as he acts casual. "She's just—"

"What?" I cut him off.

"Nice."

"What do you mean, nice?"

He shrugs.

"Nice in church or nice sucking cock?"

He rolls his lips guiltily.

"You did not," I snap as I punch him. "I swear to god I'll fucking kill you."

"Of course I didn't."

"So why are you asking?"

"I just..."

"You what?"

"I may have looked into her husband."

"And?"

"He's not who you think he is."

"What makes you say that?"

"Things don't add up."

"You had him followed?" I snap.

"Investigated," he fires back. "For interest's sake."

"Because you like her?"

"Yeah...maybe I do."

"Maybe you fucking don't. She happily married."

"If she's so happily married, why did a woman stay at his house on Saturday night while Deb was away for work?"

My eyes hold his. "*What?*"

"So..."

"So nothing. You need to stay out of this," I fire back.

This is all I fucking need.

"But it's..."

"It's illegal to stake out someone." I drag my hand down my

face. "You don't know, she could have been there with his friend. Does he have a friend? Is she his sister or something?"

"I don't know."

"You don't fucking know; you have no facts and no reason to stalk him other than to break up her marriage. Stay out of it."

He exhales heavily.

"Did you sleep with her?"

"No." He screws up his face. "She's not like that."

"What did you do?"

"Just talked to her."

"About what...your dick?"

He smirks.

"You are not to go near her, do you hear me."

He rolls his eyes, unimpressed.

"I mean it. Stay. Away. From Debbie."

Grace

Wednesday night.

The waiter arrives at our table. "Can I take your order please?"

Gabriel is sick of cooking, and between you and me, we are sick of his cooking...so we've come out to dinner when he got home from work.

"What do you want, Dominic?" he asks.

"Pasta."

"We'll have two of the spaghetti bolognese, please, and I'll have the steak." He looks over to me. "Babe?"

"I'll have the salad, please." I smile.

"Thank you," Gabriel says, the waiter disappears and the twins start to squabble.

Gabriel opens up his phone and brings Netflix up and puts a movie on, he sets the phone up against the salt and pepper shakers and they quieten down as they begin to watch. I smile and Gabriel takes my hand in his and kisses it softly.

"Hello," a woman's voice says.

We look up to see Ariana standing over us.

Oh crap.

Gabriel's face falls. "Ariana."

"I was going to come and see you tomorrow, but I guess now is as good a time as ever," she says.

"What do you mean?" he says impatiently.

"I'm pregnant."

The earth moves beneath me.

No...

"Congratulations." Lucia smiles up at her.

Dear god.

33

Grace

GABRIEL SITS BACK in his chair, unimpressed. "Don't do this."

"Do what?" She puts her hands on her hips, indignant.

"Lie."

"Not planned, obviously." Ariana smirks over at me. "It just happened."

I feel myself melting into the boiling pot of deep, dark hell.

Gabriel's brow furrows and he holds his hand up to stop Mark who is walking through the restaurant toward us.

"Let us pretend for a moment that I wasn't pulling out for the last three months that we were together."

"You were not," she snaps.

He raises his eyebrow. "I'm not stupid, Ariana."

Her eyes hold his.

"And if you are..." he frowns as he does the math... "ten weeks pregnant, can you explain to me why you've been drinking like a fish?"

Her mouth falls open.

"In fact, I believe you were at the Junction Cocktail Bar on Saturday night until two a.m., very inebriated, and left with a man who came back to your house." He folds his napkin in front of him. "He left around eleven thirty the next morning and then returned that night."

"You've had someone following me," she gasps. "You still care."

He lets out a slow, evil smile. "What I care about is you trying to manipulate me...and I knew you would try. I just wanted an insurance policy as proof for when the time came."

Thank god.

He raises his hand, and Mark walks over. "I must ask you to leave," Mark tells her as he takes her elbow in his hand.

She pulls her elbow from his grip. "Don't touch me."

"Get her out of here," Gabriel snaps.

Mark escorts Ariana from the restaurant, and I swallow the lump in my throat.

My heart is pumping hard in my chest. Gabriel takes my hand in his. "Sorry, my love." He kisses my fingertips. "I hate to say it, but I knew it was coming."

I give him a weak smile, glad he knew it was coming, because I am totally rattled.

"What's pulling out?" Dominic asks.

Gabriel frowns. "Out of that whole conversation, that's what you got?"

Dominic nods. "Yes."

I burst out laughing.

Gabriel sips his drink, unimpressed. "Something you must always do."

I put my hands on my hip as I look around my giant-sized wardrobe filled to the brim with designer clothes, beautiful shoes and swanky handbags. Surely, something in here is date worthy... But the question is, does it fit me?

It's Thursday, and tomorrow Gabriel is taking me on our first date, and he's organized for Deb to come for the weekend to look after the kids.

We're going away alone for two whole nights; I've never been away from the kids for two nights. I'm excited and nervous and had to wax my own bits because I didn't have a sitter to go to the salon.

Right... I take a black dress off the hanger and hold it up, this seems okay. I hold it up over my body and look in the mirror.

Tight sleeves...ugh, they won't go over my plaster. I hang it back up. I pull out another dress, pink and pretty, short sleeves...I could get this one on, I guess. I hold it up to my body and look in the mirror...meh.

I put it back on the hanger.

My phone rings, and the name *Deb* lights up the screen. "Hi there."

"Hello, this is jet-setter babysitter extraordinaire speaking."

I giggle.

"What are you doing?"

"I'm in the overpriced wardrobe, trying to find something to wear to our date. Did he tell you where we were going?"

"No, but I think it's somewhere exotic."

"Why?"

"Because he said he was using another jet because there wasn't time to refuel the one that I am coming in on."

My eyes widen. "So we're flying somewhere?"

"Uh-huh."

"Like where?" I really begin to panic, I am not swimsuit ready... fuck, maybe I should fake tan too. I can't do it with one hand...maybe the kids could...no. I push that pea brain idea straight out of my head.

"I don't know."

"Should I wear a dress or a skirt and top or..."

"Dress. Definitely a dress."

"But then I can't wear high heels because of my stupid ankle."

"Babe...relax. He's only going to be looking at your lingerie."

"Probably."

"And to be honest, I'm thinking you could wear a garbage bag and he'd still be impressed."

Nerves dance in my stomach at the thought. "I've waited so long for this date.

I want it to be perfect."

"It will be."

"Thank you so much for coming and doing this for us."

"Oh...because flying in a private jet to come stay in a penthouse in New York is so fucking hard...you owe me big-time, bitch."

I smile down at the phone. "I love you."

"See you tomorrow."

"Where are we going?" I ask.

"For the hundredth time, it's a surprise." Gabriel rolls his eyes as he packs his bag.

"But like...I can't wear high heels; you remember that, don't you? So if we go somewhere swanky, I'll be like a hobo in flip-flops."

"You won't need high heels." He puts a pair of boardshorts into the bag.

"So we're going somewhere where we'll be swimming?"

"Stop looking at my bag." He points to the door. "Out."

"I haven't finished packing," I fire back, that's a deplorable lie, I just want to look in his bag some more.

He walks into the bathroom and begins to pack his toiletries. "Ah, almost forgot."

Almost forgot what?

I keep pretending to pack, and he reappears with a bottle of something and throws it on top of his bag.

"What's that?" I frown.

"Lube."

"Ha." I smirk. "As if I need lube."

He raises an eyebrow as he gives me the look.

Oh...

Where does he plan to fuck me this weekend? Crap, something tells me I'm in for some deviant sex god pain.

Flustered, I keep packing. Honestly, how does he have the ability to fry my brain with just a look? "Yeah well—" I try to keep up with his dirty promises, "I packed you some Viagra."

"Needn't have bothered, I already have a double prescription," he fires back without missing a beat.

I stop what I'm doing and smile over at him, and he smiles too and then takes me in his arms. "To be honest, I'm just excited to have you to myself for a few days."

He kisses me softly.

"Me too. I don't care where we go, as long as I get to go with you."

He kisses me again, his lips lingering over mine, and these moments of just the two of us are sacred.

There's a mystical magic that swirls between us, it's been such a long time coming and yet it feels so exciting and new. Like we've always known each other...but we didn't really know each other at all.

It's utterly ridiculous how in love we are and we haven't even been having sex, maybe it's because we haven't been having sex. I don't know what it is, but we seem to have gotten the recipe right, we simply cannot get enough of each other.

This is what it's supposed to feel like.

In my past relationships, I always knew something was missing, but for the life of me, I couldn't work out what it was...now I know.

It was Gabriel Ferrara.

It's always been him.

Gabriel's phone beeps a text, and he picks it up and reads it.

"They're coming into the parking lot now. Let's go."

"Am I going to get to spend time with Deb?" I frown.

"Five minutes. The plane was delayed, and we are scheduled to leave." He zips up his bag. "Lucia and Dominic," he calls.

"Yeah?" Dominic calls.

Gabriel curls his top lip. "When I call you...please don't yell yeah," he calls back.

"Yeah, well...I'm watching television. What do you want, Dad?"

Gabriel pretends to choke the air.

I giggle, the kids' cheekiness is beginning to grate on him, the novelty of being a new father is wearing off.

"Come in here now!" I call more sternly.

"Ugh," I hear Dominic moan; he and Lucy eventually drag themselves into our bedroom.

"You two behave for Deb this weekend, please," Gabriel says.

"Yes."

"And go to bed when she tells you, none of this we're-allowed-to-stay-up-late business," I tell them.

"And nobody is allowed in the hot tub or pool." Gabriel frowns. "Actually, nobody is allowed outside without Mark or Debbie with you."

"Yes, okay."

"And you have your phones, you can call us at any time," he adds. "I put Mom's number in there for you too."

"All right."

The door clicks. "Deb's here."

"Hello," she calls.

The kids and I run to the top of the stairs to see Deb and Mark walking through the front door.

"Deb," they cry as they run down the stairs while I hobble along behind them. They hug her while I wait my turn and I grab her in a bear hug. "Oh my god, I missed you." I hold her tight.

There is no better friend in the world than my beautiful Deb.

"Holy shit. Look at this place," she gasps as she looks around.

"Hello, Debbie." Gabriel smiles awkwardly, he gives her a quick peck on the cheek.

"Hello."

"Thank you so much for doing this for us."

"It's my pleasure." She takes the kids by the hands. "Show me around, then."

Gabriel and Mark stay in the living room, chatting, and to the sounds of oohs and ahhs, the kids and I show her around. We get to our bedroom and her eyes widen. "You're fucking kidding me, right?" she whispers as she stares out over the view.

"This is my wardrobe." I open the door to show her.

Her eyes widen. "What the hell, it's bigger than my bedroom."

I get the giggles. "Stupid."

"Oh jeez." She looks around with her hands on her hips. "A weekend here is going to be tough."

"Are you sure you're going to be okay?" The kids run out of the room, bored with our conversation.

"Yep." She smiles. "And Mark is staying with me if I need anything."

"He's staying here." I frown. "In this apartment?"

"Yes. Gabriel wants him to stay with us to be safe."

My eyes hold hers for an extended beat.

"Don't." She smirks.

"Really?"

"Get your mind out of the gutter."

"I'm just saying."

"You don't need to. I'm happily married."

"Remember that."

"When have I ever forgotten?" she gasps.

"When you locked eyes with Mark for the first time."

"Stop." She smiles as she hugs me. "Go and be exotic somewhere, you rich bitch."

"I love you, thank you so much for this."

"Have fun, babe, you deserve it." She holds me tight.

I tear up, because more than anyone, Deb knows what I've been through because she's been through it with me. Every hard step of the way with these babies, Deb has been my rock. Throughout the pregnancy, the birth, their lives...she's stepped up and been their second mom and the partner I never had.

"Thank you for everything, Deb, I owe you so much."

"Stop blubbering. Your friendship is all I ever want...actually."
She looks in my wardrobe. "I'll have your hand-me-downs too."

"Deal."

We giggle and walk back out to the living room. "Let's go."

Five hours later.

The stewardess walks up the plane. "We're preparing to land, Mr. Ferrara." She smiles.

"Thank you," he replies.

I have no idea how long we've been flying; he's taken my phone and my watch. "Can I see?" I go to open the blind on the window and Gabriel snaps it shut.

"It's a surprise."

"But we're here, *this* is the surprise time."

"Not until we get there." He widens his eyes and pulls out a blindfold.

What?

Ha-ha, oh my god.

Honestly, this is the most exciting thing that has ever happened to me, being flown to a secret location on a private jet for a first date with the hottest man alive.

I feel like a Bond girl or something.

The plane pulls to a stop, and Gabriel puts the blindfold on me. "Are you serious?" I whisper as I hold it over my eyes.

"Totally." He leads me by the hand down the aisle of the plane.

"I'm totally going to fall down the stairs, you know how clumsy I am, and that's when I can see where I'm going."

"Don't remind me." He leads me to the door of the plane. "Thank you." He lifts the blindfold just a little so I can see the stairs as I walk down them. It's dark outside, and although I try to peek, I can't see anything of significance.

The wind whips my hair around, it's not as hot as I thought it would be. Maybe my dream of a tropical island isn't happening.

Where the hell are we?

We get to the bottom of the stairs and he pulls the blindfold back up and leads me to the car. "Surely you can tell me now?"

"No." He puts his hand on the top of my head and pushes me into the car and then climbs in beside me. As the car takes off, he takes my hand and holds it in his. "Not long now."

I smile as my heart races, hardly able to control my excitement. "Just tell me already."

He chuckles and takes my face into his hands and kisses me, his lips lingering over mine. "Patience," he whispers into my ear; his breath sends goose bumps up my spine, and I smile, I have no idea if anyone is watching us or what.

This is already the best night of my life.

What seems like forever later, the car pulls to a stop.

"Stay still for a moment." Gabriel holds my hand to keep me still, he readjusts my blindfold. "Keep it on," he demands.

Jeez.

"Bit over the top, isn't it?" I giggle.

"Absolutely."

He comes around to my side and helps me out. "This way."

I smile excitedly as he leads me along. "Where *are* we?"

"Somewhere special."

I stumble. "If I break my other ankle."

"Don't even think about it." He stands me still and then pauses for a moment as if waiting for something.

"What's going on?" I smile in wonder.

He slowly takes the blindfold off, and I look around...wait? It takes a moment for my eyes to focus and catch up with my brain.

Huh...I'm so confused.

We're at my house in Greenville in the back garden on the lake.

There's a picnic rug on the jetty with candles all around it, and fairy lights hang overhead from the trees. The moon's reflection dances across the water, and the stars shine bright in the sky. My eyes go to him. "I don't understand. You said you were taking me to your favorite place on earth."

"*This* is my favorite place on earth." He smiles softly.

My eyes search his.

"It's where I found you...and them...and us."

Oh.

"And if I were to be anywhere in the world, I would want to be here with you."

34

Grace

MY EYES FILL WITH TEARS. *He's good all right.*

"Well." I go up onto my toes to kiss his big lips. "You win."

"I win?"

"That is the most romantic thing that has ever been said to me."

"Yet." He smirks down at me.

"You did tell me you were bringing your A game."

"Let's see how I went." He takes me by the hand and leads me down to the jetty, the picnic blanket has padding under it and there are scattered cushions all around and a giant cane wicker picnic basket. He helps me sit down and kicks off his shoes and sits down beside me, he gets his phone out and scrolls through something. "I made you a playlist."

"Huh?"

He holds his phone out and shows me the Spotify screen.

A-Game Date Songs for Gracie

I burst out laughing. "Are you serious?"

His eyebrows flick up. "You asked for the cheese, and I am delivering." He presses play.

"You Were Always on My Mind" from Willie Nelson comes on. "This is track one," he tells me as he takes two crystal glasses from the picnic basket and fills them with champagne.

"You have a track list?"

"Yes, I've ramped them up to the finale." He passes me my glass and clinks it with his.

"There's a finale?" I ask.

His eyes twinkle with a certain something as he sips his champagne. "Grand finale."

Oh my lord...the grand finale is sex. Earth-shattering, bed-breaking sex.

That's it, I'm done. Let's skip to the grand finale now, because I'm about to orgasm on the spot.

He digs back into the picnic basket and produces a silver tray of chocolate-covered strawberries, and I laugh out loud. "What else do you have in that basket?"

"All kinds of random shit." He holds the tray out to me. "Chocolate strawberry, my love?"

"Did you make these?" I tease.

"Yes." He tips his head back and gulps his wine.

"Are you lying?"

"No comment."

Oh...I love this man.

"Can we skip straight to the grand finale right now?"

"No." He digs around in his basket and pulls out a package wrapped in brown paper with a big red ribbon bow. "I made you a present."

What?

"A present?"

"Open it." He passes it to me.

I lean in and kiss him; I hold his face in my hands because what the hell...this is the all-time of dates. I smile against his lips, lingering for a long time.

I don't want this night to ever be over.

"Open it," he repeats.

I untie the ribbon and slowly begin to peel back the paper.

"Just rip it," he tells me.

"No, I'm saving the paper."

"It's brown paper." He frowns. "Why would you want to save brown paper?"

"Did you make the paper?"

"Yes," he lies without hesitation. "I'll make you some more. Rip it."

I pull back the paper to reveal a square hardcover book, it's gold fabric and the title reads:

YOU

HUNG

THE

MOON

Hmm, weird, never took him as the type to buy me a book...but okay. I turn the page.

For Gracie

"Wait...what?" Oh, it's one of those name books, how cool.
I turn another page.

I want to hear your heartbeat from the inside.
I want to show you mine

"Oh." I think for a moment. "Wait, I've heard that before?" I turn the page.

You loved me at my worst.

462

Now let me love you at my best.

I'm so confused, what is this book? I turn another page and there's a picture of an ultrasound on the page printed into the book. Huh?

I concentrate to see that it's of a baby in the womb, oh wait... there are two babies.

I read the text on the other page.

The Lord knew that I would miss him so much that one baby couldn't fill the hole that he left
So he gave me two.

My eyes rise to meet his. "Did you make this book?"
He nods.
Oh...
His silhouette blurs.

It's not possible to miss someone this much.
It was...because I did

Realization sets in, I wrote these notes when I thought I would never see him again. "You found my box?"
"Yes."
"You read my letters?"
"Every last one."
I screw up my face in tears. "You made them into a...book?" My voice cracks with emotion, and I turn the page, I can hardly see the words.

From the moment I met her, I knew she was the one.

My heart ached for what I couldn't have.
So I loved her from afar

Oh...

He leans in and kisses me, his lips lingering over mine. "I love you, Gracie," he whispers. "I have always loved you."

"I love you." I smile against his lips. "Oh...man. You're good."

He chuckles. "How am I doing? Is this A game enough?"

"This is breaking the scoreboard."

He laughs and holds up a finger. "Ahh...but there's more."

"More?" I smile as I wipe my tears.

He texts something on his phone. "Unfortunately, I can't fit this part of our date into the magic picnic basket."

The back door of my house opens and a trail of people in white chefs' uniforms walk out carrying things.

Oh crap...was my house clean?

"What in the world?"

Two men put down a small round table and two chairs on the jetty, another man sets it with a white tablecloth and lights a candelabra in the center.

Then a stream of people carry out plates of food.

"What is this?" I gasp.

"Well..." He shrugs. "I couldn't take you to your favorite Italian restaurant in New York...so I ordered in."

"This is Becco?" My eyes widen. "You flew in Becco?"

His eyes glow with tenderness. "I wanted you to have your favorite food."

I choke up again. "Honestly, you could feed me stale bread tonight and it would be fabulous."

I see a trace of a smile cross the waiter's face as he puts the meal down in front of me. "Your entrée," he says, he takes the champagne and refills our glasses.

"Thank you." I smile.

"You may leave us," Gabriel says softly.

The waiter nods and disappears back into my house.

Gabriel listens to the song that is now playing. "Ah, yes, track seven," he says. "We are right on schedule, Gracie."

The Ed Sheeran song, *"I See Fire"*.

I imagine Gabriel picking the songs and making an agenda to go with it, and I smile as I listen. "This date is actually stupid."

"I was hoping for a bit better than stupid." He throws his head back and laughs out loud, and it's deep and velvety, it makes my stomach dance with butterflies.

"How did you even think of all this?"

"It's you." He sips his champagne.

"Me?"

"You magnify everything."

"What do you mean?" I frown.

"The way you make me feel, the good, the bad and the..." He shrugs. "You make me want to be better than I am. More romantic than I am." He tips his head as if searching for the right wording. "Just more."

I smile softly over at him...oh, *how I love this man.*

It's like every dream I had for the two of us has come to fruition. He's not the monster he is to the world, there's this deep, loving soul inside of him. I never imagined it all those years before, he felt it too.

I feel validated, I feel heard and seen...cherished.

Loved.

My eyes well with tears, overcome with emotion.

"Eat your dinner, crybaby." He smirks as he reaches over and begins to cut up my food. "We are three songs behind schedule."

I giggle as I wipe my eyes. "Sorry, boss."

Three hours later.

We've talked and laughed; we've eaten and drunk champagne. We've lain on the rug and stared up at the moon and gazed at the stars as they twinkled their magic down on us.

"It's been the perfect night." I smile over to my handsome date.

"We should dance." He stands and holds his hand out for me.

I take my time getting up.

"We are on a tight schedule, hurry up."

I giggle and stand. "This schedule of yours." He takes me into his arms and the song *"Turning Page"*, by Sleeping At Last comes on.

"Oh, this song," I whisper up at him. "This is...so dreamy..."

Like the perfect scene from the perfect movie, we dance under the moon by the lake.

I'm over here falling in love with him all over again...even more if that's physically possible.

"Gracie," he whispers.

"Yes." I smile up at him.

"It would be a privilege to call you mine...forever."

My heart stops as my eyes search his.

"Marry me." He kisses me softly and my feet float from the floor. "I know it's soon, but I cannot wait one day longer for us to be one."

The emotion between us is strong and so perfect.

"What do you say?" he murmurs into my ear.

"Yes." I smile through tears as I throw my arms around his neck. "Oh my god, yes."

He reaches into his pocket and pulls out a ring, a diamond solitaire...

It's huge.

My eyes widen. "What in the..."

He picks up my hand that's still in plaster and chuckles.

"Oh no. What?" I frown.

"The ring is not going to fit, sweetheart, your hand is still too swollen."

"Oh my god, jam it on there." I snatch the ring off him and try to squash it on, it only goes to the top knuckle.

Fucking go on.

"Wear it on your other hand until the swelling goes down."

I roll my eyes, only I could break my wrist so bad that my engagement ring won't go on...what are the chances?

He slides it onto my right hand and then kisses my fingertips.

"Can we go to bed now for the finale?" I giggle up at him.

"That was the finale." He smiles. "That's as romantic as I can do for tonight."

"It is?"

"Now I need to fuck you like I really, really, *really* hate you." He grabs my face and kisses me aggressively, and I laugh into him.

About time...

Romantic Gabriel is perfect...but dirty Mr. Ferrara is a god.

With our lips locked, he walks me into my bedroom backward, my dress is over my head, my bra is thrown to the side and he throws me back onto the bed.

"Open those pretty legs, you're about to get it," he says as he rips his T-shirt off over his head. His broad chest comes into view, his rippled abdomen, and his bronze olive skin. His dark hair is hanging in curls over his forehead, and the way he is looking at me...

Never have I seen a more beautiful man.

He unzips his jeans and slides them and his boxers down his legs and kicks them off.

My eyes drop down his body, his cock is hard and engorged with thick veins coursing down the length of it.

Good god.

I open my legs, drunk on his testosterone.

He goes to the bathroom and returns with a bottle of lube. "What are you doing?"

He puts it on his fingers and smears it through the lips of my sex. "The only thing touching you tonight is my cock."

Fuck.

Arousal screams through my body as he climbs over me. I put my hands on his thick quad muscles as they cradle inside my open legs. His teeth graze my skin and his hot breath sends shivers up my spine.

Holding himself up on his elbow, he slides the tip of his engorged cock through the lips of my sex, rubbing the lube into me as he stares down at me. I know why he wants it like this, where he's hardly touched me.

He wants me to struggle to take him.

Not a chance...I'm going to eat him alive.

He pushes forward, and I feel the burn of the stretch, I whimper and he takes my lips in his. The kiss as aggressive as the claim he's taking down below.

"Open those fucking legs," he growls.

I can hardly breathe. I open a little farther and he surges forward. In to the hilt.

My body ripples around him as it struggles with his size.

And then he kisses me, soft and with tenderness. "I love you," he murmurs as his eyes search mine. "I've waited so long for this night."

Tears escape and run into my ears. "And I love you."

He surges forward and I whimper, but it falls on deaf ears because he lifts my legs up over his shoulders and slams in deep.

I feel him sink into my bones as he takes his claim on my body.

No longer mine...but his.

Arousal so deep and primal that I can taste it.

He begins to ride me, deep, punishing pumps where the bed hits the wall and my toes curl...I can't hold it.

He's too much, too...inside every inch of me.

I cry out as I come hard, shuddering and shaking as I moan out of control.

His pumps get harder, quicker, he's no longer in control, the need to finish and come inside of me has taken him over.

He tips his head back and moans as he comes deep inside my body. We pant as we hold each other...and I am ruined forever.

But I'm not ruined, I've been saved.

My dream came true.

. . .

The morning sun peeks through the curtains, and I sneak out of bed and make my way downstairs in desperate need of a coffee. I walk into my kitchen and there's a huge bunch of red roses in a vase.

What in the world? Wasn't last night enough?

"My god." I open the card.

For the love of my life
For all of my life.
Gabriel.

I read it and smile as my heart literally flutters in my chest.

Could he be any more romantic?

"Mr. Ferrara, you are nothing like I imagined, but everything I had hoped for," I whisper dreamily to myself.

"Really?" Big hands snake around me from behind, and I feel him smile into my neck as he kisses me. "You are everything I imagined and even more than I dared to wish for." He turns me to face him and he looks down at me all serious. "I didn't give you your engagement bonus yet, Miss Porter."

I smile as he takes me back to where it all began.

I love this man.

"I thought you only gave bonuses in the office, sir."

He lifts and sits me on the kitchen table and pushes me back across it. "For you, I'll make an exception."

35

Grace

One month later.

SARDINIA.

Magic is real, I always dreamed it was, but now I have the proof.

In a twenty-eight-day whirlwind, we have achieved the impossible.

Organized a holiday, a wedding, a honeymoon, and booked in a lifetime of love.

This is it... It's actually happening.

I take one last look at myself in the mirror, my hair is out and in loose curls. Cream flowers are pinned behind one ear. My makeup is natural and I'm wearing the most beautiful flowing cream dress.

It's my wedding day, and even though I know we are having another wedding for friends and family by the lake at my house in a month, this is the one that counts.

Just the four of us, in my bucket list location with my dream man.

There are no pompous rules today, we all got ready together, and honestly, it's already been the best day of my life.

Gabriel comes out of the bathroom and I look him up and down and smile as my heart sings.

He's wearing a cream linen shirt with the top buttons undone, cream pants rolled up once at the bottom and no shoes. His dark hair is curled and even though this look is so far from the Gabriel Ferrara I thought I once knew, I now realize it's more him than ever.

Relaxed, carefree, and happy.

I've never seen anyone look so perfect in my life.

The kids are also completely dressed in cream, we wanted the photos to be natural and beachy.

Mark, our witness, and the photographer are the only two people here.

Gabriel's eyes drop to my toes and then back up to my face. "My god...look how beautiful you are." I smile into his kiss as he holds my face in his hands.

Butterflies flutter in my stomach, but not nervous butterflies, excited butterflies. The kind you get before you jump out of a plane.

"It's time," Mark says from the door.

The four of us walk out of the house hand in hand, across the lawn and down onto the beach. The priest is waiting down by the water under a giant arch of beautiful flowers.

Gabriel smiles over at me. "You ready to do this?"

Emotion overwhelms me and I nod, already teary.

We make our way to the arch and take our positions, Gabriel turns me toward him and takes my hands in his. The wind whips my hair around as I stare up into beautiful big brown eyes, and this is it.

I can hardly believe we're here, I feel like I'm having an out-of-body experience, hovering way up in the sky watching us from above.

The priest begins talking and going through the formalities...

but I don't hear a word because I am lost to the big brown eyes holding mine.

This is a monumental moment in our lives, and I want to memorize every single second. If only I could bottle the feeling of love between us.

It was worth it, every struggle and every tear...it was worth it.

Every day in each other's arms is a gift.

"Repeat after me."

"I, Gabriel, take you, Grace, to be my wife. I promise to be true to you in good times and in bad, in sickness and in health. I will love you and honor you all the days of my life."

My heart swells, I smile through tears as he tenderly kisses my fingertips.

"Repeat after me."

"I, Grace, take you, Gabriel, to be my husband. I promise to be true to you in good times and in bad, in sickness and in health. I will love you and honor you all the days of my life."

The priest blesses each of the rings and then passes them to us. Gabriel gives me a slow, sexy smile before he slides the gold band onto my finger. I hunch my shoulders up in excitement.

Is this really happening?

"In the name of the Father, the Son, and the Holy Spirit, will you take this ring as a sign of my love and faithfulness?" Gabriel asks.

"I do." I glance over to see Dominic and Lucia smiling goofily as they watch on.

Gabriel then holds his hand out, and I slide the gold band onto his finger.

"In the name of the Father, the Son, and the Holy Spirit, will you take this ring as a sign of my love and faithfulness?" I ask.

"I do." He winks playfully and my heart somersaults in my chest.

Oh, this is the best day of all time.

"I now pronounce you husband and wife." The priest turns to Gabriel with a big smile. "You may kiss your bride."

Gabriel takes my face into his hands and kisses me; his lips take mine with reverence and love, and my eyes close at the perfection between us.

He kisses me again, and again.

"Okay..." Dominic whispers, embarrassed. "Dad... That's enough already."

We giggle against each other's lips as he holds me close. "I love you."

"I love you." I hold him close. "So, so much."

We've been through hell and back to get to this moment but I'm not sure I would change a thing. Our history has made our love so much sweeter because it's something that we never thought we could have.

It's a blessing that we do.

His lips drop to my neck. "Mrs. Ferrara," he breathes against my skin as his hand drops to my behind.

The priest...

I discreetly try to edge back from him and, as if reading my mind, he gives me a breathtaking smile.

Gabriel Ferrara...my husband.

We made it.

The children casually chatter as we drive along and yet all Gabriel and I can do is stare at each other.

We're married.

Bound by the law, the four of us, a family...

The car pulls to a stop at a marina and the door opens, Mark is smiling broadly as he helps the twins and then takes my hand as I climb out of the car. "Mrs. Ferrara." He nods.

"Now, that has a ring to it." Gabriel chuckles as he climbs out behind me.

I giggle, feeling drunk with happiness, and I hold up my hand. "A diamond ring, actually."

Gabriel's eyes twinkle with a special kind of magic, and he

473

takes me into his arms as he looks down at me. "Are you ready for your honeymoon, my Gracie?"

I look down the dock to the huge super yacht waiting at the end of the pier for us, I can't believe we are sailing around Italy for three whole weeks.

"You bet I am."

I feel like I've waited my whole life for this trip.

The four of us cross the gangplank to the yacht, the staff are lined up on the bridge to welcome us aboard. "Congratulations, sir." The captain smiles.

Gabriel laughs out loud as he shakes his hand and then pulls him into a hug.

His excitement is palpable and I choke up as I watch him.

My heart.

As the children skip ahead Gabriel takes my hand and we walk onto the boat...yacht...frigging ship more like. We walk onto the deck and through the large doors, and over-the-top luxury hits us in the face. Polished timber, a grand staircase, and gorgeous furnishings. Rugs and a piano and...what the hell...

"Holy wow," the kids scream in excitement as they run from room to room.

This is more like a resort than a yacht. I look around in awe. "My god, Gabe..." I whisper. "Your yacht is..."

"Our yacht," he cuts me off, he turns me toward him and takes my two hands in his. "Do you like it?" he asks hopefully.

I nod as my eyes roam around, shocked to silence. There are no words to describe how beautiful this is. "I love it, and I love you..." I whisper.

He kisses me softly. "Our life together starts now."

My eyes well with tears. "It's about damn time."

A white light dances across the water as the full moon casts her reflection, and the sound of waves gently lapping on the yacht fills the air.

The candles flicker in the glass votives. Fresh flowers adorn the table and nothing has been left to chance. Beautiful white linen, the best silverware and a five-course meal cooked by the best chef in the world... Lobster and pasta and sashimi and oh...what a banquet we had.

"Let's get you into bed," Gabriel says as he picks up Lucia; she's half asleep and lying on the couch. "Up." He lays her carefully over his shoulder before leaning her down. "Kiss Mom good night."

I kiss her forehead. "Good night, baby."

"Night." She frowns as if I'm the biggest inconvenience and snuggles back into her father's shoulder. I kiss Dominic and give him a hug. "Good night, bubba, I love you."

"Love you too."

"Can we sleep in your bed?" Lucia grumbles.

"Absolutely not." He walks inside as Dominic follows them.

"How come?" Dominic asks.

"It's why not. How come isn't a sentence."

I smile as I listen to them squabble.

"Okay then... So why not?" Dominic continues.

"Because..." He begins to walk up the stairs. "You're a big boy now and...well."

"Well why?"

"Because I said so, that's why," he snaps. "Mom and I got married today and we want to sleep alone."

"Mom likes it when we sleep with her," he argues.

"Oh my...god..." Gabriel mutters under his breath. "Trust me, you do not want to be in our bed tonight."

"But this boat is scary."

"It is *not* scary, there is nothing on this yacht that is scary, Dominic," he snaps as he climbs the stairs. "Other than me."

"Ha, you're not scary." Dominic slaps his father on the behind. "What about the sharks, sharks can jump onto yachts, you know."

"Nooo," Lucia chips in. "Can they?"

"A shark cannot jump onto a yacht; you're just making this up now." They disappear up to the next floor.

I sip my champagne and smile. Listening to the children heckle Gabriel every day is my most favorite thing in the world. Funnily enough, when it comes to them he has the patience of a saint.

With me...not so much, but I'll happily take his grumpiness because the masochist in me finds it hot.

Smoking hot.

I refill my glass of champagne and smile into the wind. I hold my hand out and look at my rings, a diamond solitaire and the gold wedding band.

Who knew that wearing a ring on a finger would hold such a significant importance to me...but it does, somehow it means everything and then some.

What a perfect day.

We swam and laughed, drank champagne and Zoomed with the family. Not even in my wildest dreams could I have imagined a more perfect day, and to be honest, I don't even know if I want another wedding ceremony when we get home now, I mean... How could you top this?

The four of us is all I need.

For a long time, I sit and drink in the beauty of my surroundings and eventually walk to the edge of the yacht and look over to the land to see the lights of Sardinia twinkling against the blackened sky. Tomorrow we head ashore to go exploring and I can hardly wait.

I feel him before I see him, the heat radiating out of his large body behind mine as he snugs up against me. He pulls my hair to one side and his big lips drop to my neck.

"Mrs. Ferrara."

Goose bumps scatter up my spine as he pulls my hips back against his, I feel his thick length up against my behind.

He turns my head and takes my face into his hands and kisses me deeply. His tongue taking no prisoners as he claims what's his.

Oh...

There's an edge to his kiss tonight, a deeper connection running between us.

Married...

His hand slides up underneath my dress, and with his lips locked on mine, he undoes the ties on my string bikini bottoms. They fall to the floor.

My eyes flick open and I glance around as I hesitate.

"Nobody is here," he murmurs against me.

"But the . . ."

"Staff are all retired for the night and won't be coming back up," he cuts me off. His hand trails up my inner thigh and then through my legs from behind to open the lips of my sex.

My heart is racing at the possibility of getting caught. We kiss as he strokes me long and deep and my eyes roll back in my head.

Fuck...he's good at this.

His thick fingers slide into my sex and I whimper as my body contracts around them. Rippling to try to entice him to go deeper. His breathing is labored and I'm close. Dear god...he's been touching me for all of two minutes.

"Let's go to bed," I whisper.

"No." He pulls his hardened cock out of his shorts and pins me against the rail. "You always wanted to come to Sardinia...didn't you?"

"Yes," I murmur as I feel his erection against my behind, he's rock hard and ready to fuck.

"I keep my promises. I told you I would bring you here, and now... The first time I take you as my wife, you will do exactly that."

I frown, confused.

"You will come." He lifts one of my legs to open me up for him and slides in deep. "As you look at Sardinia."

He grabs a handful of my hair and pulls my head up. "Watch it," he growls as he loses control. The twinkling lights of Sardinia light up the shoreline and I smile as his thick cock slides in deep.

This is so him.

"You're perverted." I smile.

He bites my neck hard as he smiles against my skin and goose bumps scatter up my spine. With a handful of my hair in his closed fist he jerks my head back. "Look at the pretty lights while I fuck you, Mrs. Ferrara."

He slams in hard and my hormones scream into overdrive.

I married a god.

Six months later.

"Lucia, Dominic," Gabriel calls upstairs. "Your aunties are here to collect you."

He opens the front door. "Hello." He kisses his sister, Carina, before turning and kissing Helena. "Thank you for this."

"Are you kidding? This is the highlight of our week." Carina smiles.

"Hi, guys." I come down the stairs and kiss them both on the cheek. "I'm running late as usual. Are you sure you want them tomorrow too?"

"Yes. We're going ice-skating." Helena messes up Dominic's hair. "Aren't we, buddy."

"Uh-huh, and we're going to the movies tonight." He smiles goofily up at them. "Aren't we?"

"Well, drop them home as soon as you want tomorrow, we are home all day." I smile. "You two are newlyweds, I'm sure playing aunty every weekend is tiresome."

"You're newlyweds too."

"Yeah, but they're our kids. Go get your things," I tell the twins.

"Okay." They take the stairs two at a time.

"Who knew getting a night away from us would be so exciting?" Gabriel mutters dryly.

I smile, Carina and Helena are the kids' favorite people; they hang out with them at least once a week.

"We had lunch with Mom today," Carina says.

"Really?" I smile in surprise.

478

Gabriel frowns. "You did?"

"Uh-huh."

"Both of you?"

"Yeah."

"How did that go?"

"She's..." Carina shrugs. "She's been going to therapy and..." She shrugs again. "I don't know, she seems different..." She frowns as if thinking. "More herself than she has been in a long time."

Gabriel runs the backs of his fingers through his stubble as he listens intently.

"Maybe it's time you reached out too?" Carina smiles hopefully.

"How did I know that was coming?" Gabriel rolls his eyes, unimpressed.

"You know, I thought after she agreed to divorce Dad that you would come around," she says.

"There are a lot of reasons I don't come around," he replies, his eyes flick over to me. "Twenty million reasons, actually."

"Can't you just try and forgive so we can get past this?" she says hopefully. "People make mistakes, Gabriel, it doesn't mean they're bad... It just means they're human."

"Forgiveness is earned," he snaps.

"I had lunch with her the other week." I take Gabriel's hand in mine. "Didn't I?"

"You did." He exhales as if I'm a huge pain in his ass.

I don't think she's evil at all, I think she's had some kind of breakdown and control was the only way she was able to deal with it. Not that it's any excuse for her behavior, but I do believe it's the reason.

Gabriel hasn't let me take the children near her yet.

"I think we're on the road to recovery." I shrug hopefully. "Maybe one day..."

"We'll see." He sighs. "There's a lot of baggage to unpack."

The kids bustle down the stairs, carrying their backpacks. "Let's go."

"Goodbye Mom and Dad, we're going to miss you so much tonight," Gabriel says to them as he widens his eyes.

They both smile, knowing that's a complete lie.

"Goodbye, my babies." With a quick kiss for each of us, they get into the elevator.

"Thank you," I call as Gabriel closes the door behind them, he turns to me and slowly licks his lips as he gives me the look.

No matter how many times he looks at me like that...it always sends shivers down my spine.

"Finally...I have you to myself."

"Don't get any ideas." I smirk. "I'm getting ready and I'm not going to a black-tie ball in an evening gown all messy and sexed up."

He opens my robe; I'm wearing a black lace bra and panties with a suspender belt. His hungry gaze drops down the length of my body and he raises an eyebrow. "I beg to differ."

Half an hour later, I look at myself in the full-length mirror. I'm wearing a strapless red dress. My hair is out and full and my makeup is smoky and sexy.

"The car is here," Gabriel calls from downstairs.

I purposely haven't let him see me fully dressed because I knew if he saw me in a red dress, there was no way in hell we weren't having sex.

Red dresses are Gabriel Ferrara's kryptonite, a small detail that would have been very handy to know all those years I worked for him.

I grab my purse and with one last look at myself, I make my way to the top of the stairs. I look down to find Gabriel standing in the foyer in his black dinner suit, fiddling with his cuff links and the smell of his leg-opener cologne is permeating through the air.

He glances up and falters as he sees me, his eyes darken and he gives me a slow, sexy smile and begins to walk up the stairs to meet me halfway. His hands drop to my behind. "Change of plans." He grabs my hand and begins walking upstairs. "Get in my fucking bed, woman."

"No." I giggle and pull him back. "We are going out."

He readjusts the length in his suit pants. "There's no way I can wait four hours with you looking like that, I'm about to fucking blow."

I giggle, the dress having the exact desired effect I was hoping for. "Later. I want to go out."

"I want to go down."

Excitement thrums through my body, what is it about him that gets me so hot for it?

Every. Damn. Time.

We're like horny kids with each other, the attraction between us is fire.

A raging inferno.

I pull him downstairs and we get into the elevator and as the door closes he pins me to the wall. His teeth grazing my neck, his engorged cock rubbing up against my sex.

"Gabriel..." I whimper.

He hits the stop button on the elevator as he slides his hand up my thigh and beneath my G-string. "Are you wet?" He inhales sharply as he feels me. "Dripping."

"Good things come to those who wait," I breathe against his head as it drops to my breasts. He's overcome with arousal; teeth, hands and heavy breathing fill my senses.

Jeez...

I hit the go button, damn it. I really do not want to go to this ball all sexed up and messy.

The doors open in the basement, but he keeps kissing me. In my peripheral vision, I can see Mark and the security car waiting.

But Gabriel doesn't care; he's focused on one thing and one thing only.

Me...

"Stop," I whisper as I push him off me. I drag him from the

elevator by the hand, Mark smirks when he sees his state. "Good evening." He nods.

"Hello." I blush.

"Put the privacy screen up," Gabriel snaps as he opens the back door of the limousine for me.

"Of course, sir," Mark replies.

Uh-oh...

There goes my purity plan.

I slide into the limo as the screen goes up and Gabriel climbs in after me.

I feel my face go red; everyone knows exactly what's on their boss's mind.

The door shuts and Mark gets behind the wheel and we pull out of the underground parking lot; Gabriel immediately drops to his knees in front of me.

"Gabriel," I whisper as I try to push him away. "Stop it. Mark is in the car," I stammer in a panic.

"Who fucking cares." He lifts my dress up and jerks me aggressively forward in the seat as he spreads my legs. He tenderly kisses my inner thigh before sliding my panties down my legs, he takes them off and stuffs them into his pocket.

As his dark eyes hold mine he spreads me with his fingers and licks me deep.

Oh...

My back arches off the seat in pleasure.

His thick tongue takes no prisoners and watching him do this is my most favorite thing in the world.

Gabriel Ferrara is the king of a lot of things, but he is the Roman Emperor of Oral.

Never has a man loved the taste of a woman more than he does me.

He craves it, aches for it, and damn it, I'm totally fucking addicted.

He flutters his tongue, adds a finger and then another as I writhe in silence on the backseat.

Oh god...

My heart races out of control as I try to push him back from me by the forehead.

I can't come here...

He lifts my legs and holds them back, and I see stars.

I can't hold it...I can't fucking hold it.

I'm hit with a freight train of an orgasm and I shudder hard. So strong it curls my toes.

He smiles triumphantly into my sex.

I pant and glance up to see we are driving into the function center; he pulls my dress down and licks his lips as he slides back into his seat.

I'm perspiring and my heart is beating hard in my chest, I glance over to Gabriel to see he's leaning back in his seat and adjusting himself to try and hide his hard cock in his pants.

Dear god...

The door opens and Mark smiles down at me and holds his hand out. "Mrs. Ferrara."

I blush and climb out of the car to the click of cameras flashing, my heart is still beating hard and damn it, that orgasm was so strong, I can hardly see straight.

Gabriel climbs out of the car and takes my hand in his, he lifts it slowly to his lips and kisses it as he leads me up the stairs.

"Can we get a photo, Mr. Ferrara?" a photographer calls.

Gabriel turns us to face them and the cameras flash away.

"You are glowing, Mrs. Ferrara," someone calls. "Are you glad you came tonight?"

My eyes float over to Gabriel, his hair is wild and he gives me the best come-fuck-me look of all time.

"Very."

36

Grace

Twelve months later.

I CLOSE my eyes as I worship the sun. The warm vitamin D sinks deep into my bones.

Now...*this* is living.

From my deck chair I can hear the whir of the Jet Ski in the distance, Gabriel and Lucia are on one and Mark and Dominic are on the other. They're racing around and yahooing and squealing with laughter as they taunt each other.

We're on the yacht, sailing around the south of France, and just like St. Tropez, life is good.

Perfect.

If someone told me that this level of happiness was possible, I couldn't have in my wildest dreams believed it.

We live between Greenville and New York; Gabriel prefers the quiet life of Greenville on weekends and the kids are settled and have friends in both places.

And so do I.

Deb lives half her time in New York too now; her marriage to

Scott broke up and Gabriel insisted on getting her a place near us. She didn't want to take him up on the offer, but I made her. After all she's done for me, for us...it's the least we could do.

And besides, she needs us now more than ever.

Turns out that Scott was having an affair, he totally blindsided her. She has a wounded heart and a broken ego and we are very carefully limping her back to life.

Just like she did with me all those years ago.

Gabriel and she have become firm friends, and I wouldn't mind betting that Mark is a little bit sweet on her.

Cold water splashes and I open my eyes to a tall, dark and handsome Italian man standing over me. "Do you want a drink, my Gracie?"

"I'm good." I smile sleepily.

He sits down on the deck chair beside me and puts his hand over my stomach. "Kick." He gives me a slow sexy smile as he waits.

I'm six months pregnant and we are on our babymoon.

Gabriel's wish came true, he's getting to experience the whole pregnancy thing for the first time and he's obsessed with everything baby and me.

Back home we're doing a renovation on my house in Greenville, well, it's our house now, and we're moving back there permanently for a few months while we have the baby. Gabriel wants it to be born at the same hospital as its brother and sister.

We don't know if it's a boy or a girl, we wanted a surprise.

Gabriel's hand bumps as the baby kicks, and he leans down and softly kisses my stomach before kissing me tenderly, his lips lingering over mine.

"Yuck," Dominic yells as he plops onto the chair beside us. "Why do you kiss all the time?"

"I'm hungry," Lucia demands as she lies across my legs. "Can we have hot fries today?"

Gabriel exhales heavily. "Don't even," he whispers against my lips.

As usual, they have impeccable timing.

"Behave." I smile as I run my fingers through his dark stubble. "Seven thirty bedtime tonight."

"Ha." He stands and puts his hands on his hips. "I'll believe that when I see it." He looks around the yacht. "All right, Lucia... Go get your new puzzle and we'll start it."

"Really?" She gasps with wide eyes. "Dominic, we are doing the puzzle." She takes off at a million miles an hour.

"That jigsaw has a thousand pieces, you know that, right?" I tell him.

Lucia saw this puzzle in the gift store at the airport on the way here and convinced him to buy it for her, she's been badgering us to do it every day since.

"Let's just get it over with." Gabriel shrugs. "How hard could it be?"

"Piece of cake." I smile goofily up at my poor deluded fool; this tantrum is going to be especially fun to watch.

Gabriel

Ten weeks later.

Gracie rolls over in bed for the hundredth time tonight, and I reach out and put my hand on her behind. I glance at the clock, it's 11pm and yet it feels like we've been in bed for hours already. "You okay, babe?"

"Yeah." She rolls over again. "Just can't get comfortable." She punches her pillow. "Because I'm the size of a fucking whale."

I smile with my eyes closed. "A very cute whale, though."

"Ugh..." She shuffles around again. "That was the opportunity to tell me I'm not a whale, Gabriel," she snaps. "Not agree with me."

I chuckle. Heavily pregnant Gracie is grumpy.

"Do you need anything?" I ask.

"Maybe a drink."

486

I make my way downstairs, get her some iced water and then pass it to her.

"Thanks." She sits up, leaning on her elbow as she takes it and winces.

"Are you okay?" I frown as I push the hair back from her forehead.

"Yeah...I'm just...my back is aching." She shrugs. "Hot and bothered, I can't get comfortable." She sips her water and places it down on the side table. "Go to sleep, babe, I'm fine." She flops down onto her pillow. "Three and a half weeks to go."

I smile into the darkness. Twenty-five days until we meet our baby.

"Ahhh..." Gracie's voice moans from the bathroom.

I jump awake with a start. "What's wrong?"

"My back is literally killing me."

I flick the lamp on and dive out of bed. I walk in to find her sitting on the chair in the corner.

"Do you want a heat pack?" I ask.

"No."

"Maybe a hot shower would help it."

"Yeah, maybe."

I turn the shower on and hold her hand while she steps in under the water. I put my hand on her stomach as I kiss her softly, and a sharp kick hits my hand away.

"Oww." Gracie winces. "Your baby has been kicking me all night."

"Hey..." I whisper to her bump. "Be nice to Momma." I massage her back and she closes her eyes. "You like that?" I ask.

She nods sleepily as she leans up against the tiles and I strip off and get in with her, I keep massaging her shoulders to try to give her some relief.

I'm exhausted, I can't imagine how she must feel. I don't think she's slept in weeks.

I don't know how women do this shit... Between the aches and the pains, sleepless nights, the varicose veins, and heartburn. This pregnancy thing is a fucking nightmare.

I have a newfound admiration for women.

For a long time, I massage her back. Wait a minute, my hands still as a horrifying thought crosses my mind. "You're not in labor, are you?" I ask.

"No." She rolls her eyes. "I have a backache."

"What happened last time when you went into labor?"

"I didn't go into labor; I had a C-section."

"I mean..."

"This isn't labor," she snaps. "It's a backache from being a whale. And besides, the doctor said I'm probably going to go over, not early."

"Yeah, yeah, you're right. He did say that, didn't he?" I keep massaging her shoulders.

A gush of water hits the tiles and splashes up on us.

"Oh...fuck," she whispers as she stares down at the floor.

"What?"

"My water just broke."

My eyes widen. "What do you mean?"

"What else could I fucking mean...my water just broke." She holds her stomach and screws up her face in pain. "Oh no."

"Oh no what?"

"Contraction." She bends over. "Oh shit... Big contraction."

"What?" I fly out of the shower. "A contraction already? Isn't it supposed to ease into this?"

She grips the wall and winces.

My eyes widen in horror. "What the hell is happening in there?"

"We need to get to the hospital..." She doubles over in pain. "Right. Now."

"Arghhhhhh." I run into the bedroom to get dressed. "What the hell, it's too early. You said you weren't in labor not sixty seconds

488

ago." I grab a pair of shorts and struggle to put them on as they stick to my legs. "Go. On. Fucker."

"You probably should have dried yourself," Grace huffs as she walks calmly into the room.

"Don't be fucking cute, Grace." I flick my shorts in front of me as I nearly fall over. "Now is not the time for your smart-ass mouth." I throw a T-shirt on over my head, she's right though... I'm dripping fucking wet.

I run into the bathroom to grab a towel.

"You need to ring Deb to come watch the kids," she calls.

"Yes." I run back into the bedroom and begin to dial Deb's number on my phone.

"Are you getting me a towel or what?"

"You told me to ring Deb," I say through gritted teeth.

"Use your brain, Gabriel," she barks. "I'm wet."

"So help me god..."

"Get me a fucking towel." She bends over as another contraction hits.

I run into the bathroom and grab a towel and begin to dry her, she snatches the towel out of my hands. "Are you trying to rub my skin off?"

Not yet.

"Hello," Deb answers. "What's wrong?"

"Gracie's in labor."

"Yay." She squeals in excitement. "Oh my god, I'm so excited."

"Hurry up." I hang up and turn to see Gracie bent over the bed.

"Oh...oh... Oh...no..." she moans. "Not good."

"What, what, what's not good?" My eyes widen at the unfolding disaster.

"Happening fast." She screws up her face. "You need to get me to the hospital. Now."

"Okay." I snatch the towel from her and begin to dry her.

"Ow... You're hurting me."

"You have a baby coming out of your vagina, a towel drying you is the least of your fucking problems, Grace."

I call Deb again.

"What?"

"Get. Here. Now. This is an emergency situation." I hang up and run into her wardrobe, clothes. We need clothes.

I dig around in her drawers and pull out a dress and run back out.

"Not that one." She snatches it out of my hand and throws it across the room.

"Why not that one?"

"It doesn't even go over my fucking arm, you idiot."

I pinch the bridge of my nose. "So why is it in your wardrobe?"

"Get me some clothes," she growls in an *Exorcist* voice.

Fucking hell...

I run back into the wardrobe and find a nightdress; surely this will fit her—it's the size of a circus tent. "This one?"

"Yes. Sorry for screaming." She nods as she holds her stomach. "I love you."

"Stop yelling at me then."

She clutches her stomach as another contraction hits. "Stop doing stupid things then." She cries out loud as the pain runs through her.

I clench my jaw to hold my tongue. "Let's go."

"I need shoes." She looks around the bedroom.

"You do not need shoes."

"Yes I do."

"Where are you going to fucking walk to, Grace?" I grab her hand and pull her out of the room. We get halfway down the stairs and another contraction hits, she screws up her face.

"Should I call an ambulance?"

"It's fine, the hospital is ten minutes away. Quicker to drive."

I dial Deb again. "Yes."

"Where are you?" I whisper angrily.

"Calm down."

My eyes bulge from their sockets. "Oh my god...I'm going to kill you with my bare hands..." I'm interrupted as Deb comes in the

490

front door. She takes one look at Grace and her eyes widen. "How long has she been like this?"

"Seven fucking minutes, this is the quickest escalation of all time."

"Oh..." She fakes a smile. "You should go. Like...now."

"Arghhhhhh." Grace screws up her face in pain.

"Grace, you're scaring me. What do I do?"

"Get the car."

In a fluster of panic, Deb and I help her out to the car and bundle her in, Deb straps her seat belt on while I run around to the driver's side. "Call Mark."

"Okay." She kisses Grace's face. "Good luck, baby."

"Arghhhhhh. Mother...ohhhh, that hurts," Grace moans.

I take off at speed, my eyes flicking between Grace and the road. "Hold on, baby. Hold on."

"You fucking hold on," she yells. "You think I have control over this, don't tell me what to do."

I grip the steering wheel with white-knuckle force. "You know, you really need to control your temper."

Her eyes glow red, and I turn my attention back to the road.

Eish...she's like a serial killer on steroids.

"Oh no," she cries as she screams. She rears back in her seat. "Oh no."

"What, what, what?" I scream.

"The head's out, the head's out."

"What?" My eyes widen in horror and I slam on the brakes. "What do you mean the fucking head is out."

She pulls her dress up and reaches down. "It's out, the head's out."

My life flashes before my eyes, I feel faint.

"Ahhhhhh..." she cries. "I have to push."

What the fuck is happening right now?

I run around to the passenger side and open the door to see a baby's head between her legs.

"Dear god."

What the actual fucking fuck?

I put my hands on Grace's shoulder. "It's okay, you've got this." I lift her leg as she cries out and bears down.

The baby slips out to the waist.

"That's it, that's it." I kiss her forehead. "Almost there."

Damn it, I wanted to have the baby at the same hospital the twins were born in so that I could hopefully erase the bad memories Grace has of their birth.

She throws her head back and cries out as I reach down and catch the baby as it slips completely out.

It's limp and my eyes widen in fear.

Oh no.

"Flip it over," Grace pants, "flip it over."

I flip the baby onto its stomach and Grace rubs its back and it coughs and then finally...cries.

The vision of my beautiful wife blurs and I hold her head to mine. "You did it, Gracie." I hold her tight. "I love you. I love you so much."

She turns it over. "A girl."

A little girl.

I screw up my face in tears, overwhelmed with emotion.

The baby screams while I cry and Grace holds her to her chest, the umbilical cord still firmly intact.

Grace and I stare down at the perfect little girl. I should drive to the hospital, but I just want to stay right here and in this moment for as long as I can.

My heart feels like it's about to explode out of my chest.

"Can you believe that just happened?" Grace whispers.

"Of course I can, it's us," I mutter dryly. "We always do shit the hard way."

The baby settles and Grace smiles up at me. "What are we going to call her?"

"Luna." Gratitude for my life is crashing over me like an ocean. Just when you think you can't love someone any more than you do. "Luna Grace."

"Are you sure about Luna?"

"Positive."

"Why do you want to call her Luna so much?" Grace whispers.

This beautiful woman has no idea of the magic she has brought into my life.

Of how deeply she is loved.

"Because her mother hung the moon."

THE END.

Thank you so, so much for reading.
I adored writing this book.
Love always,
Tee xo

MR MASTERS EXCERPT

PROLOGUE

Julian Masters

ALINA MASTERS
1984 – 2013
Wife and beloved mother.
In God's hands we trust.

Grief. The Grim Reaper of life.

Stealer of joy, hope and purpose.

Some days are bearable. Other days I can hardly breathe, and I suffocate in a world of regret where good reason has no sense.

I never know when those days will hit, only that when I wake, my chest feels constricted and I need to run. I need to be anywhere but here, dealing with this life.

My life.

Our life.

Until *you* left.

The sound of a distant lawnmower brings me back to the

present, and I glance over at the cemetery's caretaker. He's concentrating as he weaves between the tombstones, careful not to clip or damage one as he passes. It's dusk, and the mist is rolling in for the night.

I come here often to think, to try and feel.

I can't talk to anyone. I can't express my true feelings.

I want to know why.

Why did you do this to us?

I clench my jaw as I stare at my late wife's tombstone.

We could have had it all... but, we didn't.

I lean down and brush the dust away from her name and rearrange the pink lilies that I have just placed in the vase. I touch her face on the small oval photo. She stares back at me, void of emotion.

Stepping back, I drop my hands in the pockets of my black overcoat.

I could stand here and stare at this headstone all day—sometimes I do—but I turn and walk to the car without looking back.

My *Porsche*.

Sure, I have money and two kids that love me. I'm at the top of my professional field, working as a judge. I have all the tools *to be* happy, but I'm not.

I'm barely surviving; holding on by a thread.

Playing the façade to the world.

Dying inside.

Half an hour later, I arrive at Madison's—my therapist.

I always leave here relaxed.

I don't have to talk, I don't have to think, I don't have to feel.

I walk through the front doors on autopilot.

"Good afternoon, Mr. Smith." Hayley the receptionist smiles. "Your room is waiting, sir."

"Thank you." I frown, feeling like I need something more today. Something to take this edginess off.

A distraction.

"I'll have someone extra today, Hayley."

"Of course, sir. Who would you like?"

I frown and take a moment to get it right. "Hmm. Hannah."

"So, Hannah and Belinda?"

"Yes."

"No problem, sir. Make yourself comfortable and they will be right up."

I take the lift to the exclusive penthouse. Once there I make myself a scotch and stare out the smoke-glass window overlooking London.

I hear the door click behind me and I turn toward the sound.

Hannah and Belinda stand before me smiling.

Belinda has long, blonde hair, while Hannah is a brunette. There's no denying they're both young and beautiful.

"Hello, Mr. Smith," they say in unison

I sip my scotch as my eyes drink them in.

"Where would you like us, sir?"

I unbuckle my belt. "On your knees."

Chapter 1

Brielle

Customs is ridiculously slow, and a man has been pulled into the office up ahead. It all looks very suspicious from my position at the back of the line. "What do you think he did?" I whisper as I crane my neck to spy the commotion up ahead.

"I don't know, something stupid, probably," Emerson replies. We shuffle towards the desk as the line moves a little quicker.

We've just arrived in London to begin our year-long working holiday. I'm going to work for a judge as a nanny, while Emerson, my best friend, is working for an art auctioneer. I'm terrified, yet excited.

"I wish we had come a week earlier so we could have spent some time together," Emerson says.

"Yeah, I know, but she needed me to start this week because she's going away next week. I need to learn the kids' routine."

"Who leaves their kids alone for three days with a complete stranger?" Em frowns in disgust.

I shrug. "My new boss, apparently."

"Well, at least I can come and stay with you next week. That's a bonus."

My position is residential, so my accommodation is secure. However, poor Emerson will be living with two strangers. She's freaking out over it.

"Yeah, but I'm sneaking you in," I say. "I don't want it to look like we're partying or anything."

I look around the airport. It's busy, bustling, and I already feel so alive. Emerson and I are more than just young travellers.

Emerson is trying to find her purpose and I'm running from a destructive past, one that involves me being in love with an adultering prick.

I loved him. He just didn't love me. Not enough, anyway.

If he had, he would have kept it in his pants, and I wouldn't be at Heathrow Airport feeling like I'm about to throw up.

I look down at myself and smooth the wrinkles from my dress. "She's picking me up. Do I look okay?"

Emerson looks me up and down, smiling broadly. "You look exactly how a twenty-five-year-old nanny from Australia should."

I bite my bottom lip to stop myself from smiling stupidly. That was a good answer.

"So, what's your boss's name?" she asks.

I rustle around in my bag for my phone and scroll through the emails until I get to the one from the nanny agency. "Mrs. Julian Masters."

Emerson nods. "And what's her story again? I know you've told me before but I've forgotten."

"She's a Supreme Court judge, widowed five years ago."

"What happened to the husband?"

"I don't know, but apparently she's quite wealthy." I shrug. "Two kids, well behaved."

"Sounds good."

"I hope so. I hope they like me."

"They will." We move forward in the line. "We are definitely going out at the weekend though, yes?"

"Yes." I nod. "What are you going to do until then?"

Emerson shrugs. "Look around. I start work on Monday and it's Thursday today." She frowns as she watches me. "Are you sure you can go out on the weekends?"

"Yes," I snap, exasperated. "I told you a thousand times, we're going out on Saturday night."

Emerson nods nervously. I think she may be more nervous than I am, but at least I'm acting brave. "Did you get your phone sorted?" I ask.

"No, not yet. I'll find a phone shop tomorrow so I can call you."

"Okay."

We are called to the front of the line, and finally, half an hour later, we walk into the arrival lounge of Heathrow International Airport.

"Do you see our names?" Emerson whispers as we both look around.

"No."

"Shit, no one is here to pick us up. Typical." She begins to panic.

"Relax, they will be here," I mutter.

"What do we do if no one turns up?"

I raise my eyebrow as I consider the possibility. "Well, I don't know about you, but I'm going to lose my shit."

Emerson looks over my shoulder. "Oh, look, there's your name. She must have sent a driver."

I turn to see a tall, broad man in a navy suit holding a sign with the name Brielle Johnston on it. I force a smile and wave meekly as I feel my anxiety rise like a tidal wave in my stomach.

He walks over and smiles at me. "Brielle?"

His voice is deep and commanding. "Yes, that's me," I breathe.

He holds out his hand to shake mine. "Julian Masters."

What?

My eyes widen.

A man?

He raises his eyebrows.

"Um, so, I'm... I'm Brielle," I stammer as I push my hand out. "And this is my friend, Emerson, who I'm travelling with." He takes my hand in his and my heart races.

A trace of a smile crosses his face before he covers it. "Nice to meet you." He turns to Emerson and shakes her hand. "How do you do?"

My eyes flash to Emerson, who is clearly loving this shit. She grins brightly. "Hello."

"I thought you were a woman," I whisper.

His brows furrow. "Last time I checked I was all man." His eyes hold mine.

Why did I just say that out loud? Oh my God, stop talking.

This is so awkward.

I want to go home. This is a bad idea.

"I'll wait over here." He gestures to the corner before marching off in that direction. My horrified eyes meet Emerson's, and she giggles, so I punch her hard in the arm.

"Oh my fuck, he's a fucking man," I whisper angrily.

"I can see that." She smirks, her eyes fixed on him.

"Excuse me, Mr. Masters?" I call after him.

He turns. "Yes."

We both wither under his glare. "We... we are just going to use the bathroom," I stammer nervously.

With one curt nod he gestures to the right. We look up and see the sign. I grab Emerson by the arm and drag her into the bathroom. "I'm not working with a stuffy old man!" I shriek as we burst through the door.

"It will be okay. How did this happen?"

I take out my phone and scroll through the emails quickly. I knew it. "It says woman. I knew it said woman."

"He's not that old," she calls out from her cubicle. "I would prefer to work for a man than a woman, to be honest."

"You know what, Emerson? This is a shit idea. How the hell did I let you talk me into this?"

She smiles as she exits the cubicle and washes her hands. "It doesn't matter. You'll hardly see him anyway, and you're not working weekends when he's home." She's clearly trying to calm me. "Stop with the carry on."

Stop the carry on.

Steam feels like it's shooting from my ears. "I'm going to kill you. I'm going to fucking kill you."

Emerson bites her lip to stifle her smile. "Listen, just stay with him until we find you something else. I will get my phone sorted tomorrow and we can start looking elsewhere for another job," she reassures me. "At least someone picked you up. Nobody cares about me at all."

I put my head into my hands as I try to calm my breathing. "This is a disaster, Em," I whisper. Suddenly every fear I had about travelling is coming true. I feel completely out of my comfort zone.

"It's going to be one week... tops."

My scared eyes lift to hold hers, and I nod.

"Okay?" She smiles as she pulls me into a hug.

"Okay." I glance back in the mirror, fix my hair, and straighten my dress. I'm completely rattled.

We walk back out and take our place next to Mr. Masters. He's in his late thirties, immaculately dressed, and kind of attractive. His hair is dark with a sprinkle of grey.

"Did you have a good flight?" he asks as he looks down at me.

"Yes, thanks," I push out. Oh, that sounded so forced. "Thank you for picking us up," I add meekly.

He nods with no fuss.

Emerson smiles at the floor as she tries to hide her smile.

That bitch is loving this shit.

"Emerson?" a male voice calls. We all turn to see a blond man, and Emerson's face falls. Ha! Now it's my turn to laugh.

"Hello, I'm Mark." He kisses her on the cheek and then turns to me. "You must be Brielle?"

"Yes." I smile then turn to Mr. Masters. "And this is..." I pause because I don't know how to introduce him.

"Julian Masters," he finishes for me, adding in a strong handshake.

Emerson and I fake smile at each other.

Oh dear God, help me.

Emerson stands and talks with Mark and Mr. Masters, while I stand in uncomfortable silence.

"The car is this way." He gestures to the right.

I nod nervously. Oh God, don't leave me with him.

This is terrifying.

"Nice to meet you, Emerson and Mark." He shakes their hands.

"Likewise. Please look after my friend," Emerson whispers as her eyes flicker to mine.

Mr. Masters nods, smiles, and then pulls my luggage behind him as he walks to the car. Emerson pulls me into an embrace. "This is shit," I whisper into her hair.

"It will be fine. He's probably really nice."

"He doesn't look nice," I whisper.

"Yeah, I agree. He looks like a tool," Mark adds as he watches him disappear through the crowd.

Emerson throws her new friend a dirty look, and I smirk. I think her friend is more annoying than mine, but anyway... "Mark, look after my friend, please?"

He beats his chest like a gorilla. "Oh, I intend to."

Emerson's eyes meet mine. She subtly shakes her head and I bite my bottom lip to hide my smile. This guy is a dick. We both look over to see Mr. Masters looking back impatiently. "I better go," I whisper.

"You have my apartment details if you need me?"

"I'll probably turn up in an hour. Tell your roommates I'm coming in case I need a key."

She laughs and waves me off, and I go to Mr. Masters. He sees me coming and then starts to walk again.

God, can he not even wait for me? So rude.

He walks out of the building into the VIP parking section. I follow him in complete silence.

Any notion that I was going to become friends with my new boss has been thrown out the window. I think he hates me already.

Just wait until he finds out that I lied on my resume and I have no fucking idea what I'm doing. Nerves flutter in my stomach at the thought.

We get to a large, swanky, black SUV, and he clicks it open to put my suitcase in the trunk. He opens the back door for me to get in. "Thank you." I smile awkwardly as I slide into the seat. He wants me to sit in the back when the front seat is empty.

This man is odd.

He slides into the front seat and eventually pulls out into the traffic. All I can do is clutch my handbag in my lap.

Should I say something? Try and make conversation?

What will I say?

"Do you live far from here?" I ask.

"Twenty minutes," he replies, his tone clipped.

Oh...is that it? Okay, shut up now. He doesn't want a conversation. For ten long minutes we sit in silence.

"You can drive this car when you have the children, or we have a small minivan. The choice is yours."

"Oh, okay." I pause for a moment. "Is this your car?"

"No." He turns onto a street and into a driveway with huge sandstone gates. "I drive a Porsche," he replies casually. "Oh."

The driveway goes on and on and on. I look around at the perfectly kept grounds and rolling green hills. With every meter we pass, I feel my heart beat just that bit faster.

As if it isn't bad enough that I can't do the whole nanny thing... I really can't do the rich thing. I have no idea what to do with polite

503

company. I don't even know what fork to use at dinner. I've got myself into a right mess here.

The house comes into focus and the blood drains from my face.

It's not a house, not even close. It's a mansion, white and sandstone with a castle kind of feel to it, with six garages to the left.

He pulls into the large circular driveway, stopping under the awning.

"Your house is beautiful," I whisper.

He nods, as his eyes stay fixed out front. "We are fortunate."

He gets out of the car and opens my door for me. I climb out as I grip my handbag with white-knuckle force. My eyes rise up to the luxurious building in front of me.

This is an insane amount of money.

He retrieves my suitcase and wheels it around to the side of the building. "Your entrance is around to the side," he says. I follow him up a path until we get to a door, which he opens and lets me walk through. There is a foyer and a living area in front of me.

"The kitchen is this way." He points to the kitchen. "And your bedroom is in the back left corner."

I nod and walk past him, into the apartment.

He stands at the door but doesn't come in. "The bathroom is to the right," he continues.

Why isn't he coming in here? "Okay, thanks," I reply.

"Order any groceries you want on the family shopping order and..." He pauses, as if collecting his thoughts. "If there is anything else you need, please talk to me first."

I frown. "First?"

He shrugs. "I don't want to be told about a problem for the first time when reading a resignation letter."

"Oh." Did that happen before? "Of course," I mutter.

"If you would like to come and meet the children..." He gestures to a hallway.

"Yes, please." Oh God, here we go. I follow him out into a corridor with glass walls that looks out onto the main house, which is about four metres away. A garden sits between the two buildings creating an atrium, and I smile as I look up in wonder. There is a large window in the main house that looks into the kitchen. I can see beyond that into the living area from the corridor where a young girl and small boy are watching television together. We continue to the end of the glass corridor where there is a staircase with six steps leading up to the main house.

I blow out a breath, and I follow Mr. Masters up the stairs.

"Children, come and meet your new nanny."

The little boy jumps down and rushes over to me, clearly excited, while the girl just looks up and rolls her eyes. I smile to myself, remembering what it's like to be a typical teenager.

"Hello, I'm Samuel." The little boy smiles as he wraps his arms around my legs. He has dark hair, is wearing glasses, and he's so damn cute.

"Hello, Samuel." I smile.

"This is Willow," he introduces.

I smile at the teenage girl. "Hello." She folds her arms across her chest defiantly. "Hi," she grumbles.

Mr. Masters holds her gaze for a moment, saying so much with just one look.

Willow eventually holds her hand out for me to shake. "I'm Willow."

I smile as my eyes flash up to Mr. Masters. He can keep her under control with just a simple glare.

Samuel runs back to the lounge, grabs something, and then comes straight back.

I see a flash.

Click, click.

What the hell?

He has a small instant Polaroid camera. He watches my face appear on the piece of paper in front of him before he looks back up at me. "You're pretty." He smiles. "I'm putting this on the fridge." He carefully pins it to the fridge with a magnet.

Mr. Masters seems to become flustered for some reason. "Bedtime for you two," he instructs and they both complain. He turns his attention back to me. "Your kitchen is stocked with groceries, and I'm sure you're tired."

I fake a smile. Oh, I'm being dismissed. "Yes, of course." I go to walk back down to my apartment, and then turn back to him. "What time do I start tomorrow?"

His eyes hold mine. "When you hear Samuel wake up."

"Yes, of course." My eyes search his as I wait for him to say something else, but it doesn't come. "Goodnight then." I smile awkwardly.

"Goodnight."

"Bye, Brielle." Samuel smiles, and Willow ignores me, walking away and up the stairs.

I walk back down into my apartment and close the door behind me. Then I flop onto the bed and stare up at the ceiling.

What have I done?

It's midnight and I'm thirsty, but I have looked everywhere and I still cannot find a glass. There's no other option; I'm going to have to sneak up into the main house to find one. I'm wearing my silky white nightdress, but I'm sure they are all in bed.

Sneaking out into the darkened corridor, I can see into the lit-up house.

I suddenly catch sight of Mr. Masters sitting in the armchair reading a book. He has a glass of red wine in his hand. I stand in the dark, unable to tear my eyes away. There's something about him that fascinates me but I don't quite know what it is.

He stands abruptly, and I push myself back against the wall.

Can he see me here in the dark?

Shit.

My eyes follow him as he walks into the kitchen. The only thing he's wearing is his navy-blue boxer shorts. His dark hair has messy, loose waves on top. His chest is broad, his body is...

My heart begins to beat faster. What am I doing? I shouldn't be standing here in the dark, watching him like a creep, but for some reason I can't make myself look away.

He goes to stand by the kitchen counter, his back is to me as he pours himself another glass of red. He lifts it to his lips slowly and my eyes run over his body.

I push myself against the wall harder.

He walks over to the fridge and takes off the photo of me.

What?

He leans his ass on the counter as he studies it.

What is he doing?

I feel like I can't breathe.

He slowly puts his hand down the front of his boxer shorts, and then he seems to stroke himself a few times.

My eyes widen.

What the fuck?

He puts his glass of wine on the counter and turns the main light off, leaving only a lamp to light the room.

With my picture in his hand, he disappears up the hall.

What the hell was that?

I think Mr. Masters just went up to his bedroom to jerk off to my photo.

Oh.

My.

God.

Knock, knock.

My eyes are closed, but I frown and try to ignore the noise.

I hear it again. Tap, tap.

What is that? I roll towards the door and I see it slowly begin to open.

My eyes widen, and I sit up quickly.

Mr. Masters comes into view. "I'm so sorry to bother you, Miss Brielle," he whispers. He smells like he's freshly showered, and he's wearing an immaculate suit. "I'm looking for Samuel." His gaze roams down to my breasts hanging loosely in my nightdress, and then he snaps his eyes back up to my face, as if he's horrified at what he just did.

"Where is he?" I frown. "Is he missing?"

"There he is," he whispers as he gestures to the lounger.

I look over to see Samuel curled up with his teddy in the diluted light of the room. My mouth falls open. "Oh no, what's wrong?" I whisper. Did he need me and I slept through the whole thing?

"Nothing," Mr. Masters murmurs as he picks Samuel up and rests his son's head on his strong shoulder. "He's a sleepwalker. Sorry to disturb you. I've got this now." He leaves the room with his small son safely asleep in his arms. The door gently clicks closed behind them.

I lie back down and stare at the ceiling in the silence. That poor little boy. He came in here to see me and I didn't even wake up. I was probably snoring, for fuck's sake.

What if he was scared? Oh, I feel like shit now.

I blow out a deep breath, lift myself up to sit on the edge of the bed, and I put my head into my hands.

I need to up my game. If I'm in charge of looking after this kid, I can't have him wandering around at night on his own.

Is he that lonely that he was looking for company from me—a complete stranger?

Unexplained sadness rolls over me, and I suddenly feel like the weight of the world is on my shoulders. I look around my room for a moment as I think.

Eventually, I get up and go to the bathroom, and then walk to the window to pull the heavy drapes back. It's just getting light, and a white mist hangs over the paddocks.

Something catches my eye and I look down to see Mr. Masters walking out to the garage.

Wearing a dark suit and carrying a briefcase, he disappears, and moments later I see his Porsche pull out and disappear up the driveway. I watch on as the garage door slowly closes behind him.

He's gone to work for the day.

What the hell?

His son was just found asleep on my lounger and he just plops him back into his own bed and leaves for the day. Who does that? Well, screw this, I'm going to go and check on him. He's probably upstairs crying, scared out of his brain. Stupid men. Why don't they have an inch of fucking empathy for anyone but themselves?

He's eight, for Christ's sake!

I walk up into the main house. The lamp is still on in the living room and I can smell the eggs that Mr. Masters cooked himself for breakfast. I look around, and then go up the grand staircase.

Honestly, what the hell have I got myself into here? I'm in some stupid rich twat's house, worried about his child who he clearly doesn't give a fuck about.

I storm up the stairs, taking two at a time. I get to the top and the change of scenery suddenly makes me feel nervous. It's luxurious up here. The corridor is wide, and the cream carpet feels lush beneath my feet. A huge mirror hangs in the hall on the wall. I catch a glimpse of myself and cringe.

God, no wonder he was looking at my boobs. They are hanging out everywhere, and my hair is wild. I readjust my nightgown over my breasts and continue up the hall. I pass a living area that seems to be for the children, with big comfy loungers inside it. I pass a bedroom, and then I get to a door that is closed. I open it carefully and allow myself to peer in. Willow is fast asleep, still scowling, though. I smirk and slowly shut her door to continue down the hall. Eventually, I get to a door that is slightly ajar. I peer around it and see Samuel sound asleep, tucked in nice and tight. I walk into his room and sit on the side of the bed. He's wearing bright blue and green dinosaur pyjamas, and his little glasses are on his side table, beside his lamp. I find myself smiling as I watch him. Unable to help it, I put my hand out and push the dark hair from his forehead. His bedroom is neat and tidy, filled with expensive furniture. It kind of looks like you would imagine a child's bedroom being set out in a perfect family movie. Everything in this house is the absolute best of the best. Just how much money does Mr. Masters have?

There's a bookcase, a desk, a wingback chair in the corner, and a toy box. The window has a bench seat running underneath it, and there are a few books sitting in a pile on the cushion, as if Samuel reads there a lot. I glance over to the armchair in the corner to his school clothes all laid out for him. Everything is there, folded neatly, right down to his socks and shiny, polished shoes. His school bag is packed, too.

I stand and walk over to look at his things. Mr. Masters must do this before he goes to bed. What must it be like to bring children up alone?

My mind goes to his wife and how much she is missing out on. Samuel is so young. With one last look at Samuel, I creep out of the room and head back down the hall, until something catches my eye.

A light is on in the en-suite bathroom of the main bedroom.

That must be Mr. Master's bedroom.

I look left and then right; nobody is awake. I wonder what his room is like, and I can't stop myself from tiptoeing closer to inspect it.

Wow.

The bed is clearly king-size, and the room is grand, decorated in all different shades of coffee, complimented with dark antique furniture. A huge, expensive, gold and magenta embroidered rug sits on the floor beneath the bed. The light in the wardrobe is on. I peer inside and see business shirts all lined up, neatly in a row. Super neatly, actually.

I'm going to have to make sure I keep my room tidy or he'll think I'm a pig.

I smirk because I am one according to his standards of living.

I turn to see his bed has already been made, and my eyes linger over the velvet quilt and lush pillows there. Did he really touch himself in there last night as he thought of me, or am I completely delusional? I glance around for the photo of me, but I don't see it. He must have taken it back downstairs.

An unexpected thrill runs through me. I may return the favour tonight in my own bed.

I walk into the bathroom. It's all black, grey, and very modern. Once again, I notice that everything is very neat. There is a large mirror, and I can see that a slender cabinet sits behind it. I push the mirror and the door pops open. My eyes roam over the shelves. You can tell a lot about people by their bathroom cabinet.

Deodorant. Razors. Talcum powder.

Condoms.

I wonder how long ago his wife died. Does he have a new girlfriend?

It wouldn't surprise me. He is kind of hot, in an old way. I see a bottle of aftershave and I pick it up, removing the lid before I lift it up to my nose.

Heaven in a bottle.

I inhale deeply again, and Mr. Master's face suddenly appears in the mirror behind me.

"What the hell do you think you're doing?" he growls.

Mr. Masters is coming to bookstores September 2024.

AFTERWORD

Thank you so much for reading and
for your ongoing support
I have the most beautiful readers in the whole world!

Keep up to date with all the latest news
and online discussions by joining the Swan Squad VIP Facebook
group and discuss your favourite
books with other readers.
@tlswanauthor

Visit my website for updates and new release information.
www.tlswanauthor.com

ABOUT THE AUTHOR

T L Swan is a Wall Street Journal and #1 Amazon Best Selling author. With millions of books sold, her titles are currently translated in eleven languages and have hit #1 on Amazon in the USA, UK, Canada, Australia and Germany. Tee resides on the South Coast of NSW, Australia with her husband and their three children where she is living her own happy ever after with her first true love.